I didn't know ... ... fore the renovation, but ... ... om was the size of a bas... ... ir chairs were arranged around the stone fireplace, and hanging over the mantel was a gilt-framed oil painting of some ancient lord astride a horse.

A light tap at my door.

"I'm sorry to bother you, dear," Nana apologized. "But do you suppose you could come downstairs?"

"Is there a problem with your room?"

"Just a small one. There's a dead body in it."

Acclaim for Maddy Hunter's first *Passport to Peril* mystery, *ALPINE FOR YOU*

"Delightfully fresh, with a great deal of humor."

—Creatures 'n Crooks Bookshoppe

"As funny as anything by Katy Munger, Janet Evanovich, [or] Joan Hess. . . . The laughs started on the first page and continued, nonstop, to the last. . . . This one gets five stars. It's a winner."

—Black Bird Mysteries

"[A] debut with more than a few chuckles. . . . *Alpine for You* is one to cheer the gloomy winter days."

—Mystery Lovers Bookshop

"A compelling heroine, an intriguing hero, and a great scenic tour. I'm impatiently looking forward to the next one."

—*The Old Book Barn Gazette*

Also by Maddy Hunter

Passport to Peril mystery series

ALPINE FOR YOU

Published by Pocket Books

maddy
HUNTER

A *Passport to Peril* mystery

Top O' the Mournin'

POCKET BOOKS

New York   London   Toronto   Sydney   Singapore

The sale of this book without its cover is unauthorized. If you purchased this book without a cover, you should be aware that it was reported to the publisher as "unsold and destroyed." Neither the author nor the publisher has received payment for the sale of this "stripped book."

This book is a work of fiction. Names, characters, places and incidents are products of the author's imagination or are used fictitiously. Any resemblance to actual events or locales or persons, living or dead, is entirely coincidental.

An *Original* Publication of POCKET BOOKS

POCKET BOOKS, a division of Simon & Schuster, Inc.
1230 Avenue of the Americas, New York, NY 10020

Copyright © 2003 by Mary Mayer Holmes

All rights reserved, including the right to reproduce
this book or portions thereof in any form whatsoever.
For information address Pocket Books, 1230 Avenue
of the Americas, New York, NY 10020

ISBN: 0-7434-5812-5

First Pocket Books printing August 2003

10 9 8 7 6 5 4 3 2 1

POCKET and colophon are registered trademarks of
Simon & Schuster, Inc.

For information regarding special discounts for bulk purchases,
please contact Simon & Schuster Special Sales at 1-800-456-6798
or business@simonandschuster.com

Interior design by Davina Mock
Front cover illustration by Jeff Fitz-Maurice

Printed in the U.S.A.

DEDICATION

To my cousin, Jocelyn Taylor, who means the world to me.

With love~
mmh

Top O' the Mournin'

CHAPTER 1

The guidebook says the weather in Ireland is normally wet, except when it isn't, which can be often, or not often at all. The sun *can* shine, mostly when it's not raining, but it rains most of the time, except when it doesn't.

In other words, the weather in Ireland is a metaphor for my life.

I'm Emily Andrew, twenty-nine-year-old once-married working girl with a degree in theater arts, currently employed as escort for a bank-sponsored group of Iowa senior citizens on a ten-day tour of the Emerald Isle.

Going back to my weather metaphor, my life had been sunny when I'd moved to New York City after receiving my B.A., married fellow actor, Jack Potter, and landed a part in a Broadway play. The rain started when Jack began wearing my underwear. The deluge hit when he left me a note one night telling me he was running off with his leading man's understudy.

When the shock wore off, I did what any native Midwesterner with no money to pay Big Apple apartment rent would do. I moved back to my hometown of Windsor City, Iowa, had the marriage annulled, and found a job where I could use my acting skills. Phone solicitation.

For three years I was the premier fund-raiser for Playgrounds for Tots, until the president of the organization was arrested for fraud because there *was* no organization.

He went to jail. I went to Europe. *Not* as a fugitive from justice. I had a long-standing commitment to be my grandmother's companion on a seniors' tour of Switzerland, so off I went, hoping to ease my jobless woes by experiencing the vacation of a lifetime.

It turned out to be an experience, all right. We were promised temperatures in the seventies. Spectacular views of the Alps. Gourmet cuisine. What we got was bone-chilling cold. Dense fog. A steady diet of cornflakes. And three dead guests.

The one ray of sunshine on the trip was that I met the man of my dreams. Etienne Miceli, the police inspector who investigated the three deaths. He's everything my first husband wasn't. Forthright. Dependable. Heterosexual. We've been communicating by phone and e-mail for eight months now, and you might say our relationship is at a crossroads. It's too intense not to be together. But he lives in Switzerland. I live in Iowa. See what I mean about my life? Rain. Sun. Rain. Sun. Not unlike the weather in Ireland.

"Dublin's nothin' like I imagined," said my grandmother. Her voice vibrated as we jounced down one of Dublin's most traveled thoroughfares in the back of a horse-drawn carriage. Nana was known as "a sport" in her retirement village back in Iowa. She'd won millions in the Minnesota lottery the day my grampa passed away, so in her golden years, she had the means to go anywhere and do anything, and she was taking full advantage of the opportunity. "Is it like you imagined, Emily?"

"I imagined rain." I peered skyward in search of storm clouds, but found only a brilliant wash of blue. Windex blue. Like Etienne's eyes. I sighed with the thought. In Dublin for five hours and already I was suffering the first pangs of loneliness. I needed to snap out of it, else it would be a very long ten days.

Our hackney driver tipped his head to the right. "Shaint Shtephen's Green," he said in a lilting brogue. "Firsht enclosed in 1664. Twenty-two acres of manicured lawn, ponds, and quiet in the middle of Ireland's busiest shity."

Cute accent, but he could use some speech therapy for the lisp.

"Remember that statue a Molly Malone?" Nana whispered, referring to the shapely bronze sculpture we'd seen on an earlier walk down Grafton Street. "Why do you s'pose they made her so bosomy? Did you see the cleavage? I bet she was wearin' one of them push-up brassieres. Probably where she got that nickname, 'Tart with a Cart.' "

"Wait a minute. *I* wear a push-up bra, and *I'm* not a tart."

Nana patted my knee. "Of course you're not, dear. You marry the men you sleep with. I think that's very commendable. Oh, look! A double-decker bus. I've always wanted to ride in one of those. Haven't you?"

I'd never given public transportation much thought. What I *really* wanted was to be one of the great stage actresses of the century. Windsor City boasted only a small community theater, so the odds were against me, but I remained optimistic. Entering a new century had given me an extra hundred years to make a success of myself.

"Easy, Nell." Our driver steadied his horse as she chafed against her traces. "She's frishky today. To your left is the Shelbourne Hotel." He guided us past the elegant redbrick building where our tour group was scheduled to spend its first night in Ireland. "Built in 1824. They sherve a brilliant afternoon tea in the Lord Mayor's Lounge at half-three."

The wrought-iron railings and flower-glutted window boxes reminded me of the quaint little hotel where Jack and I had honeymooned so many years ago, and, recalling our wedding night, I smiled. Poor Jack. He'd possessed the extraordinary good looks of a Greek god but the brain chemistry of a Greek goddess. And it had taken me only two years to figure it out. Am I a quick study or what? I hoped he'd found happiness with his partner, living in upstate New York, laying kitchen tile, but that didn't seem the kind of existence that would make him happy. Jack was happiest when he was onstage, sporting layers of pancake makeup and eyeliner. But he was probably happier now than when he'd been married to me. And so was I. Mostly because I didn't have to share my underwear anymore.

As we rounded the north corner of St. Stephen's Green, I sat back in my seat, soaking up the Dublin atmosphere. The hordes of people. The crush of traffic. The blare of horns. The stench of diesel fumes.

"Do you smell that?" Nana asked suddenly.

"Diesel. Must be the fuel of choice over here."

"That's not it. Smells more like"—she inhaled deeply—"alcohol." She plucked her guidebook out of her Golden Irish Vacations tour bag and flipped through the pages. "I remember readin' there's a Guinness brewery nearby, and they give away free samples at the Hopstore."

"But Guinness is dark beer. You don't like dark beer. You don't like beer, period."

"I know, dear, but I like free samples. Look here, the Guinness brewery is number seventeen on the map. Maybe our driver could drop us off if we pass by. Should we ask?"

I gave her one of my patented "It can't hurt" shrugs and

leaned forward, tapping the driver on his back. "Excuse me. If we pass the Guinness brewery, could you—"

In the next instant he slumped forward and landed on the floor of the carriage with a thump.

Nana gasped. "You didn't need to push him, Emily. A polite tap would a worked."

"I didn't push him! Oh, my God. What's wrong with him? Is he dead? He *can't* be dead. This *can't* be happening again!" I'd discovered those three dead bodies on the *last* tour we'd taken. If it happened on this trip, too, I'd be labeled a jinx and could probably kiss my tour escort job good-bye.

We popped out of our seats for a better look. "Does he look dead to you?" I asked.

"All's I can tell from this angle is that he's bald."

"I'll check his pulse."

"No!" yelled Nana. "Grab the reins!"

My gaze fell on the leather straps that were slithering out of the driver's hand. I lunged across the back of the seat, arm extended, but they disappeared over the dashboard before I could seize them. I looked at Nana. Nana looked at me.

"Uh-oh," I said. The carriage swayed suddenly, then lurched forward as Nell discovered her head. With no driver to guide her, she broke away from her traditional route, jumped the curb, and shot down the sidewalk at a full gallop. BUMPITY-BUMP. BUMPITY-BUMP. Nana tumbled back into her seat. I clutched the driver's seat for support. Pedestrians leaped out of the way at our approach. Into bushes. Onto the hoods of parked cars. People gawked. People pointed. I saw a group of Japanese tourists crowding the sidewalk ahead of us. "Get out of the way!" I screamed, flailing my arms. "Move!"

I heard excited chatter and a symphonic click of camera

shutters as we screeched around them on two wheels and swerved onto the main walkway of St. Stephen's Green.

"Do somethin'!" Nana bellowed at me.

"Like what?"

"Make the horse stop!"

"That wasn't part of my training!" On the other hand, if the horse were choking, drowning, or needed CPR, I'd be your girl.

"Cowboys did it in the old movies all the time!" Nana yelled. "Jump on her back and grab her reins. I'd do it myself if I wasn't wearin' my good panty hose."

I knew nothing about horses. I was from Iowa. I knew about seed corn, which wasn't really helpful in this situation. I did have an idea though. "HELP!" I cried. "Somebody help us!"

The park became a blur of trees, shrubs, and flower beds as Nell raced across a lush stretch of lawn that looked like the course at Pebble Beach, only without the ocean view. Fat clods of grass flew left and right beneath her hooves. Divots here. Divots there. BUMPITY-BUMP. BUMPITY-BUMP. Uh-oh. This wasn't good. Parents grabbed their children and ran for cover. Oh, my God. What if we plowed into someone and killed them?

I craned my neck to peek at our driver again. The violent jostling was causing his body to skid toward the open end of the carriage. One major dip in the terrain, and he'd shoot out of the vehicle like a log out of a flume.

I needed to do something.

"Look at that pretty circle a red flowers up ahead," Nana said in a high vibrato, as we approached a major intersection of pathways. "Be nice to stop for a picture."

We were beyond them before I had time to blink.

"I don't mean to complain, dear, but we're missin' all the good photo opportunities."

I scrambled over the backrest of the driver's seat, crouching precariously on the cushion. "Whoa, Nellie!" I yelled.

THUMP-THUMP. The carriage pitched sharply to the right, bouncing the driver across the floor. I grabbed a fistful of his jacket to keep him from falling out. I looked up.

Dead ahead was a stand of trees, and Nell was racing straight toward them. "Hold on tight!" I yelled to Nana.

I ducked low on the seat. WHUP-WHUP! WHUP-WHUP! Foliage thrashed the sides of the carriage as we whipped between two trees. I heard an ominous creak. I opened one eye to see what was ahead.

Oh, no.

We hit the pond at breakneck speed and hurdled the concrete lip like one of the losing drivers in the chariot race in *Ben Hur*. Off flew a front wheel. Off flew a back wheel. *Creeeeek! KABOOM!* The sudden stop catapulted me off the seat and into the air. I landed on my back in a foot of water that shot up my nose all the way to my brain. Snorting, sputtering, and blinded by streams of nonwaterproof mascara, I jackknifed upward to hear a man shout, "You there! There's no swimming allowed in the pond!"

I let out a startled yelp as our driver's body sluiced out of the carriage and landed eyeball-to-eyeball on top of me.

"That goes for him too!" the man added.

Most single women who visit Ireland probably dream of having their bones jumped by an Irishman as witty as Oscar Wilde, as inspiring as William Butler Yeats, and as handsome as Pierce Brosnan. That my bones were being jumped by a short, bald guy who didn't appear to be breathing was fairly typical of the direction in which my life was headed. All that was missing was the freelance photographer who would snap my picture and sell it to a tabloid newspaper. I could see the headlines now: TOUR

ESCORT HAS SEX WITH DEAD MAN IN POND! That would go over really well in Windsor City.

It was at that moment that I heard the unmistakable whirr of Nana's new Polaroid OneStep camera. "Smile, dear!"

"Here's one of the pond in Saint Stephen's Green." Nana handed Tilly Hovick a photograph as we stood at the front desk of the Shelbourne Hotel, waiting for our room keys. Tilly was a retired professor of anthropology at Iowa State University, and was slated to be Nana's roommate for the duration of the tour.

"Interesting composition," Tilly said as she inspected the Polaroid through the magnifying glass that hung around her neck. "Who is that man lying on top of Emily?"

"Our driver. He passed out and crashed us into the pond. Then he fell on top of her. We thought for sure he was dead. Then his cell phone rang, and he answered it. He would've laid right there talkin', too, if Emily hadn't done somethin'." Nana handed Tilly a second photograph. "This one's of Emily kneein' the driver in his privates." And a third. "This is the driver curled up in pain after Emily kneed 'im. And you can see there, he's still talkin' on his cell phone. That was pretty impressive."

"What caused him to pass out?" asked Tilly. "Seizure?"

"Sloshed," said Nana. She handed Tilly a final photo. "This is the policeman who dragged Emily outta the pond and gave her a written warnin' for swimmin' in an unauthorized area."

Tilly, who made ordinary mortals quake with her legendary bluntness and direct stares, stabbed a long finger at the policeman's photo. "Did you get his name? We should march right down to the Garda Station and file a complaint. This situation was *not* Emily's fault. She was treated unfairly." She turned to me. "And if I were you, I'd sue the carriage company for damages. Look at you. You look like one of the contestants on *Survivor*."

I caught a glimpse of myself in the gilt-framed mirror decorating the lobby wall. *Ehhh.* My dark brown hair was a wild, dripping mop of corkscrew curls. Mascara circled my eyes. My new rayon blouse and skirt clung to my five-foot-five-inch frame in a series of wet, misshapen folds. I didn't look as good as a *Survivor* contestant. I looked more like "Alice Cooper Meets Xena, Warrior Princess."

Nana regarded Tilly with a twinkle in her eye. "You watch *Survivor*?"

"Reality television, Marion. Anthropology for the masses. I think of it as a modern version of Margaret Mead's *Coming of Age in Samoa* without the monographic analysis."

"I think of it as *Days of Our Lives* without the script."

Tilly looked pensive. "I hadn't thought of it that way, but in a sense, you're perfectly right. That's a very astute observation. Do you have a favorite contestant?"

I'd been concerned that Tilly and Nana wouldn't be compatible as roommates. Tilly had a Ph.D. Nana had an eighth-grade education. Tilly was five-foot-eleven, built like a beanpole, and carried a fancy walking stick. Nana was four-foot-ten, built like a fire hydrant, and carried a really big handbag. Tilly had never married. Nana had been married to the same man for over fifty years. *Survivor* was the only thing they had in common, but, come to think of it, that was probably a lot more than most *married* couples had in common. Heck, they'd probably become fast friends.

I waved my arm to catch the notice of a desk clerk. My appearance was making me nervous. I needed to change my clothes before someone issued me a written warning for shedding water in an unauthorized area. "The key to room four-ten, please? And I'm in something of a hurry."

Bernice Zwerg shuffled up to us at the front desk and looked me up and down. "Is this a new look for you, or did you find another body of water to fall into?" Bernice had the body of a rubber chicken, a dowager's hump that made her clothes hang funny, and a voice that screamed of eight packs of Marlboros a day before she'd finally kicked the habit. She'd accompanied us on our earlier tour to Switzerland, so we had history.

I narrowed my eyes at her. "I was a victim of circumstance."

She flashed me a tight little smile that said she'd heard that one before. "I thought you'd want to know that the other bus just arrived from the airport."

Since our flight from Des Moines had arrived so early, the tour company had bused us the short distance to our hotel rather than make us wait at the airport for the other flights to arrive. We were expecting a contingent of people from the East Coast and a few stragglers from the Continent to add their numbers to the twenty Iowans I was escorting.

"I heard a bunch of people from New York will be joining us," Bernice continued with a sour look. "They'll probably be loud. And pushy."

Which meant Bernice would fit in with them just fine.

"What have you got there?" Bernice asked, snatching the photos from Tilly's hands. She flipped through them quickly. "Looks like Emily having sex with a dead guy in some pond."

"He wasn't dead," Nana objected. "Emily would never engage in necrophilia, would you, dear?"

I shook my head, remembering those occasions when making love to Jack had been like having sex with a corpse.

But we'd been married, so in my case, the necrophilia was legitimate.

"How come you don't have a digital camera?" Bernice asked Nana, handing the photos back. "Polaroids are old technology."

"I'm waitin' for the price to come down," Nana said in a no-nonsense tone. She might be a millionaire, but her Midwestern frugality still reared its ugly head from time to time.

"Room four-ten," the desk clerk said, handing me my key.

"I'm going up to change, so I'll see you later," I said to Nana.

Bernice gave us a squinty look. "What? You two aren't rooming together?"

"Escorts get rooms by themselves," said Nana, "so I'm roomin' with Tilly."

"Tilly?" Bernice sucked in her cheeks. "When I asked you to room with me, you said you already had a room-mate, so I assumed it was Emily. You never said you were rooming with Tilly. *I'm* supposed to be your best friend, Marion. What's the matter? I'm not good enough for you anymore?"

"Tilly asked me first."

"Oh, I get it. It's on account of the mashed peas, isn't it?"

Back in December, Nana had slipped on some mashed peas on the floor of the senior center and bruised her tail-bone. She'd had to sit on an inflatable doughnut during the entire holiday season, which didn't work out too well during midnight mass, when my nephew punched a hole in it with his Moses action figure with authentic scale-model staff. All Nana could say was that we were lucky David hadn't brought his G.I. Joe. Joe carried his own grenade launcher.

"I don't blame you for that at all, Bernice, but you *were* the person in charge a cleanin' the floor after the Christmas luncheon. And you didn't do it."

"Couldn't be helped. I had to leave early to catch the bus to the casino. But you know about the pea situation. Every time we have a luncheon for the low vision people, they leave mashed peas all over the place. How come you don't serve a vegetable they can *see*? You're on the food committee. You ever think about serving broccoli spears?"

Hmm. My guess was, Bernice was going to be the first one voted off the island.

Thinking it might be best if the ladies mediated this themselves, I waved to Nana and slipped away. As I headed to the elevator, I looked toward the lobby to find a troupe of people muscling their way through the front door behind a willowy blonde who was all legs and teeth. Ashley Overlock. Our tour guide. She'd introduced herself to us at the airport in a voice that dripped Southern charm, then sent us on our way, but the men were still suffering palpitations from the initial meeting.

I shook my head. Men were so blind. Couldn't they see all her phony reconstruction? I ticked off the list. Bleached blond hair. Collagen-injected lips. Capped teeth. Silicone-enhanced breasts. Acrylic nails, or maybe they were silk wraps. I couldn't tell from this distance. Her legs started at her neck and were definitely her own, but wearing those spike heels was bound to give her varicose veins. In a few years she'd be forced to wear support hose under that six-inch miniskirt of hers; then we'd see how many heads she turned. Of course, there was one benefit to the support hose. She wouldn't have to shave her legs so often.

The commotion in the lobby continued as every male with traceable testosterone found an excuse to mill around Ashley. Scarlett O'Hara at the barbecue. *Geesch.* The scene made me grateful I wasn't one of the beautiful people. The ogling. The gawking. The fawning. How did she stand it?

"Y'all need to proceed to the front desk to pick up your room keys," I heard her call out. "No, I don't need assistance. Y'all just take care of yourselves. Yes, I already have plans for dinner. No, you don't need to know my room number. The front desk is right through there. Just keep moving."

I pressed the elevator button and sidled up to a plant, hoping to camouflage myself as a potted palm while the tour guests swarmed the front desk area. A full five minutes later, the door opened and I scooted inside the car, followed by a woman who announced, "Fourth floor," as if I were the elevator operator. And she didn't say please. She obviously wasn't from the Midwest. My guess was . . . New Jersey.

The doors glided shut. The elevator hummed to life. "Are you on your way to a costume party?" she asked as she lounged against the handrail. It didn't help my mood any that she was a gorgeous brunette with the most exquisitely applied makeup I'd ever seen. Razor-thin eyeliner above and below the eyes. Lips perfectly outlined and stained. Foundation and blush that made her complexion appear luminous. I knew of only two groups of people with the expertise to apply makeup so precisely: makeup artists and Texans. I revised my first opinion. Okay, she was from New Jersey by way of Dallas.

"I don't always look like this," I said. "My mascara ran."

"It's a shade too dark for you anyway. Brown would be better. Have you ever had your colors done? My guess is you're an autumn."

This was handy. Take an elevator ride. Get an instant color analysis. I wondered if this was part of the tour package.

She smiled. I smiled. I lowered my gaze to the floor. Whoa! She had the biggest feet I'd ever seen, but great shoes. She must have to order out of a catalog.

"Emily?" she said suddenly.

I checked to see if I was wearing a name tag. Nope. How did she know my name? I exchanged glances with her, thinking she looked vaguely familiar, but unable to identify her. "I'm Emily, but I'm afraid I don't know who you are."

"Emily!" She rushed at me, smothering my face with kisses and enveloping me in her arms. "It's me! You don't recognize me, do you. It's Jack! Well, Jackie now."

I tried not to look as confused as I felt.

"Jack Potter!" the woman burbled. "Remember? Your ex-husband."

CHAPTER 2

"Jack?" Oh, my God. He was dressed like a flaming drag queen. I looked him up and down, my jaw hanging slack at his transformation. The hair on his forearms had completely disappeared. Had to have been a professional wax job because Jack had boasted the forearms of a gorilla. Ouch. And what was more startling, he sported a flowing mane of chestnut hair, huge breasts, a wasp waist, and fingernails like lions' teeth. He wore a little peach silk number that hugged his body like Cling Wrap and had Lord & Taylor written all over it. No denying it. Jack Potter had a real knack for cross-dressing. "Well, would you look at you," I sputtered, snapping my jaw back into place. "You . . . you changed your hair color."

"Just some henna highlights," he said, primping in the elevator's mirrored paneling. "My hair needed more pizazz, so it was either a short, sassy Sharon Stone cut or the highlights." He studied his reflection. "You don't think it makes too much of a statement, do you?"

This was *so* Jack. He was perched on four-inch stiletto

heels and worried that his hair color might attract too much notice. "Your hair looks lovely, Jack. It's you. Definitely you. So what in the world are you doing in Dublin? Did you find a gig as a female impersonator in one of the local theaters?"

"Impersonator, nothing! Honey, I'm the real thing. Feel these puppies." He grabbed my hands and plopped them onto his breasts. "Go ahead. Give 'em a squeeze. Are they perky or what?"

"Jack!" I snatched my hands away. "You shouldn't be asking people on elevators to squeeze your breasts."

"But you're not 'people,' Emily. You're my ex-wife. You've seen me naked. Okay, then. You don't have to touch them, but do you want to see them? They're pretty spectacular." He started unbuttoning his blouse.

"No, I don't want to see them! And what do you mean they're real? Oh, my God. You've been popping those breast-enhancing herbs that Nana says are advertised on the E! television network." I gave his bustline a serious look. "Wow. That stuff really works, and it's not even FDA approved."

He fisted his hand on his hip and gave me an exasperated look. "They're *real,* Emily. And they have nothing to do with herbal remedies. It's all hormone therapy. I wasn't gay after all. This is so cool. Are you ready? I've had sex reassignment surgery!"

I stared blankly. "Excuse me?"

"Sex reassignment surgery. It's the new politically correct jargon. Maybe it hasn't reached the Midwest yet. Okay, how about . . . I'm a transsexual!"

A transsexual? As in crossing over from one gender to another? As in my ex-husband had undergone a sex change? Oh, this was nice. Nana had never understood the concept of being gay. I was dying to explain transsexuality to her.

"I've had all the surgery, and taken all the hormones, and this is the result." He struck a coquettish pose that made me realize he looked better in a skirt than I did. "I'm so happy, Emily. This is who I was always meant to be. I get to do all that exciting girl stuff now. Bikini waxes. Electrolysis. Mammograms."

Yup. Three of my favorites. "Aren't you a little young for mammograms? You're only a year older than I am."

"Well, I haven't had one yet, but I can have a baseline in only five years. I can hardly wait."

Right. Slap your breast onto a glass plate so it can be crushed like a grape in a wine press. I was looking forward to that too.

"You want to know the best thing about being a woman, Emily?"

In Jack's present state of mind, there could be only one answer. "PMS?"

"No. The best thing is, I know where everything is. Remember how when we were married, I could never find anything, even when you told me exactly where it was? That doesn't happen anymore. I put something down, I know where I left it, even if it's days later. It's uncanny. Of course, I can't parallel park worth a damn anymore. Guess that's what happens when you trade in your penis for a uterus."

"You have a uterus?"

"Sure I have a uterus." He paused thoughtfully. "At least, I think I have a uterus." He frowned. "Maybe not. To tell you the truth, I have so much new equipment down there, I'm not sure what I have. But something's sure caused my spatial intelligence to take a hike."

Maybe there was a more simple explanation. "When's the last time you had your eyes checked, Jack?"

"If you wouldn't mind, Emily. It's not 'Jack' anymore. It's 'Jackie.' Jackie Thum."

"Thum? Is that your stage name?"

"I didn't tell you!" He flashed a diamond ring the size of a walnut in front of my face. "I eloped two days ago. Thum is my married name. I'm on my honeymoon!"

I was overcome by one of those feelings that had Maalox Plus written all over it. How typical was this? My ex-husband has a sex change, grows his own set of knockers, and finds a husband before I do. I might as well jump out a twenty-story window now and get it over with. I eyed the floor indicator above the elevator door. Just my luck. The Shelbourne had only six floors.

"We'd planned to have a big December wedding, but I won an Irish vacation in a theater raffle, so we decided to elope and use the trip as our honeymoon. The only annoying thing is, the invisible print on the raffle ticket specified that the winners be booked on some *seniors'* tour, so we're rubbing shoulders with a bunch of old-timers from Brooklyn. No wonder the raffle tickets were so cheap."

"Seniors' tour?" Uh-oh. I was getting a bad feeling about this.

"Something called Golden Irish Vacations. Have you heard of it?"

I struggled not to wince. "Yeah, I've heard of it. I'm *on* it."

"Get *out* of here! You are? Did you win a raffle too?"

"Actually, it's my job. I arrange tours for a local bank's senior's travel club members; then I get to accompany them on the trip. It's a great gig. I spend a few months in an office arranging travel packages through competing national tour companies; then this is my reward."

"You're a tour guide?"

"Not a guide. An escort. I'm along to cater to the Iowans if they have medical problems, need assistance with phone calls, stuff like that."

He lunged at me, smothering me in another bone-crushing bear hug. "Isn't this bitchin'? We get to spend another honeymoon together. Remember our first one, Emily? That quaint little hotel? I can see it all now. We splurged and ordered room service. You had Oysters Rockefeller. I had a lobster tail."

I could see it too. I'd had a head cold. He'd had a dick.

The elevator *pinged* to a stop at the fourth floor. The door glided open. Jack strutted into the hall like a beauty pageant contestant on a runway, head bobbing, hips swinging, boobs bouncing, and even though the carpet was slippery as a hockey rink, he was as surefooted as a mountain goat in his snakeskin stiletto heels.

"I don't see how you can wear those things," I said, nodding toward his shoes.

"You object to snakeskin? *Please* tell me you haven't joined one of those 'reptilian rights' groups. Those people are seriously demented, Emily. If it was left up to them, all footwear would be made of nonbreathable material, like brick. Brick! Can you imagine? I mean, I have hardwood floors."

"No, I don't see how you can *walk* in them without falling over. It usually takes years of practice."

"Honey, I've been waiting all my life to wear these things. Turns out I have a shoe fetish." He checked the room numbers listed on the wall and pointed to his right. "I'm this way."

I strutted along beside him, feeling the need to reminisce about the good ole days. "Remember when your only fetish was lingerie?"

"Yeah. I used to love those satin bikinis you bought. They fit so much better than the Fruit of the Looms you used to buy me. But I have a drawer full of satin undies now, so I've moved on to footwear. You should see my closet, Emily. I make the *Sex and the City* girls look like rank amateurs in the shoe department. Here I am. Room four-twelve. Where are you located?"

I held up my key so he could see the number.

"Room four-ten? Right next door?" He clapped his hands. "Just like a college dormitory! Only, I should warn you, Emily, it might get a little loud in here later on. If you hear screams and moans, don't be naughty and put your ear to the wall." He wagged his manicured finger at me in a scolding motion. "No fair listening. Remember, I'm on my honeymoon."

I unlocked my room and closed the door behind me. I wouldn't tell him that the last person I heard screaming and moaning in a hotel room turned up dead the next morning.

But that wouldn't happen again . . . I hoped.

The Shelbourne was a grand old hotel, and I'd snagged one of the plum rooms that overlooked St. Stephen's Green. As I scrubbed mascara from my face in the shower, I pondered our incredible good luck at staying here for even *one* night. Months earlier, the Vacations agent had informed me that because of the great rates they'd negotiated at a castle in the northern part of the republic, we could afford to splurge on one night in Dublin. I didn't know about anyone else's accommodations, but I was certainly thrilled with the choice. My room was spacious, the mattress firm, the decor elegant. If I swore off food for the rest of the trip, I might even be able to afford one of the liquor miniatures kept under lock and key in the minibar.

I turbaned my hair in a towel and was searching for my mousse when I heard a BANG! BANG! BANG! on my door. Great. The interruptions were starting already. I knew that's what I was being paid to deal with, but couldn't my Iowans at least wait until I had some clothes on?

Tightening the belt of my bathrobe, I marched across the floor and then took a long look through the peephole. I threw the door open. "What can I do for you, Bernice?"

"You gotta do something." She barreled into my room like a runaway freight train, then pulled up short, looking around. "Nice place. Guess it pays to be on the bank's payroll. What would I have to do to get a room like this?"

Acid rose in my stomach at her implication that I was receiving favored status, but I was a professional. I wouldn't remind her that on our last trip, one of the rooms I occupied didn't even have windows. "Rooms are assigned at random, Bernice. Maybe you'll get the room with the view at the castle."

"Who would I have to sleep with to get an upgrade? Oh, never mind. Can't use sex as a bargaining chip anymore. In my day we agreed to have sex when we wanted something. You have sex because you enjoy it. Your generation has really screwed up the balance of power for the rest of us. So here's my problem. All my money's missing."

"You were robbed? Oh, my God! When did it happen? Are you all right? Did you get a good look at the thief's face? Did he take your credit cards too? Tell me exactly what happened." I ran to the desk for pen and paper. I'd been trained for this. I knew exactly what to do in cases of burglary, robbery, and purse-snatching. You find out all the vital information, then you call the front desk and dump it in their laps. "Tell me when the incident occurred."

"Yesterday."

I held my pen in suspended motion above the paper. "But we weren't here yesterday. You mean, it happened at O'Hare?"

"Before that."

"How much before?"

"At my house."

"You were robbed at your house in Windsor City?" This was big news, since the only crime recorded in Windsor City over the past ten years was when Luther Ellis was ticketed for jaywalking. My boss getting sent upriver for fraud didn't count because he lived in Des Moines.

"I didn't get robbed," Bernice whined. "You're such an alarmist. My traveler's checks were in the drawer of my nightstand and I walked out of the house without them. I knew I was forgetting something, but when it didn't turn out to be my bloomers or my teeth, I stopped worrying."

"Did you read the leaflet I sent out from the bank? I said you should keep all your travel documents together. I said you should make a list so you wouldn't forget anything. Did you make a list?"

"Of course I made a list. I wrote 'Buy traveler's checks.' So I bought the traveler's checks. I just forgot to bring them with me."

My leaflet obviously needed major refinement. "Did you at least bring a credit card with you?"

"Don't own a credit card. Don't believe in them. I pay cash on the barrel. So I'm gonna have to borrow some cash from you."

Section 5 of the *Escort's Manual* played back in my head. *Never, ever lend money to guests. Statistics prove you'll never get it back.* But what was the alternative? Bernice was a certified pain in the neck, but I couldn't let her starve.

I grabbed my shoulder bag and pulled out my wallet. "You'll need to call Mr. Erickson at the bank and have him wire some money to you at our next stop. I only converted a hundred American dollars into Irish punts at the airport, so I don't have a lot of cash, but this should see you through dinner tonight and lunch tomorrow." I handed her three bills of varying size, each stamped with a head shot of a different dignitary—a nun, a man wearing Harry Potter glasses, and a guy with a giant balloon head the color of Bazooka bubble gum.

She stared at the bills. "That's only thirty-five pounds. I need more. We're in the shopping district." She eyed my remaining note—the one with a blue-headed man sporting an out-of-control mustache.

"I guess you'll just have to exercise a little restraint until your money arrives, Bernice."

"I got grandkids. Restraint won't cut it."

Grandkids. I understood grandkids. I wasn't Ebenezer Scrooge. "Okay. I'll give you the guy with the blue head and you can give me back the other three."

She plucked the fifty from my hand and shoved the bill with the balloon-headed man at me. "That should be enough to cover your dinner. My grandkids will be real beholden to you, Emily."

I noted the denomination of the bill. A twenty. "Wait a minute, Bernice . . ."

She was in full retreat toward the door. "I saw one of those automatic bank machines right around the corner from here. I hear you can get all the money you want from those things for just a minimal fee. And they're open all the time. I'll probably need another small loan tomorrow morning. Before the bus leaves would be nice. And I'd prefer small bills. Thanks, Emily."

I stared openmouthed at the door. That woman! I was going to strangle her! How come she couldn't be thoughtful, and polite, and unassuming like the other ladies in the group? How come she always tried to take unfair advantage of every situation? Nana always said there was *one* in every crowd, and Bernice was certainly the *one* in ours. UNNNH!

I returned to the bathroom sputtering to myself. I'd have

to find an ATM so *I* could eat lunch tomorrow. Could I handle a financial crisis or what? I'm surprised Alan Greenspan wasn't knocking down my door in search of fiscal advice.

I continued the search for my mousse. *Knock! Knock! Knock!* I stuck my head out of the bathroom and glared at the door. Too soon to be Alan Greenspan. Had to be Bernice. She'd probably come back for my 401K.

I stormed across the room and flung open the door. "WHAT?"

He was leaning against the doorjamb, all whipcord muscle and elegance, dressed in a black silk turtleneck and black pleated Italian pants. His hair was gloss black. His eyes were smoke blue and sultry. He gave me a lazy look up and down, then broke into a slow smile as he eyed my waist. My mouth dropped open in surprise as he hooked his forefinger through my belt loop and drew me against him. "Hello, darling," he whispered in his French/German/Italian accent. "I've missed you."

"Etienne? Oh, my God. Etienne! What are you doing here? You said you were working on a big case. You said you couldn't get away. You said—"

"I lied." He covered my lips with his mouth. In one lightning move he spun me around, kicked the door shut, and pressed me against the wall. His tongue entwined with mine. He wedged his knee between my thighs, parted my robe, and braced his hands on my bare hips. This is what I loved about Etienne. He really knew how to get my attention.

"I want to make love to you, Emily. Now."

I'd been thinking about taking in the brilliant high tea in the Lord Mayor's Lounge at half-three, but I liked this offer better.

"Okay." I don't believe in being coy or playing hard to get. When I fall in love with a man, I like to show it.

I yanked his turtleneck out of his pants, glided my palms up his naked spine, and sucked his tongue halfway down my throat.

Tap tap tap. The door. Again.

I hadn't had sex since my annulment. I wasn't hearing anything. I dropped my hands to his waist and fumbled with his belt.

"Are you going to get that?" Etienne rasped.

"Get what?" I unhooked his belt and probed for the metal pull tab of his zipper.

"The door. Someone's knocking."

"I don't hear a thing." No pull tab. He had a button fly. *Unnnh!* I grabbed his fly front with both hands and wrenched it apart. *Ping! Ping! Ping!* Buttons flew in every direction.

Etienne stopped breathing. "Emily, darling, these are new trousers."

"Not to worry. I have my sewing kit with me." And, it just so happened, I'd brought Velcro.

Tap tap tap.

Etienne looked at the door. He looked at me. His police inspector's expression reshaped his features. So much for the romantic mood. "It could be important," he said.

Getting laid was important too. Especially after the drought I'd had. WHY were the Swiss so practical? "If it's Bernice Zwerg, I'm not answering it."

We shuffled toward the door in tandem. Etienne squinted through the peephole. "It's an elderly gentleman."

"What does he look like?"

"Short and bald."

"That's no help." I was with a group of seniors. They were all short and bald. "Can you be more specific?"

"Very short. Very bald."

Okay. If I could get rid of whoever it was, Etienne and I

could recapture the mood and get down to some serious sex. Could I think on my feet, or what?

I slithered out of Etienne's embrace, motioned him to an alcove of the room where he would be out of sight, and readjusted my bathrobe. I cracked the door an inch and peeked out. George Farkas, dressed in a tartan plaid shirt and chinos, bobbed his head in my direction and peeked in.

George had lost his leg to a Nazi land mine in '44, his hair to a tropical infection in '55, and his wife to another man in '66. He never replaced the hair or the wife, but he bought a dandy new prosthetic leg a few years ago that set him back twenty thousand dollars. Probably a bargain considering how much a new wife might cost him in Medicare A and B payments alone.

I opened the door wider. "George? What can I do for you?"

"I'm sorry to bother you, Emily, but I got a problem."

Uh-oh. The last time he had a problem, I'd had to fish his artificial leg out of Lake Lucerne while on the upper deck of a tour boat. George might have saved Europe's butt by rescuing it from Nazi oppression in '44, but I'd saved George's butt by preventing his prosthesis from becoming fish bait in '99.

"What kind of problem?" I prayed it had nothing to do with male sexual dysfunction.

"I left my traveling alarm clock at home. Do you have one you could lend me? There's a clock radio in my room, but I can't figure out how to set the alarm. Don't want to screw up and be late for the bus tomorrow."

Iowans are never late. Ever. It's part of their genetic code. If medical science could isolate the gene and reproduce it in drug form, we could probably eliminate tardiness altogether. "You wait right there, George. I think I might be able to help you."

I raced across the floor, gave a thumbs-up to Etienne, and riffled through my suitcase. Aha! I raced back to George and handed him the clock. "I packed an extra. I just installed a new battery in this one and it has big numbers so you don't have to squint to see the time."

"Don't need to squint since my cataract surgery. I can probably see better than you. It's because of the lens implants." He pointed to a spot near my feet. "There's buttons all over your carpet, Emily. You should pick 'em up before you slip."

"I'll do that. Let me know if there's anything else I can do for you, George." Am I good or what? Even in the throes of pre-orgasmic distress, I can be helpful and courteous. I placed my hand on the door to close it.

"Wait a minute!" I heard Jackie call from down the hall. "I need an opinion."

Uh-oh. I'd forgotten about Jack. My breath caught somewhere in my chest as I considered this unexpected dynamic. Jack was on the tour. Etienne was on the tour. At some point in time, I'd probably have to introduce the man I love to the woman who *used* to be the man I loved. Oh, this was nice. Maybe leaping out the window from four stories up *would* be enough to kill me. Or at least keep me in a vegetative state until the tour was over.

"I want you to give me an honest opinion," she said as she held two garments in the air. "Which do you think for my wedding night? The sheer black babydoll with the pink satin trim and matching georgette thong, or the white chiffon with the flocked velvet vine pattern and the slit up to my navel? You're a man," she said to George, reading his name tag. "Which one do you like, George?"

The fact that Jackie was having this conversation dressed in a leopard skin bra, string panty, and nothing else might have had some bearing on George's inability to respond immediately. It's hard for an old guy to be articulate when he's collapsed against the wall and hyperventilating.

"Is he going to be all right?" Jackie asked. "Look how red his face is. Should he be breathing into a paper bag? I wish I could help out, but I don't have any paper products with me. All I have is plastic, and I'm pretty sure plastic would suffocate him. Maybe we should try giving him an aspirin."

"Maybe you should try roaming the hall in something other than your skivvies." What was wrong with her? Well, other than the fact that she'd lost all spatial intelligence and no longer sported body hair. I stepped into the hall and slapped George on the back. He pounded his chest, then waved his hand toward Jackie. "The black babydoll," he gasped out, the words barely audible. "I like that see-through stuff."

I shook my head. "I don't know. For a wedding night I prefer the white chiffon. It seems a little more . . . you know . . . sacrificial."

"The black," George countered. "And if you don't mind my saying so, young lady, your husband is one lucky man. How come all the good ones are already taken?"

"Why you sweet man," Jackie gushed. "I might have to march over there and give you a great big kiss right on top of your little bald head."

Not a good idea. He'd gone tachycardic just looking at her. I suspected body contact might kill him.

"Emily, honey!" called Ashley Overlock from the far end of the corridor. "Stay right there! I have things to give you."

Aargh! What was *with* these people and all the interruptions? I might have pulled out all my hair if it hadn't been wrapped in a towel. My heart started to pound. Prickly warmth crawled up my neck. I watched Ashley approach in her supermodel mode, blond hair spilling over her shoulders, all confidence and efficiency. "What kinds of things?" I asked as she joined us.

"Maps. Time schedules. A more detailed itinerary of the trip. Guests like to know where they're all going and what time they have to leave. If you'd hand these out to the Iowa people, you'd save me a whole bunch of time." She emptied the stack of folders into my arms. "I've written names and room numbers on each folder. No hurry about delivering them. After you dry your hair will be fine."

Etienne and I had engaged in brief sessions of cybersex over the past few months, but I figured the real thing would take a lot longer, so I needed to buy some time. "I usually let my hair air-dry."

"So you can deliver them while your hair is drying, sugar. That's even better."

Jackie waved her two wedding night selections in the air again. "I'm taking a survey," she said to Ashley. "Which one would you wear on the first night of your honeymoon?"

Ashley gave her one of those narrow looks women give each other when they discover the competition has thinner thighs, better makeup, and deeper cleavage. "You're on the tour, aren't you?"

"I certainly am. Jackie Thum. I introduced myself to you at the airport."

"Sugar, where do you think you are? Hollywood and Vine? Y'all can't run around the Shelbourne in your underwear. It's not that kind of place. You want to get us all kicked out? For God's sake, throw some clothes on and keep them on. And to answer your question, I wouldn't be caught dead in either one of those getups. They have to be the poorest example of taste and style I ever did see."

Jackie's face froze with the unkindness. I guess she had to learn sometime. Women fall into two categories. The first category say mean things to your face and smile about it behind your back. The second category say mean things behind your back but smile to your face. Ashley, apparently, fell into category number one.

"You don't like them?" Jackie's voice was small, her enthusiasm crushed.

George cleared his throat. "I like the black one."

Ashley pinned him to the wall with her eyes. "No one cares about your opinion."

"Excuse me, but *I* care about his opinion," Jackie spoke up. "If George has something to say, I'm all ears."

Uh-oh. I could see it coming. Ashley's gaze fluttered to the carpet. She went in for the kill. "Looks to me as if you're all feet. What size are those things anyway? Jumbo?"

I guess this was the downside of sex changes. A surgeon might be able to get rid of your dick, but he can't do squat about your feet.

Jackie curled her toes at the criticism, looking as if she wished she'd worn slippers. Her shoulders slumped. Her eyes welled with tears. Poor thing. She hadn't been female long enough to gain any expertise at being snide and snotty.

George plucked a clean handkerchief from his pocket and handed it to Jackie. "Got something in your eye? Why don't I walk you back to your room and have a look. I'm pretty good at making things better."

The dear man. I'd kiss his little bald head myself if I could be sure it wouldn't give him a coronary. Ashley arched an eyebrow at me when they'd gone.

"You mark my words, that woman is going to be trouble. Prancing around half naked. Titillating the old men. Flaunting what no woman should be flaunting in public. Back home in Georgia, we have a word for women like that."

"Debutante?"

She made a sound like someone choking on a peach pit. "*I* . . . was a debutante."

"Really?" I said, feigning surprise. "Who would have guessed?"

"I was presented at the Augusta Symphony Guild Cotillion." She swept her hand down the length of her leg in a dramatic flourish. "I wore a white satin gown encrusted with thousands of tiny seed pearls and long white gloves. I was crowned 'Miss Cotillion.' " She touched her hair with the memory. "I still have my tiara."

"We have cotillions in Windsor City too. But we call them pig roasts." Unlike Jackie, I'd been female for a long time, and I was good at it.

Ashley floated back to the present looking too confused to continue our conversation. "Well, I'm getting nothing done standing here talking to y'all. If anyone complains to you about the rooms, have them call me and I'll set them straight."

"What's to complain about?" I had to concede. "The rooms are great. Your company must have negotiated a really good deal at the castle to be able to afford a night here."

Ashley examined a strand of her long blond hair. "We had some wiggle room. It was simply a matter of turning a sow's ear into a silk purse."

We were definitely not on the same wavelength because I didn't have a clue what she was talking about, and I'd grown up next door to a hog farm. "What do you mean?"

"The *castle,* Emily. It doesn't have the most . . . stellar reputation."

Okay. The picture was getting a little clearer. "You mean, it got only one star in the hotel rating guide?"

"I mean, it's haunted."

CHAPTER 3

"IT'S WHAT?"

"It's haunted, but only if you believe in that kind of supernatural mumbo jumbo."

My voice rose to a pitch that was inaudible to most humans. "You booked a group of senior citizens with pacemakers . . . and hypertension . . . and predementia . . . into a haunted castle?"

"Not so loud! Do you want the whole floor to hear?"

"Yes!"

"Look, Emily, there's some cheesy ghost story connected with the castle, but it happened so many centuries ago no one even remembers the details."

"I hope you don't expect me to believe that. The Irish have memories like elephants. They forget nothing, *especially* if it's bad. Why do you think the country is still divided?"

"Oh, and I suppose you're an authority on all things Irish?"

I'd seen *The Manions of America* miniseries, so I figured

that made me something of an authority, even if I did miss one night. "I have my sources."

Ashley shook her head. "If y'all want to embrace that silliness about the castle, go ahead, but you're a modern woman, Emily. I'd think you'd know better. Who would have thought a levelheaded Midwesterner like y'all would believe in ghosts?"

She had me there. If I said I didn't believe in ghosts, I'd be admitting there was no problem. If I said I *did* believe in ghosts, I'd make myself look like a nut case. Damn. "Are you going to warn the guests about the potential for hauntings?"

"Not on your life. We don't want anyone influenced by the power of suggestion. I've been in this business a long time, sugar, and I've found that what people really want is a grand hotel at bargain basement prices. That's exactly what we're giving them, so do us all a favor and don't rock the boat." She thrust a manicured finger at me. "Remind everyone that we leave at seven o'clock tomorrow morning, so they should have their luggage outside the door by five so it can be loaded on the bus."

I returned to my room feeling as if I'd been slugged in the gut with a baseball bat. I dumped my armload of files onto the bed, then stared at Etienne, who was sitting in one of the room's four tapestried armchairs with an amused look on his face. "You'll never believe what that . . . that *woman* has done," I sputtered.

"Booked you into a haunted castle."

"You heard."

"Emily, darling, I suspect the entire fourth floor heard."

"Can she do that? You know the legal system. Isn't there some law against booking people into haunted castles without their knowledge?"

Etienne shrugged. "I suppose it depends on whether the spirits doing the haunting are deemed to be benign or malevolent. But this is Ireland, Emily. I was under the impression that all the castles in Ireland were haunted to some degree. I thought it was part of the country's charm. Or a splendid marketing ploy."

Bless his unflappable Swiss logic. I was getting the picture now. "Of course. A castle doesn't have to be haunted for someone to *claim* it's haunted. Saying a place *is* simply makes it more intriguing to tourists." For the first time in five minutes I was able to draw a calm breath, which allowed me time to bristle at how effortlessly Ashley had teased a negative reaction out of me. Boy, had she yanked my chain. Well, from now on, she could tell me the sky was falling and I'd take it in stride. Haunted castle. Right.

"We have castles in Switzerland too," Etienne continued, "and it's the haunted ones that cater to the most tourists. For whatever reason, people delight in the prospect of being frightened."

"Not me." I loosened the belt of my robe and gave him a suggestive peek of my bare shoulder. "I'm more delighted at the prospect of being ravished. Now, where were we?"

The lusty smile on his face was accompanied by a familiar chirruping in his trousers. I rolled my eyes, then drilled him with a look of pure exasperation.

"Forgive me, Emily. I'll only be a moment." He dug his cell phone out of his pocket and flipped it open. "Miceli," he said in his police inspector's voice.

Wasn't this just typical? A handsome man in my bedroom and the only thing he can whip out of his trousers is his cell phone. I plucked his buttons off the rug and placed them in the ashtray on the desk as he made a string of comments like "I see" and "Yes," ending with a definitive "I'll need to get back to you."

"Bad news?" I asked, anticipating the worst.

He stood up, his palms open in apology. "I can leave the

job, but apparently I can't escape the job. There's been a break in the case I've been investigating. I have a raft of phone calls to make, and it will probably take me the rest of the night, which means . . ."

No sex. Great. This was all my mother's fault. She maintained that having my marriage annulled returned me to "virgin" status, so she was offering up a monthly novena that I'd remain in that state until I walked down the aisle again. I tried to explain that an annulment altered a woman's marital status, *not* her anatomy, but she was having none of my argument. "If the marriage never happened, Emily, you never went to bed with Jack. That makes you a virgin. I'm mother to a twenty-nine-year-old virgin. Imagine." The awe in her voice attested to the fact that, in this day and age, she considered this circumstance to be far more extraordinary than either the Immaculate Conception or the Virgin Birth.

"I'm sorry, Emily. I signed up for this tour of yours and I intend to enjoy it. I promise that, after tonight, I'm all yours."

Sure, I thought. If my mother will stop praying long enough for it to happen.

Facing the rest of the afternoon on my own, I decided to take care of some necessary escort duties before venturing out to find the nearest ATM. I dried and styled my hair, slipped into a long almond suede skirt and a short-sleeve ivory turtleneck sweater, pulled on short leather boots with decorative front lacings and side zippers, scooped up the file folders Ashley had given me, and began knocking on doors. "Maps, itineraries, and timetables," I said as I made my deliveries. "The bus leaves at seven o'clock tomorrow morning, so be sure to have your luggage outside your door by five."

I saved Nana's room for last. She answered the door on the first knock and stepped into the hall so as not to waken Tilly, who was stretched out on the bed and snoring like a Boeing 747. "I hope she quiets down tonight," Nana said with some concern. "Your grampa used to snore loud like that until I did somethin' about it."

"Did you sign him up for one of those sleep disorder studies?"

"I moved into the guest bedroom. Worked real good. What's this folder for?"

I explained the contents of the folder and reiterated the information about the luggage and bus departure time for tomorrow morning. "So how are you and Tilly getting along?"

"Would you believe she didn't realize the man who won all the money on the first *Survivor* program is like your ex-husband?"

I stiffened. The less Nana remembered about Jack, the better. "You mean, he's an aspiring actor?"

"Nope. I mean, he walked outta a closet too."

I made an empty gesture with my hand. Okay. So her terminology was a little off. Why quibble over a verb. "Really?"

"Yup. Tilly calls it 'gender imbalance,' and she wrote a big anthropology paper once theorizin' it happens 'cause a body chemistry. Caused a big stir. She says there's gender imbalance in every culture, which means the root cause is biological 'stead a behavioral. And, listen to this, Emily, in one culture, folks with gender imbalance are given elevated status 'cause they're recognized as havin' superior social sensitivity and special knowledge. Isn't that a nice attitude to have?"

My curiosity was piqued. "Did she say which culture that was?"

"Some 'Islanders.' "

" 'Long'?" New Yorkers had always elevated gay actors, dress designers, and artists to celebrity status.

"I'm pretty sure it was 'Trobriand,' but 'Long' was a good guess." She smiled at me in the same way she used to when we'd share tea and cookies together when I was a little girl. "Tilly and me are goin' out for a bite to eat after she wakes up. You wanna join us, dear? I don't want you to think I'm ignorin' you when you're all alone."

"Thanks anyway, but I'll probably splurge on something from the minibar a little later. And, actually . . ." I paused for dramatic effect. "I'm not alone. You'll never guess who signed up for the tour."

"Inspector Miceli."

There were times when my grandmother's mental powers were absolutely scary. "You guessed. How did you guess?"

"He spoke to me in the lobby while I was waitin' for my key. Such a nice young man. A real hottie. That Ashley person thinks so too, 'cause she was all over him."

Heat sizzled up my neck and scalded my cheeks. If this was a precursor to hot flashes, I wanted nothing to do with the real thing. "What do you mean, 'all over him'?"

"Well, dear, she wanted to know his name, where he was from, what he did for a livin', if he was married. Battin' her eyelashes and attachin' herself to his arm like static cling. I'd watch out for her if I was you, Emily."

I returned to my room feeling like a juggler with one too many balls to keep in the air. I composed a mental "To Do" list. One: Keep Nana away from Jack. Even though I could trust Nana with the information about Jack's operation, there was no telling how a group of conservative Midwesterners would react if word leaked out that their esteemed escort was once married to another "female" on the tour. It wouldn't exactly be a selling point on my résumé.

Two: Keep Ashley away from Jack. Considering how well their first encounter had gone, they could very well come to blows. It would be a tragedy if they ended up killing each other, especially after all the surgery Jack had recently undergone.

Three: Keep Etienne away from Jack. I wasn't real sure how this introduction would play out. Jack probably wouldn't have any problem handling it, but I was less sure about Etienne. I was breaking new ground here. My guess was, this topic hadn't even been covered in "Dear Abby" yet.

I massaged a sudden throbbing in my temples as I contemplated my three tasks. Was it my imagination, or did most of my problems revolve around Jack? Just like when we were married. Everything *always* revolved around Jack. Maybe I couldn't juggle all the balls myself. Maybe I needed help. Maybe I should simply break down and talk to Jack. *Hmm.* I liked that idea. Simple. Efficient. It sounded like something Nana would suggest.

I marched into the hall and knocked on Jack's door. No answer. I knocked again. Still no answer. I returned to my room and downed two ExcedrinPM. Maybe it was jet lag. Maybe it was stress. Whatever the reason, my head suddenly felt as if it had a little man inside who was hacking his way out with a really big hammer. I unzipped my boots, slipped them off, and curled up on the bed, rehearsing how I could ask Jack to pretend not to know me without hurting his feelings. Maybe it was a good thing he wasn't in his room. This gave me more time to figure out what to say and how to say it.

I scratched an itchy spot at the back of my neck where my turtleneck was irritating my skin. Felt as if the tag was poking into me. I should get up and cut it off, but at the moment, I was too sluggish to even think about it. I heard a door slam in the hall and a faint echo of conversation in the room next to mine. Jack was back. Excellent. But I needed more time. Ten more minutes. Just ten more minutes and I'd have everything all figured out.

Brrrng brrrng! Brrrng brrrng!

I threw a blind hand toward the ringing phone and knocked the handset off the cradle, causing it to bungee-jump to the floor in a raucous clatter that brought me instantly awake. I stretched my neck and blinked several times. My headache had disappeared. Wow, that was a well-spent ten minutes. I reeled in the handset off the floor and spoke into the receiver in a scratchy voice. "Hello?"

"You have five minutes. If you're not *aboard the bus* in that time, we'll leave without y'all. You're an *escort,* Emily. We're not supposed to have to wait for the escorts! Not only that, our bus driver was in a car accident on his way to work and broke his leg, so they sent us a replacement. A rookie. This will be his first time out. Of all the *freaking* things to happen! Not only that, our local guide has come down with laryngitis, so she won't be joining us until she has her voice back, which could be four or five days, so the rookie will have to share his knowledge with us in the interim, if he *has* any knowledge. Not only that, *you* being late is just making my day complete!"

I paused. "Ashley?"

"Just get down here!"

I peered at the digital readout on the clock radio. "What do you mean I'm late? It's only seven oh five. Did you have something planned this evening that I didn't know about?"

"Evening? It's seven oh five A.M.! You have five minutes!" *Click.*

A.M.? I pivoted toward the curtained window. Uh-oh. That sure looked like cool morning light rather than warm evening light streaming in. *Uff da.* I'd slept the night away. *Uff da* is a pseudoreligious Norwegian saying commonly used in Iowa. Its most popular translations are, "holy smoke," "holy cow," and "holy crap!"

I leaped out of bed and shoved my feet into my boots. I combed my fingers through my hair as I raced toward the bathroom. No time to brush my teeth or touch up yesterday's makeup. I pitched all my toiletries into their bag, threw the bag into my pullman, flung my pocketbook over my shoulder, and ran out the door. I readjusted my sweater and smoothed the wrinkles from my skirt on the elevator ride down, thankful I'd fallen asleep with my clothes on. But how could I have slept so long? The jet lag? The Excedrin? The stress? A combination of the three? *Aargh!*

My neck started itching again as I rushed into the lobby. I scratched the patch with annoyance. I hadn't cut the tag off my sweater yet, so the irritation would probably persist all day. Great. A liveried doorman held the door for me as I ran out onto the sidewalk, my pullman rattling behind me on squeaky wheels. Two tour buses were parked curbside. I figured ours was the one with Ashley pacing alongside, staring at her watch.

"I'm here!" I yelled.

She spun around and glared at me. Today, she was wearing an emerald green blazer, a white three-buttoned vest that exposed cleavage halfway to her naval, a black spandex skirt the size of a postage stamp, and square-toed black slides. I rolled my eyes. How professional. If she leaned over too far, it would take her the rest of the day to get those silicone wonders of hers under containment again.

"How good of you to join us," she said, her voice dripping sarcasm. "Michael!" She motioned for the bus driver. "There's one last piece of luggage here for y'all to load."

Michael was a florid-faced man in his late thirties with a pitted complexion and muscles like those of the Incredible Hulk. His thighs were so huge, they swished against each other when he walked, knocking him left and right. Every step seemed a struggle for balance. The only thing saving him from complete inertia was the fact that he was bow-legged. And not just a little. You could have driven a Dodge Durango through this guy's legs without having to retract the mirrors.

"Get on the bus and find your seat," Ashley said to me. "We're already behind schedule."

Michael jammed the handle of my suitcase back into the housing, hefted all fifty-two pounds one-handed, and tossed it into the luggage bay. He locked the compartment, then lumbered back onto the bus without looking up or saying a word. Chatty fellow. I guess he hadn't taken time to kiss the Blarney Stone yet.

I scooted up the stairs close behind him, my nostrils suddenly assaulted by a stench more pungent than a blast of the anhydrous ammonia my father used to fertilize his fields. "My God." I crooked my finger beneath my nose. "What *is* that?"

"Michael," Ashley said in an acid whisper behind me. "He smells."

Whoa! Too bad the bus wasn't equipped with oxygen masks. I hoped Etienne was saving me a seat at the *back* of the bus. But he wasn't. He was settled into the first window seat with the much coveted "unobstructed view," which was way too close to Michael. I looked at Etienne. I looked at Michael. I wondered how long I could hold my breath. Maybe I'd turn blue and have to be resuscitated. Hmm.

One could hope. I flashed Etienne my most engaging smile and slid into the seat beside him.

"What do you think you're doing?" Ashley stood in the aisle beside me, hands braced on her hips, eyes slatted, voice pinched. She appeared to be talking to me.

"I found an open seat," I said. "I'm sitting down."

"Not there, you're not. Assigned seating, Emily." She pointed to a square of paper on the window that read: OVERLOCK/MICELI.

Not assigned seating. I *hated* assigned seating. "We had open seating in Switzerland, except for the day we visited Titisee-Neustadt."

"Open seating never works. The same people always try to hog the front seats. And the first aisle seat is always reserved for the tour guide. You should know that, Emily. It's *my* seat, and you're in it."

"Allow me to trade places with the person Emily is supposed to sit with," Etienne offered. "I'll be happy to give up my unobstructed view to sit beside Ms. Andrew." His voice dipped to a sultry whisper. "There's something very important I've been meaning to ask her."

I shot him a look. He wanted to ask me something? Oh, my God. He looked so serious. Was he thinking about popping the question? But . . . but . . . we hadn't discussed the *M* word yet. We hadn't even professed our love for each other! I was ready for sex, but was I ready for marriage again? Oh, my God. Things were moving *way* too quickly here.

"The bus is full!" Ashley sniped. "There will be no random movement. Everyone stays where I've seated them. Besides, sugar, if I break the rules for you, I'll have to break them for everyone else, and we can't have that, can we?"

Ashley Overlock was *really* starting to piss me off. But I refused to lose my temper, or make a scene, or be made to look like a whiner in front of the group. I had a position of responsibility. It was my duty to remain cool and unflappable. And with a little concentration, I knew I could force myself to do that. After all, I had a degree in theater. I'd been professionally trained to fake the hell out of people.

"Will you *please* find your seat so we can leave?" Ashley persisted.

I stood up, skewering Ashley with a pinched-lip, narrow-eyed glare that said, "One wrong move with my man and I'll rip your lungs out through your nostrils." I'd developed this particular expression as a survival technique while baby-sitting my five nephews. When they saw "the look," they ran screaming for their rooms. I didn't elicit a scream out of Ashley, but she did leap back a full step in the aisle to allow me a wide berth as I passed. I obviously hadn't perfected the adult version yet.

The bus suddenly hummed to life like a huge June bug. The engine roared. The floor vibrated. The air stank of diesel fumes. I navigated my way down the center aisle to the sound of Ashley's voice floating out to us over the loudspeaker.

"Top o' the mornin', y'all, and welcome to the Golden Irish Vacations tour of the Emerald Isle. I'm Ashley Overlock, your tour guide, and this is our driver, Michael Malooley, who'll be with us for the duration of the trip."

To the left and right I noted the Iowa contingent and the common attire and accessories for the day. For the men, plaid shirts, blue jeans, and baseball caps advertising Pioneer seed corn and John Deere tractors. For the women, elastic-waisted polyester pants, light nylon jackets, and umbrellas.

"Golden Irish Vacations is known for its unique tour packages," Ashley continued, "and that means y'all will be treated to a taste of Ireland that few other tourists experience."

I patted Nana on the shoulder on my way by and nodded at Tilly. Beyond them, I noted the attire of the New Yorkers. The men in skintight shirts opened halfway down their chests. Slicked-back hair. Lots of gold chains circling their throats. Expensive sunglasses. The women with tastefully loud blouses. Pouffy platinum, blond, and ink black hair. Bangles dangling from their ears, throats, and wrists. Lots of red nail polish.

"Our destination this morning will be an area near the Inishowen Peninsula in the north of the republic, a drive of about three and a half hours. We'll have lunch at Ballybantry Castle, which will be our overnight accommodation for the next few days. And just between you and me, y'all are gonna *love* this castle. It was built in the sixteen hundreds, and even though it's undergone extensive renovation in recent years, it still retains its original charm. It has a little something for everyone. A moat. A dungeon. Towers. Turrets."

Ghosts, if you believed in that sort of thing. The pneumatic brakes hissed. The engine revved. We nosed into morning traffic by jumping the curb and swerving blindly across three lanes of cars. Horns blared. Tires screeched. I lunged for the back of the nearest seat and dug my fingers into the upholstery. *Uff da!* I should stop worrying about the castle being haunted. If this was a sample of Michael Malooley's driving skill, he'd have us wrapped around a light pole before we ever reached the place.

"Jeezuz H. Kee-reist!" protested a man from the back of the bus. "Where'd this guy get his driver's license? In a box of Cracker Jacks?"

"This is Michael's first official tour of duty," Ashley announced in a honeyed tone, "so I know y'all will make it a good experience for him by being real understanding until he works out all the kinks."

Two seats ahead, Jackie caught my eye and gave me a

hesitant wave. She was sitting next to a man who was apparently sound asleep, slumped against the window, his head buried within the depths of a hooded sweatshirt. Must be the new bridegroom. Jackie must have exhausted him. "Rough night?" I teased as I zigzagged my way past her.

Her thickly mascaraed eyes welled with tears that sent her searching for a tissue. "I don't want to talk about it."

Uh-oh. Was there trouble in Paradise already? Had the wedding night not gone well? Holy smoke. What if Jackie hadn't told her husband about her sex change? What if she'd only told him last night? Ooh, boy. I was glad I wasn't in her shoes today. Actually, considering the size of her feet, I was glad not to be in her shoes any day.

I looked far ahead to find the last empty seat on the bus, surrounded by a sea of faces I didn't recognize, and one that I did. I winced. Okay. This clinched it. There was no God.

"Where's my money?" Bernice Zwerg demanded as I sat down beside her.

"What money?"

"You were supposed to get money out of the ATM for me. Small bills."

I scrunched my eyes and whacked myself on the forehead. "That's right."

"I hope you got a lot because I used up almost all my cash on supper last night."

I sighed tiredly. "Here's the scoop. I fell asleep early last night and didn't wake up until"—I checked my watch—"eleven minutes ago. The upshot is, I'm sorry, but I never got to the ATM."

"Oh, boy, you're some escort. What am I supposed to do now?"

This was probably a good time to remind myself that I

was being paid a lot of money to deal patiently with people like Bernice.

"There are other ATMs in Ireland, Bernice. We'll probably find one in the town near the castle. I'll get your money there."

"What am I supposed to do in the meantime?"

"I told you. The bank can wire you money. Or you could apply for a credit card. Some companies even take applications over the phone these days." I flashed her a half-smile. I was in control again, the ultraprofessional, lobbing her objections back at her like balls in a tennis volley.

"What's wrong with your neck?" she asked.

"My neck? Nothing. Why?"

"It's all red."

"I've been scratching."

"There's lumps all over it."

Lumps? Lumps weren't good. I tore open the flap of my shoulder bag and rummaged around for a mirror.

"There's no toilet on this bus," whined a woman behind me in a nasally, hard-voweled New York accent. "The brochure promised us a toilet. What are we supposed to do if we have to go in the middle of nowhere?"

"Look around, Gladys," said her male companion. "The whole country's the middle of nowhere."

"I'm serious, Ira!"

"You're always serious. When aren't you serious? I'm happy, you're serious. Tell me somethin' I don't know."

I peered at my neck in the mirror of my compact. *Ehh!* Bernice was right. My neck was cross-hatched with welts the length of my baby finger. Oh, my God. Nana had mentioned seeing a case like this on *Rescue 911*. At any moment my throat was going to swell shut from anaphylactic shock. Then I'd die. *Ehh!*

"You ever been allergic to anything before?" Bernice piped up.

"No," I said in a panic. "I'm in perfect health. I've never even had a cavity!"

"Well, you're allergic to something now."

"Look, Ernie," squawked the woman in front of me, jabbing her finger at the window. "That dump truck has a whole load of tailpipes in the back. And look how rusty they are. They were probably made in Japan."

"It's not tailpipes," said her husband. "It's probably peat. They use that crap for fuel over here."

"No way. How you gonna pump that stuff into your gas tank?"

"It's not for cars, Ethel. Jeez, you're such a genius. Fuel to heat the house. They use it in their stoves. Their fireplaces."

"How come they don't use electricity? They have electricity over here, don't they?" Silence, then in an emphatic snarl: "Ireland was your idea, Ernie. If I can't use my curling iron for the next ten days, you're gonna hear about it!"

Bernice squinted more closely at my neck. "I'm beginning to remember that my husband's neck had a notion to swell up like that sometimes."

Not encouraging. Bernice's husband had been dead for half a century. "Is that how he died?"

"You bet."

Oh, great. My throat constricted. My heart beat double-time. This was it. I was a goner.

"He was on his way to see the doc for a tetanus shot, and just before he left the house, his neck swelled up like yours. He was dead before he ever got there. Doc said it was hives brought on by the stress of thinking about that shot. Harold was awful needle phobic."

"Hives? He died from hives?"

Bernice nodded wistfully. "By the time he reached town, they'd spread all over. When he bent down to scratch his ankle, he missed a Stop sign and got broadsided by an ice truck. Back in those days, they used to deliver right to your door. They tell me he died before he ever knew what hit him."

My heart stopped racing. I discovered I could still breathe. "So your husband didn't actually die from hives. He died in a car accident."

"If he hadn't had the hives, he wouldn't have bent down to scratch. If he hadn't scratched, he wouldn't have been broadsided. He died from hives."

And I was still a virgin. Just ask my mother.

Over the loudspeaker, Ashley continued to enlighten us about our surroundings. "On your left you'll note some of the lovely stone buildings that form the campus of Trinity College, which is the oldest university in Ireland, founded by Elizabeth the First and dating back to 1592. The college is home to what is described as the most beautiful book in the world, the Book of Kells, which is a manuscript of the four Gospels in Latin, scripted and illuminated by Columban monks during the eighth century."

I angled my mirror toward the light for a better look at my throat. "So you think this looks like hives?" I said to Bernice.

"It's hives, all right. But I don't know why you'd get hives. What's someone with your cushy job got to be stressed out about?"

I dabbed pressed powder onto my neck to camouflage the redness, then, while I was at it, dug out the rest of my makeup. I could take the time to freshen up now that I wasn't going to die immediately. Ahead of me, Ethel jabbed a finger at the window once again.

"Look at this traffic! We've moved a car length in five minutes. I told you we should have gone to Venice."

Ernie snorted dismissively. "This traffic is nothin'. The Van Wyck at rush hour. Now that's traffic."

"How come everyone's driving on the wrong side of the street?" Ethel pounded on the window to a car below. "You're going the wrong way! Hey, there's no steering wheel in that car." She gave a quick look up and down the lanes of traffic. "There's no steering wheel in *any* of those cars!"

"My wife the rocket scientist. The steering wheel's on the passenger side, Ethel. Car manufacturers had to install the steering wheels on the wrong side of the car to make it easier for everybody to drive on the wrong side of the road. Get it?"

I contemplated explaining the difference between *opposite* and *wrong* to Ernie and Ethel, but I wasn't sure either one of them would "get it."

From behind me, Gladys began complaining in her singsong, sandpaper voice. "I smell something, Ira. Do you smell something?"

"Diesel."

"It's not diesel. It's worse than diesel. It smells like a sewer. I think it's coming from the front of the bus. Ethel!" she yelled past my ear. "Do you smell something?"

Ethel propped herself up to look over the back of her seat. *Ehh!* Ethel's hair was an intense burgundy rose, a shade popularized by liquid antiseptics such as Mercurochrome, and Olympic ice-skating coaches from former Eastern Bloc countries. She wore rouge that was too red and eyeliner that was too black, but at least her rhinestone-studded glasses concealed the fact that her eye shadow was iridescent blue, a no-no even in former Eastern Bloc nations. "I can smell it," she blurted to Gladys. "Phew! The toilet must be backed up. It must be the toilet. You think it's the toilet?"

"It's not the toilet. There's no toilet on this bus."

"No toilet? The brochure promised us a toilet. What are we supposed to do if we have to go in the middle of nowhere?"

"I repeat," Gladys's husband griped behind me. "Look around you. The whole country's the middle of nowhere."

I looked at Bernice. Bernice looked at me. It was kind of creepy when a conversation with Bernice started to look good.

"That's it," said Bernice. "I'm disconnecting." She popped her hearing aid out of her ear with a superior smile. "That's one of the benefits of old age. You go deaf."

Close by, a cell phone started chiming the first bars of "New York, New York." Ethel picked up. "No, I'm not having a good time. Why? I'll tell you why. There's no toilet on the bus and something stinks. How should I know if your father can smell it? Just a minute. Ernie, can you smell it?"

"I can smell it, Ethel."

"He smells it."

Another cell phone began beeping a digital rendition of "The Sidewalks of New York." "Hello?" answered the man across the aisle. "What? WHAT? YOU'LL HAVE TO SPEAK UP. I CAN'T HEAR YOU."

I leaned back in my seat and scratched my neck, my ear, my jaw. I sidled a glance at Bernice to find her sitting with her eyes shut, smiling beatifically. Some people had all the luck. What I wouldn't have given to be old and deaf right now.

Ballybantry Castle might have had a little something for everyone, but by the time we arrived, it was too dark to tell. The Golden Irish Vacations tour guests trooped into the lobby like defeated soldiers and collapsed all over the plush furniture while Ashley and I took up our post at the front desk. The clerk was a freckle-faced, redheaded man in his mid-twenties whose name tag identified him as Liam McEtigan.

"The tour group, are you?" he inquired in his cheery brogue. "We were expecting you this morning. But no harm, is there? You're only eleven hours late. Take a wrong turn, did you?"

Ashley leaned an elbow on the desk and stared him straight in the eye. "I want our keys, and I want them now."

"Yes. Brilliant. If I can trouble you for your passports. I'll be needing to check them before—"

"Y'all can check passports in the morning. Right now, I want keys." She flashed him a barracuda smile. "I'm not having a good day, sugar. Trust me. Y'all don't want to make it any worse."

Liam hesitated for only a split second before he grabbed a box filled with envelopes and shoved them at her. "Names and room numbers are on the envelopes. Keys are inside. But I'll still be needing to check passports in the morning."

My brother was right. Men find it impossible to refuse drop-dead-gorgeous blondes with big chests. Maybe I needed to change my hair color.

Ashley grabbed the keys and headed for the lobby. "If he has any questions, answer them," she called to me over her shoulder. "And find out where to get the bus repaired."

"That would be Dooley's," Liam said to me. "Two villages over. But they'll be no good to you this week because the garage is closed. Death in the family."

If the garage was located two villages over, it would do us no good anyway. Michael Malooley would get us lost trying to find it. "Tell me, Liam," I said, leaning over the desk in a conspiratorial fashion. "Why are there so few route signs posted on the roads around here? And why, when there *are* signs, are they stuck behind trees, behind overgrown shrubbery, and on buildings behind creeping vines?"

Liam shrugged. "The locals are knowing where everything is, so they're not needing signs. And if you're not local, me da would say, you've no business being here in the first place, so why tell you how to get here?"

I guess that's why most of the signs ran parallel rather than at a right angle to the road. The only way you could read them was to crank your head around and try to eyeball them over your shoulder as you zoomed past. Ireland had progressed from a nation of leprechauns with clay pipes to a nation of speed-readers with whiplash.

As I sauntered into the lobby to look for Etienne, I noted some of the interior touches of Ballybantry Castle. Suits of armor standing like sentinels around the perimeter of the room. Military shields with coats of arms displayed above a massive fireplace. Huge faded tapestries hugging the walls in an attempt to add warmth to the cold granite. Nana appeared at my side as Ashley continued to call names and distribute room keys.

"That was some day we had today. Went pretty good. I didn't even need my umbrella."

I eyed Nana warily. "You do realize we were lost all day."

"I know, dear. But we got to see lots that wasn't on the itinerary. I shot some real nice pictures." She whipped a half-dozen or more out of her bag. "Here's that pretty stone cottage that was built so close to the road in that one little village. I thought the thatched roof and all the window boxes were nice touches.

"Here's the hole in the cottage after we took out all its window boxes when we cut the corner too close.

"Here's the hole in the bus after the window boxes took out our side mirror.

"Here's the mirror lyin' in the gutter after we backed over it.

"This is a good one a Ashley. This is where she's waggin' her finger in Michael's face, callin' him a moron. Look how pretty her nails are. I wouldn't mind havin' my nails done up like that sometime.

"Here's that pretty stone fence that circled the pub where we ate lunch."

Her next photo showed a shiny sculpture twisted into a series of sinuous angles and curves. "This is different," I observed. "I don't remember seeing this."

"That's a closeup of the bus's rear fender after we rammed the stone fence. Here's another good one a Ashley. This is where she's standin' next to the fence callin' Michael a stupid twit."

I was pretty sure she'd called him a stupid shit, but Nana's hearing isn't what it used to be.

"This last one didn't come out too good 'cause we were goin' by too fast. Can you make out that crumpled thing on the pavement there? That's the door we sheared off the car that was stopped in the middle a the road when we rounded that blind curve."

I'd found it odd that the driver had left his vehicle with the door wide open on an unshouldered road boxed in by hedgerows. You had to figure it was a cultural thing. Americans liked their cars without roofs. The Irish preferred theirs without doors.

Nana shook her head. "Poor Michael. He seems to be havin' a run a bad luck on the road. Speakin' a which—" She lowered her voice. "Bernice tells me you got some real whiners back where you're sittin'. How'd you survive the day?"

I mined my skirt pocket and opened my palm. "I remembered I had these in my shoulder bag."

Nana squinted at the two short rubberized tubes that were the circumference of No. 2 pencils. "Erasers?"

"Earplugs. Once I got them in, I couldn't hear a thing."

Nana held up the earplugs with jealous regard. "You think it'd be okay to use these in my nose? There's an awful smell in that bus and I didn't think to bring nose plugs."

"It's the driver," said Tilly Hovick, joining us. "Unlike the rest of us, he doesn't feel the need to disguise his natural body odor with artificial sprays, colognes, and deodorants. I find it entirely refreshing. A man living outside the strictures of convention. He's to be admired."

I didn't agree with her about the body odor thing, but I thought it was pretty admirable that a guy who demonstrated no skill at driving or reading maps could land a job where his primary responsibility was to drive and read maps.

Tilly handed me an envelope. "Ashley asked me to give you your room key."

I peered over Nana's head toward the crowd that was rapidly dispersing in the lobby. "Has anyone seen Etienne?"

"He volunteered to help Michael unload the luggage from the bus," said Nana. "Ashley said there weren't no bellmen on duty tonight."

Okay. This wasn't so bad. I'd have time to run to my room and freshen up before he came knocking at my door.

"Refresh my memory," asked Tilly. "Etienne is the black-haired mesomorph with the stunning blue eyes. Is that right?"

I wasn't sure what the correct definition of *mesomorph* was, but I suspected it might be anthropological for "stud muffin." "Right," I said.

"There's another interesting specimen on the tour," Tilly continued. "Have you noticed? A young woman with exquisitely applied makeup and huge feet. I don't see her right now, but her skeletal structure and musculature indicate she might be something other than—"

"Shall we head for our rooms?" I interrupted. I had to discourage Tilly's anthropological observations. Too bad she wasn't a retired geology professor. Then the only thing she'd notice about Jackie would be the size of the rock on her ring finger.

I threaded my arms through theirs and dragged them along with me. "Early start tomorrow, ladies. We need our beauty sleep. What's your room number?"

Their room was three doors down from mine on the first floor, so I said good night to them at my door and raced into my bedroom. I don't know what the castle had looked like before the renovation, but the end result was stunning. My room was the size of a basketball court with a bank of windows occupying one wall. Two queen-size beds dominated the space, the headboards covered in the same rose-and-mauve flower-garden fabric that was repeated in the drapes and counterpanes. Four velvet boudoir chairs were arranged around the stone fireplace, and hanging over the mantel was a gilt-framed oil painting of some ancient lord astride a horse, surrounded by sleek hounds and barefoot children poised to dip their toes in a babbling brook. There was a mirrored double dresser, an armoire with a television inside, mirrored panels on the closet doors, and a host of other wall paintings that depicted thatched cottages, stone towers, and elaborate Celtic crosses.

I rushed into the bathroom. Wow. Whirlpool tub. Glassed-in shower. Marble tile. Aromatic candles. Jars of bath salts and bubble bath. Little bottles of shampoo, body lotion, and massage oil. I held up the massage oil. Maybe I could heat it over the candle. Oh, boy. This day might not be a complete loss after all.

I pulled the turtleneck of my sweater down to examine my neck. Okay. It didn't look too bad. No new welts had formed. If I applied more powder, Etienne might not even notice, especially if he was looking at me by candlelight.

A light tap at my door. Speak of the devil. I threw the door wide and smiled my most seductive smile.

"I'm sorry to bother you, dear," Nana apologized, "but do you suppose you could come down to our room?"

"Right now?"

"You're probably expectin' your young man. I'm sorry. You take your time then and come down when you can. There's no hurry."

"Is there a problem with your room?"

"Just a small one. There's a dead body in it."

CHAPTER 4

The deceased was a spindle of a woman dressed in a chambermaid's uniform and lying on the floor in front of the mirrored closet in Nana's room.

"You didn't touch her, did you?" I asked as I inched close to the body.

" 'Course I touched her, dear. I had to check for a pulse."

She had curly salt-and-pepper hair, pale, wide eyes that stared fixedly at the ceiling, and thin lips that were drawn apart as if in a silent scream. I placed her at well beyond retirement age.

Tilly hovered near the woman's feet. "I looked her all over and found no blood. No trauma to the body. My guess is stroke or heart attack. These people can't expect to eat full Irish breakfasts every day and not suffer the consequences. Fried eggs. Fried potatoes. Sausage. Bacon. Black pudding. Even the Samoans have switched to Special K."

"How long do you think she's been here?" I asked. As upsetting as this was, I was thankful the deceased wasn't a member of our tour group.

Nana sank to her knees for a better look at the body. "There's fixed lividity. See here. All the blood's settled at the back a her arms and legs, makin' 'em that purplish color. Her lips and nails are real pale. Her extremities are blue. Her eyes are startin' to flatten 'cause a lack of fluid. And her skin's real cool. My guess is, she's been here between six and eight hours."

I regarded Nana in astonishment. How did she know that?

"Very impressive," said Tilly. "You've been overly modest about yourself, Marion. Were you a former medical examiner?"

"Nah. I just watch a lot of them forensic shows on the Discovery Channel on Tuesday nights."

Considering the scope of my grandmother's knowledge, it was now apparent that I might have learned more from a constant diet of TV than from four years of higher education at the University of Wisconsin. I guess that said a lot about the quality of cable programming these days.

I heard a rush of footsteps in the hall and a cry of alarm as the front desk clerk burst into the room. "Oh, Jaysuz. This is terrible. She didn't sign out today, but I was thinking she'd simply forgot. Rita's getting on in years, you know, and her memory's failing. Is she going to be all right?"

Liam McEtigan obviously never watched the Discovery Channel on Tuesday nights. I patted his shoulder. "I'm sorry, Liam, but she's no longer with us."

"Are you sure? Her color's not too good, but she uses off-brand cosmetics, so her color's never that good."

I shook my head. Liam's face crumpled. "This is terrible. Terrible. What am I going to do?"

"You might want to call the coroner," I suggested.

"No, I mean, we only have one other chambermaid. Yours is the only group booked into the castle for the next few days, but one person can't be cleaning all the rooms. We were hardly managing with two."

"Only two maids?" I marveled. "Maybe you need to improve your benefits package."

"We *have* good benefits. We even include dental. It's—" He stopped short, looking as if another word would be one too many. Perspiration beaded his upper lip. He wrung his hands in nervous agitation. "I'd best call me da. He owns the local mortuary."

As he made to flee, Tilly thumped her cane on the floor. "Not so fast, young man! You can't expect us to sleep here tonight. We'll be needing other accommodations."

Liam wheeled around, looking like a deer caught in the headlights. "Of course. I'll be seeing to it right away." He sniffed suddenly, as if he were just now remembering to breathe. "I apologize for the smell, ladies. Jaysuz, this is terrible."

"It's not so bad," said Nana. "You should get a whiff a our bus."

"You'd better make your first phone call to the police," Tilly instructed. "We don't know if this woman died from natural causes or from more nefarious means. A thorough investigation must be conducted."

Liam shook his head. "Everyone will know what killed Rita. Bad heart. She was living on borrowed time, but she wasn't one to sit at home to wait for the Grim Reaper. She wanted to keep working until the end. And look at her. That's exactly what she did." He blessed himself with a quick sign of the cross. "If you'd be good enough to accompany me, ladies. I'll see about relocating you."

As Tilly and Nana hurried toward the door, I remained hovered over the corpse for a long moment. I wasn't entirely convinced Rita had died from a heart attack. Judging from the look in her eyes, I'd have guessed she'd died of fright.

My arms itched. My throat itched. The roots of my hair itched. *Scratch scratch scratch,* as I unlocked the door to my room. *Scratch scratch scratch,* as I flipped on the light switch.

"This is awful nice a you to put us up for the night," Nana said as she followed me into the room.

"A poorly run operation," said Tilly, thumping her walking stick for effect. "Imagine! A castle of this size and they haven't one room available for emergency occupancy."

I scratched my arms. My throat. My scalp. Nana was philosophical. "With only two maids to clean this place, I'm surprised they've got rooms available at all. Did something bite you, Emily?"

"I think it's hives." I rolled up my sleeve to discover a fresh crop of welts on my forearm.

"That's not good," said Nana. "Bernice's husband died from hives. Maybe you need medical attention."

I rushed into the bathroom for a better look at myself in the mirror. The welts peppered my arms and throat, but they hadn't reached my face yet.

"Did you eat somethin' you was allergic to?" Nana asked.

"I'm not allergic to anything."

"Hives can sometimes be activated by stress," said Tilly. "Are you feeling stressed by anything?"

I thought about my life over the last twenty-four hours . . . and scratched some more. "Not that I know of!" I lied. And what was worse, the more I thought about Rita, the more creeped out I was getting that she'd seen something that had literally scared her to death. What if Ashley had told the truth about the castle? What if it really *was* haunted?

"If she's not stressed out, I think we should tell her," I heard Tilly say.

When I didn't hear Nana reply, I poked my head out the bathroom door. "Tell me what?"

Tilly looked at Nana. Nana looked at Tilly, then at me. "It's about the castle, dear. I don't mean to alarm you, but . . . it's haunted."

My mouth fell open. "You know? Who told you? Bernice? How did she find out? Was she eavesdropping again? Oh, great. If Bernice knows, *everyone* will know, and they'll all want to go home. I can't go home. What am I supposed to do about Etienne? He took time off work to be with me. I think he might be planning to pop the question!"

Nana clapped her hands together. "How nice for you, dear. You want I should e-mail your mother so's she can reserve the Knights a Columbus hall for the reception? You can never book too early these days."

"No e-mails! Not yet. Now let's back up. Who told you about the castle?"

"Tilly told me last night," said Nana, "but she's kept it to herself 'cause she didn't wanna spook anyone. What with the maid dyin' like that, though, we thought you oughta know what you might be dealin' with."

"How did you find out?" I asked Tilly.

"It's a long story." She staked out one of the room's velvet boudoir chairs and sat down. With a waggle of her walking stick, she directed Nana and me to do the same.

"One of my pet courses during my years at Iowa State was a graduate seminar on Irish myth and legend, and one of the most poignant tales my students uncovered was that of a wealthy English lord who accepted an invitation from James I to settle on land the king was disbursing in Ireland. By James's edict, Irish landowners were expelled from their farms, driven into bogs, and forced to act as slave labor to the new English landowners. This particular English lord had a daughter who some say was the most beautiful female ever to set foot on Irish soil. She was light-eyed, golden-haired, and fair-skinned, and when her father commissioned a castle to be built, the girl fell in love with a handsome Irish laborer who was as dark as the girl was fair. Naturally, their union was forbidden. They didn't share the same social class or the same faith, but despite their differences, they ran off and were married in a secret ceremony by an Irish monk. No one knew what they had done until it became obvious that the girl was breeding. Her father forced a confession out of her, and they say he was so incensed, he locked her in the dungeon and forbid anyone in the family to speak to her. As far as he was concerned, his daughter was dead to him. When her lover discovered her punishment, he tried to scale the castle wall one night to save her, but his body was found floating in the moat the next morning. When the girl's father told her of her lover's fate, she went into premature labor and, after two days of agonizing pain, died in childbirth.

"Legend holds that from that time on, the two lovers have roamed the castle in search of each other, their wailing cries echoing through the halls. And when experts have chased down the cries, they've found a man's wet footprints, as if he were dripping from the moat, and a woman's bloody footprints, as if she were fresh from childbed. The name of the Irishman who dared marry an English lady has been lost to history, but the name of the castle is . . . Ballybantry."

I stared at her, spellbound. "Has anyone ever seen the ghosts?"

"A handful of people swear they've seen the girl rattling doors in the hall in search of her lover. Others claim she moves chairs close to the window so she can sit and wait for him to appear. And she's blamed with filching articles of a personal nature from guests' rooms, items that might provide small comfort to her as she wanders through eternity."

KNOCK KNOCK KNOCK!

"EHH!" I leaped out of my chair. I liked scary stories, but I wasn't so keen about finding myself at ground zero. "Don't anyone move," I said bravely, ignoring the goose bumps that were tap-dancing up and down my spine. "I'll get the door." I was pretty sure a ghost wouldn't bother to knock.

"That's an awful good story," said Nana. "Maybe they could use this place as the location for the next *Survivor* series. If you're a contestant in a haunted castle, maybe they'd even let you order takeout 'stead a forcin' you to eat rodents and bugs."

I checked the peephole and opened the door. Etienne stood before a baggage trolley crammed with luggage. "If you see your suitcase, point it out. And by the way, I missed you today." He cupped his hand around my neck and kissed my mouth. *Unh.*

"Why are you playing porter?" I asked dizzily. "You're one of the paying guests. You get to have your luggage delivered to your door."

"I haven't mastered the art of how to stand around doing nothing. If there's activity going on, I need to be in the middle of it. Besides, I assume the guests would like their bags tonight. I feared that being the bastion of inefficiency he is, Michael might not finish unloading the luggage bays until next week."

Bless his little Swiss heart. "That's so sweet," I gushed. Was this guy proving to be a perfect ten or what? He probably even liked animals and small children. He was the catch of the century, and even though I was a little squeamish about this sudden possibility of another marriage, intuition told me that if I didn't reel him in, some other woman would be only too happy to do the honors.

But what if I was jumping the gun? What if the question he wanted to ask me was more basic, like what side of the bed did I like to sleep on, or was I the type of woman who'd freak out if he left the toilet seat up? Hmm. Maybe I needed to see the whole picture before I got too far ahead of myself. "About the question you've been meaning to ask me," I hedged. "Would now be a good time for you?"

"Now?" He looked around him. "I'd envisioned a slightly more intimate setting than a hotel corridor, darling. Say, something with candlelight, and champagne, and an obscene amount of bare flesh." He trailed a slow knuckle down my cheek. "What if we synchronize our watches and meet in my room a little later? I've seen the room. I have a king-size bed."

This job was starting to cramp my style. I hesitated. "I have a teensy problem. Rule number eight of my *Escort's Manual*. I have to be available in my own room in case any of my group needs me."

He nodded supreme understanding. "Then shall I plan to come down here? Your *Escort's Manual* doesn't prohibit guests from visiting you in your own room, does it?"

I sighed. "As it happens, I have a teensy problem with that too."

Nana poked her head out the door. "I thought I heard Inspector Miceli's voice. That was real nice a you to help Mr. Malooley with the luggage. Poor man needs all the help he can get. Makes you wonder what line of work he was in before he took up bus drivin'." She eyed the luggage trolley. "My grip's right on top there if you wanna haul it down. The big red one."

"What's your room number, Mrs. Sippel? I'll deliver it to your door."

"You just did. Drag it down and I'll wheel her in. Be careful though. My laptop's in it. Tilly! You wanna step out here and find your grip?"

Etienne shot me a quizzical look. I lifted my eyebrows and shoulders in a tandem shrug. "That's what I was trying to tell you. Nana and Tilly are spending the night with me until another room comes available."

"It's on account a the dead body," said Nana.

Etienne hauled Nana's suitcase down from the top of the heap and fired another quizzical look at me. "Dead body?"

Tilly trundled into the hall and, after a moment, stabbed the tip of her cane at a tattered pullman. "This one's mine. Look at it, all frayed and patched. But I think of it as an old warrior who's fought his way through a lifetime of campaigns."

I imagined the exotic places Tilly and her pullman had visited over the years. Bora Bora. Kathmandu. The Casbah. As Etienne unloaded it off the trolley, I regarded its worn seams and scarred fabric with respectful awe. "Wow. They don't make luggage like they used to. That suitcase has to be—what?—twenty, thirty years old?"

"It's practically brand-new," said Tilly. "But you have to understand, it's been through O'Hare a couple of times."

Nana wheeled her suitcase into the room and extended her thanks, as did Tilly, who closed the door behind them. Etienne drilled me with one of his patented police-inspector looks. "Dead body?"

"A chambermaid named Rita. She died in Nana's room sometime today. The desk clerk claims she had a bad heart. We didn't see any signs of foul play, so he could be right. Nana figured she'd been dead between six and eight hours."

"How would your grandmother know that?"

"Discovery Channel."

Frustration pulled at the fine angles of his face. "Tell me again how long you have to share your room?"

"Just tonight," to which I reluctantly added, "unless there's a problem finding them another room. They're short-staffed, so . . ." I let him fill in the blank.

"The ladies could relocate to my room. I could move in here." He looked hopeful for a moment before reevaluating his solution. "I don't suppose that will look too good for you should word leak out. It could rather tarnish your professional image." He pinched the bridge of his nose as if trying to ward off a migraine.

"I'm sure there won't be any problem finding them another room," I consoled. "This is just a . . . an inconvenience."

He let out an exasperated sigh and cast a curious glance toward the palpable quiet of the lobby. "Did someone call the authorities about your dead maid?"

"A long time ago."

"Odd they haven't arrived yet. Perhaps I should offer my assistance to the desk clerk. Which room did you say the body is in?"

Uh-oh. This wasn't good. If he involved himself with the investigation of Rita's death, I'd *never* see him. I grabbed his forearm with both hands. "Remember when Ashley said the castle is haunted? I think she may be telling the truth."

He paused, looking me straight in the eye. "Why do you say that?"

"There's this legend about two star-crossed lovers searching for each other throughout eternity. People have heard unearthly wails and seen bloody footprints, and even though Tilly thinks the maid might have died because she wasn't on a Special K diet, I think she died of fright."

He digested this with typical Swiss equanimity. "Are you implying that you think the maid saw a ghost?"

"Tilly used to teach a course, so she's an expert on the subject. She says this place has been haunted since the time of James I, which was"—I searched my memory for the dates when James I ruled England—"a really long time ago."

"Over three hundred and fifty years. Close to four."

I paused to register that. These were some old ghosts. "The expression on the maid's face is chilling, Etienne. She looks terrified. If you ask me, she saw something so frightening, it killed her."

"You did say she had a bad heart. Wouldn't it be more logical to assume she died from a preexisting condition than from an encounter with some otherworldly being?"

"That doesn't explain the wailing cries or the bloody footprints. You don't know Tilly. She wouldn't tell a ghost story that wasn't authentic."

"Have *you* heard cries or seen footprints?"

"Not yet, but we've only just arrived. These ghosts have been around for almost four hundred years! They're out there."

He smiled crookedly and feathered his fingers along my jawline. "Emily, darling, do you remember when you thought a group of seniors on your tour last year was trying to kill you?"

Just my luck. He liked animals, small children, and had a photographic memory. "I vaguely remember that."

"Do you also recall that your fear was completely unfounded?"

Not too hard to guess where this was going. "I do not jump to conclusions. I am not an alarmist. If *you* recall, someone *was* trying to kill me, just not the person I suspected." If our discussion grew any more heated, we'd have to jump from cybersex to makeup sex.

"I'm simply trying to caution you against getting carried away with all this talk of hauntings and ghosts. The mind can play tricks on you, darling. If you expect wailing cries, you'll hear them. If you expect bloody footprints, you'll see them."

"In other words, you think I'm cuckoo."

"Has anyone ever told you that you have no gift at all for paraphrasing? I love you, Emily. I'm asking you to be wary of anything you see or hear but not attribute it immediately to castle lore. The terror you saw on the maid's face could simply have mirrored her realization that she was suffering a fatal heart attack. I've seen that look on more corpses than I'd like to admit. When the forensic examination is completed, we'll know more about how she died, but until that time, please consider the story of Ballybantry's haunted past as myth, not reality. Can you do that for me?"

I waited a beat. "You love me?" I stared up at him. His exact words played back in my head like an old phonograph record with a stuck needle. He'd panned my ability to paraphrase and then he'd said he loved me. I was pretty sure he'd said something after that, too, but my ears had stopped working after the "I love you" part.

"Of course I love you, darling. I wouldn't be here if I didn't love you." The sound of male voices caused him to glance toward the lobby again. "Ah. The police. I should talk to them." He frowned at the luggage trolley. "I'll have to draft someone into delivering the rest of the luggage for me."

I regarded Etienne. I regarded the luggage cart. Hoisting fifty-pound suitcases off a luggage trolley wasn't my cup of tea, but I was in love. I was walking on air. I wanted to be helpful. "I think Ashley should do it. It's probably in her job description anyway, and you know what a stickler she is for doing everything by the book."

A devious glint lit his blue eyes. A smile touched his lips. "I'll have the desk clerk ring her up." He kissed the tip of my nose. "Fetch me in the morning before you board the bus. My room is the last one down the hall on the left."

"You're not going to eat breakfast?"

"A full Irish breakfast? Emily, darling, those things will kill you."

I gazed after him as he pushed the trolley back toward the lobby, suddenly aware of a major oversight on my part. "Wait a minute! You have my suitcase."

By the time I wheeled my pullman into the room, Nana and Tilly were in their nightgowns and ready for bed.

"If it's okay with you, Emily, Tilly would like to sleep in the bed nearest the potty and I'll sleep with you."

I nodded distractedly, wondering how a man could tell a woman he loved her, then just walk away. Wasn't that the kind of revelation that should be celebrated like the Fourth of July with sparklers, and wheels, and aerial spinners? Maybe Etienne knew something I didn't know. Maybe fireworks were banned in Ireland.

My neck started to itch again as I hefted my suitcase onto a luggage rack and unlocked it. Nana stood in front of the dresser mirror attired in her favorite brown flannel nightgown, toilet-papering her head. "This brand is only one-ply," she lamented. "Two-ply cushions my curls a lot better. Hope I don't wake up with bedhead." When she was done, she yelled, "Catch, Emily," and tossed a travel-size aerosol container across the room at me.

"What's this?" I asked, bobbling the catch.

"Weaponry. After what happened on the last trip, I wanted to be prepared, so I brought a whole arsenal with me."

My heart thudded in my chest. "An arsenal? You mean,

like Mace? Nana! This stuff is bad news! It can weaken your lungs. Damage your skin. Ruin your sinuses."

"All's your grampa used to claim was that it gave him a headache."

"You used this stuff on Grampa?" I looked at Nana. I looked at the canister. I read the label. "Strawberry Shortcake Room Freshener."

"I was gonna buy one called Florida Sunshower, but it smelled too much like mildew. There's a canister for each of us. Remember what we learned in Switzerland. A burst of spray into the ole eyeballs will bring down a two-hundred-pound man real good, especially if he has allergies. I'm not sure if it'll work on a ghost, 'cause I don't know if a ghost *has* eyeballs."

Clutching my room freshener in my hand, I crossed the room and gave Nana a little hug. "This was very thoughtful of you."

"Think nothin' of it, dear. Us girls need to stick together so's we can watch each other's back."

Maybe this was my wake-up call. Sure I was disappointed about not being able to spend the night with Etienne, but I realized that I had a pressing duty to perform that far outweighed my desire for romantic satisfaction. I needed to watch out for Nana and Tilly. I needed to protect them from whatever Etienne claimed wasn't out there, because if any harm came to them, I wouldn't be able to live with myself. My mother wouldn't be able to live with me either. If anything happened to Nana, she'd annihilate me.

After Nana climbed into bed, I located my bank-supplied medical bag that was full of every over-the-counter painkiller and ointment known to man, dug my nightgown and toiletries out of my suitcase, and turned down the lights. At the bathroom door I paused to consult my watch. Okay. Any time now.

In the next instant a door down the hall banged so loudly it vibrated our walls and set all our pictures to rattling. A growl of Southern irritation echoed in the corridor, followed by hissing, sputtering, and the charge of angry footsteps toward the lobby. "My goodness," Nana whispered from across the room. "Who do you s'pose that is?"

"Ashley." I smiled wickedly. She was right on time.

I performed my regular getting-ready-for-bed routine, rubbed anti-itch cream that promised a "New Improved Fresh Clean Scent" onto my arms and neck, and prayed the welts would miraculously disappear before morning. I sniffed my arm, wrinkling my nose at the odor. The cream didn't exactly smell bad. It just smelled strong, like something a desert dweller would rub onto an ailing camel. I didn't want to think about what it had smelled like before someone had thought to improve it.

I navigated through the darkness to my side of the bed, then sat for a full minute listening to the snores of my two roommates as they wheezed and sawed like the wind section in a symphony orchestra. There was no ebb and flow. The noise was a constant clash of whistles and snorts and grunts that filled the room to bursting. And the volume was so jacked up, I guessed we were beyond the decibel level that was considered safe for humans, which illustrated an astonishing point: This castle might be old, but it had really good acoustics.

I listened for another minute before I realized there was no way I could fall asleep in this racket. Not without some help. I cracked the drapes to allow a narrow shaft of light to guide me, then located my shoulder bag by the fireplace and mined the contents for my earplugs and mini Maglite. As I closed the drapes again, I regarded the landscape that was illumined by the castle's solitary floodlight—the moat directly beneath my window, an expanse of lawn sweeping

toward the parking lot, two cars with police markings
marooned in the middle of the lot. Beyond the spill of the
floodlight lay an infertile, untillable wasteland, scarred by
ancient stone and steeped in darkness. And as I stared, I
thought I saw a ripple in the darkness. A movement amid
the crags. A shadow within a shadow. Skulking. Slinking.
Hovering. Watching the castle with sightless eyes.

I blinked. I couldn't actually be seeing this. Could I?

I snapped the drapes shut and flew into bed. I needed to
get a grip. I was scaring myself.

CHAPTER 5

Fueled by hunger, I showered, slipped into a black funnel-necked jersey, cropped red leather jacket, and black cigarette pants, and was out the door before Nana or Tilly stirred the next morning. I followed the signs to the dining room and stood gaping at the sight that greeted me. This room had obviously once served as the castle's Great Hall because it rose two, maybe three stories into the air, like a great underground cavern carved into the stone. A chandelier as big as a carousel hung from the ceiling, shining light onto dozens of tables set with white linen tablecloths and fine china and a breakfast buffet that extended the length of one wall. A handful of guests were scattered at various tables about the room, but the only person I recognized was the very person I wanted to talk to.

"Mind if I join you?" I asked as I pulled out a chair at Jackie's table.

She looked up from her coffee with a long face and a half-pound of concealer under her eyes. I winced. "I know you're on your honeymoon, but there's probably one thing more vital to honeymooners than sex. It's called sleep."

"Sleep? Who can sleep with all the noise in this place?"

"Yeah, Ashley wasn't exactly quiet delivering all that luggage last night." I stared hungrily at Jackie's plate, eyeing the scrambled eggs, fried eggs, potato cakes, grilled tomatoes, fried potatoes, and three different kinds of toast slathered with jam. All right! This was like the Hog Wild breakfast special offered at the Windsor City Perkins Restaurant during harvest. I pointed curiously at a shoe-leather-black object wedged between her eggs and tomatoes. It resembled a mini-Oreo cookie minus the white stuff. "What's that?"

"Black pudding. I didn't know what it was before I bit into it. It's made from blood or intestines or something like that. Don't eat it. It tastes like a hockey puck. And I wasn't talking about Ashley's crashing the luggage trolley into the wall last night. I was talking about the moans from someone's sexual acrobatics. It kept us awake most of the night."

"Moans?"

"You didn't hear them? I thought we were the only honeymooners on the tour, but from the sound of things, somebody else was going at it until dawn. Have you seen the people on our tour, Emily? They're all over sixty. They're *really* old! Jeez, they must be spending a fortune on pharmaceuticals to maintain that kind of stamina. And our room is freezing. Like subzero. Is your room cold?"

I shook my head. "I was pretty toasty last night, but I was sleeping with Nana, and she tends to generate a lot of heat, especially since menopause."

Jackie's face lit up like a hundred-watt bulb. "Mrs. S. is on the tour? I *thought* the lady with the big handbag looked familiar, but the last time I saw your gran, her hair was blue, so I wasn't sure."

"She's keeping up with the times. She scrapped the blue

rinse for a silver one. Blue is out unless you're Marge Simpson or a drummer for a rock band."

Jackie looked around the dining room. "Where is she? I always thought you had the coolest gran. Do you think she'll recognize me?"

I bolstered my courage and charged straight ahead. "I've been meaning to talk to you about that," I said delicately. "I don't think she's going to understand what's happened to you, Jack."

"Why wouldn't she understand? Oh, no." Her voice became a confidential whisper. "Is it because . . . she has some degenerative mental disorder?"

"It's because she spent seventy-six years in Minnesota."

She pondered that for a moment. "Huh?"

"Minnesotans are pretty isolated out there in the middle of the country, so they stay focused on what's important to them. Hard work. Church. Family. World Wrestling Alliance death matches. They don't have to face too many issues outside the norm, which means a lot of seniors are clueless about issues that are fairly common to the rest of us. You were a guy, Jack; now you're a girl. How that happens is a really confusing issue to people of Nana's generation."

"They've done a slew of documentaries on the subject. Didn't she watch TV in Minnesota?"

"Her cable networks were pretty limited," I prevaricated. "She watched things like the Hockey Channel, the Speed Skating Channel, the Ice Fishing Channel."

Jackie paused, her bottom lip suddenly quivering in a pout. "Don't lie to me, Emily. I've been through this kind of humiliation before. You don't want to tell your grandmother about me because I've become an embarrassment to you. Admit it. You're afraid how people will react if they discover you were married to a man who's become a woman."

"If you tell Nana someone is gay, she's thinks you mean they're happy."

"Oh, right."

"For *years* she had you coming out of a wardrobe instead of a closet."

"A wardrobe? Is that like an armoire?"

"She was taught by nuns!"

"I went to a party dressed in a nun's habit once. It's so freaky. I've had this strange aversion to patent leather ever since."

"I'm telling you the truth, Jack! Nana just doesn't get it. But if you insist on telling her about your operation, that's your prerogative. I'm simply surprised that you're so obsessed with people knowing who you *were* instead of who you are."

The expression on Jackie's face shifted from hurt to guilt. "Do you really think I'm obsessing?" She fluttered her hands like hummingbird wings. "Of course, I'm obsessing. I always obsess. You're right. I shouldn't insist that people know about my sex change. It's more important that they see me for who I am instead of who I used to be. You're so insightful, Emily." She squeezed my hand with heartfelt emotion. "Okay. Our little secret can remain our little secret. No need to spill the beans to Mrs. S. I apologize for questioning your intentions. But not everyone is as understanding as you, especially people in my immediate family. Talk about narrow minds."

"That doesn't include your husband, does it? I mean, you told him about your operation before you married him, didn't you?"

She clutched her throat in distress, her plum nail polish the perfect complement to her dusty mauve sweater set. "Of course I did! It would have been *so* dishonest not to. How can you even ask such a thing?"

"You were pretty weepy when I saw you on the bus yesterday. It made me think something might have gone wrong on your wedding night."

She lowered her eyes to her plate and sniffled. "You know me so well, Emily. Something did go wrong. The worst thing you can ever imagine."

I lit on the most likely possibility. "Your husband freaked out when he saw you without makeup?" I'd heard this reaction was epidemic among bridegrooms south of the Mason-Dixon Line.

She shook her head and stuck her hand into her pocketbook for a tissue. She looked as if she was going to cry again. I hoped she was wearing waterproof mascara. "Worse than that."

"There's something *worse?*"

She blew her nose at a decibel level that rivaled cannon fire. The sound echoed upward for three stories, filling the room and rattling the flatware. Heads turned. People stared. I smiled at the guests whose names I hadn't learned yet and whispered to Jackie out the corner of my mouth. "I hate to tell you this, but you blow your nose like a guy."

"I know," she snuffled. "I haven't mastered noseblowing yet. I can't figure out how to do it daintily. Being female can be a real bitch at times, Emily. It's so restrictive. No groin scratching. No butt slapping. No belching. No spitting. How do you remember all that?"

"It's pretty easy, unless you watch a lot of professional baseball. Getting back to your wedding night. What happened?"

"*Nothing* happened. That's the problem."

"Nothing? You mean—"

"I mean, I'm still a virgin!"

I sighed in commiseration. "Yeah, me too."

"You? How can you be a virgin? You jumped my bones every chance you had when we were married."

"Talk to my mother. It's a long story." As she dabbed tears from her eyes, I suddenly realized the upshot of what she'd revealed. "Wait a minute! If you're still a virgin, does that mean you and your husband never . . . that before you were married you didn't . . . you know . . . do it?"

Jackie's eyes looked like bottle corks on the verge of popping. "Emily! I'm not that kind of girl!"

"You were that kind of guy!"

"That was different. Guys are expected to have loose morals and sleep around. I was only following the norm."

"So what does that say about me?"

"That you were . . . easy?"

"WHAT?"

"Bad choice of words. You were . . . willing. Jeez, people get *so* freaked out about semantics these days."

I glared at her. She cast a furtive glance around and grabbed my hand, pleading in a desperate voice. "All kidding aside, Emily, this is serious. I don't know what to do. You've gotta help me."

Uh-oh. Ripples of heat pricked my neck. "This doesn't have anything to do with male sexual dysfunction, does it?"

"No! Tom's not the one at fault. *I* am. He wants to do it, but . . . I can't. I just can't."

"Why not?"

She leaned across the table to within a half-foot of my face. "Everything is so new down there, Emily." She dipped her eyes to the area below her waist. "I don't want Tom to mess anything up. I mean, what if he's not a perfect fit, or his aim is off, or he puts too much oomph into it. I could be ruined for life. I can't help it. I want to keep everything intact for a while longer. I want to savor the newness. Do you think I'm being selfish?"

"You didn't consider this *before* you got married?"

"Who has time to think about sex when you have all those bridal magazines to pore over? Do you know how many separate publications appear on the newsstand each month? It's overwhelming. And that doesn't include the special double issues on honeymoons and modern contraceptive techniques. Eloping didn't help. Everything happened too quickly. I need more time, but Tom isn't being very understanding. Will you talk to him?"

"Me? Why would he listen to me?"

"Because you're a woman."

"So are you!"

"But you've been a woman for decades longer than I have. That makes you more credible."

"Tom—is that his name? Tom doesn't even know me!" I regarded the Golden Irish Vacations name tag that hung around her neck, zeroing in on the surname for the first time. "Your last name is Thum? You married . . . Tom Thum?"

"Don't even *think* about going there, Emily. I've had it up to here"—she made a slashing motion across her throat—"with the midget wisecracks. Or is it more politically correct to say 'little people'? Of course, you say 'little people' over here, and everyone is looking around for a leprechaun. Anyway, Tom's parents were sadistic wretches to name him what they did. And Tom does know you. In a sense. I've told him all about you. Unfortunately, that seems to be part of the problem." She winced slightly. "I talked you up so much, he got a tiny bit jealous. He thinks the reason I don't want to have sex with him is because I still have 'a thing' for you."

"WHAT?"

"That's why you need to talk to him. You have to convince him that you and I are no longer an item. And then you might want to explain to him the psychological reasons behind why I can't have sex with him right now."

I stared her eyeball to eyeball. "Are you NUTS?"

"You can do it, Emily. You're the most clever person I know. You've gotta buy me some time. The success of my marriage depends on it."

Uff da. No pressure there.

Her facial muscles froze suddenly as she looked over my shoulder toward the doorway. "Oh, great. Don't look now, but Miss Georgia Peach has entered the room. How often do you think she has to dye her hair to keep her roots looking so good?"

I rubbed my temples in thought. "Exactly how much time do you need to savor your new parts, Jack?"

"Do you suppose her skirt could possibly be any shorter? I have headbands that are bigger than that. And she's wearing my sweater set! The same style. The same material. The same *color.* The bitch."

I glanced over my shoulder. "It looks better on you."

"You think so? You're not just saying that?"

I watched as Ashley sashayed across the room to an unoccupied table by the buffet. "Okay, listen to me, Jack. You need to make a date with yourself to lose your virginity. Savor the newness for another couple of weeks, then on the appointed day, lose it. Write it in your day planner if you have to. The trick is, you need to give yourself permission to be indulgent with yourself, and then you need to do your thing with Tom. That way, you both get what you want. Trust me. It'll work."

"Like the Nike commercial, right? 'Just do it.' " She exhaled an anxious breath. "What if Tom doesn't go along with it?"

"You have the rest of your lives together. Will two weeks matter that much?"

"I guess in the scheme of things, two weeks isn't so very long." She gnawed thoughtfully on her bottom lip until she worked her plum lip liner right off. "Will you still talk to Tom?"

"No! He has no reason to be jealous of us because there *is* no us. You told him the truth. He's simply going to have to believe you."

Jackie nodded. "You're right. That's a trust thing. We'll have to work that out ourselves. But I *love* the idea of sex by appointment! It even sounds a little naughty. I think Tom will go for it. I *knew* you'd find the solution, Emily. I'm so excited!" Grabbing my shoulders and pulling me toward her, she gave me a loud, mushy kiss on my lips. "There! That's for being so nice." She scrutinized my mouth as she pulled away. "I like that lipstick. Do you suppose I could borrow it sometime?"

From across the room I noticed Ashley looking our way with the oddest smile on her face. Lovely.

A half hour later I stood outside Etienne's door, feeling pretty good about myself. Maybe advice-giving would turn out to be my greatest strength in the escort business. People would seek me out for my wisdom and counsel. For my levelheadedness and logic. Emily Andrew: Adviser to newlyweds, seniors, and transsexuals. There was no situation I couldn't handle. No problem I couldn't solve. Was I pumped or what? My hives didn't even itch anymore.

"You're looking immensely pleased with yourself this morning," Etienne said as he opened the door. He wore a bath towel knotted around his waist and a silky slate gray shirt that he'd probably bought in some expensive little boutique in Zurich. I gave his bare legs the once-over. They were long and lean and muscled, as if they'd been chiseled by some famous Italian sculptor. *Unh.*

"No trousers today?" I licked my lips in appreciation. "I

like this look on you." He yanked me into the room and shut the door behind him.

"Please tell me you still have the buttons you popped off my trousers."

"Buttons? I . . . I . . ." I replayed the incident in my head. *Ping ping ping.* Off flew the buttons. *Tap tap tap.* George Farkas at the door. *Chirp chirp chirp.* Etienne's cell phone. That's when I'd picked up the buttons, walked across the room, and dropped them into . . . "Oops."

"Why do I always cringe when I hear you say that?"

"They're—uh—they're in the ashtray that's sitting on top of the writing desk, that's in my room . . . back in Dublin. I'm sorry! I'll call the hotel. I'll have them overnighted to you."

He waved off my suggestion, looking a little distracted. "I'll ring up the front desk. They might have an emergency sewing kit with a few stray buttons for guest use."

"Can't you wear the pants you wore yesterday?"

"They're gone."

"Gone where?"

He shrugged. "I hung them up last night. Now I can't find them. They've disappeared."

"How can trousers just disappear?"

"Check the closet. If you can find them, I'll eat them."

I slid open the closet door to find one article of clothing hanging up. A black suede sportcoat. I peeked left and right and scanned the floor. No trousers in sight. "You're right. They're not here. Did you try the dresser drawer?"

"I never put trousers in a drawer." He sighed his disgust. "I suppose this means I'll need to find a men's clothing store."

Clothing store? The gravity of the situation hit me like a twenty-ton brick. "Are you saying you packed only two pairs of trousers?"

"I packed one pair. I was wearing the other."

This was such a guy thing. Pack light. Anticipate no fashion emergency. End up wearing a towel. To avoid this problem, women packed everything in sight, had stickers labeled HEAVY slapped onto their suitcases at check-in, and developed rotator cuff problems lugging the things around. Women usually ended up having to undergo months of physical therapy when they arrived home, but at least they had the satisfaction of knowing they'd looked really good on vacation. It was purely a matter of priorities.

I looked Etienne up and down. "Do men wear kilts in Ireland? A little fringe, a fancy pin, you'd be right in fashion. But you'd better decide what you're going to wear pretty quickly because the bus will be leaving before long."

"I need to investigate some things here at the castle today, darling, so I'm afraid I'll have to miss today's outing."

My good humor spiraled downward into my shoes. "You're kidding, aren't you?" His mouth was set in his police inspector's mode, however, so I knew he was serious. "But why?"

"Did you sleep well last night, Emily?"

"Like a log."

"You weren't disturbed by noises?"

"Snoring." I emptied the contents of my jacket pocket into my hand. "But I stuck these in my ears."

He peered into my open palm. "Erasers?"

"Earplugs. They really work. I didn't hear a thing the rest of the night."

"No moaning? No crying?"

"You heard moaning and crying? Someone else heard the moaning, but she thought it was a couple of the guests high on Viagra." I paused as reality set in. I wheezed in panic. "Moaning and crying? I *told* you this place is haunted! The ghosts must have been crying out to each other last night. You heard it with your own ears! This is *so* creepy."

"There are any number of explanations for what I heard last night, Emily. The wind. Faulty pipes."

"Ghosts."

"I'm not willing to admit that yet." But I saw a glimmer of unease in his eyes that indicated everything he knew of the world was being severely tested. "That's why I'm staying behind to snoop around the castle today. Something caused those noises last night. I intend to find out what." He shivered suddenly, then strode across the room to check the setting on the thermostat. "One thing is definite. The management needs to check the heating system. It was so cold in here last night, I could see my breath."

I frowned. "That's funny. The person I ate breakfast with complained about the cold too. I'll stop at the front desk on my way out to see what the problem is." I sighed with resignation and gave him a puppy dog look. "I'm going to miss you today, but we're on for dinner tonight, right?"

He opened his arms and gathered me tightly against his chest. "I wouldn't miss it." He buried his lips in my hair, then worked his way lower, kissing my face with soft touches of his mouth. But despite his show of affection, he still seemed distracted.

"What's bothering you?" I asked gently.

"I think you'd be better served by being left in the dark about this one, Emily."

"I hate the dark. Please tell me. I'm not a wuss. I lived through the reformulation of the old Coca-Cola to the New Coke. I can handle anything."

He smiled at that and hesitated long enough to make a decision. "I suppose you have a right to know, but I'd prefer you keep the information to yourself."

"Okay." Considering what I knew already, what was one more secret?

"I suspect you may be right about what killed the maid yesterday."

I gasped at his words. "You do? You saw the look on her face? The fear in her eyes? I knew it. She had to have died of fright. Did the coroner agree?"

"The coroner suspected she died from a heart condition . . . until he moved her body."

I gasped alarm. "Did he find evidence of foul play? A stab wound to the back? A pool of blood we didn't see?"

"There was blood, but not from a stab wound. On the carpet beneath the maid's body we found a set of footprints. Bloody footprints."

A tingling sensation slithered down my spine. My mouth went dry. "What kind of footprints?"

"They show bare feet that manifest an unusual physical anomaly. There are no separations between the toes. They're all conjoined. In essence, the footprints belong to someone with webbed feet."

This was a real shocker. "You think the maid was frightened to death by a duck?"

"I think the maid was frightened by something in that room, Emily, but I doubt it was either fowl or beast. From the configuration of the footprints, I'd say she was frightened to death by a woman."

"Were either one of you cold last night?" I was back in my room, pitching odds and ends into my shoulder bag for our day trip to the Carrick-a-rede Rope Bridge and the Old Bushmills Distillery in North Antrim. Nana and Tilly had finished breakfast and were making up the beds, but my question caused each of them to straighten up and stare at me.

"People at breakfast were complaining about the cold," Tilly volunteered, "but I didn't offer an explanation. I didn't want to upset anyone."

Uh-oh. "Don't tell me. You checked at the front desk and they told you the furnace is broken and they don't expect the new spare parts to arrive until next week." Like we really needed heating problems in addition to a dead maid, eerie cries, and a ghost with feet like a duck. I gave my jaw a vigorous scratch.

"The cold air in the castle has nothing to do with the heating system," Tilly announced. "It indicates the presence of malevolent spirits."

Great. Not only was the ghost saddled with foot problems, it had a bad disposition as well. I lowered my gaze to my own feet, wondering what it would be like to have webbed toes. It couldn't be much fun. It would really limit your choice of stylish summer sandals. And you could forget about toe socks altogether.

But that led me to another thought. What if the ghost was in a bad mood *because* of the foot problem? Hmm. Maybe Ballybantry Castle didn't need an exorcist. Maybe what it needed was a podiatrist.

Tilly continued. "Paranormalists have documented that rooms haunted by hostile ghosts are subject to temperature shifts, cold spots, and icy breezes."

"That can't be good for people with circulatory problems," I said.

"Bernice has poor circulation," said Nana. "And I bet you anything she forgot to pack her support hose."

"Wait'll I get my hands on that Ashley," I seethed, mindlessly scratching my neck and jaw. "This is some great place she booked us into. If the ghost doesn't get us, the frostbite will."

"Are the police suspicious the maid might have died

from a ghost-related incident?" asked Tilly. "She did have a frightful expression on her face."

"I bet she ate one a them black puddin' things they served us at breakfast," Nana said. "The taste probably killed her. It nearly killed me."

"It's pretty early in the investigation. I don't think the police have drawn any conclusions yet." The ladies didn't need to know about the bloody footprints under the maid's body. At least, not yet. I zipped up my bag and threw it over my shoulder. "Is there any chance you could search the Net for more information about Ballybantry Castle and its ghosts, Nana? I could use more details about sightings through the centuries, attempted exorcisms, related deaths. Anything you can find would be helpful." Nana was second to none when it came to Internet searches on her laptop, so I knew she'd be able to shed further light on the subject. I had to be prepared, but I needed to know what to be prepared for.

"You want I should do that right now?" Nana asked.

"No-no. You and Tilly get ready to board the bus. Tonight will be soon enough."

"Are you plannin' to touch up your face before you go out, dear?"

"I hadn't planned on it. Why?"

"Remember that problem you was fussin' over yesterday?"

I fingered my jaw to feel a fresh crop of welts snaking across my skin.

"From the looks a things, it's back."

After spending ten minutes in the bathroom with my anti-itch cream, I headed for the front desk. The morning desk clerk was a big-boned brunette in her thirties with a broad face, a warm smile, and hands the size of catcher's mitts. Her name tag identified her as Nessa O'Conor.

"Excuse me," I said by way of greeting, "but I've had several complaints about the temperature in the rooms last night."

"Too cold for them, is it?" she inquired. "We're always fielding complaints about the cold spots in the rooms at this time of year."

Aha! I leaned over the desk and lowered my voice to a no-nonsense whisper. "And we all know why that is, don't we? But I'd like to hear it straight from the horse's mouth."

The clerk leaned close to me and replied in an equally no-nonsense whisper, "We shut the furnace down in May and don't turn it on again until September."

Right. Like I was going to believe such a logical explanation. "How convenient. Blaming the cold on the furnace."

"It's hotel policy, miss."

Enough pussyfooting around. "What about the ghosts?"

"If it's ghosts you're after, miss, you might want to ring up Castle Leslie in County Monaghan. They have a popular ghost who appears in the Red Room. Quite friendly, he is. They've even documented it on the Travel Channel."

"What about the malevolent ghosts in Ballybantry Castle?" I demanded.

"Ghosts? In Ballybantry?" Her laughter trilled outward. "Ballybantry is famous for its moat, not its ghosts. Someone's been pulling your leg, miss. Ballybantry's not haunted. I wouldn't be working here if it was. Excuse me for a moment."

She left to answer the phone, leaving me more confused than enlightened. If she was telling the truth about the furnace, that would explain the cold, but it did nothing to explain the cries in the hall or the bloody footprints under the maid's body. And how could she miss the rumors about the castle being haunted? Tilly and Ashley lived an ocean away and they knew. Were the employees in denial? Or was someone paying them to play dumb?

Figuring I wouldn't be getting any more answers out of the desk clerk, I wandered into the lobby and made the rounds to greet some of the Iowans who had gathered to await the commencement of the day's activities. We were scheduled to depart at eight o'clock, so I wasn't surprised when, at seven-thirty on the dot, my group moved en masse to form a sudden line at the door. Same old thing. By Iowa standards, with only a half hour left before departure, we were already late.

"You don't have to stand there," I called to Nana from the comfort of a plush velvet chair. "The bus is right outside the door. It's not going to leave without you."

"What did she say?" asked Osmond Chelsvig, who was eight-eight and wore hearing aids in both ears.

A ripple of panic. A scuffle of feet. "She said the bus is leaving without us," Bernice yelled.

"The bus is leaving," confirmed Alice Tjarks from the back of the line. Alice had been the voice of radio station KORN's early morning farm report for years, so she was used to announcing things. "Okay, folks! Let's move it!"

I shook my head as they shuffled out the door on each other's heels. No sense trying to reason with them. Once they were in motion, there was no turning them back. I waved to the last person out the door, then reviewed the passenger list and the day's itinerary while I waited for everyone else to show up.

I waited five minutes. Ten minutes. I watched a custodian maneuver a carpet sweeper like an unwilling dance partner around the furniture in the lobby. He was a tall, gangly limbed man who probably fancied himself as Fred Astaire with all the rapid quicksteps he was executing. He wore his thick salt-and-pepper hair tied back in a short ponytail, and I could see the sparkle of a rhinestone stud in his ear. He was dressed in forest green coveralls that were etched, front and back, with what must have been the castle's coat of arms: two really big fish emblazoned on a white background with the head of a warthog sandwiched between them. Kind of like a seventeenth-century advertisement for surf and turf.

I heard them before I saw them.

"What do you mean I woke you up? It's ten of eight here. What time is it there?"

I immediately recognized the voice of the Mercurochrome-haired woman who had sat in front of me on the bus yesterday. Ethel Minch. She wandered into the lobby with her husband at her side and a cell phone attached to her ear, outfitted like Gloria Swanson in a scene from *Sunset Boulevard*—white turban, flowy tunic and pants, fifty pounds of costume jewelry around her throat and wrists. Ernie was the same diminutive height as his wife, and, like many men his age, wore his trousers jacked up to his armpits, which is where his waist began. He had a weak chin, a head like a hard-boiled egg, and ears like satellite dishes.

"It's WHAT time?" Ethel yelled into the phone. "SPEAK UP! WE HAVE A BAD CONNECTION!"

Ernie looked around the lobby. "I told you we were too early. You see this, Ethel? Nobody's here. We're the first ones. What'd I tell you?"

Ethel punched her antenna back into her phone and stuffed it into her pocketbook. "So go back to the room already. Who's stopping you?"

"What'd Ernie Junior have to say?"

"KRRRRRRKKKKK."

"Piece-a-crap phone. I don't care how many trillion countries it can connect with, it's still a piece of crap."

Okay. That was my cue. I was out of here. I stuffed my papers back into my shoulder bag and stood up.

"Hey, doll!" Ernie swaggered over to me. "You're on the tour. Where's everybody?"

I pointed toward the front door. "Outside."

He swiveled his head in that direction. "What're they doing out there?"

"Surrounding the bus." I figured that might need further explanation. "They're worried it might leave without them. They're from Iowa."

"I was in Iowa once. Selling shoes outta the trunk of my Edsel. Those were the days, when a trunk was a trunk, before people started filling 'em up with sound systems the size a refrigerator-freezers." He held his hand out to me. "Ernie Minch."

"Emily Andrew," I replied, shaking his hand.

"I'm Ethel," said his wife. "I could be in Venice, but Ernie had to visit Ireland to find his roots. I ask him, what's so important about finding your roots? All those ancestors you're looking for? They're dead! What good are they to you dead?"

It was obvious the only "roots" Ethel felt needed attention were the ones attached to her head. She squinted at me intensely. "Did you know you have bug bites all over your face?"

"I'm taking care of it."

"If there's bugs in this place, I'm gonna have to stop and buy repellant."

"So you're in the shoe business," I said to Ernie.

"Used to be. I turned the business over to Ernie Junior a few years back. But I still keep my thumb in the pie. Someone's gotta keep Junior on top of what's hot. Take these little numbers, for instance." He swept his hand toward Ethel's feet. "Stick your foot out, Ethel."

Ethel stuck out her foot and hiked up her flowy pants.

"These are the latest thing from Taryn Rose. Fits like a second skin. Wide toe box. An insole that massages your foot. Made from Italian leather that's soft as butter. Stylish. Orthopedically designed. Is it comfortable, Ethel?"

"It's comfortable, Ernie."

"Three hundred and fifteen bucks," said Ernie. "A steal for that kind of shoe. 'Course, we don't have to pay full price. Ernie Junior gives us a senior citizen discount."

I stared at Ethel's foot. "Very nice," I heard myself say as shock set in. Her shoe consisted of two thin straps of platinum leather lashed across her foot and attached to a perfectly flat sole. But it wasn't the price of the two leather straps that caused my shock. It was the rest of her foot. Her toenails were dark burgundy overlaid with painted daisies, which smacked of a recent pedicure. No small feat, considering Ethel Minch's toes were all stuck together.

CHAPTER 6

"On yer right," Michael Malooley announced into the microphone of the bus, "that ruin on top of the hill was once an ancient watchtower. Oliver Cromwell blew it apart. You've no doubt heard of Cromwell, the English Lord Protector who lived by the motto that the only good Irishman is a dead Irishman."

We were cruising along a narrow road somewhere in Northern Ireland en route to our first destination. Ashley had apologized for our late start by explaining that things in Ireland operated on "Irish time," which always ran a bit late. I suspected if my group had known this, they would have opted to return to Switzerland, where the weather had been damp, the fog thick, and the food tasteless, but at least everything had run on time.

Ashley was sitting at the front of the bus this morning with a large map unfolded on her lap. She'd probably decided to navigate today to ensure we actually *did* arrive at our first destination. Michael was therefore acting as driver *and* guide, alerting us to sights that appeared in the infrequent spaces between hedgerows. He'd obviously spent years studying local history, because he was a real wealth of information.

"Did you see that bunch of stones in circles back there?" Ernie Minch called out to Michael. "Why are they there?"

"Dunno."

"What're they used for?"

"Dunno."

"Who built them?"

"Dunno."

I'd read that ancient peoples had used stone circles as calendars or astronomical blueprints, but my personal theory was that some primitive civil engineer had built them as a form of traffic control, to lend order to the constant flow of farm wagons and carts. The first roundabouts. The guy later moved to Massachusetts and built some more, but he changed their name to "rotaries."

Ssssppt! Sssssppt!

I caught a sudden whiff of something strong and aromatic in the air. "What's that smell?"

Bernice Zwerg, who was seated beside me, stuck her nose in the air and inhaled deeply. "Pine-Sol."

"Smells more citrusy to me. Like some kind of expensive eau de cologne." Your average Iowan is blessed with a remarkable sense of direction. Iowans never get lost. They're always aware of magnetic north, even when the sun isn't shining. It's uncanny. I didn't get that gene. I got the gene that allows me to identify just about any smell that comes my way, which isn't always the best gene to have when you grow up next to a hog farm.

Sssssppt! A fountain of mist shot into the air from the seat in front of us and rained in our direction. Ethel Minch poked her head over the top of her seat. "Do you like that?"

She waved the bottle in front of us. "It's from Guerlain. Some kind of orangy toilet water. Expensive as hell."

Orange! All right. Was I good, or what?

"A bunch of us talked at breakfast and decided to take matters into our own hands about the smell in this place. Isn't that right, Gladys?"

Gladys Kuppelman, who was occupying the seat behind us, answered with an emphatic *Pssssssssttt!* A cloud of spray floated over the top of my head. I sniffed. This one was easy. Right Guard spray deodorant. My dad still used it. Oh, this was nice. We were having fragrance wars.

"Ira didn't want me to bring perfume bottles on the trip," shouted Gladys. "He said they might break. This works fine, though. Good thing I decided not to bring a roll-on."

Michael's voice sounded over the microphone once again. "To yer left. In that field. That pile of rocks used to be an abbey before that God-cursed bastard Oliver Cromwell reduced it to rubble. For nine months he reigned death and destruction on Ireland. May he burn in Hell for it!"

Silence. Murmurs. An undercurrent of unease. I looked at Bernice. Bernice looked at me. "Did you get to an ATM to get me my money yet?" she asked.

I rapped my knuckles against my head. "Your money. Unh! I'll speak to Ashley. Maybe we can stop someplace along the way today."

"You better. I'm down to a few coins. Good thing our meals are included today."

"Did you call the bank back home to wire you some cash?"

"Can't. You need some kind of card to make a long-distance call on the room phone. In my day you could give the phone a crank, tell the operator who you wanted to talk to, and she'd make the connection for you. These days you

pick up the phone and they've made so many improve-
ments, you can't make a call at all."

"I have a phone card. I'll show you how to use it when
we get back tonight."

"If that's like a credit card, you can forget it. I don't want
anyone stealing my identity."

"Bernice," I said evenly, "no one can steal your identity
from a phone card."

"I'm not taking any chances. If I can't use coins, I'm not
making any phone call."

The itching started again. My throat. My jaw. My
cheeks. I dug my anti-itch cream out of my shoulder bag.

"What's wrong with your face?" Bernice inquired.
"Looks like measles. Weren't you immunized? You should
of gotten immunized. In my day if people got measles, they
usually died."

"I've been immunized," I snapped. "It's not measles." I
uncapped the tube and smeared ointment all over my face.
Bernice wrinkled her nose.

"That stuff smells like camel dung. You should have
bought the kind that comes in an improved fresh clean
scent."

"This *is* the improved fresh clean scent!"

PSSSSSSSSSSSSST!

I shielded my arm over my head to avoid the geyser of
spray the man across the aisle released into the air, but
the fumes stung my eyes and clogged my windpipe anyway. *Uff da.* I waved my arms in front of me to scatter the
mist.

"Furniture polish," the man said proudly, holding the
aerosol can at the ready. "Lemon scented. The maid's closet
was open, so I kind of borrowed it. It was the best I could
do on such short notice. Doesn't linger too long, though,
does it?"

PSSSSSSSSSSSSST! He gave another blast in my direction. I guess I hadn't choked enough for him the first time.

"To yer right," Michael announced again, "those stone walls with the cannonball dents in them over by the river. Used to be a fine church over there before that goddamned son-of-a-bitch Cromwell and his son-of-a-whore bastard troops"—I heard a rush of footsteps—"*bnnrk ig athwart.*"

Bernice tapped my arm. "What's 'bnnrk ig athwart'?"

Gladys Kuppelman stuck her nose into the space dividing my seat from Bernice's. "I think it's Gaelic. He must be bilingual."

I looked down the aisle to find Ashley looming over Michael with her hand firmly planted over the microphone. *KRRRREEOOOO!* Feedback blared out at us as she wrenched the mike in her direction. *KRRRREEOOOO!* I winced as Michael wrenched it back. *KRRRREEOOOO!* Fifty pairs of hands flew up to cover their ears.

"I'd like to thank Michael for his excitin' narration," Ashley finally announced in a breathy calm, "but to get y'all in the mood for the day's sights, I think a little Irish music is in order. So y'all just sit back and enjoy the scenery."

As I twisted the cap back onto my small tube of anti-itch cream, I could read the handwriting on the wall. One tube wasn't going to be enough.

We pulled into the parking lot of the Carrick-a-rede Rope Bridge a mere hour behind schedule. Ashley presented us with a short narrative, explaining what we were about to see. "The bridge connects the mainland to a small island that's the site for a local salmon fishery. It spans a distance of sixty feet and hangs eighty feet above the sea. If any of y'all have vertigo, I don't recommend you attempt the crossing. The handrails are sturdy, but the flooring consists of wooden planks strung between wires that begin twistin' and wobblin' the minute you step onto them. It's about a mile walk to the actual site, so bring your cameras and some bottled water with you, but leave all your extra baggage behind. You'll want to leave your hands free for the crossing. Michael will lock the bus, so y'all don't have to worry about someone stealing your valuables."

I heard a groan of voices around me as people stretched their cramped muscles and aching joints. I hadn't brought any water with me, so I retrieved my camera, wedged my shoulder bag into the overhead compartment, and waited my turn to exit through the back door. I was a little apprehensive about the height thing. Iowa is so flat, a lot of people might be unaware they have vertigo. I mean, riding the escalator to the second floor of Younkers department store is high enough to give some Iowans a nosebleed. I didn't want to think about anyone from my group growing so paralyzed with fear they'd get halfway across the bridge and not be able to make it back. More specifically, I hoped that person didn't turn out to be me.

I exited the bus behind Gladys and Ira Kuppelman, who were dressed in matching chocolate brown jerseys, cherry microfiber vests, yellow spandex leggings, and really cool sunglasses with mirrored lenses in the shape of rhomboids. Or maybe they were trapezoids. Some shape like that. Geometry had never been my best subject.

Bernice nudged me from behind. "Check out the Bobbsey twins. They look like a couple of banana splits."

I shrugged. "Maybe they own a Dairy Queen franchise." But you couldn't fault their physiques. Ira and Gladys had gleaming silver hair, razor-cut into easy-care, classic styles, and complexions that were bronzed and wrinkle-free. And they didn't sport an ounce of fat between them. They looked like the kind of people who spent vacations skiing in Vail, snorkeling in Bermuda, snowshoeing in Vermont, and scuba diving off the Keys. They were a real inspiration. I hoped I'd be that fit when I reached sixty, or whatever age they were.

"Emily! Over here!" I pivoted toward the sound of Nana's voice and, with Bernice in tow, elbowed my way through the crowd toward her. "Is your young man here, dear? I didn't see him board the bus."

"He couldn't come today."

"That's too bad. No interest?"

"No pants."

"No kiddin'?" She nodded her understanding. "I can see's how that might be a problem. Could be one a the other fellas on the tour would be nice enough to lend him a pair." She paused to evaluate the men milling around us. Ernie Minch. George Farkas. Osmond Chelsvig. "Guess that's not such a good idea. Everyone else has shrunk." She wrinkled her nose. "I thought it smelled bad on the bus, but it's followed us right outside. What in the world is that odor?"

"Me," I said, offering my jacket and hair up for inspection. "Take your pick. Spray deodorant or furniture polish."

"I smell it too," said Tilly. "It's not a synthetic odor. It's more organic. Earthy. Pungent."

"Smells like garbage," said Bernice.

Tilly continued. "Considering the Irish have access to an alternate supply of fuel for cooking and home heating, I would suggest what we're smelling is peat."

"Which one's Pete?" asked Bernice.

Nana grabbed my arm. "Look, Emily. There's a tall one. Maybe you can borrow his pants. They look pretty nice too. Dockers."

As if on cue, the "tall one" turned to face us. He had a lion's mane of shoulder-length frosted blond hair, cheekbones like sculpted granite, and eyes that were a dazzling shade of aquamarine. He flashed a killer smile at Nana, and while we all stood gawking, he sauntered toward us. "Forgive the intrusion, ladies, but did I overhear one of you say you wanted to borrow my pants?"

Drop-dead gorgeous men sometimes affect women in inexplicable ways. Our body temperatures increase. Our brain function decreases. Speech deserts us. It's really annoying. Especially the speech part. Nana was first to recover. "The pants would be for Emily's young man. He hasn't got none."

"There you are, lovebug!" cried Jackie, barging into our circle. She wrapped her arms around the "tall one" and preened like a prom queen. "One minute you're there, and the next you're gone," she scolded him. "I hope I don't have to spend this entire vacation keeping track of you. Have you introduced yourself to Emily yet?"

"Emily?" he said, redirecting his gaze to my face and narrowing his eyes. "You're Emily?"

Ehh! Jackie's husband. Why was I getting the impression that the pleasure of meeting me was running a distant third to root canal and sigmoidoscopy?

Jackie graced Nana with an affectionate smile. "And you must be Emily's grandmother. She told me all about you at breakfast this morning. I'm so happy to meet you!" To show just how happy, she rushed at Nana and lifted her off her feet in a bone-crunching hug that knocked Nana's visor off her head and raised the eyebrows of a few people who had joined our circle.

"I hope she's not that happy to meet *me*," Bernice grumbled.

"I should introduce myself to the rest of you," Jackie said to the group, waving her name tag. "I'm Jackie Thum, and I'm here on my honeymoon with my husband, Tom." She held up his name tag for our collective perusal.

"Your name's Tom Thum?" Ernie Minch grinned, hik-

ing his pants up higher under his armpits. "You any rela-
tion to that midget colonel who played the circuit with
P.T. Barnum?"

Gladys Kuppelman gasped. "You're not supposed to say
'midget' anymore. You're supposed to say 'little person.'
You have to be politically correct."

"Tom Thumb was a midget?" puzzled Ethel Minch. She
grabbed her turban as a fierce wind blew across the parking lot. "I thought he was a dwarf."

"I thought he was a general," said Bernice.

Tilly thumped her walking stick on the ground and said
with authority, "It's more politically correct to refer to a
diminutive person as 'vertically challenged,' whether he's a
colonel *or* a general."

"Says who?" Ira Kuppelman objected as he raised his
arms above his head in a series of stretching exercises. "My
money's on 'height impaired.' "

"You can't say he was 'impaired,' " Gladys corrected.
"That implies there was something wrong with him."

"There *was* something wrong with him," shouted Ernie.
"He was a midget!"

Nothing circular about this conversation.

"So what's the story?" Ernie prodded Tom. "Are you
related or not?"

Jackie stuck out her hip and posed her fist on it. "He's
over six feet tall. Does he *look* like he's related?"

"How should I know? Maybe he wears lifts."

"Ernie used to sell lifts," Ethel said with pride, "but there
wasn't much call for them in Brooklyn. In order to make
any money at it, we woulda had to relocate to Hollywood."

"All right, y'all!" shouted Ashley from somewhere at the
front of the throng. She poked a green-and-white-striped
umbrella into the air so we could locate her. "We'll proceed
through the gate and hike slowly along the trail. Watch

your footing because the trail's uneven. Please don't crowd each other! Everyone'll get to see the bridge once we reach it. And whatever you do, don't wander from the trail."

Good advice, considering the path wended along the lip of a cliff that dropped off precipitously to the sea below.

With mumbles of anticipation the crowd started forging toward the gate. "Would you like me to take a picture of you and your grandmother before we hit the trail, Emily?" Tilly asked.

"That would be great." I handed Tilly my new palm-size Canon Elph, showed her which button to push, and struck a pose with my arm around Nana's shoulders. "So what's your opinion?" I looked down fondly on all four-feet ten-inches of her, from her visor to her new white tennis shoes. "Would you rather be called vertically challenged or height impaired?"

"Say 'Cheese,' " instructed Tilly. CLICK.

" 'Short' works fine for me, dear."

That's what I loved about Nana. She was so basic.

Tilly held up my camera. "It's rewinding, Emily. You'll need to reload."

"A timely reminder. My film's back on the bus. You ladies go on ahead. I'll catch up to you in a minute."

Bernice tugged on Tilly's sleeve as they fell in behind the rest of the group. "Will you point out that Pete fella to me so I can stay upwind of him?"

I scooted up the back exit stairs of the bus, spied Michael at the front of the bus checking gauges and making notations in a log, yanked my shoulder bag down from the overhead compartment, and slipped unobtrusively into my seat to search the contents. Sanitizing hand wash. Anti-itch cream. Pepto-Bismol tablets. Band-Aids. Breath mints. A package of semicrushed cheese crackers with peanut butter filling. I peeked out the window to find the group filing quickly through the main gate. Pen. Mini Maglite. Lipstick. Sunscreen. Change purse. Blush. I heard a soft shushing sound. Mini umbrella. A Fleximap of Ireland. Dental floss. Had I forgotten to pack extra film? I upended my shoulder bag onto Bernice's seat and riffled through the pile. Emory board. Collapsible drinking cup. Compass. So *that's* where it was! I thought one of my nephews had eaten it on our last camping trip to Wisconsin. A dog-eared copy of Frommer's *Ireland*. A canister of Kodak Advantix film. My film! Yes!

I grabbed the film, reloaded my camera, then opened the mouth of my bag wide and shoveled all my stuff back in. Good thing I'd only brought the essentials. I gave the lumpy contour of my bag a satisfied pat. And Ernie Minch thought the trunk space in his Edsel had been impressive.

I peeked out the window. The last of the group had disappeared through the gate. I'd have to hurry to catch up. I stashed my bag in the overhead again and ran to the back exit.

The door was closed.

Closed? Why was it closed? I looked toward the front of the bus. No Michael. I descended the step well and pressed the exit bar, but it didn't depress. I tried again. Same result. I pushed on the door. It rattled but didn't open. I pushed harder. It didn't budge. I threw myself against it.

Nothing.

Uh-oh. I was beginning to get a bad feeling about this.

Suppressing a twinge of panic, I raced down the aisle to the front of the bus and sprinted down the step well. I braced both my hands against the exit bar and pressed downward.

Nothing. I angled my shoulder against the door and shoved with all my might.

The door remained stubbornly closed. No creaking. No

rattling. No nothing. Okay. This was a no-brainer. The bus was locked.

But how could it be locked? I WAS STILL INSIDE!

"Let me out of here!" I pounded on the door. "Can anybody hear me? I'm not supposed to be in here! Can somebody open the door?"

We were parked at the far end of the lot, beside a field of scrubby grass, so there wasn't much foot traffic around us. If I expected anyone to hear me, I was going to have to draw attention to myself in another way.

I hurried back up the stairs and regarded the windshield, the dashboard, the steering wheel. Aha! I slammed the heel of my palm down onto the horn.

Nothing.

Nothing? How could there be nothing? I pressed it again, and again, and again. Okay. Another no-brainer. The horn was broken. Maybe it had gotten damaged in the mishaps with the side mirror and rear fender yesterday, though I'm not sure how that would be possible. Great. Now what?

I wandered back down the aisle, opening windows as I went. "Can somebody help me?" I yelled to nobody as the wind threw the words back in my face. I eyed one of the windows, thinking I could escape out the top, but it was a long drop to the ground, and to be perfectly honest, I wasn't dressed for the occasion. I mean, I was wearing kidskin mules with a two-inch stacked heel. Probably not the most practical shoes for a hike to a rope bridge, but they made my feet look really small.

I slumped into a seat and sighed my disgust. "Well, Emily, you're going to have some sensational photos of the Rope Bridge to show people back—" A muffled tone interrupted me. A digital tone that sounded much like the song, "New York, New York." Ethel Minch's cell phone! Of course! I could phone 911 for help! If there was such a thing in Ireland.

I dug my *Ireland* guidebook out of my shoulder bag and found a listing for emergency numbers. Yes! Nine-nine-nine worked in both the republic and Northern Ireland. I tried not to let my head swell too much with my own genius.

Ethel's phone continued to ring, leading me to its whereabouts in her pocketbook, which she'd hidden beneath the seat in front of her. When it stopped ringing, I entered a series of codes that were conveniently taped to the housing, then punched up 999. "Police, Fire, Ambulance," the dispatcher answered.

"I'm *so* glad you're there," I said breathlessly. "This is Emily Andrew from Windsor City, Iowa, and I'm locked in a bus in the parking lot of the Carrick-a-rede Rope Bridge."

Silence. "Is this a crank call?"

"No! I'm locked in a tour bus. Really."

I heard the click of computer keys. "Where is the bridge located?"

"Beyond the parking lot. A mile's hike down the trail."

"What *town* is it near?"

"I didn't notice the name of any town. It's a major tourist attraction! You don't know what town it's near?"

"Can you identify any distinct geographical markers?"

I peered out the window. "There's a parking lot, and cars, and grass that's kind of yellow and scruffy, and cliffs, and the ocean. Haven't you ever been here?"

"Never."

"How come?"

"No curiosity about the place."

"Well, you should make it a priority because I hear it's quite spectacular, unless you have vertigo. Are you acro-phobic?"

"I'm agnostic, actually. We'll send a unit straightaway."

I disconnected, feeling much better about my situation than I had a few minutes earlier. I replaced Ethel's phone, returned her handbag to its hiding place, and breathed a sigh of relief. All I had to do now was sit back and wait to be rescued. I'd catch up with the group and everything would be fine.

So how come I couldn't relax?

I retreated to a seat overlooking the parking lot and pressed my forehead against the window. I knew exactly why I couldn't relax. I couldn't get Ethel Minch's feet out of my mind. Etienne had said the maid might have been frightened to death by a woman with webbed toes. Ethel had webbed toes. Did that mean Ethel caused the maid's death? Granted, Ethel's hair and iridescent blue eyeshadow were pretty scary, but I didn't think they were enough to scare anyone to death. And the timing wasn't right. The maid had died while our bus was toodling around the countryside, clipping window boxes and ramming fences. There was no way Ethel could have been on the bus and in the castle at the same time. Hmm. Ethel had said Ernie was in Ireland looking for his roots, but what about *her* roots? Was she a small piece in a larger puzzle?

Just who *was* Ethel Minch? She might look like a colorized version of Gloria Swanson, but maybe her flamboyance was a deliberate ploy to disguise something more sinister. Looks could be deceiving. I'd found that out in Switzerland. I hoped I was wrong about Ethel, but I was getting some pretty bad vibes about the whole thing. This meant I'd have to dig into her family history to see if I could find some kind of Irish connection, but in the meantime, I'd fire my theory past Etienne to see what he thought. After all, he was the police inspector.

I could hardly wait to get back to the castle to tell him.

* * *

Two hours later I was still waiting. I guess the rescue team was operating on what Ashley called "Irish time." Good thing I wasn't choking on a fish bone.

I was speed-reading all 561 pages of Frommer's for the second time when a soft shushing caused me to look up. Michael stood at the top of the step well at the front of the bus, pointing an accusatory finger at me. "Bugger me! What are you doing in here?"

Up I popped, elevating my voice to match the volume of his. "You locked me inside! That's what I'm doing in here!"

"The bus was empty when I left."

"If the bus had been empty, I wouldn't be here now, would I?"

He rubbed his brow as if trying to figure out how this had happened. He wasn't a good-looking man. His jaw was too heavy, his mouth too wide, his eyebrows too thick. His hair was thin and mousy brown, but I saw an intelligence in his eyes that I hadn't noticed before—a spark of intensity that belied his inability to read a map or maneuver a bus. He speared me with an irritated look. "Why didn't you shout for me to come back?"

"I *would* have if I'd seen you go! Shouldn't you be yelling 'Clear' or something before you leave?"

"I'm driving a bus, not using defibrillator paddles. How come you didn't leave with everyone else?"

"I did leave with everyone else! But I had to come back." I shrugged. "For film."

He threw his hand out in a dramatic flourish. "There you go. It's yer own damned fault. You should have made some noise so I'd know you were here. You managed to open all the windows. You couldn't yell to a passerby to help you out?"

"We're parked in the 'back forty,' for crying out loud!

Do you see any foot traffic out there? I *tried* to beep your horn."

"Didn't get too far, did you? It's broken."

"I noticed. Isn't that illegal for a vehicle this size?"

He gave me another of his glowering looks. "Why didn't you hit the Emergency button?"

I opened my mouth to parry further, then snapped it shut again. "Emergency button?"

He beckoned me closer and pointed to a button the size of a paperweight angled over the top of the door. "The Emergency button. You press it. The door opens. It prevents you tourists from getting locked inside. How else would you be able to get out?"

I didn't feel this was a good time to mention the 999 rescue team.

"So you've missed it all then, have you? The coastal path. The bridge. The view of Scotland."

Now that I was standing close to him, I realized the smell clinging to him wasn't so much body odor as bad cologne or aftershave, and lots of it. Wow! He needed to think about switching to a name-brand product. "I haven't missed everything yet." I scooted down the stairs, trying not to inhale. "I can still catch up with everyone. It's only been two hours. They're seniors. They walk slowly."

"I wouldn't be so sure. Have a look across the car park. Aren't those the folk from yer group heading this way?"

I visored my hand over my eyes and squinted toward the entrance gate. Nuts! There was Tilly in her red velvet beret, red blazer, and tartan plaid skirt and Nana in her Minnesota Vikings windbreaker and purple polyester slacks. They were leading the group back at breakneck speed, which led me to draw one conclusion: Nana had enrolled in the step-aerobics class I'd been encouraging her to sign up for at the senior center. Look at her! She was really hauling.

I walked across the parking lot to meet them, noting one other detail as I drew closer. Everyone's hair was standing on end. Literally. Had crossing the bridge frightened them that much? If being eighty feet above the water could scare them like this, I shuddered to think what seeing a ghost would do to them. I started to count heads, hoping we hadn't lost anyone.

Nana waved a handful of photos at me in greeting. "Emily, dear! Where were you? I was worried."

"I ran into a little problem," I said sheepishly. "I—uh— I got locked inside the bus."

"That happened to me once," said Bernice. "Going up to Mystic Lake Casino. I fell asleep, people flew the coop, and no one bothered to wake me up."

"That must have been frightening for you," I said, reliving my own experience.

"You bet. And it was cold up there in Minnesota. Subzero. I thought I might freeze solid before anyone found me."

Poor Bernice. She probably wouldn't have thought to blow the horn to attract attention, and I doubt she'd had access to a cell phone. What a traumatic episode for an elderly person to suffer through! Maybe that explained why she always seemed to focus on worst-case scenarios, why she tended to be so prickly. I studied Bernice's face, feeling as if I was finally learning what made her tick. "How did you finally get out?"

"I hit the Emergency button."

Okay. Maybe I should fling myself off the cliff now and get it over with.

"Aren't we lucky Emily didn't do that," Nana stated emphatically. "Can you imagine what might a happened to our valuables if she'd hit that button and left the bus wide open? Some thief could a cleaned us right out. That was a big sacrifice you made stayin' behind, dear. We all appreciate it, don't we, ladies?"

Nana had this wonderfully subtle way of turning my most miserable blunders into my most noteworthy achievements. That's what I loved about grandmothers. They made you feel good about everything, even your mistakes.

"You wanna see my pictures?" Nana asked, barely able to contain herself. "You can have a look-see at what you missed." She thrust the top photo at me. "These are the stairs leadin' down to the bridge. Musta been about a thousand of 'em."

The staircase sure wasn't going to win any awards for aesthetics or engineering design. It consisted of primitive tiers of wood, bare earth, and stone following the slope of the cliff in a steep, crooked path downward. I got dizzy just looking at it.

"Here's one a the whole group at the top a the stairs. They don't look too good 'cause they're all wheezin'. And lookit everyone's hair. Standin' straight on end. The wind was blowin' something fierce right there."

I regarded the faces in the photo. "It's not exactly the whole group. Where are the people from New York?"

"A lot of 'em started complainin' that the path had too many dips. Too many rises. Too many potholes. Then they whined that they was havin' to stop too much to shake gravel outta their shoes, so they called it quits halfway down the trail. They never made it to the stairs. Good thing I took your advice and signed up for that exercise class at the senior center, else I might a had to call it quits with 'em."

"Step aerobics?"

"That class was full, so they signed me up for my second choice." She offered me another photo. "This is lookin' east over the cliffs. You see this land mass pokin' out into the water at the tip here? That's Scotland. Isn't that somethin'?"

She showed me three more photos in rapid succession—a close-up of the stairs that showed how narrow and uneven they were, a body lying faceup near the stairs, a section of a chain-link fence that formed a protective barrier along the ledge side of the stairway. Didn't look as if I'd missed too much so far.

I paused. I blinked. I stared at the photos in Nana's hand. "Could we go back to the one of the man on the ground beside the stairs?"

Nana separated it from the others and squinted at it rather critically. "I shoulda got a better angle on this one. And the light's all wrong. Makes the fella look all washed out."

"He was alive? He wasn't dead?"

She scrutinized the photo more closely. "He didn't sound dead when he give me the okay to take his picture. You s'pose I missed somethin'?"

"Who *is* this guy?"

Nana shrugged. "Some stranger gaspin' for breath. Climbin' those stairs really done him in. I think him suckin' air like that lends the place real verisimilitude."

Whoa! " 'Verisimilitude'?"

"That's one a Tilly's fancy words. Isn't it a dandy? Means somethin' looks kinda authentic."

I shook my head. "Did you take any pictures of the bridge?"

"We never seen the bridge."

"You WHAT?"

"We couldn't get past the stairs."

"You walked all that way and didn't see the bridge?"

"We was afraid once we climbed down, we wouldn't be able to climb back up again. Imagine how bad that woulda thrown our schedule off."

"Some people saw it," said Tilly. "That young honeymoon couple. And George Farkas."

"George climbed those stairs with only one good leg?"

Nana lowered her voice and spoke close to my ear. "I never realized before what a stud George is, Emily. He can do things on one leg that most men can't do on two. Makes you wonder what else he can do, don't it?"

She waggled her eyebrows. Oh, no. My seventy-eight-year-old grandmother was entertaining lusty thoughts about George Farkas. My mother would have a bird.

"This is the last snapshot," Nana said, handing me a glossy print of a blonde woman splayed facedown on the crooked stairs above the bridge.

"Oh, my God!" I recognized the flowing bleached hair, the mauve sweater, the skirt that was the size of a head-band. "That's Ashley! What happened to her?"

"She thought the newlyweds were spendin' too long wanderin' around that island on the other side a the bridge, so she went over to fetch 'em. On her way back up the stairs, she tripped on somethin' and took an awful spill. I guess she'd a been better off not wearin' them spike heels today."

"Where is she?" I searched the crowd. "Is she all right?"

"Somebody's helping her back," said Bernice.

"She hit her head fairly hard when she went down," Tilly added. "I'd venture she may have suffered a concussion."

"From the way she was screamin', I bet she broke a bone or two," said Nana.

"She probably suffered massive internal injuries and is as good as dead," said Bernice. "And we all know what that means. It means the person next in line to take over the tour is Emily."

CHAPTER 7

"No-no. Nuh-uh." I waved off Bernice's suggestion as if I were undoing a curse. "I'm sure Ashley is fine. She probably just stubbed her toe or something."

"I believe that's her now," said Tilly, gesturing toward the entrance.

I looked in that direction. I saw a horde of people milling around the gate, frantically brandishing cameras. Ernie Minch was waving people out of the way so he could get an unobstructed shot of Tom Thum bookended by Gladys Kuppelman and Ethel. George Farkas looked to be snapping multiple pictures of the same group using each of the four or five cameras he had draped around his neck. Alice Tjarks was shooting a picture of George Farkas shooting pictures. Cute. Kind of like one of those infinity things. I looked left. I looked right. I didn't see Ashley.

"Where do you see her?" I asked Tilly.

She elevated her walking stick and stabbed the air like a pointer. "There," she said, holding it at an unwavering angle.

The crowd shifted. Heads turned. Shoulders swayed. A

slight path opened up and out squirted Jackie, red-faced and breathless, lumbering sluggishly with a body that was hoisted over her shoulder like a sack of potatoes. "Coming through!" she gasped, while Ashley whined hysterically, arms and legs flopping around like fish out of water. Oh, this was nice. I loved the way Jackie had mastered the art of keeping a low profile. This wasn't going to attract any attention at all.

"Looks like we better call an ambulance," Nana advised.

From far off we heard a soft whirr of sirens that erupted into a deafening blare as a fire truck roared into the parking lot, followed by an ambulance with lettering on the door that identified it as "999 RESCUE UNIT."

"My stars." For once, Bernice was dumbfounded. "It's a miracle."

"Like I always say—" Nana lifted her eyes to heaven and blessed herself with a solemn sign of the cross. " 'Ask and you shall receive.' "

I smiled brightly. Gee. That had worked out well.

The rescue squad worked to stabilize Ashley for a half hour before they could finally transport her. I stood beside Jackie in the parking lot watching the ambulance speed onto the road, siren blasting.

"I wouldn't have given her painkiller for that injured foot of hers," said Jackie. "I would have given her a muzzle. Did you ever hear so much whining in all your life? Well, other than when Nancy Kerrigan lost the gold medal to Oksana Baiul in the '94 Olympics."

"She was in pain."

"She *is* a pain."

"So how come you're the one who ended up carrying her back?"

"I couldn't just leave her there, could I?" She gave me a tormented look. "Oh, shit, I hope that wasn't an option."

I indicated we should start walking back to the bus. "You were very nice to take on the burden yourself, but— wouldn't it have been better if you'd let Tom carry her back? I mean, Ashley is an Amazon. Tom is more physically equipped to do the Tarzan thing, don't you think?"

Jackie inhaled sharply. "That is *such* a sexist remark! Women are every bit as capable as men. I ran track in high school and college. I lift weights three times a week." Then in a more conversational tone, she added, "I figure it's never too early to take measures to ward off osteoporosis. But Tom couldn't have done it, anyway. He has rotator cuff problems. No heavy lifting. Occupational hazard."

The only people I knew to suffer consistent shoulder injuries were athletes and circus performers. Since Tom didn't strike me as a trapeze artist or clown, that left only one practical choice. "Does Tom play professional baseball? Has he thrown too many fastballs?"

"Too much snipping, clipping, and curling. He's a hair designer. He runs a very upscale salon in Binghamton. Headhunters. Isn't that adorable? He serves champagne and caviar even if you're only having a cut and blow-dry. His prices are outrageous, but women like the soft lighting, the New Age music, the fountains, the aromatherapy candles. He does a land-office business. That's how we met."

I got my hair cut at Midge's Beauty Palace in Windsor City. The palace was located in Midge's house and occupied a back room that had once served as her children's playroom. It smelled of Play-Doh and Crayola crayons, but her rates were reasonable and in the summer she sometimes served iced tea to compensate for the fact that the place wasn't air-conditioned. "You married your beautician? No wonder your hair looks so great. You'll save a fortune on weaves over the years. I'm so jealous!"

"Tom isn't a beautician," Jackie corrected. "He's a color artist, not to mention a master razor cutter."

My dad got his hair cut by a master razor cutter too. His name was Hugo. He ran the local barbershop on Main Street.

"Should I ask Tom to have a look at your hair?" Jackie asked as we rounded the corner of the bus. "He does free consultations."

I stopped in my tracks to finger my windblown locks. "You think I should do something different with it?"

"You've been wearing it the same way since we were married, Emily. Don't you think it's time for a change?"

I followed Jackie onto the bus. She'd obviously forgotten. I was cursed with hair that only knew how to do one thing. Frizz. But I was a sport. If Tom thought he could do something with it, maybe I should let him try. Who knew? Maybe it would help us establish some kind of bond.

The bus burst into applause as we climbed aboard. "There she is!" someone shouted. "The woman of the hour!" I thought they were referring to me until people started popping up to slap Jackie on the back and shake her hand.

"If I'm ever in trouble, you're the one I'm calling on to help!" yelled the furniture polish man from the back. "JA-CKIE. JA-CKIE," he began to chant.

"JA-CKIE. JA-CKIE," chanted the rest of the bus. Feet stomped. Hands clapped. Someone in the front even started the wave.

Nope. She hadn't drawn any attention to herself at all.

After Jackie took her seat and everyone finished having their picture taken with her, I addressed them over the microphone. "You'd probably like an update on Ashley's condition, so I'll tell you what I know. She appears to have racked up her foot pretty badly, so the ambulance is taking her to the nearest hospital to have it looked at. Until she rejoins us, she's asked me to take over her responsibilities with the group and make sure the rest of your day isn't disrupted."

"How about we stop at a rest room!" Ira Kuppelman called out.

"Can we eat soon?" Ethel Minch's voice. "We're starving back here."

"I'd like to stop someplace to do some shopping," Jackie shouted.

"You need to find a cash machine!" Bernice squawked.

I looked down the length of the bus, a little daunted at the prospect of taking the reins, but feeling suddenly energized by an inexplicable surge of power. I was woman. I could do this. Either that or I was being electrocuted by the microphone and didn't realize it yet.

Osmond Chelsvig raised his hand. "What are we supposed to see this afternoon, anyway?"

"Hold on." I rummaged through Ashley's Golden Irish Vacations bag. Road maps. Guest rosters. Yellow highlighter pens. A pack of Virginia Slims cigarettes. Ashley smoked? *Hunh.* Obviously not in front of the guests. A glossy brochure of the rope bridge. A small-caliber gun.

My hand froze. A gun? I stood paralyzed . . . until I saw the curious hole at the rear of the barrel that housed a little striker wheel that would produce a flame. I rolled my eyes. A novelty lighter. Cute. But didn't she know that smoking caused wrinkles? I shuffled some more things out of the way. A finely detailed room map of the castle. Gee, I should look at that. I'd like to know how to find my way into some of the towers. A folder marked "Bushmills." Bingo.

I scanned the first page, eyeing all the pertinent facts. "This afternoon we're scheduled to take a tour of the Old Bushmills Distillery, which, it says here, is the oldest distillery not only in Ireland, but in the world. Famous for its single-malt, single-grain Irish whiskey. You can use the rest room facilities in the visitors' center before the tour. After the tour we'll have lunch at the Postill Bar, where we'll be treated to a sampling session of the distillery's many whiskeys. There's also a gift shop on the premises for shopping. And we'll stop at a bank somewhere along the way so that those of you who need money can get some. That should take care of everything. Any questions?"

I looked up to find everyone nodding their heads in approval. No questions. No complaints. All right! There was a trick to this tour guide business. Act like you know what you're doing and you'll keep everyone happy. Now all we had to do was get there. I stepped back to speak to Michael. "Do you know the way to the distillery?"

"It's down the road somewhere. I'll find it."

I had no doubt he would, but I was concerned about when. We needed to find it today. I caught George Farkas's eye and motioned him to the front of the bus. "I bet you've never been lost a day in your life, have you, George?"

His cheeks flushed in embarrassment. "Folks shouldn't tell you that. Makes me sound like a blowhard."

"Are you good with maps?"

"Don't have much use for maps. All I need is the general direction of a place and a sunny day."

I handed him Ashley's map of Northern Ireland and pointed to a tiny black dot superimposed on a thin red line. "This is the town of Bushmills. Can you get us there?"

He squinted at the dot at the tip of my finger. "You bet. You mind if I sit in the front seat with you so I can give directions?"

"Be my guest." I scooted by him to claim the window seat. He removed his reading glasses from his pocket and slid them onto his nose, then, after a glance at the map and a peek at the sky, settled down to business.

"When you come out of the parking lot, you'll want to head west," he instructed Michael, who threw him an irritated look over his shoulder.

"You'd best be telling me whether it's left or right I'm turning. None of this east or west malarkey."

"Make a right turn," said George. "And don't turn again until I tell you."

Oh, yeah. George would get us there.

We pulled into the parking lot of Ballybantry Castle at precisely six thirty that afternoon, a full fifteen minutes ahead of schedule. "Remember, people!" I announced as Michael cut the engine. "If you didn't get a chance to show your passport to the front desk clerk this morning, do it now." I assumed a post outside the front door of the bus, helping people off the stairs while exchanging pleasantries and smiles. I had to admit, I kind of liked being in charge. And what was even better, I was realizing I was pretty good at it.

"Good job, Emily," said Alice Tjarks as I assisted her to the ground. "I really enjoyed that tour. And look at the time. You even got us back early."

"An interesting place," said Osmond Chelsvig. "I think I got a little drunk on the fumes though. Any chance we could go back and tour it again?"

The tour had gone off like clockwork. No one tumbled down any stairs or fell off any of the many catwalks in the plant. Everyone appeared satisfied with their luncheon fare. No one got loud, drunk, or obnoxious after sampling shots of the original Bushmills, Black Bush, and Bushmills Malt. People wandered the gift shop after lunch and picked up a few souvenirs. We even stopped at the First Trust

Bank in Limavady on the way back so I could withdraw money from their automatic teller for Bernice and myself. And we didn't get lost. Not even once. The whole afternoon played back like a Disney movie—a little too good to be true.

Nana and Tilly were the last people off, followed by George, who looked immensely pleased that his navigational prowess had come in handy. "We couldn't have done it without you, George." I gave his arm an enthusiastic rub. "How can I thank you?"

"Shucks. That was nothing. Anyone in the group could have done it. But you better stop thanking me else you'll have me blushing in front of your gramma."

Nana's eyes sparkled at the recognition. Her mouth slid into a coy smile. "George, would you like to join Tilly and me at our table for dinner tonight? We wanna hear what it was like crossin' that bridge and what you saw when you was over there. Don't we, Tilly?"

"I'd like that," said George, leaping at the opportunity before Tilly could answer. "And if you want, I could have my photos duplicated so the two of you can see what you missed. Pills Etcetera runs a special deal on photo developing on Tuesdays."

"How very kind of you," said Tilly in an uncharacteristically girlish voice, her studious eyes twinkling at the same wattage as Nana's. "We'd like that, wouldn't we, Marion?"

Uh-oh. I hoped Tilly and Nana didn't have their romantic sights set on the same target, but let's face it, George Farkas possessed the kind of modest charm that women find irresistible. It didn't seem to matter that he'd lost his youth, his hair, his muscle tone, and one of his legs. He was still a babe magnet. Guys had it *so* good. Then again, given the disparity in life expectancy between the sexes, women were probably delirious that he was simply alive.

"Would you ladies allow me to escort you back to the hotel?" asked George, offering an arm to each of them. I hoped a ménage à trois wasn't in the offing, but I was pretty sure that wouldn't happen. Nana didn't speak a word of French.

I scurried back onto the bus to collect my belongings, grabbed Ashley's Irish Vacations bag, and thanked Michael for his services. He drilled me with a curious look, his expression that of a man who had never been thanked for anything before in his life and was therefore unaccustomed to saying "You're welcome."

"That old gent there," he said, nodding toward George. "He's not a local."

"Nope. He's a tourist."

"Then how did he know his way around so well?"

"He's from Iowa."

Michael frowned his confusion. "So?"

"So don't be too impressed. They can all do stuff like that."

I meandered across the parking lot studying the granite exterior of Ballybantry Castle with a leisurely eye, thinking it looked like something whipped up in a bakery. It was as solid and dense as a pound cake but divided into angles and tiers as asymmetrical as a half-eaten wedding cake. Turrets and towers shot up like birthday candles, and along the roofline the stonework formed a border that was chiseled into shapes as delicate as decorative icing. Ivy had found a toehold in some places, framing itself around bay windows as it crept upward toward the battlements, adding a splash of green to the cold gray wash of granite.

As I crossed the drawbridge, I peered over the railing into the moat. It was a murky green-brown that looked incapable of sustaining any kind of aquatic life. I wondered if they'd ever drained the water from it, and what they might have found lying at the bottom. I thought of the poor Irish boy who had been floating dead in it four hundred years ago, and I shivered at what a grisly sight it must have been. It seemed so unfair. He'd been guilty of nothing more than falling in love with the wrong woman, and for that sin, his punishment had been death. It made me want to cry, but more than that, it made me want to find Etienne so he could enfold me in his arms and tell me he loved me.

The redheaded clerk named Liam was minding the front desk again. I requested my room key, but the slot was empty, meaning Nana had already retrieved it. "There's a message for you though," he said, handing me a slip of white paper.

Receiving messages while I'm on vacation gives me the willies. I always think the worst. Somebody back home was in an accident. A tornado wiped out my apartment complex. My VCR malfunctioned and recorded a rerun of *Baywatch* instead of *Sex and the City*. I unfolded the paper.

Emily darling,
    I've taken a taxi into town to look for a clothing store. Will try to be back for dinner. If I'm late, go on without me. Have much to tell you . . . not the least of which is . . . I love you. Tonight I want you to myself.

Etienne

I felt a tingling below my navel that traveled to my toes and fingertips. Every nerve ending in my body quivered with anticipation. The down on the back of my neck stood on end. I felt weightless, as if I'd been pumped full of helium and was in danger of floating away. I wondered if this was the human version of being in heat. I read his words again. "I love you. Tonight I want you to myself." His sentiment filled me with so much excitement I thought I might explode, until reality slapped me upside the head. How could Etienne have me all to himself when I was sharing my room with two other women?

"Oh, by the way, Miss Andrew, I've given Mrs. Sippel and Ms. Hovick the key to their new room. The custodian volunteered to take over Rita's duties today, so we were able to open up a new room. It's across the hall from yours. I'll be happy to help the ladies move their bags when they're ready."

"They're being moved to their own room?" Was this a sign from Above or what?

Liam motioned me closer and said in an undertone, "Mind you, now, Archie's not the housekeeper Rita was, so the room might not be up to our usual standards. But you tell the ladies, if they find the least thing out of order to make a note of it, and we'll take care of it as soon as possible. 'Service' is our motto here at Ballybantry Castle."

Liam seemed friendly enough. Maybe he'd be more forthcoming than the desk clerk I'd questioned this morning. "How long have you worked here, Liam?"

"Off and on for six years now, not including the eighteen months we closed down for renovations. I worked for me da in his mortuary that year."

"Have you ever seen the ghosts that are creeping around this place?"

He didn't skip a beat, but I could see a wariness in his eyes that hadn't been there before. "Ghosts? Here? Go on with ya, now."

"Let me phrase it another way. Why are you afraid to admit the castle is haunted?"

He forced an unconvincing smile. "You'd be confusing us with Ballygally Castle. It has a tower room that people claim is haunted and a grisly legend to accompany it."

"Worse than the Ballybantry legend?"

He looked genuinely confused. "What legend would that be?"

"The one about the forbidden marriage, the boy floating in the moat, the girl dying in childbirth, and . . . the duck."

He shook his head, absolutely deadpan. "Not familiar with it, but it does sound a bit like one of those American soap operas of yours."

Stonewalled. Again. Maybe I needed to try another tack. "Who owns Ballybantry Castle?"

"A family by the name of McCrilly, and a group of investors from America. The family decided to sell stock in the castle when they learned their B-and-B license was being revoked and the building was going to be declared uninhabitable. It's something of a white elephant, isn't it now?" He gave the lobby a sweeping look. "A brilliant structure, but who can afford to foot the bill for its upkeep? 'Twas the investors from America who put up the capital for the renovations. I heard it was millions."

McCrilly. Now we were getting somewhere. If Ethel Minch's maiden name was McCrilly, I'd have a small piece of the puzzle. "It must have been traumatic for the family to give up ownership of their ancestral home."

Liam nodded. "Aye. But mind you, the McCrillys only owned Ballybantry for twenty years. They bought it from the previous owner when they won the Irish sweepstakes back in the late seventies. Ownership has changed hands at least a dozen times."

I drew a black line through my mental image of the McCrilly name. Back to square one. "Do you happen to know the name of the family who built the castle?"

He shook his head. "Don't know."

"Do you know the names of *any* of the former owners other than McCrilly?"

"Me da might know. I'll ask him if you like. But he'll want to be knowing why you're asking."

"Because it's history! How can you work in a place this old and know so little about it?"

He shrugged dully. "I've no curiosity about it actually. Besides, the first owners were English, so why would I want to be remembering their names?"

Hadn't Ethel Minch said much the same thing this morning? *Hmm.* "Tell me, Liam, since your father runs the mortuary, have you heard any more about what caused Rita's death?"

Liam hung his head woefully. "Sad thing, that. 'Twas her heart. Her arteries were clogged worse than a backed-up pipe. The coroner said 'twas surprising she lasted as long as she did. Me da blames it on our full Irish breakfasts. Too many trans-fatty acids, you know. He's a cornflakes man himself."

Etienne had warned me about the health risks of Irish breakfasts, but I hadn't listened. I thought about the bacon and sausage I'd chowed down this morning and imagined the backup in my own arteries. I vowed to eat a more sensible breakfast tomorrow morning. But learning that Rita's death was heart related didn't provide me with any clear answers about the incident. She still could have been frightened to death, but how could we ever prove it?

As I gathered up my belongings, I heard footsteps scuttling across the lobby. "Have they started serving dinner yet?" Bernice asked, breathless.

"Dinner's at seven thirty," I said, checking the wall clock. "You have forty-five minutes. What's the rush?"

"I want a good seat."

I wasn't sure what made one seat any better than another, but I decided not to ask. With my luck, she might tell me. "Hey, Bernice, this is a good time for you to call the bank and have them wire you some money."

"I don't need any money. You already got me some."

"Not enough to last you for the rest of the trip." I beckoned her with my index finger. "Come on. It'll be painless. And I'll wait here until you're done."

Two phones hung on the wall opposite the front desk. One had a silver casing and was designated as a coin-operated phone. The other was encased in gray with a turquoise strip slashed down the front and labeled "Card Phone." I dug my address book out of my bag, inserted my TE callcard into the turquoise phone, punched up the number for the Windsor City Bank, and handed the receiver to Bernice. "Tell them to wire your money right here to the castle. They do things like that all the time."

While she explained her problem to a clerk in Iowa, I returned to the front desk and hefted Ashley's Golden Irish Vacations bag onto the counter. "Would you leave a note in Ashley Overlock's box telling her that Emily has her tour bag and she should pick it up in my room when she gets back?"

While Liam penned the message, I noted the minute hand on the wall clock and hoped Bernice talked fast. My phone card was only good for twenty minutes.

While I waited, I looked over a display of postcards that came in the shape of frothy glasses of Guinness, black-faced sheep, Celtic crosses, and old-fashioned red phone booths. From behind me, Bernice continued her conversation with the bank clerk. "No, I'm not giving you my account number. This phone could be tapped."

I shook my head. Hindsight was telling me I should have bought the one-hundred-minute card. I heard Bernice's voice increase in volume. "Let me talk to Mr. Erickson. He knows who I am." I checked the clock again, watching another minute tick by.

I pulled a Celtic cross, a glass of Guinness, and a black-faced sheep from the postcard display and dug out a ten-pound note to pay for them. I didn't really enjoy writing postcards, but it was more economical than buying another callcard. Liam regarded my ten-pound note.

"I'm sorry, but I can't accept that."

"What?"

"That bill isn't considered legal tender here in the republic."

"I got it at a bank. What's wrong with it?"

"It's provincial money. Issued by one of the provincial banks in Northern Ireland. It's only good in the North."

"Aren't we in the North?"

"We're in the republic. We're a stone's throw away from the North, but it's still the republic, and your money's no good."

"You can't do some kind of exchange thing?"

"I could if the bill were pounds sterling, but as you can see, it's not."

This was nice. I had a wallet full of cash that was worthless in 90 percent of the places we'd be visiting. Unfortunately, so did Bernice. I was going to have a great time explaining *this* to her.

"Emily, will you come here and talk to these people?" Bernice held the phone out to me. "They're making my blood pressure go up."

I took the receiver from her. In the eight months I'd worked at the bank, I'd become buddies with Mr. Erickson, the bank president, so I was only too happy to talk to him. "Greetings from Ireland," I said into the receiver, expecting to hear Mr. Erickson's rich baritone in reply. What I heard instead was elevator music. I frowned at Bernice. "Where's Mr. Erickson?"

"He's on coffee break. I'm on hold." The phone suddenly started to beep like a digitized Gatling gun. Bernice tented her arms over her head and ran toward the front desk. "Move, Emily! It's gonna blow!"

I hung up the receiver and removed my phone card from the slot, holding it in the air so Bernice could see. "The beeping alerts us that we've run out of time, *not* that the phone is going to explode." Our lesson in international calling obviously needed a little more work. "Were you able to arrange for any money to be transferred before you were put on hold?"

"I arranged nothing. The clerk was an idiot. That does it. No more phone calls. I'm heading for the dining room."

"Wait a minute, Bernice." I chewed my lip, contemplating what kind of word picture I could draw to explain our money problem. I snapped my fingers with inspiration. "Do you remember the Civil War?"

She shot me a narrow look. "Just how old do you think I am?"

Bad start. Take two. "Do you remember how the South issued their own currency during the war, and that after the war, the money was declared worthless?"

"If this is a joke, I hope you remember the punch line. My husband used to try to tell jokes, but he'd always forget the punch line. It really used to irritate me, especially after he'd go on . . . and on . . . and on . . . setting the thing up. Harold wasn't very funny." She looked suddenly nostalgic. "But his Mr. Peeper was as long as my arm. That kind of made up for things. What were you saying about Confederate money?"

I stared at Bernice, my mind bombarded with images of her and Harold that were far too disturbing for any human to process. I couldn't deal with the money issue right now. That crisis could wait. I'd withdraw more cash from an ATM in the republic. I waved her off. "Nothing. Never mind. It's not important."

My eyes were still glazed over when Nana let me into the room. "We're about ready to make the move across the hall," she announced as she closed her suitcase.

I dumped my stuff on the bed and regarded the two of them. Maybe it was the unflattering dullness of the room's fluorescent lighting, but they suddenly appeared very old and vulnerable. "Are you sure you're going to be all right?" I asked, suffering a pang of conscience. "You don't have to move if you'd feel safer in here with me."

"You're sweet to offer, dear, but to be honest, Tilly and me like to be on our own. We didn't sign up for this trip to be a bother to you. We can take care of ourselves." With a herculean grunt, she swung her suitcase onto the floor and popped the handle up. I stared in horror.

"Nana! You shouldn't be lifting suitcases by yourself! What are you thinking? You'll hurt your back!" As I hurried across the room to assist Tilly in closing her bag, Nana rolled hers toward the door.

"It's on account of exercise class, dear. I can do all sorts of things now that I couldn't do before."

"The desk clerk said he'd help you with your bags," I said as I headed for the phone.

"Save your breath," Tilly advised, joining Nana at the door. "He's probably operating on Irish time. By the time he walks down the hall, your grandmother and I can be unpacked."

I saw them to their door, but Nana shooed me away before I could gain more than a peek at the flowers and flounces in their room. "I'd invite you in, dear, but you need to get ready for dinner and so do we." She let Tilly go ahead of her, then in a confidential whisper said, "Do you think George would find me too brassy if I rouged up my lips a little tonight?"

I gave her the thumbs-up sign. "Before I forget, make a list of anything untidy in your room and give it to me so I can inform the front desk. The custodian cleaned your room, so I've been warned it might not be up to usual standards. You know how men are about cleaning. They miss a lot of details."

She returned my thumbs-up. I scooted back to my room, checked the time, and geared up to warp speed. I set out a long red matte jersey dress with a slit to mid-thigh, red thong sandals with a three-inch heel, and drop pearl earrings. Understated but elegant. I liked that. I ran into the bathroom. *Eh!* My anti-itch cream had turned my skin yellow. I'm surprised no one had mentioned that I looked like a summer squash. I removed my eye makeup, washed my face with foaming cleanser, and examined my complexion in the mirror. My hives were less visible than they'd been earlier, and they'd stopped itching, which meant that even though my anti-itch cream smelled terrible, it worked. Or maybe I should attribute the improvement to the fact that nothing disastrous had happened on the afternoon tour. Yeah. That was more likely. I felt in control again.

I pulled my hair back into a ponytail and twisted it into a simple ballerina's bun, then began applying fresh makeup. Light foundation. Eyeliner. Mascara. A smudge of brown eye shadow for depth. Blusher high on the cheekbones. As I reached for my lip pencil, I heard a knock on my door, and hurried to answer it. I checked the clock again. Probably Etienne picking me up for dinner. *Hmm.* I wondered how he'd feel about having a little appetizer before the main event.

"Here's the list you asked for, dear," said Nana when I opened the door. She handed me a sheet of castle stationery. "And if it wouldn't be too much trouble, you s'pose I could borrow some a your lip rouge? I couldn't find none in my toiletry bag, then I remembered why. I don't usually wear none."

I took the note from her and scooted into the bathroom. I searched through the dozen tubes of lipstick I'd brought with me, selected one, and pressed it into her hand. "The perfect color for you, Nana. Shell Pink Passion."

"No kiddin'. I like it already."

I returned to the bathroom, outlined my lips, and, as I riffled through my stash of lipstick tubes again in search of one called Lusty, glanced at the note I'd set on the vanity. The list was short and was printed in Nana's distinctively neat and precise hand.

Cigarette butt left in ashtray
Lightbulb burned out in floor lamp
Dead body in closet

I inhaled a calming breath. "NANA!"

CHAPTER 8

"I slid open the closet door to hang up my dress, and there he was," said Nana. "Crumpled up like an accordian."

I peered at the body lying in near fetal position on the floor of Nana's closet, recognizing immediately the pony-tailed man wearing the green coveralls with the fish and warthog emblazoned on it. "It's the custodian," I said. "I saw him in the lobby this morning, carpet-sweeping the rug. Did you check for a pulse?"

Nana nodded. "He hasn't got no pulse, but he's still warm, so he hasn't been dead too long."

I dropped to my knees in search of bloody footprints, but from what I could see, the area around the body was clean. There was no trace of blood on either the carpet or the body. But the man's eyes were wide open and glazed with what looked like terror, and his mouth was contorted into a shape that suggested that he hadn't prayed with his last dying breath. He'd screamed. Pinpricks of ice needled my flesh. "I'd better call the front desk."

"I just did that," said Tilly, and no sooner were the

words out of her mouth than we heard the sound of foot-steps racing pell-mell down the corridor. Liam McEtigan burst into the room so white-faced with panic, even his freckles looked pale.

"Oh, Jaysuz, not another one." He peeked into the closet, then pressed the heels of his palms into his eye sockets as if to erase the image. "It's Archie. Jaysuz. Two people in two days. This'll be our doom for sure. What am I going to do?"

Tilly thumped her walking stick on the floor. "You could recommend that all your employees have stress tests before they begin work. That could reduce your mortality rate considerably."

Liam raked his fingers through his hair as he continued to regard the custodian. "He was a good worker, Archie was. He might not have given attention to every detail, like making sure the labels of the body washes and shampoos were facing outward and folding the corners of the bathroom tissue into a point, but he always got into every corner with that carpet sweeper of his. He even did closets."

I looked across the room to find Archie's carpet sweeper leaning against the stone facade of the fireplace. "So if he was carpet-sweeping the closet, what's his sweeper doing over there?" I asked, nodding toward the fireplace.

Liam looked from Archie to the sweeper, bewilderment stamping itself on his face. "I wouldn't be knowing that. But if he wasn't cleaning the carpet, why was he in the closet?"

"Maybe he was tryin' to tell us somethin'," said Nana.

Hmm. I hadn't thought of that, but I remembered seeing a movie once where a long-decayed skeleton indicated the correct path through a complex cave system by extending a bony forefinger in the right direction. I gave Archie's corpse another look. He wasn't pointing at anything. "What do you suppose he could be trying to tell us?"

"Look at the expression on his face," said Tilly. "I think he was frightened of something in the room and was hiding from it. Why else would he squirrel himself away in a closet?"

Liam paled another shade lighter. "Oh, Jaysuz."

"Nana?" I said, soliciting her opinion.

"I think it's obvious." Three sets of eyes riveted on her, awaiting her pronouncement. "He was tryin' to tell us he was gay."

I knew my decision to avoid explaining the gay and lesbian movement to her in rabid detail would one day come back to haunt me.

"You're being too literal, Marion," Tilly explained. "The term 'coming out of the closet' is merely a euphemism to describe a person's decision to reveal his lifestyle to the world. There are no actual closets involved."

"No kiddin'? What about wardrobes?"

Tilly shook her head. "No wardrobes either."

Nana mulled this over for a half second. "You mighta known that, but how do we know *he* knew that?" She nodded toward Archie. "Maybe he didn't understand about euphemisms either."

"I need to be calling the authorities," Liam stammered, wringing his hands. "And I'll need to be asking you ladies to pack your bags and move to another room before the police arrive, else they might be wanting to include your belongings as part of their investigation."

Nana nearly tripped over Tilly's cane in her rush to start throwing things back into her suitcase. "I been that route with Emily last year," she said as she gathered the contents of a drawer into her arms and dumped them into her grip. "That Swiss hotel lost her luggage and she couldn't wear none a the pretty things she brought with her. No way that's gonna happen to me, specially not with all the fancy undies I got with me. I bought 'em, and by glory, I'm gonna wear 'em."

I could hardly believe my ears. "You brought fancy underwear with you?" I teased. Nana had always favored flannel bloomers, but that was logical considering the longest season in Minnesota was winter, with an occasional warm weekend in July that passed for summer.

"I been rethinkin' my options in intimate apparel since I made the move south," Nana replied as she scooped out the contents of another drawer.

Tilly waggled her cane as if calling us to order. "What room are you sending us to, young man?"

Liam scrunched his face into an agonizing grimace and massaged his forehead. "Let me think. Oh, Jaysuz, I've no rooms available."

I felt my stomach sink to my knees. No. No! This was my mother's doing. Her prayers of intercession were killing me.

"I'm afraid you ladies will have to be returning to Miss Andrew's room, if she'll be having you."

"What about the room we checked into yesterday?" asked Nana. "You got that clean yet?"

"We do, yes. Archie scoured it today. Even washed the carpet. But—"

"We'll take it," she said, rushing into the bathroom.

Liam looked horrified. "I'll not be asking you ladies to sleep in a room where someone died only yesterday."

"Won't bother us a bit." Nana scurried across the floor with her toiletry bag, pitched it into her suitcase, and slammed the lid shut. "It'll be like visitation at the funeral parlor, only without the body."

Liam gave Tilly an Are-you-sure-you-want-to-do-this? look. Tilly assumed her professor's demeanor. "In comparison to some of the places I've done field research, this should be a cakewalk. Why, I've slept in huts in New Guinea where the main decorative feature consisted of a hundred human skulls dangling from the roof."

Good thing Martha Stewart hadn't been along. She probably would have wanted to turn them into something adorable, like lampshades . . . or door knockers. "Okay," I said, liking the plan. "Liam will call the police, then see the two of you to your new room. I'll scoot back to my room to finish dressing and will plan to see you in the dining room in a little while."

I picked my way around small clumps of New Yorkers who had stopped to socialize with each other as I walked across the hall to my room and unlocked the door. They apparently weren't concerned that it was seven twenty-five, and by Iowa standards, they were really late for dinner. I envied their ability to ignore the schedule and to live life at their own pace. Of course, they ran the risk of cold food, bad seats, and disapproving stares by being late, but they could remedy this easily enough by whining to the management. Unfortunately, New Yorkers had earned a reputation for being consummate complainers, but no one ever asked *why* they complained. I figured the reason was health-related. Complaining was a way of preventing ulcers. They didn't get the ulcers themselves; they gave them to other people. New Yorkers were really serious about preventive medicine.

As I changed into my dinner dress, I tried not to think about the body in Nana's closet, but the look on the man's face kept haunting me. It was Rita the maid all over again, minus the bloody footprints. Was Tilly correct in thinking Archie had been trying to hide from something in the room? Is that why Rita's body had been found near a closet too? Had she been attempting to hide? Or had she been trying to escape? But from what? Cries? Apparitions? Cold spots? A really big duck?

Whatever the explanation, it seemed statistically impossible to me that two members of the castle's staff would die of natural causes on two consecutive days. I'd taken statistics in college. I knew about these things. I might even be able to work out the math if I could remember what I'd learned. Liam McEtigan might not want to face the truth, but I thought it was as clear as the freckles on his face. Something in Ballybantry Castle was killing people, and my greatest fear was that once it finished off the staff, it would start on the guests. I had to make sure that didn't happen, but I wasn't exactly sure how. The only recourse I had at the moment was to keep my eyes open at dinner and see if I could root out any new information.

I smoothed my dress over my hips and thighs, slid into my shoes, and plucked out a few wisps of hair to float around my neck and temples. It was seven thirty-five now, and since Etienne still hadn't shown, I followed his directive and trotted off to the dining room by myself.

The place was abuzz with conversation and laughter. Chairs scraped the floor as people headed out to join the buffet line. Glasses tinked. Dishes clinked. Flatware chinked. A soft Irish melody played in the background. I noticed my people all bunched together in groups of four and six at the tables closest to the food. I guess these were considered the "good" seats—where you simply had to tilt your chair back on its legs to grab more dinner rolls. The New Yorkers occupied the tables flanking the good seats, but they all seemed content, at least for the moment. I spied George Farkas down front at a table for six, wedged contentedly between Nana and Tilly, who had somehow managed to beat me there. Their table was full, so I searched for another open space and found one where I could both mingle outside my social circle and snoop. A brief acquaintance had once told me that the fun of travel isn't the sights you see but the people you meet. This was the perfect time to put the theory to the test.

"Do you mind if I join you?" I smoothed my fingers along the back rail of the last empty chair at a table occupied by the Minches, the Kuppelmans, and my ex-husband. "Or are you saving this seat for Tom?" I asked Jackie.

"Tom has a migraine, so he can't even look at food. I'll save the seat for you, but don't stop to sit. Get your food before it's all gone. The Iowans arrived first and they have voracious appetites."

I grabbed a plate still warm from the dishwasher at the end of the buffet table and proceeded slowly through the line, agog with the variety of culinary fare available. Two members of the cleaning staff might be dead, but the cooks were alive and kicking. There were three tureens of soup: green pea, creamy mushroom, and a butterscotch-colored broth that had green herbs and seashells floating around in it.

I skipped the soup and went on to the appetizers. Fresh oysters. Pale pink smoked salmon. I forked a piece of salmon onto my plate. I pondered a bowl of crisp lettuce, then passed it by, not wanting to waste my appetite on food I could eat back home. Next came the vegetable choices. Potatoes in every incarnation: mashed, boiled, roasted, fried, and flattened into cakes. Boiled cabbage. Kale. Broccoli. I scooped a little of each kind of potato into my plate and added a spear of broccoli for color, then moved on to the chafing dishes.

I wasn't sure what each dish contained, but it all smelled delicious, and since I'd made a vow to expand my rather pedestrian "meat and potatoes" palate, I decided to sample everything. A spoonful of some kind of stew with carrots, onions, and a meat product that looked like sausage. A nibble of something resembling a stuffed mushroom cap covered with breadcrumbs. A dollop of mashed potato with a crab claw sticking out of it. A spoonful of another kind of stew with onions, mushrooms, carrots, and shredded beef. A scoop of a fluffy golden casserole with onions and some other ingredient I couldn't quite identify. I passed up the baked ham as too ordinary and the bread selections as too filling and headed back to the table.

"I'm sorry to hear about Tom's migraine," I said as I took my place between Ethel Minch and Jackie. "Does he get them often?"

"Only when he's stressed out. This thing with Ashley today did a real number on him."

I nodded, understanding. Poor Tom. Crippled by the stress of watching his wife carry another woman down a rugged path for over a mile. Life could be hell. "So, is everyone excited to taste authentic Irish cuisine?" I gazed around the table to discover that no one else's plate looked like mine. Jackie's was glutted with potatoes, cabbage, broccoli, a bunch of lettuce, and a single slab of salmon. "You didn't take any ham? You used to love ham."

"Did I forget to tell you? I've become a vegetarian! I've changed so much since I saw you last, Emily. No burgers. No steak. No ham."

No dick.

"You two dolls go back a ways?" asked Ernie Minch, whose plate held a pile of lettuce supplemented by potatoes, cabbage, kale, and broccoli, with a cup of pea soup on the side.

"We're old friends," I said, staring at Ernie's meatless selections. "Don't tell me you're a vegetarian too."

"We're vegans," Ethel answered for him. "We don't eat anything with a face, a mother, or a liver."

They ate nothing with a face? Wow. That eliminated meat, fish, fowl, Nabisco Teddy Grahams. They could probably still eat gingerbread men, but they'd probably have to break the heads off first.

Ira Kuppelman waved his fork at Ethel's plate. "You're still eating too many unhealthy vegetables." Ira's dinner consisted of cabbage, kale, broccoli, and a single slice of bread. "Potatoes are on my 'Do Not Consume' list and I eat lettuce only occasionally."

"You're too extreme with that diet of yours," warned Ethel. "One of these days someone's going to find you dead from malnutrition."

I regarded the five different kinds of potatoes on my plate. "What's wrong with potatoes?" I asked Ira.

"They don't allow the body to achieve a harmonious and dynamic state with the natural environment."

I wondered if that was worse than eating too many calories. It kind of sounded like it. I pushed my potatoes to one side of my plate.

"So what do you eat if you don't eat potatoes?" Jackie asked Ira.

"I eat what every macrobiotic eats." He ticked off a litany on his fingers. "Bok choy, burdock carrots, daikon radishes, azuki beans, and your common sea vegetables like nori, wakame, hiziki, and agar-agar."

The man ate prickly carrots and questionable produce that sounded like creatures who'd tangled with Godzilla. *Hmm.* Disharmony with the natural environment was looking pretty good about now. I nudged my potatoes back toward the center of my plate.

"Are you on the same diet as your husband?" Jackie asked Gladys Kuppelman.

I figured the answer to that was no since the food on

Gladys's plate was divided evenly between lettuce and broccoli.

"I'm a fruitarian/raw-foodist," said Gladys. "And let me tell you, it's not easy sticking to your diet when you're on vacation. The fruits are overripe. The vegetables are over-cooked. And just *try* asking for condiments or beverages. Watch this." She motioned a server to our table. "I'd like to order something to drink. Do you have roasted bancha twig tea?"

"I'm sorry?" the girl asked, looking confused.

"How about roasted brown rice tea?"

"We have green tea."

"Do you have any sesame seaweed powder?"

"What?"

"Never mind." Gladys motioned her away. "You see what I mean? The tour company promises that all your dietary needs will be met, but once you arrive at your destination, they serve you the same old slop that everyone else is eating." Her eyes dipped to my plate. "I bet you don't even know what half that swill in front of you is."

This was authentic Irish cuisine! How gauche of her to call it swill. I skewered some food on the end of my fork and held it up for her perusal. "Boiled potato." I stuffed it into my mouth and flashed a satisfied smile.

"I know what's she's eating," said Ethel Minch. "I got a book." She whipped it off her lap for us to see. "It lists every kind of Irish dish there is and shows a color photograph. You see that mound of mashed potatoes on her plate there with the crab claw sticking out of it? That's called Seafood Pie and it's a real delicacy."

A delicacy, was it? Nice choice, Emily. I dug into the seafood pie.

"You better have all your business in order," Ira Kuppelman warned me, "because that food is poisoning your system. Wait and see. It'll end up killing you. You young people treat your bodies like refuse dumps. You'll never live as long as Gladys and me."

All the tables in this place and I had to pick the one patrolled by the food police. Brilliant idea I'd had to socialize outside my immediate circle.

"How old are you?" Jackie asked Ira as I forked a whole mushroom cap into my mouth.

"Take a guess," Ira said proudly.

Jackie shrugged. "Sixty-one?"

"Here's a picture of that little nibble you just put in your mouth," said Ethel, pointing out the photo to me with her brightly lacquered nail. "It's a stuffed heart."

"I'm ninety-two," bragged Ira, "and Gladys is ninety."

EH! My eyes froze open in shock, but I was unsure what freaked me out more: learning Ira Kuppelman's age or discovering what I'd just sunk my teeth into. I tried to remain calm as I mumbled around the pulp in my mouth, "Wot kind of hart?"

"It says here they use any kind of fowl or small game heart. What kind of heart do you think she's eating, Ernie?"

"Gotta be a chicken," he replied. "Or a turkey."

Ira shook his head. "I bet it's a duck."

Oh, God!

"Could it be a Cornish hen?" asked Jackie. "They look like they'd have bite-size organs."

"Maybe it was a capon heart," said Gladys.

Jackie looked confused. "What's a capon?"

"A capon is your standard male chicken with one basic difference," said Ernie. He scissored his fingers in the air. "He's been castrated."

Jackie clutched her throat and sucked in her breath. Uh-oh. I hoped she wasn't having a flashback.

"How can they castrate a chicken?" asked Ethel. "I thought all chickens were female."

Ernie rolled his eyes. "There's girl chickens and boy chickens. The girls are called hens. The boys are called cocks. When there's too many boys, Farmer Brown snips off their stones and—zap!—they can forget about knocking up Clucky Lucky anytime soon."

Aha! A perfect example of the incredible strides the feminist movement had made in the poultry industry.

"I thought the boy chickens were called roosters," said Gladys.

"Clucky Lucky was not a hen," Jackie corrected Ernie. "He might have acted like a hen, but I think it's obvious he was a cock . . . with gender-identification issues."

"Would that make him a dyke?" asked Ira.

Gladys shook her head. "It makes him a capon."

"You know what I think? I think you people are all talking *bull*," wailed Ernie.

Why was this discussion sounding so familiar? I swallowed the half-chewed mush in my mouth and sat straight up in my chair, stricken.

"Tasted pretty bad, huh?" asked Ethel.

I shook my head. "It's not that. I just realized I've had this conversation before. In Switzerland." The topic had been bovines instead of fowl, but the level of confusion had been exactly the same. I studied the remaining food on my plate with apprehension.

"You want me to find pictures of the other stuff you got there so you know what you're eating?" Ethel asked helpfully.

"That would be *so* sweet of you," I said with relief. I snatched the water pitcher from the middle of the table, filled my glass, and chugalugged the whole thing in one gulp to get rid of the aftertaste in my mouth.

"I hope that's well water," said Ira. "Or spring water. Those are the only kinds of water you should ever drink. And never with ice."

Sounded like advice Ponce de Leon might have given his men during their search for the mythical fountain of youth. Of course, ice hadn't been an option back in the 1500s. Especially in Florida. But it seemed the Kuppelmans had discovered the elixir of youth that had eluded Ponce. I regarded their smooth, tanned complexions. Their taut flesh. Their full heads of hair. Their athletically trim bodies. The superior muscle definition beneath their matching jerseys. "Are you really ninety-two?" I asked Ira.

"Born April second, 1908. You do the math."

"That fluffy casserole you got there," Ethel said, referring to her book. "That's tripe and onions."

I scooped a portion of the casserole onto my fork for a better look. "What's tripe? Some kind of fish?"

"It's cow stomach," said Gladys. "Or sheep. Or goat. They sell it at our corner market. Some people make handbags out of it."

Not the Irish. They made casseroles. I dumped it off my fork and scooted it to a remote section of my plate.

"How come you don't have any wrinkles?" Jackie marveled at the Kupplemans. "Most people who look as good as you do have had a ton of face-lifts."

Ira gestured toward his plate. "Anyone who follows our diet can look just like we do. They won't develop wrinkles. Ever."

I guess my mom had actually been on to something when she'd told me to eat my vegetables. But was it worth living to the age of ninety-two, wrinkle-free, if I could never eat another potato chip or doughnut hole? I mean, what was the point?

"That concoction in the middle of your plate with the

onions and mushrooms and carrots," said Ethel. "That's rabbit stew."

Rabbit stew. Finally. Something both recognizable and tasty. I poised my fork over a mound of mushrooms, meat, and carrots only to have Jackie seize my hand.

"You can't possibly eat that."

"Not until you let go of my hand, I can't."

"How can you stoop so low?"

"Because I'm hungry!"

"That's no excuse! You could be about to eat Flopsy, Mopsy, and Cotton-tail. How can you live with that on your conscience?"

I gave her a long, hard look. She couldn't be your average, run-of-the-mill transsexual. *Noooo.* She had to be a *vegetarian* transsexual.

"Is that 'the look'?" she cried. "Oh. My. God. You're giving me 'the look.' Don't deny it. I remember it quite vividly from when we were in New York together. Go ahead then." She released my hand and crossed her arms over her chest, her lips puffed out in an exaggerated pout. "Eat the baby bunny. And to think that's the mouth I used to kiss!"

Gladys did something with her face that might have been a failed attempt at a frown. Ira and Ernie exchanged curious glances. I smiled stiffly and kicked Jackie under the table.

"OW!"

"We played the theater circuit together on Broadway," I explained. "And you know modern theater. It can be very avant-garde. One of the plays actually required us to kiss."

"Cruibins," said Ethel.

"You saw these two acting together on Broadway?" Gladys gasped in astonishment. "Was that the name of the play?"

"It's the name of that gunk on her plate next to the

rabbit stew. Says here it's a mixture of carrots, onions, and pickled pigs' trotters. What are trotters?"

Gladys's complexion turned chalky. "Pigs' feet." She covered her mouth in horror. "You're going to eat pigs' feet?"

Pigs' feet or Benjamin Bunny. Some choice.

"I got a lot of sympathy for pigs," said Ethel, closing her book. "They're the size of Sherman tanks, but they have to tiptoe around on these little tiny feet. They must develop some major foot problems. I've had foot problems all my life, and believe me, it's no fun."

Oh, my God! She was admitting to foot problems? This was perfect! Here was my opening. "What kind of foot problems do you have?" I asked in a voice that I hoped expressed concern and interest without sounding too eager.

"What problems *don't* I have? You name it, I got it. Good thing I married a shoe salesman. Would have cost me a fortune for footwear otherwise."

"You sell shoes?" Jackie perked up beside me, obviously more concerned with her own feet than pigs' feet. "Do you happen to carry . . . large sizes?"

"So, Ethel," I continued, cutting Jackie off, "what are you struggling with? Bunions? Calluses? Corns?"

"I got deformed bones in my feet. Not much I could do about it though. My podiatrist says deformities like mine are usually hereditary."

My anticipation started to build. "So your relatives all have the same foot problems?"

"Only on my mother's side of the family. The Quigley side. My father's side never had so much as an ingrown toenail."

" 'Quigley' is Irish, isn't it?" Gladys asked.

Ethel nodded. "It used to be O'Quigley, but when my great-grandfather arrived on Ellis Island, the *O* got lost somewhere in the paperwork."

"Did your relatives emigrate during one of the potato famines?" I asked, growing more excited. I had only deformed feet and Ethel's Irish heritage to go on, but I could smell a connection. Was it possible the O'Quigleys had been involved with the castle in some bygone era? I tried to suppress the trill of emotion in my voice. "Do you know if your relatives were originally from this area?"

Ethel threw me an annoyed look. "How the hell should I know? And why would I care? Haven't you ever heard that proverb? 'He who boasts of his descent is like the potato; the best part of him is underground.' If you ask me, all that genealogy stuff is a waste of time. What's the sense? It's all ancient history. What good's it gonna do me to know I was related to some spud farmer in Ireland two hundred years ago? Is that gonna make me any richer? I don't think so."

This was the second time she'd expressed her apathy toward all things historical. Could her disinterest be genuine? Or was this a deliberate tactic to shift attention away from herself and her family?

"That's the right attitude!" Ira tapped his fist on the edge of the table. "I said the same thing to Gladys, but she had an inkling there was *royalty* in her family's past, so we had to spend thousands finding out who all her ancestors were. Let me tell you, there are some things better left buried, but Gladys *had* to know. Didn't you, Gladys? Go ahead. Why don't you tell your friends who you're related to?"

Gladys's eyes became daggers as she pivoted her head around to glare at her husband. "I don't want to talk about it."

Goose bumps crawled up my arms. Geez. What had she found out?

"I'm not even sure why she wanted to visit Ireland after—"

"So help me, Ira, if you say one more word, I'll make the rest of your vacation a living *hell!*"

"I bet you're related to Hitler," said Ethel. "I wouldn't tell anyone if I was related to Hitler."

"I wouldn't tell anyone if I was related to Jack the Ripper," said Ernie.

"I wouldn't tell anyone if I was related to Peewee Eck," said Jackie.

A hushed silence ensued as all eyes trained on Jackie. Peewee Eck? Yeah. A real biggie in the annals of criminal history. "Peewee Eck?" I repeated.

"First baseman on my grade school Little League team," Jackie explained. "We were playing for the city championship, and Peewee flubbed up and let a ball scoot right through his legs into right field. The other team scored on his error, and we ended up losing the game and the championship. Peewee was so despised, his family eventually had to move out of town. I think they had to go into the witness protection program or something."

"You grew up in a real progressive town," Ethel commented. "Co-ed Little League teams. Imagine. We never had anything like that in Brooklyn."

I doubted they had anything like that where Jack grew up either, but why confuse the issue?

"That same exact play happened in the '86 World Series!" Ernie enthused. "The ball rolled right through Bill Buckner's legs, and the Mets ended up stealing the series from the Red Sox in seven. I bet that Eck kid was related to Buckner." He puffed out his chest like a prideful pigeon. "I played a little ball before I got drafted. Batted lefty. Used to give the pitchers fits. What'd you bat?" he asked Jackie. "Righty or lefty?"

Jackie smiled with equal pride. "I was a switch-hitter actually. I could go either way."

A definite precursor of things to come.

"All right!" Gladys sobbed in an agonized voice. "I can't stand this any longer! The secrets. The guilt. I'll tell you! But you have to promise that what I'm about to reveal will go no further than this table. Do all of you give your word of honor not to repeat anything I'm about to tell you?"

We all leaned back in our chairs, stunned by Gladys's sudden turnaround. I guess this proved something I'd suspected for a long time: Some women would do anything to avoid a lengthy discussion about baseball. We nodded in agreement and hunkered low over the table to catch Gladys's every word.

"Ira's right," she said in a confidential tone. "I never should have dug into my genealogy. I discovered I'm related to the most contemptible, the most vicious, the most brutal person ever to walk the face of the earth."

"Oh, my Lord," said Jackie. "You're related to Joan Rivers?"

"Worse than that," said Gladys. "I'm related to . . . Oliver Cromwell!"

Breath hissed through Jackie's nostrils like air through a leaky valve. "That's the son of a bitch who destroyed all the watchtowers and abbeys and churches with his son of a whore bastard troops . . . *bnnrk ig athwart.*"

Ethel tapped my arm. "What's 'bnnrk ig athwart'?"

"I had no idea the man was so ruthless," Gladys continued, "or that his name was so cursed over here. I thought he might have captured a couple of villages and treated the people according to the rules of the Geneva Convention, but that wasn't his style. He leveled everything! Did you see all those ruins today? He left nothing standing! He was a monster. A monster! And I'm related to him! Honestly, I wish I were dead."

"You better not tell our driver about this or you might get your wish," warned Ernie. "You heard him on the bus today. He's got a real grudge against Cromwell. I wouldn't wanna be in your shoes if he finds out you're related to the guy."

The backs of my knees went weak. Oh, this was nice. I'm surprised the castle's brochure didn't read, "Welcome to Ballybantry, an equal-opportunity hotel, where you're as apt to be knocked off by a ghost with webbed feet as by a bus driver with a grudge."

A sick feeling roiled in the pit of my stomach. I scratched a sudden itch at the back of my neck. I pushed my plate of half-nibbled food away from me. There was only one way to deal with a crisis of this magnitude. "Dessert, anyone?"

CHAPTER 9

The hotel had arranged for our tour group to be entertained by a troupe of Irish fiddlers and dancers in the dining room after supper, so while the furniture was being rearranged to provide some open space, I excused myself to check at the front desk to see if Etienne had returned.

"He picked up his key about ten minutes ago," Liam informed me.

Thirty seconds later, I was standing in front of his door at the end of the hall.

"Missed you at dinner," I said when he answered my knock. I did a visual scroll down the length of his legs. "Nice pants."

He closed the door behind me and drew me into his arms, nuzzling my neck. "I thought you preferred me in a towel."

"I'd prefer you in nothing at all," I said, breathless and light-headed from being cocooned against him.

"That can be arranged."

"When?"

"After I make one phone call."

"How long will that take?"

"Far too long for what I have in mind for you this evening." He lowered his hand to stroke my leg, found the slit in my dress, then glided his palm upward over my bare thigh to ride the curve of my hip. "Nice dress." His lips lingered at my ear. His tongue made slow, teasing explorations of my lobe, arousing both a surge of desire and an irrational fear that my earring was about to become snack food. I never should have worn studs. Hoops would have been a better choice. They're harder to swallow.

"I missed you today," he rasped against my earlobe. "I had to hit three different towns before I found anything that resembled a men's clothing store. I'm not sure how the natives tolerate having such limited access to goods and services."

"L.L. Bean." I stroked the back of his arm, holding him close. "They mail anywhere in the world, except maybe to some of the lesser known archipelagos in the South Pacific."

Our bodies were fused together so perfectly that I could feel the rapid beat of his heart, the lean sinew of his body, the hard steel of his gun. Gun? The fact that he was packing heat inflamed me more, not to mention its opening up great opportunities for fantasy role-playing.

"I imagine your day was more exciting than mine," he said as his mouth grazed the outer edge of my ear, causing my heart to pound, my knees to sag, my instep to tingle.

"It was pretty average," I said in a breathless whisper.

"How average?"

I moistened my lips and rushed through the litany. "I got locked in the bus. Ashley had to be rushed to the hospital. Bernice thought the phone was going to explode. Ethel Minch has webbed feet. And Nana found another dead body in her room."

He stiffened. His breath rattled in his throat. His voice grew strained. "Emily, darling?"

"Yes?"

"Are you suggesting that your grandmother's finding a dead body in her hotel room is an average part of the day?"

"It seems to be an average part of *my* day."

He held me away from him and searched my face, his eyes losing their fire to become darkly serious. "Who died?"

"The custodian. Archie. Nana found his body crumpled in the closet of her new room. There was no sign of foul play and no visible wounds, but he had a really terrified look on his face. His death looks just like Rita's, except I didn't see any evidence of bloody footprints anywhere around him."

"Does anyone know why he was in the closet, other than the most obvious reason?"

There was a reason that was obvious? I thought about Nana's theory. Had she been on to something? "The most obvious reason wouldn't be that he was gay, would it?"

He regarded me oddly. "The most obvious reason would be that he was hiding from someone. Or some-*thing*."

"That's what Tilly said!"

He massaged the back of his head, looking distracted. "I wondered why the police cars were in the parking lot just now. I suspected they were here to follow up on Rita's death, not to investigate a new case. Though I'm not sure how much investigating these village departments actually do. I paid a visit to the local Garda Station today and thought I'd stepped back into the last century. They're understaffed, poorly equipped, and totally unreceptive to the idea of outside police help. The only reason I found out any information from them was that I happened to be standing there when the call came in from the lab."

"Information about Rita?"

"Results from the blood samples they took from the footprints on the carpet. The blood wasn't human. It was animal."

The news calmed my nerves a small degree. I was relieved the blood wasn't human, but I knew not everyone would share my relief. If the animal rights people ever got wind of the findings, they would *not* be happy campers. Better to face a malevolent spirit than a pissed-off PETA member. "So does this mean the ghost isn't some centuries-old spirit who's still dripping fresh blood?"

"That would be my guess. My instincts tell me that our ghost, if there is a ghost, is very human. All we have to do now is determine who the person is and why they've decided to target Ballybantry Castle."

"I bet you anything it has something to do with ill will between the Irish who were kicked off their land and the Englishman who built this castle."

He looked at me askance. "Who did you say has webbed feet?"

"Ethel Minch. One of the ladies on the tour from New York. She has relatives who emigrated from Ireland during one of the potato famines, but she claims she's not interested in her family history, so she doesn't know anything about them. I think she's trying to cover up the fact that one of her relatives might be involved with the hauntings. She has webbed toes! I saw them this morning. And she admits her foot problem is genetic and that lots of people on her mother's side of the family have it. Her maiden name is O'Quigley, and I'll bet that's a very popular name around here."

His eyes flickered alertly, as if they were reacting to

some internal flash going off in his head. "You could be right." He walked to the desk and jotted a note on the castle's stationery. " 'O'Quigley,' you said. I'll have someone look into it." He flipped open the phone book, found a page, and ran his finger down its length. "Right again. If she needs accomplices, there's at least two score to choose from in the area."

I came up behind him and threaded my arm through his. "The front desk clerk told me that the castle has had a dozen owners since it was first built, none whose name he knows. But the current owners are a group of American investors and a family by the name of McCrilly. He also told me that Rita's death was being attributed to natural causes."

"How would he be privy to information about Rita?"

"His father is the local mortician."

"So the police are going to ignore the bloody footprints altogether so the coroner can sign off on the cause of death."

"Not only ignore. The custodian has already cleaned the carpet."

He shook his head in disgust. "At least they took pictures of the prints. I conducted my own investigation of the castle this morning but got no farther than a padlocked door leading to what I suspect is the dungeon."

"You didn't try to open it?"

"I asked the front desk clerk to open it."

"Liam?"

"It was a woman. Big-boned. Brown hair. Unusual name. Nessa, I think it was. She said she didn't have a key. I asked her what was down there. She said she didn't know because she'd never set foot through that door. I asked her why not. She said because there's no electricity below ground level, she's heard it's full of spiders, she doesn't like spiders, and she basically has no curiosity about dungeons."

I was starting to see a pattern with this lack-of-curiosity thing. I guess this explained why the quest to discover the New World had been turned over to an Italian.

"Something peculiar is going on in this place," he allowed, "and I'll wager the answer to the whole affair is in the dungeon. I need the key to that padlock. The custodian probably has one." He looked across his shoulder to the door. "What room did you say his body is in?"

Uh-oh. His police inspector genes had kicked in bigtime, which didn't bode well for a romantic end to the evening. I needed to divert him, and fast. "Speaking of affairs." I waltzed two fingers up his arm. "Do you suppose you could make your phone call so we could get started on ours? I have the room to myself, the whirlpool accommodates two, and there's a decanter of bubble bath just waiting to be poured."

That got his attention. "Bubble bath? I've never taken a bubble bath."

"Not even with your first wife?"

"Especially not with my first wife. Our apartment didn't have a tub. It only had a shower."

"Trust me," I whispered in a sultry voice close to his ear. "You're in for a treat."

He smiled with anticipation. Cupping his palm around the back of my head, he covered my mouth in a long sizzling kiss before he deliberately set me away from himself. "I'll make my phone call. You fill the tub."

"And don't forget. There's something you want to ask me."

He trailed a knuckle down my cheek and regarded me with his electric blue eyes. "I'm not likely to forget."

Okay, I wasn't going to win any awards for subtlety, but if we *did* decide to plan a life together, we had some serious issues to discuss, like living arrangements, jobs, children. Would he want me to move to Switzerland with him? Living in Switzerland might be romantic. Switzerland had Alps, lakes, castles, chocolate. But Iowa had something Switzerland couldn't offer—Blimpie's Grilled Chicken Sandwich. Could I survive being separated from my family *and* edible meat products at the same time? I didn't know. I mean, it could prove to be unbearable. We had *so* much to sort out. *Unh.*

I headed for the door, turning back to face him when my hand touched the knob. "Can I ask a favor?"

He opened his arms in a palms-up gesture. "Anything, darling."

"When you come down to the room, will you bring your gun?"

"I'm not carrying a gun."

"You're not?" My voice sank with disappointment. So much for fantasy role-playing. "Then what's that thing in your front pocket that feels like a gun?"

He slid his hand into his right pocket and withdrew the item in question. "My wallet. Sorry to disappoint you."

I smiled brightly as I watched him slip the wallet back into his pocket. "I'm not disappointed." What I'd felt had been in the *other* pocket. Hoochimama!

I hurried back down the corridor, pausing outside the room where Nana had found Archie. The sound of fiddles blared in the hall. The dancers' rhythmic foot-stomping vibrated the floor. I could hear muffled conversation on the other side of the door, but the music drowned out the words. If Archie was still in there, I hope they removed his body before everyone returned from the dining room. One death was bad enough. The guests might get really creeped out and want to go home if they learned there were two.

I unlocked my door, flipped on the overhead light, and set to work. I rushed into the bathroom and turned on the water full force in the whirlpool. I ran back into the bedroom and stopped short when I noticed that one of the four boudoir chairs in the sitting area was missing. Huh. Had someone moved it to another room? Shrugging off the disappearance, I hurried toward the bed, only to stop short again.

The chair wasn't missing. It was angled close to the window, as if someone had wanted a comfortable chair in which to sit while they kept vigil over the castle grounds. Choosing to ignore what Tilly had revealed about the ghost's penchant for furniture rearranging, I told myself that maybe the maid had moved it earlier and I'd been in too much of a rush to notice. Furniture got moved around all the time in hotels. This meant nothing. Absolutely nothing.

I dragged the chair back to the hearth area, then threw myself back into my preparations. I folded down the bedcovers, plumped the pillows, and spritzed the whole place with the Strawberry Shortcake room freshener Nana had given me. I inhaled deeply. Nice. It smelled like real strawberries. I thought about the odor on our bus. *Hmm.* Locating my shoulder bag, I stuck the canister in one of the outer compartments for future use.

Darkness had gathered beyond the windows. I drew the drapes halfway to create a more cozy atmosphere, switched on the bedside lamps, turned off the overhead, then returned to the bathroom. I set out two fluffy bath towels and a bottle of scented body oil on the vanity. I arranged a cluster of votive candles on the ledge of the tub and unstoppered a container of lavender bubble bath that sat perched on the same ledge beside a dish of seashell soaps and bath salts. When the tub was full, I set the single power/timer switch for thirty minutes and stood for a moment watching the circular jets shoot streams of air into the water, stirring up the surface like monsoon winds.

HRRRRRMMMM! Water bubbled. The jets roared, reverberating off the ceiling and tiles. I frowned. The whirlpool needed a muffler. If Etienne decided to whisper sweet nothings into my ear, I hoped I could hear him. HRRRRRMMMM!

As I reached for the little plastic scoop in the bubble bath container, I noticed the handwritten label attached to the jar:

> We kindly ask that you use bath salts when the whirlpool is in operation. For long, quiet soaks without the whirlpool, we recommend liberal use of our bubble bath.

Hmm. Okay. This wasn't so bad. We could frolic in the whirlpool tonight and indulge ourselves in a hot bubble bath tomorrow night. Something to look forward to.

Returning my attention to the jar beside the bubble bath, I dumped a small scoop of bath salts into the tub, then looked over my handiwork. Okay, the bathroom was ready except for lighting the candles. Now I had to get *me* ready. I closed the bathroom door, muting the sound of the whirlpool to a softer *hrrrrrmmmm.*

I opened my suitcase, stashing clothes into drawers and hanging them up as I considered what to wear. Since I'd packed for warmth, I was short on sexy sleepwear, so I figured I needed to improvise. I stripped down to my undies and covered up with a teal satin wrap that hung to mid-thigh and tied at the waist. Now the question was, should I unpin my hair from its bun, or should I let Etienne have the pleasure of doing it while we were in the tub?

Knock knock knock.

I peered at the door. Wow. That was quick. Lucky me to fall in love with a man who boasted the competence of a German, the grace of a Frenchman, and the testosterone of an Italian. Jittery with excitement, I crossed the room and opened the door.

"Men can be such pigs!" cried Jackie as she burst into the room. "I sneak out of the entertainment to check on Tom, and guess what I find him doing?"

My first choice would have been "boinking the maid," but since one maid was dead and the other had probably punched out for the day, I went with choice number two. "Trying on your underwear?"

"No! He was talking on his cell phone. Long distance. To his high school girlfriend!"

"I thought he had a migraine."

"He gave himself one of those expensive injections and it went away."

I peeked into the hall. No Etienne. Good thing. I closed the door on the music and foot-pounding and eyed the pocketbook Jackie had tossed onto the bed. Actually, it was a little bigger than a pocketbook. It looked more like— Uh-oh. "What's that?" I said, nodding toward the bag.

"My overnight bag. I'm spending the night."

"WHAT?"

"I can't stay with Tom! He's cheating on me! Where else am I going to go?"

"Well, you can't stay here! I'm about to have sex!"

Jackie flung herself into one of the boudoir chairs by the fireplace and made a sweeping gesture with her hand. "Have at it. It won't be anything I haven't seen before."

"I am not about to have sex in front of you!"

"There was a time when all you could *think* of was having sex in front of me." She flopped her hand back and forth at the wrist as she elucidated. "In front of me, behind me, on top of me, beneath me." She cocked her head toward the bathroom. "What's that noise? It sounds like an outboard motor."

"It's the whirlpool. I've planned the perfect evening, and much as I adore you, Jack, YOU'RE NOT PART OF IT!"

She regarded me despairingly. "You're kicking me out? After all we've meant to each other?"

"Yes! You need to go back into that room and talk to Tom. You'll probably discover the call was really innocuous, like the woman is his best friend or something."

"*I'm* supposed to be his best friend!" She folded her arms across her chest and set her mouth stubbornly. "I have nothing to say to Tom. The two-timer. You should have heard the conversation he was having. It was disgusting!" She paused. "At least . . . I'm pretty sure it was disgusting. I couldn't hear all the words with that music blaring in the hall."

I scratched a sudden itch at the back of my neck. "Talking on the phone to an old girlfriend is not what I'd call cheating."

"It is when you're on your honeymoon."

"Well, you're not exactly filling up his dance card!"

She gasped. Her eyes narrowed with reproach. "Are you implying that by postponing our wedding night, I'm driving him into the arms of other women?"

"Their arms, no. Their ears? Maybe."

"I can't believe you said that! He's cheating and you're blaming *me*? You know who you sound like? You sound like a guy!"

I startled at the accusation. Oh, my God. She was right. The threat of sexual deprivation was causing a major malfunction in my hormonal levels. I did sound like a guy. Next thing out of my mouth would probably be "He started it!"

I tried to make amends. "Look, Jack, some husbands have short attention spans, so if a wife doesn't keep them occupied, they'll find other ways to entertain themselves. Ask Nana. They've probably done studies!"

She slumped lower in her chair, her expression despairing. "Did we have problems like this when we were married?"

"Nah. You were easy to entertain. If you ever got bored, I'd take you shopping."

"Tom doesn't like to shop. Come to think of it, he doesn't enjoy any of the things I like. Chick flicks. Pedicures. ESPN SportsCenter."

"Why did you marry him?"

"Because he's gorgeous! And he drives this great little red Porsche. I mean, those are the important things, right?"

"Right. IF YOU'RE IN HIGH SCHOOL! Geez, Jack, what happens when he gets old and wrinkled?"

"He could go on that diet the Kuppelmans are on. They're not wrinkled. But I wonder if all those fruits and vegetables would give him gas."

"What if he loses his hair?"

"Rogaine, hair plugs, hair transplants. Scientists have made great strides with male-pattern baldness."

"What if his Porsche rusts out?"

She grew deathly still. "That could be a problem. You wouldn't believe how much salt they use on the roads in Binghamton during the winter. I wonder how Tom would feel about Florida?" She nibbled the nail of her pinky with worry. "Do you think I made a mistake by marrying him?"

You bet I thought she made a mistake, but I couldn't exactly tell her that. "I think you need to give it a chance," I counseled. "It's only been three days. Give yourself some time to work the kinks out."

She hung her head and sighed with resignation. "Yeah,

yeah. I suppose you're right . . . but I'm still not going back in there tonight!" She popped out of her chair, snatched her overnight bag off the bed, and headed toward the door. "If you won't let me stay with you, I'll have to find someplace else to go. Mrs. S. is a sport. I bet she'd put me up."

"No!" I chased after her. "Five minutes with Nana and you'd blab everything; then she'd be at my door wanting to know why my former husband has breasts. There aren't enough days on this vacation for me to explain the process to her, and I'm not going to start tonight because, as I told you . . . I HAVE PLANS!"

She folded her arms across her chest and gave me a dour look. "I would not blab everything."

"You would so. You almost gave it away at dinner!"

"A slip of the tongue. I got lost in the moment. So what's it going to be? Your room or your grandmother's? Frankly, I think Mrs. S. and her roommate would love to have me. Tilly asked me all kinds of inquiring questions on the way to the rope bridge today. We had what you would call a wonderful bonding event. In all my years as a man, I never experienced anything like it. It's so emotionally fulfilling." She gave her nails a quick buff on the sleeve of her sweater, then regarded them admiringly. "I think Tilly is rather taken with me." She looked up suddenly. "She's not gay, is she?"

"No, she's not gay. She's an anthropologist."

Jackie's face froze. "An anthropologist? Oh, Jeez. She probably noticed how big my feet and hands are in comparison to the rest of me. And you know what that means? It means she was only being nice to me so she could study me like a bug under a microscope!" She sucked in her breath. "She wasn't trying to bond with me at all! She was being dishonest, and . . . and conniving. I hate that about women! A guy would never sink that low. The only time a guy is going to bond with you is when he wants to get you into bed, and that's not really dishonest. It's just shallow." She seized my arm. "Are you going to send me in there to be scrutinized by that woman? What if I can't handle it? What if I crack under the pressure? You *have* to let me stay here, Emily. If you don't, I refuse to be held responsible for what might happen."

She was right, of course. Sending her off to spend the night with Nana and Tilly would be like sending her into a minefield. If I was serious about wanting to keep our former relationship under wraps, there was only one safe place for her to sleep.

Disappointment weighted my limbs. Despair flooded through me. *Nuts!* Sometimes I hated my life. "All right," I said glumly, disbelieving that I was agreeing to this. "You can stay here. But only for one night! Tomorrow night you're back with Tom."

She wrapped her arms around me and lifted me off the floor, covering my face with a flurry of kisses. "Oh, thank you! We can pretend it's a sleepover! This is going to be so much fun. I've never been involved in a sleepover before, except in college at the frat house, and that was more like a drunken orgy, so it probably doesn't count." She set me back on my feet and made a beeline for the bathroom. "I'll just go slip into my pj's. It's always been a mystery to me what girls *do* at a pajama party, but I'm really excited to find out." She paused at the bathroom door. "You won't kick me out if I don't have standard-issue pajamas, will you? See you in a sec."

I stared at the door, numbed. How had this happened? My perfect evening. Gone. Kaput. I walked to the telephone in a daze, convinced that in her own inimitable way my mother had something to do with this. I punched up Etienne's room.

"Hi," I said when he answered. "I don't know how to tell you this, but something's come up."

"Something has been up since the moment I kissed you," he confessed in his beautiful French/German/Italian accent. "I'm anxious to ease the strain."

Unh! Have I mentioned before that I hate my life? "What I'm trying to say is"—I choked out the words—"we have to postpone until tomorrow night."

Silence, punctuated by intermittent bouts of heavy breathing.

"Etienne?"

"The missile is ready to fire."

"Can you freeze the countdown?"

"It can be severely damaging to a missile when the launch sequence is interrupted."

Especially when the missile was the size of Rhode Island. "I'm so sorry. I can't *tell* you how sorry. But I have to spend the night with one of the female guests who's having a problem with her husband. I tried to get out of it, but I can't. I'm stuck."

A pause. "Is there physical violence involved, Emily? Do you need my assistance?"

"No, no. It's just a misunderstanding."

Another pause. "What about my room? Can the woman stay here tonight?"

That's just what I needed. An opportunity for Etienne and Jackie to meet each other. "Um . . . that won't work. She's pretty distraught. I'll probably be up half the night listening to her vent."

More silence, followed by, "I suppose that's part of your job. One of the many hazards of being employed. I understand it, darling, but I don't like it. Don't let me keep you then. Have a good evening, and I'll see you tomorrow." CLICK.

I held the receiver at arm's length and studied it for a long moment before hanging up and throwing myself onto the bed to replay the conversation in my head. The polite words. The supreme understanding. The solicitous tone. Boy, was he miffed! And here I thought the Swiss were too unemotional to display fits of temper. Hah! I guess it was best to find this out before the engagement ... if there was an engagement ... if Jack Potter hadn't completely ruined my chances of marital bliss for the second time in as many centuries.

I stared mindlessly at the canopy above me, unable to think, unable to move, until I heard a tentative knock at the door. I was up like a shot. Maybe it was Etienne. Maybe he was here to apologize for losing his temper. I threw open the door.

"There was a note in my mailbox sayin' y'all had my tour bag in here."

Ashley. *Nuts.* I eyed the crutches under her arms and the plaster cast that constricted her right leg to mid-calf. "Wow. You really did a number on yourself. I guess the cast means you broke something."

"My, my, aren't you the clever one. I broke my medial malleolus." She gave me a smug look. "You probably don't know what that is."

"A bone." I lowered my gaze to her cast, catching a glimpse of the bare toes that were bundled inside the thick casing of white plaster. "In your foot."

Her face fell. "How did you know that?"

Duh? "Lucky guess."

She shifted her weight on her crutches, looking as if she wished she hadn't stopped by.

"You probably want to get back to your room," I encouraged. "I'll get your bag."

"I suppose the whole day fell apart after my untimely

departure today," she said as I charged across the room. "That was so unkind of me to land in the hospital and dump all my responsibilities in your lap. How did y'all ever manage?"

"We did okay. We toured the distillery, ate lunch, bought souvenirs, and arrived back here fifteen minutes ahead of schedule."

Her eyes narrowed to slits. "Really?" She sounded disappointed. "You didn't run into any problems?"

I retrieved her bag and headed back to the door. "None."

"Well." She smiled stiffly. "Isn't that nice."

"We've run into a few problems at the castle though. Wailing in the halls at night. Cold spots in the rooms. Bloody footprints on the floor. And lest I forget, two people have died!"

She looked taken aback. "Tour members?"

"Castle staff! A maid and a custodian. And they looked like they'd been frightened to death! This is all your fault!"

"*My* fault? Why is it my fault?"

"Because you booked us into this place knowing full well it's haunted!"

"I thought you didn't believe in ghosts."

"I believe in them now!"

"The tour company made the decision to stay here, Emily. And they based their decision on economics, *not* on some old wives' tale about the castle being haunted. Look at this place! It's a five-star hotel. Where else can y'all find accommodations like this for the money we're paying? In another hotel at our rate you'd be looking at single beds, bare walls, and a communal bathroom down the hall. You think the guests would settle for that?"

"I think they'd settle for staying in a place where people aren't turning up dead every day!"

"Ready or not," yelled Jackie over the roar of the whirlpool, "here I come."

I wheeled around toward the bathroom to see a leg kick out from behind the door in the style of a Vegas showgirl. In the next instant the door opened wide to reveal Jackie striking a sexy pose in sheer black babydolls with pink ribbon trim and a matching G-string panty. "Boop-oop-a-doop!" She hoisted up her leg, flung out her arm, and snapped back her head. "Okay. What's next?"

Oh, this was nice. Alone in the bathroom for five minutes and she turns into Betty Boop.

Ashley hobbled up beside me for a better look. She stared at Jackie. She stared at me. A knowing smile curled her lips. "Looks like y'all have plans for the evening. I better go. I wouldn't want to keep you girls from anything."

Jackie looked our way. "Oops! I didn't realize we had company."

"You don't. I was just leaving." Ashley nodded toward the tour bag in my hand. "Loop that around my neck, would you?"

"I can carry it down to your room for you."

"No!"

Uh-oh. I was getting a bad feeling about this. "Jackie's being here isn't what you think," I explained as I maneuvered the handles over her head. "We're having a"—I forced the words out—"a pajama party."

"Is that what y'all call it up North?"

"Too bad about your injury!" Jackie bellowed over the noise echoing behind her. She thrust her foot out and gave it a little wiggle. "That's one of the advantages of having enormous feet. You don't fall on your face and make a fool of yourself so often!"

Wow. I had to hand it to Jack. He was really getting the hang of this female thing.

Ashley fixed Jackie with a withering look. To me she said, "Does her husband know about y'all?" Then with her canvas tote hanging like a feed bag around her neck, she hobbled briskly out the door.

"Cretin," Jackie mouthed after her. "And did you notice? She didn't even thank me for hauling her butt all the way back from those stairs today. The ingrate."

I closed the door to the hall, an uncomfortable feeling churning in my stomach. I'd explained well enough, hadn't I? Ashley didn't think Jackie and I were . . . that the two of us were about to—

"If the whirlpool's available, do you mind if I hop in?" Jackie asked. "Seems a shame to let it all go to waste."

I waved her on with a listless gesture. "Go ahead. Someone might as well enjoy it."

"Oh, good. You want to join me?"

"NO!"

"What? Girls don't do that at pajama parties?"

"No! They don't. They . . . they have scavenger hunts. They make crank phone calls. They do inventive things with toothpaste and feathers."

"Sounds boring."

"They paint each others' toenails."

"Ooh. That's a little better. Maybe we can do that when I come out." She gave me a little finger wave and disappeared, thankfully, into the bathroom. I stumbled across the floor, collapsed into a chair, and practiced some mindless staring again.

Okay, I told myself, things weren't *that* bad. My love life was on permanent hold and I had to spend the evening entertaining Gypsy Rose Lee, but at least I was coping. I mean, despite the stress, I didn't have hives galloping all over my body.

I pondered that for a millisecond before racing to the

dresser to check out my face. I squinted into the mirror. Uh-oh. Little red welts were creeping up my throat. And there was a huge one on my jaw. Okay. Things were really bad.

The lights suddenly dimmed, then flickered, then went out completely, pitching the room into total darkness.

And now they were worse.

CHAPTER 10

"If this is a pajama party prank, I don't think it's funny!" yelled Jackie from the bathroom. "Turn the light on! I can't see a—"

CLINK! CRASH! *Tinkle.* PLOP! Glug glug.

"Jack? Are you all right?"

Silence.

Uh-oh. "Hang on! I'm coming!" I felt my way through the darkness like a blind person, arms waving like antennae, toes testing the floor before each step. I located the bathroom door and curled my hand around the knob, giving it a turn. It wouldn't budge. I listened intently for a moment. The silence was eerie. I banged on the door. "Jack? Are you okay? Can you hear me?"

"Loud and clear, now that you've killed the whirlpool. Are you going to turn on the light or not?"

"I can't. Must be a power outage. Everything is dark out here too. Why can't I get the door open?"

"Because it's locked."

I rested my forehead against the door and waited a beat.

"Here's a thought. Why don't you unlock the door and come out of there?"

"Because I'm in my bare feet, there's glass all over the floor, and I can't see my hand in front of me! You have any other bright suggestions?"

"Are you close to any towels?"

"Just a minute." A pause. Shuffling. SPLAT! *Plink.* CRASH! "Damn. Okay. I found a couple of towels."

"Keep them folded, set them on the floor, then step onto them and glide your way to the door. Pretend you're ice-skating." I hope she'd found bath towels. Given the size of her feet, hand towels would never cut it.

"You're sure it's all right to use these towels on the floor? If I dirty them, what'll I use to dry off when I finally get to use the whirlpool?"

Back when she'd been a guy, she used to grab our white Royal Velvet towels with the ribbon-and-lace embroidery to dry off the car. Megadoses of estrogen and progesterone had worked wonders with her brain matter. "We can request more towels at the front desk. Just unlock the door and get out of there."

"Okay." After a half-minute's wait that was accompanied by muffled epithets and sounds of broken glass scraping the floor tiles, I heard the lock click and the knob rattle. The door creaked open. "Emily?" she asked tentatively.

"Right here." I inched my hand into the blackness, connected with her arm, and yanked her into the bedroom.

"Wow." Her voice was a whisper. "It's really dark in here. Isn't this fun? How long do you think the power outage will last?"

"Don't know. Let's see if I can find out." This was eerie. Even the outdoor floodlights were out. I inched my way to the sitting area, located my shoulder bag on the chair where I'd left it, and fingered every object inside until I found my flashlight. I turned on the beam, walked to the bedside phone, and hit the button on the phone pad for the front desk. It rang, and rang, and rang. "No one's answering."

"Listen. The music's stopped. I bet they had to shut down the entertainment. Those cloggers could trample each other to death in the dark. That's probably where the desk clerk is. In the dining room, directing traffic with a big flashlight."

I hung up. "Maybe you're right." I flashed the light on her. "EH!" Not only was she right, she was buck naked. "Where are your clothes?"

"In the bathroom. What's the problem? You used to see me naked all the time."

"Your hardware was different back then. I'm not used to the new stuff yet."

"You better cough up a robe for me then, because I'm not going back into that bathroom until the lights come back on."

"You outweigh me by ninety pounds, Jack! I own nothing that'll fit you."

"I love that little teal wrap you're wearing. That might fit. It's loose enough."

I sighed with defeat. What the heck. My evening was ruined anyway. I shrugged out of my wrap and set it on the bed for her. "Here it is. Knock yourself out." I pulled a pair of Joe Boxer pajama bottoms and a cotton top out of the dresser drawer, and yanked them on. "How's it fit?" I asked as I aimed the narrow beam back at her.

"You tell me." She twirled in place like a music-box dancer. It was too short, too tight, and entirely the wrong color, but at least she wasn't naked anymore.

"Perfect," I said, cursing under my breath when my little Maglite suddenly dimmed. I slapped it against my palm and rotated the head, narrowing and widening the beam.

"Looks like your batteries are getting low. Do you have matches here someplace?"

"By the ashtray on the desk." I heard commotion in the hall as I panned the light left and right over the fireplace. Excited voices. High-pitched laughter.

"I told you they must have ended the entertainment," said Jackie from the direction of the desk. "Party's over. Everyone's headed back to their rooms."

My beam was holding steady, but as I focused on the gilt-framed painting of the aristocratic lord with his horse, hounds, and frolicking children, I slatted my eyes in astonishment, noticing something I hadn't seen before. "*Uff da,*" I said in an undertone. I hurried closer for a better look and squinted up at the painting, but it was too high on the wall for a close-up inspection. "Jack, come over here. And bring a straightback chair. You need to drag this painting off the wall for me."

A hesitation, then, "Oh, I get it. This is part of the pajama party festivities. You take a painting off the wall and hang it in another place and see if anyone notices." She lumbered through the darkness with the requested chair and set it down on the outer hearth. "Girls really get off on some pretty stupid stuff. I think getting bombed at the frat house sounds like a lot more fun."

She stepped onto the chair and braced a hand on either side of the painting, hefting it slightly. "Whoa. This baby's heavy." She wiggled it up, down, left and right. "It's hung up on something." She wrenched it back and forth several times before she was finally able to free it from its wall hooks and hand it down to me. She was right about the painting being heavy. It had to weigh a good fifty pounds. I leaned it against the stonework and steadied the beam of my Maglite on the youthful figures in the foreground.

"Okay. What do you notice that's different about this

painting?" I asked in my best Sherlock Holmes imitation.

Jackie hopped down from the chair and gave the picture the once-over. "It's dusty."

"Besides that. Look at the three children. Do you see anything unusual about them?"

"They're not fighting with each other. That's pretty unusual for kids of that age."

"Their feet, Jack. What's odd about their feet?"

She hunkered down, studying the composition intently. "Oh, wow. Their toes look like they're all stuck together. I've heard of that condition. There's a name for it, but I can't remember what it is."

"What would you say if I told you Ethel Minch has the same condition?"

"I'd say she probably saved a lot of money not having to buy beach thongs every year. Which reminds me. Do you happen to know what room she's in? I bet ole Ernie could tell me where I could order classy shoes in extra-large sizes. Most catalogs only advertise up to size eleven."

She wasn't getting the point. "Don't you think it's a little coincidental that Ethel Minch has the same foot condition as the family in the portrait?"

She hoisted herself to her feet and pursed her lips in thought. "No."

"But *think* about it! You heard the conversation at dinner. Ethel's maternal side of the family has roots in Ireland. The condition is hereditary. The people in this portrait could very well be part of the O'Quigley clan."

Jackie shrugged. "So what if they are?"

"That would prove Ethel and her family have some connection to the castle."

"So?"

"So that might lead us to the person who left the bloody footprints."

Jackie grew very still. "The what?"

"The bloody footprints they found under the maid's body. The imprint showed it was someone with webbed feet. Probably not Ethel, but it could be someone related to her."

"A maid died? When did a maid die?"

"Yesterday. In Nana's room. The custodian died today in Nana's closet, but they didn't find any footprints under his body. He still looked like he'd been frightened to death though."

Her voice rose two octaves. "Excuse me?"

"Did I forget to mention that the castle might be haunted?"

"I'LL SAY YOU FORGOT TO MENTION IT! Bloody footprints? Dead bodies?" She locked her hand around my arm and steered me to the nearest chair. "Okay, Emily. Talk."

For fifteen minutes, sitting in the pitch black, I told her everything I knew about the star-crossed lovers, the demise of the maid and the custodian, the inexplicable noises and cold spots in the castle, and what I perceived to be Ethel Minch's connection to it all. When I finished, I fired up my flashlight again to find Jackie's eyes looking pinched and frightened, her face drawn and sallow. Either I'd really creeped her out, or this was the way she always looked when the makeup came off.

"So that moaning I heard last night wasn't some old geezer with a six-pack of Viagra? It was a ghost?"

It was my turn to shrug. "Either a ghost, or someone trying to convince us it was a ghost." I shined my flashlight at the portrait again and regarded it through the dimness, bothered by something I couldn't quite put my finger on. Jackie followed my gaze.

"If those are the O'Quigleys, they certainly looked prosperous enough four hundred years ago," she observed.

"How can you tell the portrait was painted that long ago?"

"Look at the guy on the horse. I wore a ruff, doublet, and cloak-bag breeches just like that when I had a part in *A New Way to Pay Old Bills.* The long hair parted in the middle. The small, neat beard. It's all seventeenth century. You have to wonder what happened to change the family fortunes."

Her words jarred me. Of course! That's what had been bothering me. I smacked the heel of my palm against my forehead. "Duh! What was I thinking? This family can't be the O'Quigleys. The Irish were impoverished during the sixteen hundreds. They couldn't own a horse, much less land or a castle."

Jackie leaned back in her chair. "So if Ethel Minch is related to these people, but they're not the O'Quigleys"— she threw me a long questioning look—"who are they?"

There could be only one answer to that question, and the shock of it had me counting sheep at three o'clock that morning.

I'd finally gotten through to the front desk clerk, who informed me that power outages happened all the time at Ballybantry and electricity might not be restored until morning. So having nothing better to do in the dark, we'd stayed up past midnight, reminiscing about our days in New York and scaring each other with ghost stories. Jackie had rehung the portrait over the mantel, but it would need tweaking in the morning because it was hanging at a disturbing slant.

"It looks like it's about to fall," I said, tilting my head in the same direction.

"Trust me. It'll be fine until morning."

I'd slipped into some walking shoes and ventured into

the bathroom to retrieve Jackie's clothes and my toiletry bag with my anti-itch cream. Using the dull beam of my Maglite for illumination, I picked some larger chunks of glass off the floor and disposed of them, but I could still hear the crunch of shards and slivers and other substances under my feet, so to be safe, we closed the bathroom door and set a chair in front of it to remind ourselves not to go into the bathroom without shoes on our feet. Having experienced numerous power outages in our collective lifetimes, we also remembered to turn off the switches of the bedside lights that had been on when the power went out so we wouldn't be blinded by them if the power came back on in the middle of the night. We'd thought of everything to ensure ourselves a peaceful night's rest.

So how come I couldn't sleep?

I turned over on my side and punched my pillow, knowing exactly what was keeping me awake. The portrait.

If the people in the painting weren't seventeenth-century Irish, they had to be seventeenth-century British. And if they were British, the reason their picture was hanging in Ballybantry Castle was undoubtedly because they had once lived in the castle. If my hunch was right, the family in the portrait was the same one that had emigrated from England to Ireland and commissioned the castle to be built. The original owners of Ballybantry. And if that were the case, one of the fair-haired children in the picture had been disowned and suffered a grisly death in the dungeon, and after four hundred years, might still be walking the halls of the castle.

And Ethel Minch was related to her.

She wasn't Irish at all. She was English. But why had she lied? Was she playing a role in the hauntings? And if she was, what was in it for her?

I flopped over onto my other side and hit the illumination bar on my travel alarm: 3:05. I groaned, then, feeling a sudden chill, pulled the bedclothes up to my nose. I knew the furnace was off for the season, but even given that, it seemed inordinately cold in here.

Hrrrrrmmmm.

I lifted my head off the pillow, listening.

Hrrrrrmmmm.

The whirlpool. The power must have come back on again. Great. We'd turned off all the lights, but we hadn't thought to turn off the power switch on the tub.

Hrrrrrmmmm.

I buried my head under the covers and clapped my hands over my ears. I wondered how many minutes were left on the timer. I curled up into a cozy ball, waiting for the time to run out. I didn't have to worry about the noise disturbing Jack. He always slept like the dead.

"How long are you planning to listen to that damn thing before you decide to get up and turn it off?" rasped a groggy Jackie from the opposite bed.

I poked my head out of its makeshift cocoon. "What are you doing awake? You used to be able to sleep through anything."

"Yeah. That was one of the benefits of being a guy. I could sleep through a nuclear blast. Not anymore. It must be estrogen related. So are you going to kill the tub?"

"It's too cold in here to get out of bed. Besides, what's wrong with *you* killing the tub?"

"With all that glass on the floor? Get real, Emily. You're the one with the rugged shoes. Mine are open-toed."

I burrowed deeper under the covers. "I don't want to move."

"It's your room. If I wasn't here, you'd have to turn it off yourself anyway."

Not true. If Jack wasn't here, Etienne would have been,

so I'd have asked *him* to do it. And I probably wouldn't be so cold right now either.

Hrrrrrmmmm.

I grunted my disgust with the situation, then, feeling completely out of sorts, threw off my covers, jammed my feet into my shoes, and stomped across the floor in the dark.

"Don't bump into the chair in front of the door," Jackie called out helpfully.

"Yeah, yeah." I shoved the chair out of the way. I opened the door.

WOOOOOSHHHHH!

"EEEEEEE!" I screamed as a tidal wave of wet, frothing goop smacked into me full force, knocking me to the floor. HRRRRRMMMM went the whirlpool. "EEEEEEE!" I screamed again, flailing at the slop that was enveloping my body. "Help me!"

I heard Jackie's feet hit the floor and pound toward me. "What's— EHHH!" She hit the slop at full throttle, skidded out of control across the carpet, and landed in a heap beside me, whacking the slime with hands and fists. "What *is* this?" she shrieked. "Feel it. It's alive. It's breathing." THWACK. SPISH. "It's eating my foot!"

HRRRRRMMMM!

It oozed around me like quicksand. "It's some kind of secretion," I said, swatting it away. "I hope it's not intestines!"

Jackie raised herself onto hands and knees. "Whatever it is, it sure smells good. What is that? Lavender? Lavender is supposed to be very good for headaches, you know."

Lavender? I stopped swatting and started sniffing. It *was* lavender. I squinted in the direction of the bathroom. Uh-oh.

HRRRRRMMMM!

I struggled to my feet and slogged my way through the billowing goop to the bathroom door. I flipped on the light.

Bubbles were spewing out of the tub like lava out of a volcano. Frothing. Gushing. Swelling. "What did you do?" I cried over the roar of the motor to Jackie. I plunged through the knee-deep foam and batted clouds of bubbles away from the tub.

"What do you mean, what did I do?" she shouted back.

HRRRRRMMMM! I dug through the spume like a dog after a bone, located the power switch, and snapped it to the OFF position.

Silence.

I looked around the room. There were bubbles everywhere. Crawling over the vanity. Oozing out of the toilet. Slithering down the walls. I heaved a sigh before turning around to regard Jackie, who was standing calf-high in soapsuds in the doorway. "Bubble bath!" I wailed. "Lavender bubble bath! Didn't you read the label? You're not supposed to use bubble bath with the whirlpool!"

"I didn't touch the bubble bath!"

"Then how did this happen?"

"How should I know! Unless . . ." I watched her expression change from stubborn denial to conceivable guilt. "Hmm. Do you suppose I knocked the container off the ledge when the lights went out?"

"You knocked everything else off. Why not the bubble bath?"

"Hey! It was dark in there!"

"*HHHHRRRRRRRRRHHHHH . . . HHHHRRRRRRRR-HHHHH!*"

I looked at Jackie. Jackie looked at me. I stood riveted to the spot, chills needling up and down my spine. "What's that?" I whispered.

Jackie poked her head into the bathroom and studied the ceiling as if the answer to my question lay imbedded in the porcelain tile. "That's the same noise I heard last night. The orgasm heard round the world. I bet it's Gladys Kuppelman. She probably drinks pureed kelp to enhance sexual potency."

"It's a sad sound." I cocked my head, listening. "I think she's crying."

"Maybe Ira launched his torpedoes early. Premature ejaculation is no laughing matter."

"Hhhhrrrrrrrrrhhhhh . . . Hhhhrrrrrrrrrhhhhh!"

"Where's it coming from?" I puzzled. "It sounds like it's right inside the room."

Color drained from Jackie's face. She looked suspiciously left and right, then swallowed with apparent difficulty. "Oh, my God. This is what you were talking about. The legend. The hauntings. The cries are from that dead girl who's looking for her husband. Those are the sobs of the ghost, aren't they?"

"Somebody's sobbing. I think we need to find out who." Jackie stiffened. "We?"

"Hhhhrrrrrrrrrhhhhh . . . Hhhhrrrrrrrrrhhhhh!"

"If we don't find out who's crying, no one will *ever* get a good night's sleep in this place."

She wrung her hands nervously. "It's not so bad. Earplugs would probably help. Do you have some I could borrow?"

I sloshed past her through the disintegrating bubbles. "Here's the deal. We can either lie in bed and listen to this all night, or we can try to find the source." My shoes made squishy sounds on the carpet as I flipped on the overhead light.

"Why are you being so brave?" She chased behind me as I armed myself with flashlight, matches, and the aerosol spray can from my shoulder bag. "You said the ghost may be responsible for the death of two people! What if she sets her sights on us? I'm not ready to die! There's too much I haven't experienced yet. Regular sex. Make-up sex. Childbirth."

I stopped dead in my tracks. "Childbirth?"

"*Hhhhrrrrrrrrrhhhhh . . . HHHHrrrrrrrrrhhhhh!*"

"Okay, since I've remembered I don't have a uterus, that could be a stretch. But there's always surrogacy. Which reminds me, when Tom and I decide to start a family, would you be willing to consider carrying our baby for us?"

I sucked in a mouthful of air and tried not to choke on it. "ARE YOU NUTS?"

"Maybe you need time to consider. You're probably under a little stress right now."

"I . . . You . . . Aargh!" I threw my hands into the air and stormed to the door.

"Is that a no?" she called after me.

The corridor was illuminated by a series of frosted-glass wall sconces that shot naked light upward, toward the ceiling, and muted light downward, toward my sodden Joe Boxers and cotton top. I cast a long look down the hall toward the lobby area. I wondered if the desk clerk could deny hearing this. I jogged to the front desk and looked around. No one on duty. No wonder they never heard anything. I hit the *Please Ring Bell For Service* bell and waited. Nothing. Shaking my head, I struck out in the opposite direction.

"*HHHHRRRRRRRRRHHHHH . . . HHHHRRRRRRRR-HHHHH!*"

The cries were louder in the hall than in my room. I scrutinized the celery-and-cream-striped wallpaper and darker green wainscoting that lined the walls, my finger poised on the nozzle of my air freshener, ready to spray the hell out of the first thing that moved. I wasn't exactly sure what I was looking for, but I was hopeful I'd recognize it if I saw it.

I listened for telltale sounds beneath numerous pictures of grazing sheep and crumbling abbeys that were suspended on wires from the crown molding. Nothing. I snooped around vases of fresh flowers that sat atop marble stands in shell-shaped niches cut into the wall. Nothing. I was standing outside Etienne's room at the end of the corridor, wondering if I should enlist his help, when I heard a sudden "Pssst!" Since I wasn't smelling strawberry shortcake, I was pretty sure I hadn't misfired the air freshener. When I heard the sound again, I looked over my shoulder to find Jackie running barefoot down the hall toward me. She was wearing my satin wrap over her babydoll, which wasn't much of an improvement over her nightie except that at least it wasn't see-through. "What?" I called out in a stage whisper as she approached.

"I changed my mind. I'm coming with you. It's too scary in there by myself."

"You're sure you want to do this?" I insisted.

"No, but it beats the alternative." She danced from foot to foot and patted her arms for warmth. "Can we keep moving though? It's *freezing* out here."

With Jackie in tow, I bypassed Etienne's door and proceeded to the end of the corridor, where a sharp turn to the left led us down a short passageway that terminated in an arched door upon which were painted, in Old English script, the words: NO ENTRY. A metal hasp was attached to the door's deeply scarred wood and was secured to a D ring on the wall with a padlock. "This must be the entrance to the dungeon," I said, remembering what Etienne had said. I yanked on the padlock, but it was one of those heavy-duty kinds that looked like a miniature version of a Brink's truck.

"Tough break," said Jackie. "All locked up. Guess we'll have to go back to the room." She wrapped her hand around my arm and tried to pull me away, but I shook her off.

"You can go back if you want," I said, poking at the padlock as I turned it upside down and right side up. "I'm staying. There must be some way to open this thing up without a key."

"How about a stick of dynamite?"

I flashed a hopeful smile. "You have some on you?"

"Jeez, Emily, you really want to get down there, don't you?"

I pressed my ear to the door. "There's something in this dungeon that someone in Ballybantry Castle doesn't want us to find out about. I want to know what."

Jackie heaved a huge sigh. "Oh, all right, but it's going to cost you. How about you fork over that lipstick you were wearing today. It's the perfect shade for the outfit I'm planning to wear tomorrow."

I stared at her doubtfully. "Are you telling me you can open this door?"

She plucked a hairpin from the bun at the back of my head. "Piece of cake. Out of the way, please." She inserted one arm of the hairpin into the plug at the bottom of the padlock and worked it up and down with the skill of a master jeweler. "When I was in high school, I was always losing the key to the padlock on my gym locker, so I got a lot of practice picking locks. My best friend used to tell me if I didn't make it as an actor, I'd make a great petty thief." The metal shackle sprang open. Jackie gave it a quarter twist, lifted it out of the D ring, and swung back the latch. "Is it a deal on the lipstick?"

"I have the matching nail polish," I said excitedly. " I'll throw that in too."

We touched fists in agreement before Jackie depressed

the tongue on the door handle and opened the door. *Creeeeeeeeeeeeak.*

A blast of foul-smelling air rushed up from the bowels of the castle, sweeping over us like the fetid breath of some prehistoric beast. "Phew!" said Jackie. I pressed the back of my hand to my nose, but the odor had already settled in my nostrils. The dankness of moist earth and decay. The mustiness of unlit subterranean chambers. The stench of once-living things moldering in the darkness. I eyed the uneven stone steps, plunging downward into what looked like a pit of infinite blackness, and took a step backward, my courage wavering.

"Where's the light?" asked Jackie, searching the inner wall for a switch.

"Umm . . . there's no electricity down there."

She snapped her head around. Fire leaped from her eyes. "This gets better all the time. Two dead bodies, ghosts roaming the halls, and no lights in the dungeon. Anything else you forgot to mention?"

I could have told her the ribbon binding on her baby-doll nightie had ripped away and was dangling to her thighs, but that might have been a little too upsetting for her to cope with right now. "That's all I can think of at the moment."

"*HHHHRRRRRRRRHHHHH . . . HHHHRRRRRRRR-HHHHH!*"

My mouth went dry. My heart leaped into my throat. I stared at Jackie. She stared at me. "Okay," I said nervously. "We might as well get this over with."

"You carry the flashlight," said Jackie. "Give me the Mace."

"It's not exactly Mace." I handed it over to her. She held it up to read the label.

"Strawberry Shortcake room freshener?"

"Air deodorizer can be a very effective weapon in the war on crime," I defended. "It's nonviolent, nontoxic, and causes no permanent damage, though it might leave you a little uncomfortable if you have allergies. It'll work best if you can get off a sustained squirt to the eyes."

Jackie shook her head. "And women wonder why they put men in charge of the military. How about you hand over the matches too? I'm not going to be caught down there without a light source."

"Don't drop them. It could be wet down there." I gave up the matches reluctantly, turned on my Maglite, and with an intrepid gulp, stepped down onto the first riser.

The damp coolness raised gooseflesh on my skin. The smell of mold, mildew, and stagnant water cloyed my nostrils. I shone the light before me to guide the way downward, and after descending more than a dozen ancient stairs that angled beyond the ring of light from the hall, I reached the floor of the dungeon, immersed in the kind of blackness that felt alive and crawling. Somewhere in the darkness I could hear the soft sounds of water trickling and plinking.

"This is so gross," said Jackie beside me. "My pedicure's getting shot to hell. What are we looking for?"

"I'm not sure yet." I panned the light across the floor. The hard-packed earth was worn smooth, dipping and rising in places where ancient feet had strode. Small piles of avalanched rock were scattered about like cemetery stones, waiting to stub the toes of the unwary. Shallow pools of water lay like open wounds along the way, crusted with scum that gleamed slimy and yellow in the light. The walls were constructed of rough-edged stones cemented together with mortar, but water seeping in from the outside had caused the mortar to erode and dozens of stones to fall away, leaving the walls looking like a mouth full of crumbling teeth.

Pssssst. Pssssst.

I shone the light on Jackie. "What are you doing?"

"Spraying your air freshener. It stinks down here."

"Cut it out! You'll use it all up."

"Not my fault. You should have bought the large economy size. Hey"—she sniffed the air—"this stuff isn't bad."

"Well, stop wasting it."

I inched my way forward and directed my Maglite at a small barred window cut into a door whose hinges were dark with rust. Cobwebs hung from the corners like bridal netting and formed a gauzy tapestry over the window, making it impossible to see into the chamber beyond.

"Bet this is one door that hasn't been opened in a while," said Jackie.

"Can you get rid of the spiderwebs?" I asked.

She stepped in front of me. *PSSSSSSSSST!* She stepped back and squinted at the impenetrable mesh that still crosshatched the window. "Looks like air freshener doesn't work on cobwebs. You think Eloise would consider that a helpful household hint?"

"You could use your hands."

"Oh, sure. Like *that's* gonna happen."

We forged ahead into the blackness, me in the lead, Jackie following close behind. A multitude of doors studded both sides of the passageway, each one pockmarked and grimy and looking as if it hadn't been opened for centuries. "How far do you think this thing goes?" asked Jackie. "You think there's a torture chamber behind one of these doors? Remember that old Vincent Price movie, *The Pit and the Pendulum*? He had some pretty cool instruments of torture in—"

Blackness enveloped us.

I stopped dead in my tracks and slapped my Maglite against my palm. "Shoot!"

Psssssst! went Jackie's trigger finger.

"Not you!" I yelled, choking on the cloud of strawberry spray that surrounded my head. I waved my hands in front of my face, gasping when my flashlight escaped my grip and went flying into the air. It smashed into the stone wall with a kind of tinny sound and thunked onto the ground.

"What was that?" wailed Jackie.

"Don't ask. You still have those matches?"

After a few moments I heard a sharp *phtttt* and saw Jackie hold up a solitary match that blazed eerily bright in the blackness. I searched the ground at my feet. "Do you see anything that resembles a flashlight?"

"Maybe it's up ahead of you," she said, cursing when the flame burned out.

I inched my way forward in the dark. *Phtttt!* Jackie struck another match. I hunkered down on my haunches, my eyes roving the shadows, and in a pocket of darkness close to the wall, I spied an object that was shaped like my Maglite. "I see something."

The light faded to blackness again.

"It's over this way," I said, scuttling in the direction of the object. "Right about here."

Phtttt! Jackie held another match up and tiptoed toward me, hunkering down and angling the light above the place I indicated. I hunkered beside her, ready to snap up my flashlight, until I saw what I was about to grab. "Ooh!" I snatched my hand back. "A mouse."

Jackie cocked her head, observing the dead rodent from another viewpoint. "It does kinda look like a flashlight though. Must be the rigor mortis." She hoisted herself to her feet. "Okay, I say we forget the Maglite and blow this joint before we run out of matches. There's nothing down here except puddles and cob— Ouch!" Blackness blanketed us once again as the match burned out. "That hurts," she spat. I heard soft, slurpy sounds as she sucked her fingertips.

She was probably right. Even if there *was* something suspicious down here, we'd never find it without a flashlight. I stood up, discouraged, but secretly happy not to have to spend another minute in this place. "Did you burn your fingers very badly?" I asked.

"I'll live."

"You want me to take over the matches?"

She groped for my hand in the darkness and slapped the matchbook into my palm. "Be my guest."

I fingered the matchbook, flipped open the cover, ripped off a solitary match, and struck it against the friction strip on the back. *Phtttt!* I pivoted in a slow half-circle to get my bearings, then nodded hesitantly to my left. "That's the way we go back, isn't it?" Where was George Farkas when you needed him?

Jackie seized my arm, her voice a high vibrato, her eyes riveted on something behind me. "Emily? You'd better turn around."

Alarmed, I spun around to face another dungeon door, but this one was vastly different from the others along the passageway. There was no barred window, no cobwebs, no scarred wood, no rusty hinges. Forget *The Pit and the Pendulum*. This puppy was classic Home Depot, with an added charge for the arch. "This is our door," I said in excitement. "It has to be." I tried the knob.

Locked.

The backplate for the knob was designed with an old-fashioned keyhole. "How are you with keyholes?" I asked Jackie, flicking the match to the ground before it burned my fingers.

"Not my speciality."

I lit another. "I'll buy a new flashlight tomorrow. And

maybe we can find a hardware store that sells skeleton keys."

"This stuff is weirding me out, Emily. Can we leave now?"

I lowered my eyes to the ground to see where I was stepping, and it was then I saw the footprints—footprints tracked onto the dirt floor in an intricate pattern of slashes and dots. Footprints that were still dark with wetness. They trailed off in a direction that led deeper into the dungeon, but they originated from behind me. From the door with the new hinges and the old-fashioned keyhole. *"Uff da,"* I said. "Look at this."

Jackie followed my gaze. "Is it the ghost? Do you think those belong to the guy they found floating in the moat?"

I scratched my nose, catching a whiff of something that teased my senses with familiarity. "It's not a ghost," I said with sudden awareness. Despite the potent fetor of must, mildew, and damp earth that hung in the air, no smell could mask the overpowering reek of Michael Malooley's cologne.

CHAPTER 11

Nana and Tilly were exiting the dining room as I headed in for breakfast the next morning. "You're runnin' late, dear," Nana said, checking her watch. "You look a little groggy. Were you up late last night?"

I stared at Nana's hair, trying not to look as horrified as I felt. "New hairdo," I said, nonplussed. Her cap of tidy white fingerwaves was sticking straight out in mutilated tufts all over her head, like cottonballs that had been attacked by dull lawn shears and finished off by a pack of wild dogs. I'd been on the receiving end of a few bad hair-cuts, but this haircut wasn't bad. It was criminal.

"It's the latest in Hollywood ultrachic," said Nana, primping like a schoolgirl. "I think it makes me look twenty years younger. Don't you love it?"

"Love it," I repeated numbly. I was in no hurry to witness my mother's reaction when my grandmother returned home looking like a French poodle.

"It's called a choppy cut," Nana continued. "That nice Tom Thum person has some a his stylin' equipment along and gave a few of us makeovers last night after the power went out and they shut down the entertainment."

I guess that explained the ragged clumps and bald spots. He'd cut her hair in the dark. I gave her head a quick once-over to make sure her ears were still attached. "Funny he could see anything with the lights out," I commented.

"On the contrary," said Tilly, "we weren't lacking for light. We gathered all the candles from our collective rooms and used those for illumination. It was very New Age. Tonsorial artistry by candlelight."

He'd actually been able to *see* what he was doing? I wondered if you could sue a hair designer for malpractice. And to think Jackie suggested I consult him about my problem hair. Huh! I'd rather have problem hair than no hair at all.

"Tom and his bride had a little spat last night," Nana said under her breath, "so he didn't have nothin' better to do. You shoulda seen him work, Emily. He'd stretch out a hunk a hair and whack it off with his razor so quick, it made you wonder if he knew what he was doin', but I shouldn't a fretted. That young man has vision. If his wife is still mad at him tonight, he says he'll have time to add color."

Eh! That settled it. I didn't care how good Jackie was at picking locks. She was going to spend this evening with her husband. I hadn't reached the age of twenty-nine without learning a few lessons in life, the most basic of which was: It's a lot more desirable to live with a malevolent ghost than a bad dye job.

"I don't want to be a bother, dear, but did you happen to notice if I left my bathrobe in your room?" Nana asked. "I thought I packed it in my grip with the rest a my stuff, but I can't seem to find it."

"I don't remember seeing it, but I'll double-check for

you." Nana's age must be catching up to her. It wasn't like her to misplace anything.

I said my good-byes to Nana and Tilly, and proceeded into the dining room, standing on the periphery for a moment to scope out the diners. Jackie had headed back to her room about an hour ago, but I saw neither her nor Tom at any of the tables. I hoped their absence meant they were taking the time to iron out their differences. Michael Malooley was seated by himself at a table in the far corner, reading a paper. Shocking he was up so early after his covert operation last night. He had to be tired. I sure was. I was surprised he wasn't sitting with Ethel Minch, or maybe that would have been too obvious. They probably needed to keep their distance from each other to disguise the fact that they were in cahoots. I was sure the two of them were a team. Ethel Minch was the brains of the outfit, and Michael Malooley was her henchman. But how had they connected up with each other? What kind of sickos got a thrill out of scaring people to death? And what exactly did they think was in store for them, other than a lengthy jail sentence? I had a lot of questions that needed answering.

Putting a bead on an unoccupied seat, I wove my way through the maze of tables in the dining room, greeting members of the Iowa contingent as I passed. "Top o' the morning," I said, noting the plates everyone had heaped with fried eggs, scrambled eggs, omelettes, bacon, sausage, and potatoes. I didn't know about the rest of the country, but from the size of some of the girths around here, Iowans were definitely winning the war on bulimia.

"Mind if I join you?" I asked the Minches and Kuppelmans when I reached their table.

"Glad to have you, doll," said Ernie Minch.

I seated myself next to Ethel and surveyed the bowls of cold cereal sitting in front of everyone. Ethel, Ernie, and

Gladys were taking their cereal with water. Ira was eating his dry, which looked only a little less appealing than eating a cardboard box. "How did everyone sleep last night?" I asked cheerfully.

Ira and Gladys exchanged glances. I think they were trying to smile at each other, but their expressions never quite made it. "Like logs," said Ira. "We always sleep like logs. It's the result of having proper nutritional equilibrium in our diets."

"I heard some weird sounds next door," said Ernie. "I think it was the honeymooners. Remember when we used to boink like that every night, Ethel?"

"That was the pre-Viagra era," Ethel commiserated. "Sex is a lot more expensive these days. If you're on a fixed income, who can afford it?"

I felt a hand on my shoulder and looked up to see Alice Tjarks standing behind my chair. "I'm sorry to bother you, Emily, but is it true? Have two people died in the last two days?"

Uh-oh. So much for trying to keep our little secret under wraps and not causing a panic. "Um . . . What did you hear?"

"Bernice complained to the desk clerk this morning that her room hadn't been properly cleaned yesterday, and the clerk said she could probably expect the same today, what with two of the cleaning staff having dropped dead in the last two days."

Leave it to Bernice. She could stir up trouble even when she wasn't trying. "I guess it's probably true then."

"Do you know what killed them?" Alice pressed.

"I can tell you what killed them," announced Ira Kuppelman. He flung his hand toward the buffet table. "Breakfast! Look at the toxins these people cram into their bodies. Dead animals. Unhealthy fats. Massive doses of carbohydrates. Who can exist on a diet like that and live? And if you eat what they're serving, you'll be next!"

Alice, who ate a full country breakfast at the Windsor City Perkins every day of her life, sucked in a sharp breath. "Is that right, Emily? Did they die from eating too many Irish breakfasts?"

I hedged, not knowing what would cause the greater panic—bacon with too much fat or a ghost with deformed feet. I decided to play middle of the road. "Well, I have it on good authority that even the Samoans have switched to Special K."

Alice gave me a puzzled look. "I see. Thanks. I'll pass the word along."

"Who died?" asked Ethel when Alice left.

I stared at her through narrowed eyes. What a con artist. As if she didn't know. "A maid and a custodian have both been found dead since we arrived. Curious, huh?"

"Why is that curious?" she asked, digging into her cereal. "People die all the time back home."

"Not under circumstances like this, they don't," I said in a ghoulish voice.

Gladys's spoon slipped from her hand and clattered against her bowl with a sound that gave us all a start. "What kind of circumstances are you talking about?" she asked in a rush of breath.

"Hey, there's Ashley," Ernie interrupted. "She's on crutches. With a cast on her foot. Must've broken something."

I glanced over my shoulder to see a few men hurry over to Ashley, their body language smacking of genuine concern. She was all smiles as she tossed her blond hair over her shoulder, looking helplessly pathetic as she allowed herself to be escorted to a nearby table, cooing and fluttering like an injured bird. I rolled my eyes. I was developing a keen aversion to the drop-dead-gorgeous people of the world.

I returned my attention to Gladys Kuppelman, picking up the thread of our conversation. "The authorities found a set of extremely suspicious footprints beneath the first body, and they're pretty sure that if they find the person who made the footprints, they can prove the deaths were murders instead of deaths from natural causes." Of course, the authorities had made no such claim, but I might as well make Ethel squirm a little. Let her know I was on to her.

"There's a murderer on the loose in the castle?" gasped Gladys, her eyes showing terror, but her face wearing the same placid expression she always wore.

Ethel flipped her an "Aw, go on" gesture. "What are you worried about, Gladys? Who'd want to murder you? I've gotta agree with Ira. It's probably the saturated fats and trans-fatty acids that got 'em."

Aha! Just what I thought she'd say. Talk about trying to shunt guilt away from yourself. She was in my trap. All I had to do now was tighten the noose.

"Excuse me, Emily," said Osmond Chelsvig, coming up behind me. "Alice just mentioned that a couple of people on the tour dropped dead from mad cow disease over the last couple of days. Is that true?"

I craned my neck to look up at Osmond. "They weren't on the tour. They were on the castle staff. And I'm not sure about the mad cow disease. I don't know what they died from."

He nodded and returned to his chair. I was glad I'd decided not to tell Alice about the ghost. She'd already gotten the story wrong, but I guessed that was to be expected, considering how many years she'd spent working in the media.

"I'm worried, Ira," Gladys complained. "What if someone finds out I'm related to Oliver Cromwell? Everyone in Ireland hates Cromwell. What's to stop them from hating me as well? And killing me. I could be dead by morning! This is serious. You're one of the people in charge, Emily. What do you and Ashley intend to do to protect me?"

I stared at her bowl of cereal. Section two of my *Escort's Manual* had dealt with "Protection," but if memory served, its main concern was to list new products designed to assist with bladder control. "Uh . . ."

From my left I heard the digital tones of "New York, New York." Ernie Minch fished his cell phone out of his shirt pocket and flipped it open. "It's Junior," he said, checking the readout on the display screen. "What's up?" he asked into the phone.

I heard chairs scrape the floor behind me and looked over my shoulder to see a quartet of Iowans head for the buffet table. I watched them as they bypassed the warm chafing dishes and clustered around the huge bowls of cold cereal at the end of the table.

"Okay, okay," Ernie said into the phone, then to Ethel, "Junior says your podiatrist left a message on our machine that they wanna change your next appointment to the day after we get back from vacation. That okay with you? Junior will call them back."

"I suppose, but have Junior tell that doctor I don't like all this changing-around business." Her face grew stern. "These hoity-toity doctors think *their* schedules are sacred, but they think nothing about telling us to change *ours.*"

Alice Tjarks blew by me in a rush to join the other Iowans around the cereal section of the buffet table. Hands flew every which way as she tried to muscle her way toward the remaining bowls. I frowned at the commotion but dragged my attention away to focus on Ethel. "You have regular appointments with a podiatrist, do you?" I asked matter-of-factly.

"Honey, these feet have put all five of his kids through college. I'm there once a month, every month. When the pain gets bad, I'm there more."

"I guess it must hurt having your toes all stuck together like that."

She looked taken aback. "Why would that hurt?"

Osmond Chelsvig raced past us to join the huddle at the cereal table. I startled as a bowl crashed to the floor. "Don't your toes get sore not being able to operate individually?"

Ethel laughed. "That's why I had them sewn together. They were all cockeyed before, crossing over each other, crossing under each other. Now they're just fine."

"You did WHAT?"

Bernice and George popped out of their seats and charged toward the swell of bodies fighting over the stash of cereal bowls. I couldn't help noticing that Bernice looked unusually stylish this morning with a print scarf turbaned around her head.

"I—had—them—sewn—together," Ethel enunciated slowly for my benefit. "You never heard of that? My podiatrist does it all the time."

"You weren't *born* with webbed toes?" I asked, feeling a bit like champagne that had lost its fizz. But what about the ghost? What about Michael Malooley? She'd just ruined my theory. She'd ruined everything! I jumped as another bowl hit the floor.

"Shoot, I had them stitched together forty years ago," Ethel said.

"So how come you have to see the podiatrist so often if you already got your toes fixed?" asked Gladys.

A white-coated server flew out from the kitchen and

dashed toward the sound of breaking glass, dustpan and broom in hand. Five more Iowans followed in his wake to join the fracas.

"I keep telling you," grated Ethel, "my metatarsus is deformed. How many times do I gotta tell you that? You ever think about listening when people talk to you? They'd have me in orthotics if I'd let them."

"Junior says hi," said Ernie as he slipped his cell phone back into his pocket.

Ethel turned on him. "You hung up without letting me talk to him? I wanted to talk to him! Why's he up at three o'clock in the morning? Don't you wanna know what he's doing up at this hour of the morning? Call him back. Is he sick? Are the kids sick? Do you hear me, Ernie?"

"I'm not calling him back, Ethel."

"If she wants to talk to her kid, let her talk to her kid," griped Gladys.

"Anything to shut her up," said Ira.

Ethel shot him a hostile look. "I beg your pardon?"

"You're causing disharmony in the environment!" he shouted at her.

"Are you going to let him talk to me like that?" Ethel screamed at Ernie.

Drawn back to the commotion beyond Ira, I watched in stunned silence as my polite, well-behaved fellow Iowans knotted themselves into a gridlocked clump of bobbing heads, writhing limbs, and flying elbows. Yup. They really knew how to queue up at the buffet table. I heard grunts and heavy breathing, a cry of "Get off my foot!" then watched a fistful of what looked like Cheerios geyser haphazardly into the air. "Cut that out!" someone shouted. "You're wasting it!"

"Stop!" cried the server, waving his dustpan and broom at them. "There's other food besides cereal for you to be eating!"

"Not on your life!" I heard Bernice wail from some- where within the center of the throng. "Everything else has botulism!"

I rose calmly from my seat. "Would you excuse me?" I skirted around tables cluttered with abandoned plates heaped with full Irish breakfasts. I shook my head as I headed toward the melee. Good going, Emily. Did I know how to avoid causing a panic or what?

When I left the dining room sometime later, Etienne was at the front desk handing something to the female clerk I'd spoken to yesterday—the one with the name of a deep-sea monster and the body of a football tackle. I admired him from afar for a moment. His style. His ele- gance. His really nice trousers and Italian knit sweater. I crept up behind him and wrapped my arms around his waist. "Top o' the morning."

He stroked my hands with his fingertips and turned around, placing a kiss on the tip of my nose. "Good morn- ing, darling."

I wrinkled my nose at him. "Is that the best you can do?" This didn't bode well. I hoped he wasn't still miffed about the change of plans last night.

"My best is for private consumption only. Hold still. You've something in your hair." He spent a half-minute plucking things from the crown of my head, then offered them up for my inspection.

"Cereal," I confirmed, peeking at the smattering of toasty brown crumbs in his palm. "There was a run on cornflakes at breakfast. I probably have Cheerios on me too," I said, patting down my cowl-neck sweater, "but I don't know where they are."

"I won't ask how you ended up wearing your food instead of eating it. You Americans do have peculiar ways

about you." He deposited the crumbs in the nearest ashtray, then caught the desk clerk's attention. "Nessa, could I
trouble you to hand me the note I just asked you to place
in Miss Andrew's box?"

A note? Uh-oh. Notes were bad news.

With freshly penned note in hand, he motioned me to
accompany him into the lobby. We sat down on a velvet
settee nestled in an alcove guarded by two sentinels wearing highly polished suits of armor. "I guess that's for me,
huh?" I said, staring at the paper in his hand.

"Something's come up, I'm afraid, darling." His tone
was apologetic as he unfolded the note for me. I read his
words aloud.

Emily,

My superiors contacted me this morning to inform
me that there might be an Irish connection to the case
we're working on in Lucerne. Unfortunately, darling,
this means I must spend the day interviewing some
likely suspects in a nearby village. I'll return as quickly
as possible, but I fear this means I'll miss the day tour
again today. However, we'll be together tonight, no
matter what. This I promise you. I know you'll understand my dilemma. You're always so accepting of the
duties and limitations of my job. That's one of the
things I love about you.

E.

My face fell with disappointment, but it was kinda hard
for me to rage and whine when he'd made me sound like
Mother Teresa. However, a warning bell clanged in my
brain, alerting me to the possibility of trouble ahead.

Would it be like this after we were married? Would his job always come first? Was he such a workaholic that we'd be forced to lead separate lives even when we were together? I'd already chalked up one failed marriage. I didn't want to risk another. That clinched it. We needed to have a long talk about our relationship, only I couldn't let on about it. Men enjoyed relationship talks about as much as they enjoyed a visit to the proctologist.

I let out my version of the long-suffering sigh. "So when are they going to let you enjoy your holiday? You *are* on holiday. Remember?"

"I shouldn't have rung them up to have them look into the O'Quigleys. It was too vivid a reminder that I was already over here and available to do their footwork for them. But you'll be happy to know, they have complaints about this castle on file, so, amazingly enough, the wheels of progress are turning. They're checking out your O'Quigley angle and might even be asking assistance from Interpol."

Terrific. The wheels of progress take off like gangbusters for once and I have to bring them to a grinding halt. "About the O'Quigleys." I winced. "There's a good chance . . . I've sent you on a wild-goose chase."

"I'm sorry?" His eyes probed my face, as if he'd misheard.

"Ethel Minch came clean at breakfast. She wasn't born with webbed toes. She had them sewn together. Deliberately. Her feet are deformed, but not in the way I thought they were. So unless all her relatives have had their toes sewn together, which is highly improbable, the O'Quigleys are a dead end. Our ghost is a web-footed being with another last name."

"Are you sure Mrs. Minch was telling the truth about her condition?"

"She sounded pretty convincing. She was using words like *metatarsus* and *orthotics*."

"I suppose *metatarsus* isn't a word one throws around casually." Sparks leaped behind his eyes as he considered his next step. "I could phone the department and tell them not to waste their time on the O'Quigley link, but I don't think I'll do that. Who knows? Maybe they'll turn something up. Unfortunately, if they don't, we'll probably find ourselves back at square one."

"No! Not at square one. I made a discovery last night. Did you hear the cries in the hall around three in the morning?"

Etienne shook his head. "I followed your example and bought earplugs when I was in town yesterday. I have to confess, I didn't hear a thing."

"Well, I heard it, and I'm convinced you're right. Whatever is happening is originating from the dungeon. All the chambers down there are closed off by doors that are rusted shut and cocooned with cobwebs. All except one particular chamber that was sporting a new door with shiny hinges and a set of wet footprints that I'm positive belong to—Are you ready for this?—Michael Malooley."

"The bus driver? You think he could actually *find* his way into the dungeon?"

"Trust me. He's smarter than he looks. I thought he was in cahoots with Ethel, but maybe he's running the operation by himself. You've seen him. I don't mean to stereotype, but have you ever seen a more shady, unfriendly character? He's the culprit. I know he is. If we could coax his shoes off him, I bet we'd find he has webbed toes. Could you flash your badge and commandeer his shoes and socks so we could check?"

Etienne laughed softly and lifted my hand to his lips. "You've become a footprint expert, have you, darling?

Might I inquire how you decided these particular footprints belong to Malooley?"

"It wasn't the footprints exactly. It was the smell. It's pretty hard to disguise a stench like that." He feathered kisses across my fingertips with a gentleness that lifted the down on my arm from my wrist to my shoulder. *Unh.* Okay, maybe a long talk wasn't as necessary as I thought. So he was a workaholic. I could live with that.

"As an aside, darling, would you care to tell me how you got into the dungeon to smell him?"

This could be a little sticky. I didn't know if what I'd done would be considered breaking and entering, but I needed to play it safe. "It took a little ingenuity, the details of which I'm not willing to share at this time."

"You picked the lock." He shook his head and tried to suppress a smile. "If I'd known you were so adept at breaking and entering, I'd have asked you to do it myself."

"You would? You wouldn't have scolded me for setting out to perform an illegal act?"

"Emily, darling, I might be an officer of the law, but I've learned that laws can sometimes be bent without being broken. Even I can turn a blind eye every so often." His gaze shifted from my eyes to a spot above my right ear. "Though it's increasingly hard to turn a blind eye when your hair is full of foreign matter. Hold still."

"More cornflakes?" I asked as he caught something between his fingers and coaxed it down the length of my hair. I eyed the BB-sized piece of grit in his palm. "Nope. Grape-Nut."

Etienne studied the morsel with appreciation. "Cheerios. Cornflakes. Grape-Nuts. They have an excellent assortment of breakfast cereals available here."

Good thing. They were going to need them.

From the parking lot we heard the loud blare of a car

horn. Etienne rose from his chair. "That's probably my cab."

"Your cab?" I popped up beside him. "But . . . but . . . I haven't finished telling you what else I found out."

He grasped my hand and pulled me along with him as he strode to the door. "Is it life or death, or will it hold until evening?" The horn blared again. He gave me one of those anguished looks that punctual people always give anything that is threatening to make them late.

"It's not life or death. It's about a painting in my room."

"Your room. Perfect. Tonight then. You won't have to tell me; you can show me." He bent close to my ear, his breath warm against my lobe. "I hope this doesn't interfere with your showing me the other intimate details in your room that crave my attention." He kissed my mouth and bolted out the door, leaving my hand elevated in farewell and the rest of me in need of a cold shower. But remembering my dilemma with the dungeon door, I ran outside after him.

"If you happen to pass a hardware store, would you pick up a flashlight and a skeleton key?" He waved to me as he stepped inside the cab. I watched the vehicle squeal out of the parking lot, not knowing whether he'd heard me or not. Oh, well, I guess it would be a surprise.

As I made my way back across the lobby, I noticed Ashley standing at the front desk, jabbing an angry finger into the air in the vicinity of Nessa's nose. I wondered what the desk clerk had done, or not done, to warrant Ashley's wrath, but figured it didn't have to be much to set Ashley off. She was so fond of reaming people out, I was amazed she could hold on to a job that required her to be nice for extended periods of time. All that phony Southern charm was such a crock. Funny no one had exposed her for what she really was. Knights might have lived and died by the sword, cowboys might have lived and died by the gun, but tour guides lived and died by the all-important standard evaluation form. Strange that it hadn't proven Ashley's downfall already. *Hmm.* Maybe Golden Irish Vacations used a new form that excluded the really profound questions, like: *Was your guide informative? Was she courteous? Was she careful to avoid poking your eye out when she jabbed her finger in your face?* That had to be it. The company had sanitized the forms to be more politically correct. They didn't dare give guests a chance to say Ashley was hostile, two-faced, and crabby because the truth would hurt her feelings and she might decide to sue the hell out of them, which could plunge the company into bankruptcy. *Geesch.* I hated political correctness.

As I rounded the corner of the front desk on my way to my room, Ashley stopped rebuking Nessa long enough to call out to me, "Did y'all enjoy your evening with your . . . friend last night, sugar? You'll have to tell me what you did to amuse yourselves, especially dressed like you were. Loved the see-through babydolls."

Nessa took advantage of the interruption to escape to the grid of mail slots behind her and busy herself with extraneous pieces of paper. But she wasn't so busy that she failed to toss me a grateful look over her shoulder. I smiled inwardly. I'd consider that my good deed for the day.

"We had a lovely evening," I fired back at Ashley. "It was especially exciting after the power went out."

"I'm sure it was." Ashley faked a honeyed smile. "Lots of heavy breathing was there?"

"Lots of . . . bubbly."

"Champagne? Y'all were able to order champagne? I tried to order champagne, and they told me they didn't have any."

"Maybe it's your accent. I bet they couldn't understand you. You should try again."

She squinted at me like a clueless Neanderthal before trying to gain the advantage. "Not to rain on your parade, Emily, but if you can't control your people any better than you did this morning, I might have to write you up. And you really don't want that to happen. It could ruin your career as a tour escort."

She . . . I . . . *Uff da!* "My people wouldn't be *out* of control if someone could explain why two people died in the last two days. When they think they might be next in line, they panic!"

"Nonetheless, I don't expect them to start food fights. If there are cleanup costs, you're footin' the bill."

I drilled her with one of Nana's patented steely-eyed looks. "Lest it escape your notice, you're not the only one around here who can complain about the people in charge, or ruin careers."

She propped herself up higher on her crutches, oozing confidence. "Try it, sugar," she challenged, "but I mean to tell you, that dog don't hunt."

"Oh, yeah?" *Hunh.* She wasn't the only one who could throw around trite catchphrases. "Well, the pen is mightier than the sword."

She smiled a saccharine smile. "My daddy owns the company."

Yup. That explained a lot of things.

Fuming about the unfairness of nepotism, I returned to my room and was about to unlock my door when I noticed Ira Kuppelman and Michael Malooley engaged in quiet discussion in the shadows at the end of the hall. Now that was odd. What would a man whose wife was related to Oliver Cromwell have in common with a man who professed unmitigated hatred of Oliver Cromwell?

Ira handed Michael a sheet of white paper that Michael initially rejected, then stuck in his shirt pocket begrudgingly, shaking his head all the while. What had Ira asked him to do? And why was Michael saying "No," then changing his tune and nodding yes? Strange bedfellows, Ira and Michael. Had I paired up the wrong people? Was Michael doing Ira's bidding instead of Ethel's? But why would Ira want to frighten anyone to death? What was in it for him? What was his motivation? And then it hit me. The oldest motivation in the world. Uh-oh. I didn't like the looks of this. I opened my door with the sudden fear that if we discovered body number three today, it might belong to Gladys Kuppelman.

CHAPTER 12

As we pulled into the parking lot of the Giant's Causeway on the North Antrim coast, Ashley threw a few details at us in a voice that could melt butter. "Some folks call this site the eighth wonder of the world, and after y'all see it, you'll know why. What y'all are about to see is a geologic puzzle."

The word *geologic* caught my attention as I sat catnapping beside Bernice. Wow. A four-syllable word. She was pulling out all the stops this morning.

"The site consists of about thirty-seven thousand columns made of a volcanic rock called basalt. They start at the base of the cliff and descend like stepping-stones into the sea. Some of the columns stand forty feet high, and what y'all will notice is that they're mostly shaped like perfect hexagons. Not all, mind you. You'll see some columns with four, five, eight, or ten sides, but the regularity of the six-sided ones have geologists baffled. I guess it's unusual for nature to be that consistent, especially when you consider there are no two snowflakes that are alike."

"What does she know about snowflakes?" Bernice muttered. "Listen to that accent. She's probably never even seen snow."

Bernice was in a particularly sour mood this morning. I figured it had something to do with the Grape-Nuts she'd inhaled up her nose in the food fight. "That's a really attractive turban you're wearing, Bernice. Magenta is a good color on you."

"It's not mine. It belongs to Alice Tjarks."

"Well, that was nice of her to lend it to you. I've never had much success with scarf turbans. They keep unraveling on me. Yours looks pretty secure."

"Why are you telling me? Tell Alice. She's the one who tied it."

Bernice could accept a compliment with such grace. "It looks very smart." And it added a touch of class to her sweatshirt with the Monster Truck emblazoned on the front and her red polyester pants.

"I think it looks stupid. Paisley. Who wears paisley anymore? But it was either this or a paper bag."

Ashley's voice sounded over the loudspeaker again. "When you get off the bus, head toward the visitors' center and proceed through the back door to the circular walkway that wends down to the shore. It's a lovely hike for those of y'all who enjoy a scenic walk. If walkin's not your thing, you can catch the shuttle bus at the designated area behind the visitors' center. It'll drop you right off at the Grand Causeway. We'll plan to meet back at the bus in three hours, so check your watches and make a mental note."

"What did you say about a paper bag?" I asked Bernice as the bus rumbled to a stop.

"I got made over last night," she snarled. "By an idiot. Your grandmother got made over, too. She looks like she got her head caught in a SaladShooter, but her eyesight's going, so she doesn't know yet how bad it is. At least I know enough to hide mine."

I cringed. "How bad is it?"

As the people around us stood and stretched and crammed into the aisles to disembark, Bernice pulled the turban off her head. "You tell me."

Eh! It was worse than Nana's, if that was possible.

"It's called a choppy cut."

More like the machete cut. What hair she had left fanned over her scalp like sheaves of mangled wild grass, crisscrossing in random directions. This was really bad news. "The good news is," I said, feigning optimism, "it'll grow back. Let me help you get your scarf back on."

As I snugged it back over her head, the whole thing unraveled in my hands like cascading silk, slithering over her ears and halfway down her neck. *Nuts.* I did a quick sleight of hand with folds and knots and tail ends, then paused to observe my handiwork. "I like it."

Bernice stared at me, deadpan. "It didn't droop over my eye when Alice did it."

"This is a good look for you. It's sassy. Coquettish."

"Maybe I didn't make myself clear. I CAN'T SEE!"

"Okay, okay." I tucked the overhang into a fold at her hairline. "There. Perfect." Well, almost perfect, if you overlooked the fact that it was a little crooked. "If it falls apart again, have Nana give you a hand. She does the turban thing every night, only with toilet paper."

By the time we gathered our belongings and left the bus, the rest of the group was far ahead of us, heads down and arms swinging, trying to outpace each other in what looked like a spirited dash toward the visitors' center. The Iowans were in power-walk mode because they wanted to be on time for the next event. The New Yorkers were in power-walk mode because fast is the only speed they know. I figured this phenomenon was a holdover from the days when streetcars were first introduced in Brooklyn. So many city dwellers were run over by the unwelcome new vehicles, people were forced to move really fast to dodge them. Streetcars may have disappeared, but New Yorkers seem to have retained the genetic imprint to move it, move it, move it. I guess that's how the Brooklyn Dodgers ended up in Los Angeles.

The visitors' center was a one-story structure that looked newly remodeled, with lots of glass and layers of fresh paint. Once inside, we found ourselves in the middle of a gift shop, with an airy cafeteria-style eatery located at the back and a ramp that led to the shuttle bus area, with a turnstile at the bottom. While some of the group milled about the gift shop, I located a sign for the comfort station and headed toward the opposite end of the building. As I approached the area, the door to the men's room swung open. I stopped short when a sheepish-looking Jackie, dressed in a sexy striped tank dress and leather wedges with a high wooden heel, shot a look both ways and slunk out the door.

"Damn," she complained, joining me. "I hate it when that happens."

I shook my head, admiring her chutzpah. "Let me guess. There weren't enough stalls in the ladies' room, so you decided to sneak into the men's."

"I didn't sneak in. I walked into the rest room, headed for the urinal, got ready to whip out my equipment, and realized I don't *have* any equipment. Jeez, you'd think I'd remember I don't whiz standing up anymore, but every so often, I have these little mental lapses and end up in the wrong room. Old habits die hard."

"Guys have it so good," I said grudgingly. "External plumbing. Zippered access. No lines. No waiting."

Jackie nodded. "I have one male acquaintance who decided not to make the leap into transsexualism after he saw the ridiculously long lines women had to wait in to use the rest rooms at Yankee Stadium. He figured he could discover a cure for cancer in the time he wasted queuing up to pee."

We made our way to the ladies' room around the corner and took our places at the back of the line. "Is Tom here with you today?" I inquired, unable to locate him in the crowd .

"He's here. But we're not speaking. He's hidden my fuzzy pink slippers on me, the creep. He knows I love those slippers. They're better than comfort food. He swears he didn't touch them, but I can't find them anywhere in the room, so you tell me. Did they decide to walk away by themselves? I don't think so. He hid them. I didn't realize how petty he can be."

Jackie's slippers. Nana's bathrobe. Etienne's trousers. What was going on here? "Please tell me you're going to make up before tonight."

"Why? What's happening tonight? Oh, God, you're not going to invite him to join in one of your dungeon adventures, are you? I'll tell you right now, he won't go. He's allergic to certain kinds of mold, and he doesn't like mice."

"Have you seen my grandmother today?"

"Yeah. She looks like Peter Rabbit on speed. What happened?"

"Your husband happened. He decided to give her a makeover last night to kill time. The choppy cut. If he's free tonight, he's going to apply color."

Jackie shook her head. "He wanted to give me the choppy cut, but I wouldn't let him anywhere near me. That choppy cut is bad news. They love it in Hollywood, but that's not a good barometer. Normal people sneak weird looks at you and ask if you'd like to borrow a comb."

"No color," I stated emphatically. "Nana's probably going to have a hard time clearing airport security with the haircut alone. I don't want to see what'll happen if her hair is pink."

"Tom has never done pink hair. Not even by accident."

"No color!"

Jackie planted her fist on her hip and gave me an exasperated look. "So what do you suggest I do to keep him occupied this evening?"

"You're on your honeymoon," I said in a meaningful whisper. "You figure it out."

After we did our thing at the comfort station, we passed through the turnstile near the cafeteria and exited out the back of the building. A blue-and-white shuttle bus was loading up passengers, but people were crammed in so tightly, I decided to wait for the next one. I'd been pinched, crushed, and pickpocketed too many times on crowded New York subways to ever want to repeat the experience. But I spotted George Farkas with his nose pressed to one of the windows, and Bernice, and then I saw a lot of people who weren't from Iowa: the Minches, the Kuppelmans, the guy who borrowed the furniture polish from the maid's closet, Tom Thum. I shook my head. Nice of him to leave his wife behind. I took a quick inventory of the people still standing on the pavement and realized that all the New Yorkers except Jackie had made it onto the bus, and most of the Iowans hadn't. This was one of the drawbacks of living in a state without a highly developed system of public transportation. You never learn how to shove people out of the way when you're trying to board a vehicle with limited capacity.

Ashley hobbled onto the step well of the bus and

maneuvered herself around on her crutches to deliver a few last-minute instructions. "The shuttle runs every fifteen or twenty minutes, so the rest of y'all can either wait here for the next bus, or stroll down to the shore at your own pace. I see Emily's here with y'all, so if you have any problems, you just give her a holler." She flashed me a syrupy smile before hopping up the stairs, aided by a swarm of men who all but body-passed her to the front seat. The door hissed shut. As the bus pulled forward, I regarded the tangle of bodies squished together in the narrow space and nearly swallowed my tongue when I saw an unexpected face profiled in the window of the very last seat.

Michael Malooley? What was *he* doing in there? Bus drivers never took the tour with the guests. They always hung out in the nearest café with the other bus drivers so they could drink coffee and tell bus driver stories. Pinpricks of unease rode my spine. I didn't like this one bit. Michael and Ira had to have something heinous planned, and I figured Gladys was the target. Ira Kuppelman wouldn't be the first well-to-do senior to want to knock off his wife. He looked good enough to attract younger women. That had to be the scheme. Get rid of Gladys in favor of a younger, prettier trophy wife. Gladys probably didn't have a clue what was in the works, which meant that by the time the shuttle returned to pick us up, she could already be dead. I needed to warn her, and I needed to do it fast.

I stuck my pinkies in my mouth and let out an earsplitting whistle. Chatter ceased. Bodies wheeled around. I waved my hand above my head so everyone could locate me, then raised my voice so I could be heard. "I don't know about the rest of you, but I think we can make better use of our time than to stand around here for twenty minutes waiting for a bus. We could all use the exercise after that meal last night. I say we walk. Are you game?"

"I'm not game," said Jackie. "How far a walk is it? I'm not wearing the right shoes and I already have a blister on my foot from yesterday."

"I'm game," said Nana. "We've sat on buses long enough as it is."

Alice Tjarks nodded. "I agree with Marion. Besides, that shuttle will need to be aired out before anyone boards it again. Did you see?" She lowered her voice. "Our bus driver is on it."

"All those in favor of walking say, 'Yea,'" Osmond Chelsvig instructed. Osmond had served as the president of Windsor City's electoral board for decades, so he was a natural to call for votes, though with his hearing loss, I feared we might be facing a lot of recounts. "Opposed, say, 'Nay,'" he continued.

"Nay," shouted Jackie.

"By my count we have a bunch of yeas and no nays, so the yeas have it. We walk."

Jackie thrust her hand into the air. "Wait a minute. I said nay!"

"Give it a rest," I advised. "You're outnumbered."

"My vote was properly cast. It shouldn't be discounted on someone's whim. That's only supposed to happen in presidential elections."

"Maybe we should line up according to height," Tilly Hovick suggested, directing people with her walking stick. "Short people in the front, tall people in the back." I suspected Tilly might have taught kindergarten before she hit the college circuit, but I noticed confusion in the ranks as people stood shoulder to shoulder, trying to decide who was taller. Everyone had shrunk to about the same height.

Uh-oh. We might never get out of here if a few people demanded to have measurements taken.

"Tell you what," I called out. "Just start walking. You don't have to be in any kind of order." Tilly shot me a disapproving look, then shook her head in a way that suggested if mass chaos broke out, *she* would not be held liable. Jackie let out an exaggerated sigh beside me.

"Well, I'm not doing any more walking. I walked enough yesterday. I'm staying put and waiting for the next bus."

I shrugged. "Suit yourself. I'll see you down there."

She sucked in her breath. "What? You're going to go off and leave me?"

"Come on, dear," Nana shouted to me. "You don't wanna be left behind."

"Duty calls." I waved my forefinger at Jackie in farewell and caught up with Nana and Tilly as they began the downhill march to the shore. We fell in line at the back of the group, soaking in sights that were completely alien to the Iowa landscape. A mountainous slope of lichen-encrusted rock flanked us on the right, while to our left, a wide border of scorched yellow grass skirted an endless span of shoreline where rocks were strewn helter-skelter, seaweed blackened even the palest stone, and the midnight blue waters of the North Atlantic churned up foam as thick as the froth on a pint of Guinness. The waves made a whooshing sound as they rushed onto shore, and I found their soothing, steady rhythm rather hypnotic. The locals probably had some secret way of determining whether the tide was coming in or going out, but I'd have to live around the ocean for a long time before I'd ever be able to figure it out. The sea certainly inspired romantic notions, but for overall practicality, the Tidal Wave at the water park a few towns over from Windsor City suited me just fine.

I threaded my arm through Nana's, like a hitchhiker

catching a ride on a speeding train. "How many days a week does your exercise class meet?" I asked, breathless from trying to keep up.

"Three days a week usually, but I opted for the accelerated class, so we meet every day except weekends."

"Great," I panted, feeling a stitch in my side. I wondered if Nana's class was open to nonseniors.

A gull circled above us and let out a whining shriek as it glided on a downdraft. I wondered if gulls always shrieked like that, or if this was its gut reaction to Nana's new hairdo.

"I found some information about the castle for you, dear. Just like you asked. I woulda had it sooner, but that power outage last night messed me up. You're right to be suspicious about the place. Either Ballybantry is home to one mean ghost, or there's an awful lot a sick people takin' vacations in Ireland when they should be in hospitals back home. Folks are dyin' left and right in that place, Emily. Mostly since the renovations were done."

"The extensive redecorating inside the castle may have angered one of the ghosts in residence," said Tilly. "Or worse yet, it may have disturbed a supernatural presence that had lain dormant for centuries and released it into the world. Either way, the cluster of deaths at Ballybantry Castle is far too great to deem it a natural occurrence. It's statistically impossible for that many people from different parts of the world to die from heart disease at one chance location."

"Is that how the deaths were explained?" I asked.

Nana took up the story. "The village paper printed notices of the deaths. They were all members of various tour groups, all in their seventies and eighties. Most a the write-ups said that the deceased had probably suffered a heart attack. I guess if you're eighty years old and you drop dead suddenly, people always think it's your heart. But there wasn't no mention of the police doin' any more investigatin'."

"How many deaths have there been?" I asked.

"Forty-eight," said Nana. "Over two years."

"FORTY-EIGHT?" My God, the Irish might have a lack of curiosity, but you'd think that forty-eight deaths in one small castle might raise the eyebrows of *someone* in law enforcement. Or was the castle simply located in too remote an area to raise any blips on the radar screen?

"I found some death notices when the castle was a bed-and-breakfast," Nana continued, "but only one or two over a period of some twenty years."

"That's more consistent with statistical probability," Tilly added. "Tell her about the exorcism, Marion."

"Oh, yeah. Back in 1832 the owners of the castle sought out the local village priest to perform an exorcism. They complained of wanderin' spirits who slammed doors, cried in the night, left footprints on the floor, and were a general nuisance. So the priest performed the exorcism and blessed the castle, and everything seemed pretty peaceful for over a hundred and sixty years."

"Until the remodeling project," I offered. We were narrowing the field, but I still had lots of unanswered questions. "A board of American investors share part ownership of the castle. Did you happen to find out the names of any of the board members?"

"I didn't run across no information about a board of investors, dear. If you like, I'll check when we get back."

"Were you able to find out anything about the Englishman who was the original owner of the castle?" I asked. "I'm pretty sure there's a portrait of him and his children hanging in my room. And the children all share a really peculiar trait. Their toes are stuck together."

"No kiddin'," said Nana.

"Syndactyly," said Tilly.

"Sin-*what?*" I asked.

"Syndactyly," Tilly repeated. "It's a birth defect in which two or more fingers or toes are fused together, either with partial or total webbing. If I recall the statistics, the condition occurs one in every three thousand live births in the United States. Fusion of the third and fourth digits of the hands is most common. Fusion of the toes is more rare, but I can't be specific about how rare. And it doesn't happen out of the blue. The condition is an inherited trait, passed on from one generation to the next in a family bloodline."

"So if Ballybantry's original owners showed signs of the defect back in the sixteen hundreds, their descendants would still exhibit the defect today?"

"Not all of them, of course. The condition seems to manifest itself randomly within families, but yes, the defect would certainly exist. Though it would have been impossible for the family who originally built Ballybantry to have passed the trait on."

"WHAT?" I screeched to a grinding halt, nearly tearing Nana's arm out of its socket as she continued forward. "Why couldn't they have passed the trait on?"

Tilly paused in the middle of the roadway and turned around to face us. "You haven't finished your story, Marion. Go ahead. Tell her what you found."

Nana rubbed her shoulder protectively. "I enjoy walkin' with you, dear, but these quick stops are murder on my joints. All right, then. The rest a the story. The man who built the castle was an English lord by the name a Ticklepenny. He had three children. We know one daughter died tragically after he disowned her, and he didn't have a day a luck after that. His wife and two remaining children fell victim to a fever some months later, and they died within days of each other, so with no family to keep him here, he abandoned the castle and moved back to England, where he pretty much became a recluse. He didn't have no other relatives. He was last in the line a Ticklepennys, so when he died, the family name died with him."

"How did you find all that out?" I asked in amazement.

"You can find anything on the Internet, dear, so long's you know where to look."

"So you see, Emily," Tilly recapped, "it would have been impossible for the Ticklepennys to pass on their congenital anomaly because, unfortunately, with the death of the children, the entire bloodline was wiped out."

My mind was working at warp speed. "What about his wife? Could she have been the one to carry the gene? Could she have had siblings who passed on the condition?"

Nana shook her head. "There wasn't no good information about her on-line, except that she was the only child a Lord and Lady Pluckrose a County Sussex, England."

"She was an only child?" Drat. So if it wasn't a Ticklepenny or Pluckrose ancestor who was making the bloody footprints in the castle, who *was* making them? Why couldn't I connect any of the dots? Why wasn't any of this making sense?

As we broke into a near run to catch up with the rest of the group, the terrain grew more dramatic. In the distance, set against the blue of a cloudless sky, a plateau of sheer rock rose hundreds of feet into the air, then sloped toward the sea in uneven terraces that were as jagged as sharks' teeth. Horizontal bands of red rock striated the cliff and looked like open wounds slashed into the stone.

Tilly pointed to the cliff with her walking stick. "You see that bright ochre color in the stone? The rock here has a high iron content. That's why it's red. And if you look very closely, you can make out a single column of rock on the first terrace below the plateau. That's known as the 'chimney stack.' "

I squinted at the column in question. It looked like another Cromwellian ruin to me.

"If you don't mind, I'm going to hurry ahead and tell the others. They might not have noticed." Off she went at double-time, leaving us in the dust. I stared after her.

"Is Tilly in your exercise class too?"

Nana shook her head. "She gets a real good pension from the university, so she hired a personal trainer."

"And how does she know so much about this place if she's never been here before?"

Nana unzipped her fanny pack and pulled out a cream-colored pamphlet. "She read the brochure. Maybe you didn't get one. They were in a plastic dispenser on the wall in the visitors' center. You wanna borrow mine?"

I hesitated as a sound echoed out from behind us. *Clop-clop. Clop-clop. Clop-clop.* I scooted Nana toward the shoulder of the road and whirled around, expecting to see a horse galloping toward us, but it wasn't a horse.

"Wait up!" Jackie ran awkwardly toward us in her wedges with the high wooden heels. "It's no fun waiting up there all by myself!"

"However do you run in those shoes, dear?" Nana asked when she caught up to us.

Jackie bent over at the waist, clutched her side, and sucked in air. "These are nothing," she gasped. "Good thing I didn't wear my two-band leather stilettos. Those would have been a real bitch."

We waited long enough for her to catch her breath, then took off down the road again. "We're really laggin' behind," Nana fretted. "By the time we get to the causeway, it'll be time to head back. I hope George takes good pictures. That might be the only way I'll get to see anything."

"How was George able to maneuver his way onto the bus when the rest of you couldn't?" I inquired.

"The bus driver made a special concession for him 'cause of his leg. It was painin' him some today."

I recalled George's leg aching last year in Switzerland too. "The pain has something to do with barometric conditions, doesn't it?"

"I suspect it has more to do with all the cloggin' he done last night."

"George was clogging? With his prosthetic leg?"

"He's very agile and light on his feet, dear, even with the prosthesis. When the dance captain asked for volunteers, George was the first one up there. Him and Bernice. His steel-toed boots worked out real good for cloggin'. He mighta danced all night if the power hadn't went out. He told me later he mighta had a career in competitive dancin' if his leg hadn't got blown off in the war. He done real good up there with the pros. And you know, Emily, I never noticed before, but George has one fine heinie on him. All the ladies were commentin'. The bubble-butts get all the praise, but I'll take a tomato-butt like George's any day." She locked her hands about a foot apart in the air. "I like somethin' substantial to grab on to."

Oh, God. Was this normal? Did other people's grandmothers discuss men's heinies with such enthusiasm? Maybe I should check out what she was reading these days. Whatever it was, I bet it wasn't on the Legion of Mary's ten hot picks for summer. "So how did Bernice do?" I asked in a quick change of subject.

"She done good until the power failed. She lost her balance in the dark and butted heads with the dance captain. Knocked him out cold. And it didn't help none that the other dancers ran into each other and accidentally stomped on his face."

Jackie smacked my arm. "You see? I told you that could happen."

"Bernice wasn't hurt, was she?"

"She's fine, dear. Bernice's head is like a rock."

Far ahead of us, at the foot of the great stone plateau, where the rock had eroded to lesser heights, a rugged spit of land knifed into the sea, its choppy terrain visible even from where we were. "That has to be the causeway," I said by pure deduction. Not only did the road terminate at that point, but the blue shuttle bus was parked there and loading up passengers.

"You s'pose I could ask you girls' opinion about somethin' before we join the others?" Nana asked somewhat reluctantly.

"I love rendering my opinion," gushed Jackie, abandoning my side to tag along beside Nana. "Fire away."

"It's about George." Nana sighed. "I think I'm losin' him to Tilly."

"No," I soothed, curling my arm around her shoulders to lend moral support. "What makes you say that?"

"Men like hot babes, Emily. I'm not hot anymore."

"And Tilly is?" I questioned.

Jackie made a *pshaw* sound. "Shoot, Mrs. S., you're a lot hotter than she is. If I were a guy, which, of course, I'm not, but if I *was*, or ever had been, you'd be the babe for me."

I shot Jackie a nervous look over Nana's head. Okay. Other than showcasing the fact that she was pretty rusty with the subjunctive mood, she hadn't given anything away. Had she?

"Emily's husband used to call me Mrs. S.," Nana reminisced fondly. "He was such a nice young man. Handsome too. You ever hear from him, Emily? I wonder what he's doin' these days."

Jackie looped her arm through Nana's. "You thought he was handsome?" she prodded, seemingly delighted. "How handsome?"

"Real handsome. Emily's grampa told me he thought Jack Potter was too pretty to be a boy."

Grampa Sippel had always been a bit psychic.

"Really?" Jackie preened, giving me a disgusted look. "I wonder why Emily never bothered to tell that to Jack? An actor's ego can always use a boost."

I rolled my eyes. "Do you mind? We're discussing someone else's problem at the moment. Go ahead, Nana."

Nana's mouth drooped in discouragement. "It hurts to admit, dear, but when you stack me up against Tilly, I come out lookin' pretty pathetic. She's everything I wish I. was. Taller. Smarter. She's got her own teeth."

"She is not smarter," I protested.

"She uses bigger words. That makes her sound smarter."

"You could buy a thesaurus," Jackie suggested.

"Tilly looks like Cindy Crawford," Nana sulked. "I look like that singer who lives on Long Island."

Since I hadn't I clue who that was, I made a wild guess. "Jennifer Lopez?"

Nana shook her head. "I think his name is Billy Joel."

"You do not look like Billy Joel!" I balked. "You look like"—I stared down at her, trying to come up with a complimentary example of another person who sported three chins, Howdy Doody ears, and the hair from hell—"like . . . a Boyd's Bear. A sweet-faced, huggable Boyd's Bear."

"Men don't want their women to look like stuffed animals," Jackie argued. "They want them to look like Barbie dolls."

"In New York, perhaps." I gave Jackie the eye and

snarled silently at her. "Men in the Midwest have a different value system."

"What a crock," said Jackie. "Listen to me, Mrs. S. Men are men. If you want to snare this George, there's only one way to do it."

"Give it to me straight," Nana pleaded. "That's why I asked."

"Naughty lingerie," Jackie announced. "Parade past him in a satin thong, and he'll follow you anywhere."

Nana looked crestfallen. "My bum's not my best feature. It slid down to my knees some years back. You think that'll be a turnoff?"

"If he has cataracts, he might not notice," Jackie said optimistically.

"He got 'em removed."

"Okay, a see-through bra then. Picture this. A nylon cup. Light underwire. Front closure so he doesn't have to fumble with hooks and eyes at the back. Those can be such a nuisance, especially if a guy is older and has arthritic joints."

This idea seemed to perk Nana up a bit. "I tried on one a them sheer lace brassieres at the Victoria's Secret in Ames, but it didn't give me no support. I need underwire that's industrial strength. The salesgirl was real sweet, though, and she worked on commission, so I ended up buyin' one a them lacy cleavage-enhancin' Miracle brassieres with what they call Liquid Lift."

"That's fabulous," Jackie cooed. "I have one of those, too. George will love it. One small word of caution, though. Avoid contact with sharp objects. I punctured my left cup with a toothpick at a party one night and spent the rest of the evening lopsided. Did you bring along something low and plunging to show off your décolletage?"

"Sure did."

Jackie clapped her hands with excitement. "Tell me what."

"My Minnesota Vikin's sweatshirt."

Jackie arched an eyebrow. "You might want to think about something a little more daring. A scoop-necked tank top. A V-necked blouse. You need to wear something with a neckline that *reveals* your assets."

"My sweatshirt reveals enough. When I strap that brassiere on, my assets get hiked to my chin."

"Would you take a minute to listen to yourselves talk?" I scolded. "Women do *not* have to be sex kittens these days to attract a man's attention."

"Maybe not, dear, but it can't hurt none."

"I can't believe this!" I fussed. "What happened to the concept that everyone drilled into my head when I was growing up? 'If you want to catch a man, just be yourself.'"

"Who taught you that, dear?"

"You did!"

Nana looked stunned. "I did? I'm sorry, Emily. That was an awful misguided thing for me to do."

I rolled my eyes so far back into my head I saw the top of my skull.

"Well, would you look at that," Nana marveled as we approached the causeway. The site was a vast boneyard of twelve-inch-wide upright stone columns that were chimney-stacked against each other like patio tiles in a supplier's warehouse. Some columns had eroded down to nubs, with smooth, flat surfaces. Others were tall as a man, while others reached the height of a two-story house. "I never seen nothin' like it," Nana said. "All these rocks look to have the same shape. They're all six-sided. How'd that happen?"

"Ashley said it was an anomaly of nature," I answered.

"Ashley's an anomaly of nature," Jackie wisecracked.

"Oh, look. There's Tom. If you'll excuse me, ladies, I'm going to wander over and ask him how many old people he had to knock over to get that seat on the shuttle."

Nana staked a claim on a low, squat rock and did a slow three-hundred-sixty-degree rotation. "Check out the rocks at three o'clock," she said, pointing to a sprawling cluster of uneven spires. "They look like skyscrapers in the New York skyline, only smaller. And look at the big clump at high noon. If they was silver, they could pass for the pipes attached to the organ at Holy Redeemer. And would you look at those behind you. They kinda remind me a the little piles a chips on the craps table at the Meskwaki casino."

"You play craps?"

"Don't tell your mother. She don't even like me playin' the one-armed bandits. I don't know about your mother, Emily. I raised her Catholic, but sometimes I think she's got a touch a Southern Baptist in her."

"Marion!" Tilly shouted from a higher elevation, waving her walking stick in the air. "Yoo-hoo! Over here!"

"Be right there!" Nana shouted back. She turned to me. "You don't mind if I abandon you, do you, dear? I gotta make sure Tilly don't hog George."

"You and Tilly would never come to blows over George, would you?" I asked a little anxiously. These rocks would be the perfect place to put someone out of commission.

"Emily! Tilly and me wouldn't let no man spoil our friendship. We like each other too much. But just between you and me, I think I got a slight advantage. I seen her underwear. A hundred percent cotton with maximum coverage. She don't stand a snowball's chance in hell with him."

"Watch your footing!" I called after her, as she charged in Tilly's direction. I spied Ashley not too far from Tilly, rattling off some kind of spiel to a semicircle of listeners

from the tour. I saw other members of the group clustered in little pockets, snapping pictures of each other
against the rocky backdrop of skyscrapers, and organ
pipes, and casino chips. I shielded my eyes and looked
seaward, noting long spines of black rock arched above
the surface of the water like huge humpbacked whales.
Some outcroppings were farther out to sea. Others were
nearer to shore, close enough for a few brave souls to step
across a narrow channel of water and scramble onto
them, climbing like mountain goats onto their barnacle-
encrusted peaks.

The longer I regarded the terrain, the more uneasy I
grew, my own recent thoughts ringing in my ears. *These
rocks would be the perfect place to put someone out of commission.* Oh, my God! Where was Gladys Kuppelman?
Where was Michael Malooley?

I whirled around to check out the group listening to
Ashley. They were clumped too close together for me to
distinguish who was there, so I hurried off in that direction, my feet skimming across the rocks as if they were
stepping-stones in a brook, my mind racing.

If what Tilly had told me about the Ticklepenny family
was true, I was at a huge impasse. No family member could
have passed on the syndactyly trait because they'd all died.
But it was too much of a coincidence that the ghost should
leave footprints with the same genetic defect that the
Ticklepenny children displayed in the portrait. There *had*
to be a connection, yet how was that possible if none of
Lord Ticklepenny's children had survived?

I clambered up a ministaircase of ochre-colored stone,
arriving at the back of the crowd gathered around Ashley.
As I searched for Gladys Kuppelman, Ashley continued
talking in her gooiest Georgia-peach drawl. "Legend has it
that these columns were placed here by the giant Finn

MacCool. He had a ladylove on the island of Staffa in Scotland, so he built this causeway as a way to reach her and not get his feet wet. Interestingly enough, the only other place in the world where y'all will find rock formations like this is on the island of Staffa in Scotland."

I checked out all the heads in the group. No Gladys. No Michael. I headed off in another direction, back toward the road. I'd start there and work my way systematically toward the shoreline.

When I reached the road, I eyed a towering stack of columns to my left and a pathway that curved around it, skirting the base of the plateau. These columns were fractured into horizontal chunks that resembled hundreds of ottomans piled on top of each other. I pitied the poor giant who'd had to construct them. He probably wouldn't have had the energy to visit his ladylove once the causeway was complete, but the idea of a ladylove led me to a sudden, more daring thought.

A man could have many loves in his lifetime, and could father children inside and outside of wedlock. What if Lord Ticklepenny had engaged in an affair with an Irish maid or serving girl while he'd lived in Ireland? Highborn lords did that as a matter of course, didn't they? What if the girl had become pregnant and given birth to Ticklepenny's illegitimate child?

A tingling sensation crawled up my spine. Could that be it? If Ticklepenny was the one carrying the syndactyly gene, was that how the birth defect had been passed down to the present generation? Not through his official bloodline, but through an illegitimate bloodline? Was it a descendant of that illegitimate heir who was leaving bloody footprints at the castle and scaring people to death? That had to be it! Someone was seeking revenge for centuries of being abused, demeaned, and shunned. Someone had his sights on Ballybantry Castle and would apparently do anything to wrest it out of the hands of its present owners in payment for past wrongs. But who was the heir? Ira Kuppelman? Michael Malooley? Could the two of them be related? There was only one sure way to tell. I needed to get their shoes off them; then the truth would be as clear as the little webbed toes on their feet.

"I don't believe these things just happened," I heard Ethel Minch say as she rounded the corner of the towering columns, heading toward me.

"Ashley said they were a natural phenomenon," Gladys Kuppelman said, strolling beside her.

"They're too perfect." Ethel rapped her knuckles on the stone, as if checking to see if they were hollow, or made of Styrofoam. "I think some guy built this whole place so he could call it the eighth wonder of the world and charge people an entrance fee. The whole thing's a scam."

"You don't know what you're talking about," Gladys whined at her. "The place is real. It says so in the brochure." Gladys saw me and motioned for me to join them. "These rocks are real, aren't they, Emily?"

Relieved to see Gladys alive, I jogged over to them. "They sure look real to me." But I thought Cinderella's castle in Disney's Magic Kingdom looked real too, so maybe I wasn't a good judge.

"They're fake," Ethel reiterated. Then to Gladys she said, "The only reason they look real to you is because you don't know the difference between what's real and what's phony anymore."

"What do you mean by that?" Gladys huffed, her bland expression belying the anger in her voice.

"Oh, get off it," Ethel shot back. "Sometimes your innocent routine makes me want to gag."

"Really? Speaking of gagging, when's the last time you

had your hair colored by a professional? I hate to be the one to tell you, but that color went out with the dinosaur."

Uh-oh. "Where'd you leave your husbands?" I jumped in, hoping to avert the squabble that seemed to be brewing.

Ethel tossed her head toward the shore. "They're looking for some rock called the Wishing Chair. If you make a wish while you're sitting in it, it's supposed to come true."

I wondered what a guy like Ernie Minch would wish for. I knew what I'd wish for if I were a bald-headed vegan whose waist started under my armpits. I'd wish for a pound of hamburger.

"Bunch of nonsense," Ethel continued. "I wish my feet would stop hurting, but sitting in some stupid chair isn't going to make it happen."

"So you ladies aren't up for a little frolicking over the rocks like everyone else?"

"Those rocks are a disaster waiting to happen," said Gladys. "You wait and see. Someone's going to fall down and break a leg, or crack his skull, but it's not going to be us, is it, Ethel?"

Ethel shook her head. "We're staying on level ground, but I hope we're not here much longer. Staring at fake rocks is downright boring."

"They are not fake," protested Gladys.

Okay. They were back to where I came in.

I was feeling much better about Gladys's well-being as I returned to the Grand Causeway. If she stayed away from the rocks and remained with Ethel, she'd be safe, unless she made another snide comment about Ethel's hair. Then it could get a little messy. I still wasn't entirely sure that Michael Malooley had been hired to kill her, but maybe my best option would be to find Michael and keep my eye on him. I'd tailed people before on my trip to Switzerland and I'd discovered I was pretty good at it.

I leapfrogged from one level of rock to the next, exchanging pleasantries with other tour members, my gaze ranging in a wide arc in search of Michael Malooley. I whipped out my Canon Elph and snapped a panoramic shot of the waves that seemed to be breaking higher on the shore, a wide-angle shot of the formation that resembled a pipe organ, a classic shot of the New York skyline cast in stone.

Ten minutes passed.

Twenty.

I found the Wishing Chair, a wobbly horizontal stone that tourists used as a primitive rocking chair, and waited my turn to sit down and make a wish. Ira Kuppelman and Ernie Minch had become the official photographers at the site, so they were too preoccupied snapping pictures of the chair's occupants to get into any trouble. After I took my turn and made a simple wish that Etienne and I would be able to spend one quiet evening together, I wandered over every inch of the causeway and finally found Michael leaning against an errant boulder close to the shoreline, smoking a cigarette.

I imagined the wise thing to do would be to hang back, stretch out on a rock, and watch him, but I'd learned something about myself that I hadn't realized before I accepted my escort job. I'm not the "hang back" type.

"Top o' the morning to you," I called out as I approached him. He stared at me through a fog of smoke, neither acknowledging my greeting nor looking happy to be interrupted. "Quite a place you have here!" I stopped in a spot that I prayed was downwind of him.

He scowled at me and blew a mouthful of smoke into the air. "It's not my place, but they tell me you tourists like it well enough."

"It's nice you decided to join us at the site. I mean, usually the bus driver waits at the visitors' center and never gets to see the attraction."

"Does he now?"

"But you're a rookie. Maybe they forgot to tell you the drill."

He took another drag on his cigarette and turned his head away from me to glance out across the North Atlantic. *Geesch,* this guy really did need to kiss the Blarney Stone.

"So . . . if you don't mind my asking, what line of work were you in before you decided to become a bus driver? I used to be in phone solicitation before I became a tour escort."

"Brilliant," he said, throwing his cigarette to the ground and crushing it beneath his heel.

Hmm. This was going well. Maybe I needed to change my strategy. "Do you live close to the ocean?"

"Close enough."

"You probably know all about the tides then. I live in the Midwest, so I don't know diddly about these things. Can you look at the ocean right now and tell if the tide is coming in or going out?"

"It would be comin' in. Be high tide in about"—he checked his watch—"ninety minutes."

"You see? That's what baffles me. How can you tell? What's the secret?"

"Tidal charts. They print them up in the paper every day."

"HEEELLLLLP!" I heard someone yell in the distance. "HELP!"

I spun around, trying to locate the person in trouble. Heads turned. People froze. Fingers pointed toward the water. I looked in the direction they were pointing and visored my hands over my eyes.

"There's yer problem," said Michael Malooley, pushing off from the boulder.

"HEEELLLLLP!" echoed the cry again.

I squinted at a figure waving her hands frantically over her head. She was hunchbacked, wore a paisley scarf, and didn't look to be injured, but the spiny black pinnacle of rock on which she stood was no longer surrounded by dry ground. It was surrounded by water.

Bernice had ignored the incoming tide. Now she was stranded.

CHAPTER 13

"Oh, my God!" I cried at Michael. "How deep is that water?"

"How would I be knowin' that? I've never been here before."

I did a quick double take. "The eighth wonder of the world and you've never been here before?" I held up my hand. "Let me guess. No curiosity about the place. Right?"

He shrugged his beefy shoulders.

I riveted my gaze back at Bernice, trapped on her little barnacle-encrusted island. I stared at the rough, foamy water enveloping the rock, the tangled clumps of seaweed floating in the water, the kite tails of kelp whipping around in the surf. Great. This was just great. I cupped my hands around my mouth and yelled, "Hold on, Bernice! Someone will be right out to help you!"

"Hurry!" she yelled back. "I can't swim!"

Like that was a surprise. Footsteps stampeded behind me. Gasps. Wheezing. "Is that Bernice?" panted Osmond Chelsvig.

"It sure is," choked out Alice Tjarks. "I can tell 'cause she's wearing my scarf. MIND MY SCARF!" she bellowed at Bernice. "IT'S SILK!"

"What's that water doing there anyway?" Osmond puzzled. "It wasn't there before." Observations like this are common among Midwesterners who are only acquainted with nontidal bodies of water, like town drinking reservoirs.

Tour members scuttled toward us. George Farkas and Nana and Tilly. Ira Kuppelman. Ernie Minch. Tom Thum. Ashley hobbled over the rocks on her crutches, her face pinched like a California raisin. Either she was really ticked off, or she was definitely showing signs of premature aging. Probably from sneaking too many smokes. Michael reached into his pocket for another cigarette and stuck it between his lips. "Whoever's in charge, you'd best be fetchin' the old girl back before the tide carries her away," he said matter-of-factly.

I looked at Ashley. Ashley looked at me. "She's all yours, sugar," Ashley drawled. She regarded her cast sympathetically. "I'm not dressed for the occasion."

Oh, sure. And I was? I was wearing flared leather jeans, a cashmere sweater with an angora cowl, and square-toed harness boots—none of which would be enhanced in appearance by a dip in the Atlantic.

"SAVE ME!" cried Bernice.

Nuts. I sank down onto the nearest rock, yanked off one boot, then the other. I peeled off my trouser socks and tossed them into my boots. I marked my watch. I'd bought it new before leaving Iowa. Guaranteed to withstand water pressure up to two hundred meters. No amount of water was going to ruin this baby. It was called a dive watch. I gave it an affectionate pat. I'd learned at least *one* lesson in Switzerland last year.

I stood up with reluctance, grimacing at the undulating strands of seaweed and kelp littering the surface of the water. Yuck! I once saw a movie where the heroine got entangled in seaweed like that and drowned. That wouldn't happen to me, would it?

Gooseflesh pricked my skin. I wondered if I had time to run back to the Wishing Chair.

"Hey, doll," yelled Ernie Minch. "I hope you're not gonna get those slacks of yours wet. Salt water does a real number on shoe leather. I can't even begin to tell you what it'll do to pant leather. It's too painful."

I looked down lovingly at my two-hundred-dollar jeans. I needed to write a memo to remind myself that . . . I HATE THIS JOB!

"Better take 'em off," Ernie urged. "You probably dropped a couple of C-notes for 'em. You gotta think about protecting your investment."

"But there's no time!" Nana sounded panicky. "Bernice is about to drown."

Ira Kuppelman checked his watch. "High tide's at noon. If she doesn't lose her footing, she's good for another ninety minutes." Ira must have read the morning paper.

"That gives you plenty of time to lose the slacks," coaxed Ernie. He raised his camera to his eye and poised his finger on the shutter button.

"I am *not* taking my clothes off!"

"I can help with the rescue," George Farkas offered, limping toward me.

I flashed him a grateful smile. He was sweet to offer, but with those steel-toed boots of his, he was liable to sink faster than the Dow Jones in a bear market.

"Thanks, George, but—"

"The ocean's got an undertow. I learned all about it in

the war. So I'll try and hold on to you when you wade out there so the undertow won't grab on to you and sweep you out to sea."

Undertow? I'd read my *Escort's Manual* from cover to cover. Never once had it mentioned the word *undertow*. I wondered if this would turn out to be a critical oversight.

We heard a deep roar heaving up from the bowels of the earth, then felt the rocks beneath us vibrate as a towering breaker crashed against the shore, raining spume and seawater high into the air. I shot a quick look at Bernice. She was no longer standing but was flat on her butt, soaked to the skin, with her turban plastered against her face like a roll of prepasted wallpaper. "EHHHH!" she screamed, flailing blindly. Clawing the scarf off her face, she lunged sideways and anchored herself to a narrow column of rock, clinging to it for dear life.

I gulped. I winced at the seaweed. I winced at the thought of an undertow. Lake Lucerne in Switzerland was one thing; the ocean was a whole other matter. I felt my knees wobble. I considered George's offer. I got an idea. "George is right!" I said in a quick rush of breath. "Maybe we could form a human chain—you know, everyone holding on to everyone else, so no one"—specifically me— "will get swept away by the undertow."

"Like a conga line," said Nana. "I like conga lines. Only the last time I was in one, I wasn't in such good shape, and I threw my back out."

"I like the Chicken Dance myself," said George. "Too bad we only get to do it at wedding receptions."

"I tried teaching the Chicken Dance to a group of Polar Eskimos decades ago," Tilly recalled. "They did remarkably well, considering none of them had ever seen a chicken before."

Alice Tjarks marched to the front of the crowd. "The line forms behind me."

"I hope y'all signed your release forms!" Ashley sniped as the little group fell into line behind Alice. "If any of y'all gets hurt, Golden Irish Vacations will not be held responsible. That means, you can't sue! You got that? We are not liable!"

I was happy to see Ashley so concerned about the welfare of the tour guests.

"If you're wearin' good shoes, take 'em off," barked Ernie as he untied his shoestrings. "Letting the salt water at 'em is the same as introducing 'em to cancer."

"We have to go barefoot?" asked Osmond. "I'm not sure that's the best thing for my corns."

Barefoot? I almost leaped with excitement. What a brilliant idea! Ernie Minch may just have put this mystery in the can for me. "Ernie has a point!" I reiterated. "Don't take a chance with your good footwear. Get rid of your shoes and socks."

I watched Ira Kuppelman wiggle his feet out of his Bass Weejuns. Hot damn! This was almost too good to be true. Now, if I could just get a closer look. Jackie's husband stood apart from the crowd, watching the shoe-shedding activity like *The Lion King* observing his minions. "You're not joining us?" I questioned.

"Crabs," he said.

I wasn't sure whether this was his opinion of the people in the group or if he was confessing to a personal hygiene problem. "Excuse me?"

"There are crabs in the water. I'm not about to lose a finger to a crustacean. My hands are my livelihood." He sheltered one hand in a protective gesture against his chest. "I'm sure you can understand why I don't dare take any chances."

I rolled my eyes and turned to Michael, who was puffing nonchalantly on his cigarette, looking aloof and detached. I clapped my hands at him. "Let's move it. Chop-chop," I said, salivating over his shoestrings. "We could use a hand from you too."

His already florid complexion grew redder. "Bugger off."

Okay. I was really sorry his ancestors had been abused, demeaned, and shunned, but that was no excuse for bad manners. "Maybe you need some help," I said, squatting down and pulling on his shoestrings.

"WHAT ARE YOU WAITING FOR!" cried Bernice. "HELP ME! THIS ISN'T GOING TO LOOK GOOD ON YOUR EVALUATION, EMILY!"

Clop-clop. Clop-clop. Clop-clop. "Stay where you are!" someone's voice echoed in the distance. I looked up to find Jackie racing pell-mell across the rocks from the direction of the Wishing Chair, hair flying, arms pumping, shoes clacking, dress hiked up to her hips. "I'll save her!" She stumbled slightly on some loose stones, hopped one-footed, kicked off her shoes, then charged toward us like the human version of Road Runner. "Don't worry about me!" she yelled, as she bounded past. "I was a member of my high school swim team!" Displaying an uncanny amount of athletic grace, she *jetéd* over a tidal pool, *pirouetted* onto a flat shelf of rock, *relevéd* to her toes, then—

KERPLUNK!

I knew about the swim team, but she'd kept the ballet lessons a real secret. Wow. She could execute some great moves.

Michael tapped his foot against my hand. "Seein' as how Sheena has come to the rescue, I'll be thankin' you to tie my lacin's back up now."

My fingers froze on his shoestrings. But . . . but . . . I was so close! This wasn't fair! I pouted at the secrets that would remain hidden in Michael's shoes before lifting my eyes to squint fiercely at Jack. That did it. I didn't care how expensive his surgery had been or how short a time he'd had to enjoy it. I was going to kill him. I was freaking going to *kill* him.

"This here's a picture of Jackie climbin' outta the water after the big rescue," Nana explained, handing the snapshot to Etienne later that evening. We were huddled together on one of the plush sofas in the lobby area, Nana and I on either side of Etienne and Tilly seated on a chair opposite us. "That thing danglin' from her left shoulder is kelp. The thing danglin' from her other shoulder is Bernice."

It was seven forty-five, and we were waiting for the dining room to open. We'd been informed earlier that dinner would be delayed this evening because of the massive cleanup the kitchen staff had had to undertake after the food fight this morning. I was actually enjoying the wait. I was using the time to chill out with Etienne and talk myself out of coldcocking my ex-husband.

"There's something real deceivin' about that Jackie," Nana continued. "She might look real feminine, but I mean to tell you, she's strong as an ox. Girls today aren't delicate like they used to be when I was growin' up. Must be all the vitamins they pump into young people these days."

I raised my eyes heavenward and tried not to bite my tongue in half. Etienne studied the photo. "I assume Bernice wasn't paying attention to the tide and found herself stranded?"

"Yup. But it wasn't her fault on account a the only tide we got in Iowa comes in a plastic container." She handed him another photo. "This here's Bernice shakin' the water off herself. She coulda used a towel, but the closest thing we had to a towel was George's handkerchief, and that turned out to be way too small. But at least it was clean."

Etienne lifted the photo closer to his face. "Did she seek medical attention? It looks as if she sustained major trauma to her head."

Nana leaned over for a better look. "That's just her new hairdo. It don't look too good wet." She passed him the next photo. "I really like this one. This is where everyone started clappin' for Jackie and congratulatin' her on savin' Bernice's life. That Jackie was sure eatin' up all the attention. Lookit the smile on her face." Nana jabbed her forefinger at a far corner of the photo. "Ashley don't look too happy here 'cause she was havin' to hold herself up on her crutches and couldn't join in the applause. See how disappointed she looks?"

Oh, please! "May I see that photo?" I asked, curious. Etienne handed it to me. I scrutinized Ashley's tiny image. Disappointed? Huh! That look on Ashley's face wasn't disappointment. It was hostility, and it was being directed at Jackie. I guess ole Ashley wasn't real thrilled about having to share the limelight. She looked as if she'd like to cold-cock Jack too.

"This last one's got some real good color," Nana said as she placed the final photo into Etienne's hands. I glanced sidelong at a glossy print bright with a powder blue sky, cottonball clouds, slick black rocks, marine blue surf, and a streak of crimson snaking through the water.

"What's this?" asked Etienne, pointing to the streak. "Red kelp?"

"Alice's scarf. I don't know if you can tell there, but it was real silk."

Etienne smiled. "Exceptional photos, Mrs. Sippel." He handed the prints back. "I obviously missed out on quite an exciting day. How is Bernice handling the stress of the incident?"

"She went shopping," Tilly piped up.

I stiffened. Shopping?

Tilly continued in her professor's voice. "A number of university studies have proven that in times of stress, an average woman can relieve more tension by visiting a mall than by taking tranquilizers."

Not if the merchants wouldn't accept her money. Uh-oh. I felt my stomach do a loop-the-loop. This could spell trouble. "Do you happen to know where she went shopping?" I asked nervously.

"Londonderry," said Tilly.

I exhaled the breath I'd been holding. Northern Ireland. Thank God. Her provincial money would be good there.

"But shoppin' wasn't Bernice's idea," Nana informed us. "When Alice found out dinner was gonna be late, she told Bernice the two of 'em was gonna take a cab into Derry so's Bernice could buy her a replacement scarf. They're still not back yet. Paisley's hard to find anymore."

"How long have they been gone?" I asked, concerned. I'd fallen into bed when we got back from the causeway, trying to catch up on some of the sleep I'd lost the night before.

"Four hours," said Nana. "That don't surprise me, though. After they get the scarf, Bernice needs to find a new camera to replace the one that washed away when she got knocked on her beam today. That could take a while. Bernice might not dress too good, but she's real picky when it comes to camera equipment."

I sensed a shift of energy in the room as Osmond Chelsvig got up from his chair and headed toward the dining room. He'd started a buzz. Voices rose. Feet shifted. Ethel Minch popped up. Then Ernie. Then the whole lobby came to life as everyone joined in the usual mad dash.

"Dining room must be open," said Nana, catapulting

herself to her feet. "C'mon, Tilly. Sorry, dear." She blew me a kiss. "Gotta run before all the good seats are taken. You want we should save you each a place?"

"Sure," I called at her retreating back. In the space of ten seconds, the guests were gone and the lobby was empty. I nuzzled against Etienne, resting my head on his shoulder. He kissed my forehead and laughed.

"Your grandmother displays amazing stamina for a woman of her advanced years. What's her secret?"

"Senior aerobics. She's in the accelerated class." I inched my arm around his waist, enjoying the quiet bliss of the moment. "Tell me your day was better than mine."

"It was rather a mixed bag. I conducted my interviews but discovered nothing of consequence. I stopped at the Garda Station again to urge them to contact a forensics expert about the bloody footprints, but a big brute of an officer by the name of O'Conor told me to bugger off."

I wondered if *bugger* was the Irish equivalent of *uff da*. It sure was a popular expression over here. "O'Conor. Isn't that the desk clerk's last name?"

"The officer is her brother. If I had to guess, I'd say they're twins. And since there were no police cars in the parking lot when I arrived back at the castle this evening, I would venture your grandmother didn't turn up any more dead bodies in her room today."

"There's always tonight," I said, not trusting the status quo.

"It doesn't matter what happens tonight, darling. It will be of no concern to you." He found the lobe of my ear and stroked it softly with his thumb. "You'll be otherwise engaged."

A tingling sensation arrowed down to my toes. I liked the sound of this. Could that Wishing Chair really work? Nuts. Maybe I should have included an addendum about an open date for the Knights of Columbus hall. Hindsight was always twenty-twenty.

"Are you ready for dinner?" he whispered against my hair.

I had a better idea. "If we skipped dinner, we could toodle down to my room and get a head start on the evening."

"In the interest of our continuing investigation, I'd like to sit down with some of the guests this evening to see if I can tease any information out of them. A relaxed setting, a little food, a little drink—even the most recalcitrant of people can be forthcoming."

Despite my eagerness to cut to the chase, I could see merit in his suggestion. He was the crime expert. Who knew what would happen if he had a chance to strut his stuff? "All right," I conceded. "But I'll warn you ahead of time, these people are hard nuts to crack. All I've come up with is goose eggs." As I started to detach myself from him, I thought about the footprints I'd found in the dungeon last night and wondered if he'd thought to pick up the flashlight and skeleton key I'd asked for earlier. "Did you happen to run across a hardware store in your travels today?"

He snapped his fingers. "I nearly forgot. I didn't have any luck at the hardware store, but I believe I found just the thing at a craftsworks gallery two villages over." He removed two small packages from the inside pockets of his sportcoat, freed them from their tissue paper wrapping, and set them on my lap.

I looked down at a paperweight and a dog. The paperweight was the size of a bagel with a series of triangular kites in bright jelly-bean colors floating in the center of the crystal. The dog was a shaggy little porcelain terrier who stood about two inches high, was attached to a wooden base, and carried a shamrock in his mouth. They were lovely, but terribly impractical. I wouldn't dare use them for breaking and entering, especially if the paperweight was Waterford.

"A paperweight and a dog," I mumbled, confused. *Hmm.* Okay. Maybe the paperweight lit up. Maybe the terrier's tail doubled as a key!

Etienne seemed confused by my confusion. "Isn't this what you asked me to pick up for you this morning? A glass kite and a Westie?"

"Umm . . . not exactly. But you were close. I asked you to pick up a flashlight and a skeleton key."

As far back as the days of the caveman, women have accused men of not listening to them. A recent study explained why. A man listens with only half his brain. That's because the other half is too crammed with thoughts of sex, money, football, beer, and maintaining possession of the remote control to absorb any new information.

"I'm sorry, Emily. I misheard. The taxi . . . the engine . . . Vehicles are much quieter in Switzerland."

"No problem." The study further indicated that this erosion of listening skills only occurred in married men. Etienne had been married once, so I guess he'd already suffered partial damage. "I'm going to be otherwise engaged tonight anyway," I assured him. "Why would I need a flashlight and a skeleton key?"

When we entered the Great Hall, I noted the configuration of the dining tables had changed. Instead of dozens of separate tables, arranged in random order around the room, the staff had pushed all the tables together in an E pattern, with chairs situated on all sides. And the buffet tables were empty. I guess this meant we were being served our meal tonight, and if any rowdiness broke out, we'd be confined in a small space rather than spread out all over

the room. All the better to deal with the uprising. Good thinking.

I scoped out the diners, apprising Etienne of a few odds and ends as we made our way to the seats Nana had saved for us. "I caught Ira Kuppelman in a private discussion with Michael Malooley this morning. A paper passed hands. Instructions? Money? Who knows. It's very suspicious. Something is definitely going on there. But at least Gladys made it through the day so far. Ira might be trying to knock her off, but I still don't see how that relates to our ghost. And I think the Englishman who built the castle fathered an illegitimate child whose present-day descendants might have reason to haunt the place, but I don't have anything concrete to go on yet. I don't see Michael here tonight. That's not a good sign. I bet he's in the dungeon. I bet he— Hi, Nana. Thanks for saving us a place."

She'd reserved two chairs for us in the middle of the E, at the junction of where the short, center table right-angled with the long, outer table. Etienne pulled out the corner chair for me, then seated himself beside me. "I'm glad you came along when you did," Nana confessed. "I didn't know how much longer I could hold those chairs. They're in a real prime spot."

People surrounded us at every compass point. Nana and Tilly were seated opposite us at the short table. To Etienne's right sat the Minches. Opposite them, on Tilly's left, were the Kuppelmans. To my left, on the outer side of the long table, were Jackie and Tom. Behind me sat Osmond Chelsvig. Behind Nana sat George Farkas. We were packed in tighter than sardines. If anyone moved, he'd bump into himself. But it wasn't the close quarters I was worried about. It was the group dynamic. With Jack on my left and Etienne on my right, I feared I was one step away from disaster.

"You dried out pretty good," Ernie Minch called down to Jackie. "That was a real heroic thing you did today."

Jackie shrugged modestly. "It was nothing. My outfit was wash 'n' wear, so it wasn't a big deal. Besides, I bet all of you have done things in your lives that were a lot more heroic than plucking an old woman from the jaws of imminent death."

A thoughtful pause traveled around the table. "I never done nothin' heroic like savin' someone from drownin'," Nana offered. "Mostly on account of I can't swim."

Tilly chimed in next. "When I was doing field work in the Amazon fresh out of grad school, I lopped the head off an anaconda who was crushing my guide to death. Of course, in subsequent years I've come to think that what I did was based more on survival than heroics. Without a guide, I never would have found my way out of the jungle."

"And you never woulda seen the *real* survival show on CBS." Nana gasped her horror. "Think what you woulda missed."

"I once took a taxi ride with a cabbie who didn't speak English," Ethel volunteered. "I thought that was pretty heroic. I didn't know if I'd ever get to the place I wanted to go."

"That surprises me," Etienne said to her. "I've discovered that cabdrivers in foreign capitals sometimes speak four, maybe five languages. Where were you traveling?"

"Manhattan."

"Pretty stupid, huh?" hooted Ernie. "She ends up in Newark and I gotta fight rush-hour traffic to pick her up. I ask you, who's dumb enough to get in a cab with a guy who don't speak English?"

Ernie obviously traveled exclusively by subway these days.

"Are you starting with me?" Ethel fired back. "I'm warn-

ing you, don't start with me because I got stories to tell too."

"You got a short one?" asked Nana. "The food's not here yet."

Ethel boosted her elbows up on the table. "Heroic? You want to hear heroic? I'll give you heroic. I get up last night to use the toilet. I hear someone crying in the hall. I peek out and I see wet footprints all over the carpet."

I came to attention. Wet footprints in the hall? Wet, not bloody? Oh, my God. The other ghost. I'd seen footprints in the dungeon that I knew belonged to Michael, but how could I have missed the ones in the hall? Had Michael made those too? Busy guy, being able to be in two places at the same time. I wonder how he did that.

"I run back to the bed to get Ernie," Ethel continued. "I drag him out to the hall. I point at the footprints. 'There's something not right here,' I says to him. 'Look at these footprints. There's something real odd about them.' "

Uff da. I bent forward to catch Ethel's eye. "Were they webbed?"

"No. They were big. Really big. Abominable Snowman big."

"Had to be at least a size eighteen," Ernie conceded.

I swallowed slowly. I knew the footprints in the dungeon belonged to Michael, and they hadn't been that big. So if the supersize prints in the hall didn't belong to Michael, who *did* they belong to?

Ethel went on with enthusiasm. "So Ernie opens an eye and looks at the footprints and says, 'This guy has flat feet, a narrow heel, and probably stands seven foot tall. You see someone like that, let me know. I'll be in bed.' Some hero, huh?"

The ghost was a giant? A ghost, I could believe. A giant seemed a little over the top. "Did you notice any smell in the hall when you were studying the footprints?" I asked Ethel.

"I sure did. It about knocked me over."

Ta da! Michael Malooley.

"It smelled like lavender. And lots of it."

Lavender? As in lavender bubble bath? Uh-oh. Not Michael Malooley. I swung my head around to slant a look at Jackie. She slanted a look back. Oops. We both slumped in our chairs and tried to look invisible.

"What's the most courageous thing you've ever done, Emily?" Tilly asked in her professor's voice.

"Umm . . ." No-brainer. *Sitting between Etienne and Jack and worrying what was going to happen next,* but I couldn't really say that. "I don't know if I've ever done anything really courageous," I admitted.

"That's not true," Nana objected. "She rescued a hairpiece from the River Reuss last year," she announced to the table.

"She saved my leg from sinking to the bottom of Lake Lucerne," George proclaimed.

"She faced a maniacal killer single-handedly," Etienne said softly, holding my gaze to his, lifting my hand to his lips, warming my flesh with his mouth. *Unh.* Excuse me while I melt. "Emily is the bravest woman I have ever known."

I blushed at their flattery. They were making me sound pretty good. Etienne had even remembered about my facing the maniacal killer. What a good memory he had. It was nice to be in love with a man who could remember what you were like on your good days.

"I didn't hear anyone crying in the hall last night," said Gladys Kuppelman. "Why didn't I hear anyone crying?"

"It's your snoring," accused Ira. "Who can hear anything over that racket?"

"Oh, sure, and I suppose if I'd heard something, you would have run right out to investigate, you being so heroic and all. Bugger you."

Gee, Gladys was really picking up the language.

"I always thought Ira was pretty heroic to agree to the number of operations he's been involved with," said Ethel.

Ira froze in place. Gladys froze too—everything except her mouth. "I told you *never* to say anything about that," she spat at Ethel.

"What? You think people don't know? People aren't as dumb as you think." She addressed the rest of us. "You all know about their little secret, don't you?"

I *knew* it! I knew Ira Kuppelman was involved in illegal operations. "I know," I said, shooting my hand into the air as if expecting to be called on. Ira snapped out of his deep freeze to fix his gaze on me.

"There's nothing wrong with what I did," he defended. "Everyone else is doing it. Why not me?"

I imagined a laundry list of crimes everyone else was doing. Insider trading. Embezzlement. Extortion. Murder for hire. Jaywalking. Boy, Ira was going to have the book thrown at him.

"Why don't you tell us what everyone else is doing," Etienne encouraged with the ease of a master interrogator.

"Aesthetic surgical recontouring," confessed Ira.

Nope. That wasn't on my list.

Nana sidled a look at Tilly. "You know what that is?"

"I think it has something to do with landscaping."

"It's plastic surgery!" squealed Ethel. "You've never heard of aesthetic surgical recontouring? Where are you people from? Mars?"

"Iowa," said Nana. Although I'd seen it happen where news of certain trends had indeed traveled faster to Mars than to the Midwest, mostly in the fashion industry.

"Ira's had more surgery than the Frankenstein monster," Ethel cackled. "He's had a full face-lift, a mid face-lift, cheek implants, drooping eyelid repair, a chin implant, collagen injections in his lips, nose surgery, pectoral implants, calf implants, and laser resurfacing. He's practically bionic."

"Don't forget the abdominoplasty," Gladys said. Then to the rest of us, she explained, "Tummy tuck. He used to be a real porker."

My mouth fell open so far it almost banged on the table. "You said your youthful appearance was a result of your diet!"

"It is!" Ira shot back. "Diet . . . enhanced by a modest amount of facial and body rejuvenation. Mother Nature needs a little help every once in a while."

Eh! What a bunch of bull he'd fed us. What a phony! Diet, my foot. He'd had more bodywork than the Six Million Dollar Man. "Have you had all that surgery too?" I asked Gladys.

"Not as much as Ira's had. There's only so much money, so we're talking big out-of-pocket expense, because Medicare won't cover it. We used to be rolling in dough, but with the expense of some recent investments and the cost of our quarterly Botox injections, we're about living on the edge."

Recent investments? How could people living on the edge afford to make investments? I guess everyone was looking for that elusive pot of gold, whether they could afford it or not. And that thought tripped something in my brain. Investments? Pots of gold? That was it! That was the connection! All the pieces fit together now. I narrowed my eyes at Ira Kuppelman. Hadn't heard any crying in the hall last night, had he? Huh! Not only was he a phony, he was a liar to boot!

"I've heard a those Botox treatments," said Nana. "They jab a needle full a food poisonin' into your face and it makes your wrinkles go away. That's real progress. Used to be all food poisonin' could do was make you barf."

"The botulism paralyzes the facial muscles," added Tilly. "You can always tell a person who's had Botox injections because his face becomes virtually expressionless."

"That's not true," argued Gladys. "I have full range of motion of every muscle in my face. You want to see? This is happy." She strained the corners of her mouth and looked bland. "This is sad." She strained the corners of her mouth and looked bland. "This is frightened." She strained the corners of her mouth and looked bland.

"Can you do bewildered?" asked Ernie.

She strained the corners of her mouth and looked bland.

"Are you sure that's bewildered?" questioned Nana. "I think it looks more like happy."

"I think it bears a rather strong likeness to frightened," said Tilly.

"Can we cut the million-dollar-makeover crap?" griped Ernie. "I wanna know who was doing all the crying in the hall last night."

"The ghost," said Jackie.

A beat passed before all eyes riveted to the end of the table. "What ghost?" Ernie asked her.

"The one who's haunting the castle. Emily and I tried to find her last night, without any success, I might add."

Uh! I gave her "the look." She furrowed her brow at me. "What? Is the ghost a secret? You didn't tell me it was a secret!"

"What the young lady is referring to," Etienne interjected, diffusing the situation, "is the fanciful legend of a . . . friendly ghost who was purported to have roamed the halls of Ballybantry in centuries past."

"Like Casper?" asked Ethel. "Ernie junior used to read all those Casper comic books when he was growing up. I wouldn't mind seeing a little ghost like Casper. You think the image would show up on Fujifilm? Maybe I should have bought Kodak. The grandkids would like that a lot better than a picture of some fake rocks."

"It's Ireland," Etienne explained in his beautiful French/German/Italian accent. "Ghosts are part of the country's charm. But I assure you, you're all quite safe."

I could feel the tension level decrease with Etienne's assurances. He really did have a wonderful knack for handling potentially volatile situations. I squeezed his knee under the table, beside myself with pride.

"Say, doll," Ernie called down to Jackie, "what was your husband doing while you and Emily were out ghostbusting last night?"

Jackie looked at Tom askance. "He inflicted his choppy cut on some unsuspecting victims, hid my fuzzy pink slippers on me, and then he probably continued his conversation over the phone with the woman who's trying to break up our marriage!"

Tom threw his napkin down on the table. "That does it! You want to know who I was talking to? I'll tell you. It was the president of your class reunion committee. They voted to surprise you with a special award at your high school reunion, but I didn't have a chance to talk to her before we left, so I called last night, and I haven't heard the *end* of it since!"

Jackie's eyebrows inched higher on her face. "An award? What kind of award?"

"Are you sure you want me to tell you?"

"Tell me, already!"

"It's an award presented to the person who's changed the most in the last twelve years. It's going to be crystal and gold with before and after photos. A real master-piece."

"Really? That's so . . . so touching." Her expression changed suddenly. She gave Tom's shoulder a thwack. "Dammit! Why did you tell me? You spoiled the surprise."

"How have you changed?" asked Gladys. "Were you a porker like Ira? What system did you go on to lose weight? Weight Watchers? Jenny Craig?"

"Old news," said Ira. "I want to know how the three of you manage to work out that thing you're doing. I thought I was liberal, but you three take the cake."

"Thing?" Jackie frowned. "What 'thing'?"

Ira twisted his fingers in the air to signify the "thing." "You know. The thing with your hubby and Emily."

Uh-oh. I didn't like the sound of this.

Tom leaned forward to eyeball Ira. "Would you care to be more specific?"

"You want me to be specific? I can be specific. We're all adults here. Ashley spilled the beans when we got back from the causeway about the—uh—special relationship the two girls have there. I just wanted to say, it takes a real prince to share his wife with another woman, especially on his honeymoon."

Tom nodded thanks to Ira before swinging around to face Jackie. "You swore it was all over between you and Emily!"

"It is!" Jackie cried. "I was only with her last night because I was mad at you! Ashley has it all wrong. Tell him, Emily."

Etienne braced his elbow on the table and angled his head in my direction. "Yes, darling. Tell him."

Shit.

"I had a hard time believing Ashley when she told us," said Gladys. "Sometimes it's pretty obvious when a man's gay, but I never would have guessed it of you, Emily. You hide it so well. Don't you think she hides it well, Ethel?"

"I am *not* gay," I protested.

"Of course you're not." Ira smiled.

"You people are gettin' everythin' confused," Nana corrected. "Emily's not gay. It's her ex-husband who's gay."

Jackie shook her head and rolled her eyes. "Now, see? That is just *sooo* inaccurate. I've been biting my tongue, but I can't bite it any longer. Now hear this! I'm not gay! I never was. I had gender issues. I underwent sex reassignment surgery. Now I'm straight. Get it? I'm straight! Emily was my past. Tom's my future. The end."

Heads turned. Mouths hung open. Eyelids flapped upward like jet-powered window shades. I hung my head and expelled a breath. Ooh, boy.

Nana stared at Jackie with much the same expression Gladys wore when she was looking happy, sad, frightened, and bewildered. "Sex reassignment surgery? I don't s'pose that has anything to do with landscaping, does it?"

"The doll used to be a guy!" hooted Ernie. "I'll be damned! I never would've guessed. And the two of you used to be married?" He howled and slapped his hand on the table. "I love it! This is better than *Ripley's Believe It or Not.*" He stopped laughing suddenly to eye the ceiling and walls. "Hey, we're not on *Candid Camera,* are we?"

Jackie speared Ernie to his chair with an angry look and stabbed her finger at him. "Okay, buster, listen up. I do not wear size eighteen shoes! I wear a size fourteen, so let's cut the seven-foot-giant crap, okay? My feet are not proportionally out of line with the rest of my body, although if you happen to be carrying any catalogs that advertise plus-size footwear, I'd *really* appreciate looking at them."

"So Ashley lied to us?" asked Ethel. "You and Emily aren't an item?"

"How can we be an item?" Jackie pleaded. "I'm married! Emily and I are just girlfriends—the kind who have sleepovers and borrow each other's lipstick. Isn't that right, Emily?"

"Someone should put that Ashley in her place," Ethel said, thumping her fist on the table for emphasis. "Spreading vicious gossip like that. I think she was jealous of all the attention the two of you were getting today. She's put out that you girls are so competent. All she can do is break her leg."

"Her foot," I corrected, though, in hindsight, I kinda wished it had been her neck.

Nana stared quizzically at Jackie. "Do you mind if I ask you a question, dear?"

"Go right ahead, Mrs. S."

"Who are you?"

"Jack Potter. Remember? Jack Potter? Emily's ex-husband. Now I'm Jackie Thum."

"And you've got breasts."

"Real perky ones," Jackie gushed. "You want to feel them?"

"No thank you, dear. And you're not gay anymore. I'm sorry to hear that."

She sounded so despondent, I reached across the table and patted her hand. "You should be happy for Jack," I soothed. "He's finally found his niche."

"Oh, I'm happy for him . . . her . . . him. But the thing is, I'm the only member of the Legion a Mary who could say she'd ever met a gay person. It kinda gave me special status. Now I don't know no one."

"On the contrary, Marion," Tilly said, sounding thrilled to be of help. "You know me!"

CHAPTER 14

"Are you sure they're hives?" Etienne asked as he hovered over me an hour later. "They look more virulent than hives. Can you breathe?"

"It's nothing really," I said as I clawed at my face and neck and scratched my arms. "I've had them before. It's just a nervous reaction. They'll go away pretty soon."

"Do you have medication?"

"Oh, sure. But you know us Midwesterners. We like to tough things out before we give in to drugs." Which, translated, meant I'd rather suffer than smell like camel dung for the rest of the night. I guess it was a girl thing.

I was nestled in a chair before the fireplace in my room. Etienne was sitting on the armrest, smoothing his hand with a tender motion over the crown of my head. "What are you nervous about, darling?"

I shook my head and forced a laugh. "How much time do you have?"

He feathered two fingers along the curve of my ear. "I have all night."

The Wishing Chair hadn't failed me. I was getting my romantic evening alone with Etienne. I should be ecstatic! I should be entertaining lascivious thoughts about sex. But I couldn't. I was too distraught, too preoccupied. "Could anything else have gone wrong at dinner?" I asked glumly.

"Ah. The cause of your nervous reaction. Dinner. What seems to have distressed you the most? Having to introduce me to the woman who used to be your husband, or learning that your grandmother is rooming with a woman who bats for the other team?"

"Actually, I think that's great about Tilly. Nana was delighted too. She gets to maintain her exalted status with the Legion of Mary, and it knocks Tilly out of the running with George, so the coast is clear for Nana to make her move. Couldn't have worked out better. And you sounded as if you really enjoyed talking to Jackie and Tom."

Etienne laughed. "Your ex-husband does have a certain amount of charm about her . . . him . . . her. Very affable. Though you might want to mention to her that asking strangers if they'd like to feel her breasts isn't such a good idea these days. And her husband offered to give me a complimentary trim." He patted his hair. "Just a little off the top. He's supposed to be something of a master stylist. The bottom line is, darling, everything resolved itself. You've nothing to be nervous about any longer."

I cranked my head around to look up at him. "Nothing has resolved itself! What about the dead bodies, and the crying, and my furniture being rearranged, and personal items going missing, and the Kuppelmans?"

"What about the Kuppelmans?"

"Think about it. They've run out of money to perform any more plastic surgery. They need more. What would happen if they were partners with a man who stood to inherit a castle?"

"They'd suffer a lot of headaches, I imagine. The upkeep on these places is enough to throw you into bankruptcy." He eased off the armrest, removed the crystal paperweight and porcelain Westie from his jacket, and set them on a side table. "I thought you were concerned that Kuppelman was conspiring to eliminate his wife."

I gnawed the corner of my lip while Etienne slipped out of his jacket and folded it neatly over a chair. "That was my theory before dinner. Now that I know about all the reconstructive surgery, I've changed my mind. I didn't understand their motive before. Now I do."

Etienne sat down on the chair opposite me and untied his shoes. "Are you going to share?"

I scratched my chest and forearms as I watched him pull off his socks. "Okay. Here's the way I see it. The original owner of the castle was an English lord by the name of Ticklepenny." I thrust my hand toward the painting over the mantel. "Please note the feet of the children in the portrait. The toes are webbed in the same manner as the bloody footprints you found beneath the maid's body, meaning that our purported ghost is no doubt related to the guy sitting on the horse there. However, all Lord Ticklepenny's children died in their youth, so who was left to pass on the congenital anomaly from generation to generation?"

"If the bloodline was wiped out, no one."

"Exactly, which means, the bloodline wasn't wiped out. Someone survived. My money says Ticklepenny got frisky with one of the Irish serving girls while he was living here and fathered an illegitimate child who *should* have inherited the castle after Ticklepenny's legal heirs died, but since the Irish weren't allowed to own land, that didn't happen." *Scratch scratch scratch.* "When Ticklepenny returned to England, the castle fell into disuse, the government probably took it over for delinquent taxes, and it passed from one owner to another until some long-lost relative of the bastard child did his homework and realized *he* was a direct descendant of Ticklepenny and was entitled to the castle."

"And you think Kuppelman is the relative?"

I buzzed him wrong. "Michael Malooley is the relative. You said yourself the key to the problem is in the dungeon. I think Michael is directing some kind of operation from one of the chambers down there. Forty-eight people have died since the castle was renovated two years ago, which tells you that someone is doing something. I bet you anything Michael was involved in the renovation project—as a carpenter, or a plumber, or an electrician. He refuses to say what he did before he became a bus driver, which has me very suspicious. But if he worked on the castle, he installed a lot more than light fixtures. He wired the place for sound, and cold, and who knows what else. He wants the castle back and he's willing to kill innocent people to get it."

"I suppose that makes sense. Bad publicity will dry up the tourist trade and force the present owners to dump the castle. Michael buys it back for a song, he makes a show of having the place exorcized, the deaths suddenly stop, and he's in business again. A brilliant plan, actually. But how does Kuppelman fit into the picture?"

He unbuttoned his shirt, stood up, and yanked the tails from his waistband. My eyes lingered on his naked torso as he slid the shirt down his arms. *Scratch scratch.* "I—uh—I think Ira might have bankrolled Michael's project. Sound systems are pricey, and Michael doesn't look as if he was born with a silver spoon in his mouth. I don't know how they met, or how they ended up involved with each other—that's a big unanswered question—but the Kuppelmans might have looked at this as an investment. They pay initial cash up front, and they receive dividends later to pay for more surgery. It's probably a lot less risky than the stock market these days."

He pondered this as he stroked his long fingers through the dark hairs of his chest. His skin was the most beautiful color—like warm mocha and cream. His shoulders were wide. His stomach flat. His arms lean and muscled. My brain numbed and my eyes burned at the sight of him. "So do you have authority to arrest Michael and Ira?"

"I have no authority in Ireland, Emily. But even if I did, I'd need more evidence than what we have to make an arrest. Your theory is entirely plausible, but at the moment, it remains just that. A theory."

"But if we wait to check out the details, someone else might get frightened to death. Me, for instance. Or Nana!"

Etienne shook his head as he unzipped the fly front of his trousers. "Not to make light of the situation, darling, but it's more likely your grandmother would frighten the ghost to death. Whatever happened to her hair?"

"Tom gave her a complimentary haircut. Just a little off the top, I think."

"That's Tom's handiwork?" Some of the mocha color drained from his face. "Well, then . . . since the man is on his honeymoon . . . I probably shouldn't bother him with that trim."

"So what are we going to do?" I persisted. "We need to take the bull by the horns. We can't wait for our boat to come in. We have to row out and get it." *Scratch scratch scratch.* "I say we camp out in front of Michael's room tonight and catch him red-handed when he starts his monkey business." *Scratch scratch.*

Etienne dropped his pants. "All right. He can't very well cause any trouble tonight if we're following him. Tomorrow we can look deeper into his background and see if we can make a case for his guilt. Is that agreeable with you?"

I nodded. I thought about being more verbal, but my tongue was pretty preoccupied licking my lips. I'd always considered Etienne a boxer shorts kind of guy, but he was standing before me wearing a plain black thong, and nothing else. The pouch hung halfway down his thigh and was so full, it was bulging at the seams. Not to state the obvious or anything, but my aristocratic Swiss police inspector was hung like a horse. *Unh!*

He removed his watch after checking the time, then sauntered toward me, all sooty-eyed and hard-limbed. He braced his hands on the armrests on either side of me, then bent down and kissed my mouth.

Scratch scratch. Scratch scratch. "I never pictured you in a thong," I whispered numbly against his lips.

"What did you picture me in, darling? Boxers? You Americans would have everyone in boxers."

"Boxers can be quite attractive. Especially the fitted kind. Calvin Klein makes—"

"They're too confining." His voice grew low, husky. "A thong makes me feel as if I'm wearing nothing at all."

"You don't think it's a wee bit . . . showy?" I tried not to hyperventilate as he pressed his mouth against my throat.

"It's a decidedly European vice," he whispered.

"But you're not like other Europeans. You're Swiss."

He looked me square in the face, an earthy glint smoldering in his eyes. "You forget, darling. I'm half Italian."

UNH! Still . . . "Are you planning to camp out in front of Michael's room dressed like that?"

"We have several hours to kill before we head to Michael's. I have other plans for you until then." He drew my lower lip into his mouth, cutting short my next question. Almost.

"Can I ax you somethin'?" *Scratch scratch scratch. Scratch scratch scratch.*

He released my lip. "Ask me anything, darling, but when you're done, I have a rather critical question of my own to pose."

This was it. He was going to pop the question. But was I ready? Oh, lordy. I didn't know. I DIDN'T KNOW.

"Emily?"

My question. Right. I dipped my eyes to the package between his legs. "Is that real?"

"Why don't you peel off the thong and find out."

My breasts tingled. My throat grew hot. A swell of erotic sensation arrowed downward from my navel. *Scratch scratch scratch scratch scratch.* AARGH! "Okay! I can't STAND it anymore!" *Scratch scratch scratch.* "Where's my anti-itch cream?" I scrambled around him and raced for the bathroom. "Hold that thought. I'll be right back."

"Would a bubble bath help?" he called to me.

Bubble bath. Sure. Water might help. I turned on the faucet full blast. I'd promised him a bubble bath anyway. I grabbed my toiletry bag and dug out my anti-itch cream. Maybe if I applied just a little, it would stop the itching long enough for me to open his surprise package. Oh, geesch, the *size* of that thing. Sonny Corleone, eat your heart out. I unscrewed the cap. From the next room I heard snippets of Etienne's voice being drowned out by the roar of the bathwater.

"I . . . my imagination . . . the portrait . . . of someone."

"I can't hear you!" I yelled, as I slathered my neck with cream. "Say again?"

"I SAID, MAYBE IT'S MY IMAGINATION, BUT THE CHILDREN IN THE PORTRAIT REMIND ME OF SOME-ONE."

"Really?" I yelled back. "Who?"

A pause. "HOW DID THE PAINTING GET SO CROOKED?"

"That happened last night! It's not hanging too securely, so don't touch—"

CRAAAASH!

The bathroom mirror wobbled. The wall shook. The floor jumped. I screamed at the sound and ran into the bedroom. "Oh, my God!"

Etienne lay still as death, sprawled on his back by the fireplace, his head and torso buried beneath the cumbersome weight of Lord Ticklepenny's portrait. "Etienne!" I sprinted to his side and, trembling with fear, levered the heavy painting ever so slowly off his body and angled it against the fireplace. I fell to my knees beside him, terror gripping me when I saw blood pooling onto the carpet beneath his head. "Etienne," I soothed. He was out cold. I cradled his head in my hands and with gentle fingers found a gash near his crown that was turning the ink-black of his hair red with blood.

My mind operating on automatic pilot, I rushed into the bathroom and returned with an armful of towels that I pressed against his head to stanch the flow of blood. I ran to the telephone and dialed 999, giving the operator the necessary information for the ambulance. "Please, hurry!" I cried, hanging up. I prayed the driver could find Ballybantry Castle a lot faster than he'd found the Carrick-a-rede Rope Bridge. If not . . .

I didn't want to think about "if not."

I raced back to Etienne's side. "It'll be all right, sweetheart." I flattened my palm against his cheek, willing him to wake up. "Help is on the way. You'll see. They'll be quick."

BAM BAM BAM. I darted a look at the door. Not that quick. I dashed across the room.

"Your people are really starting to piss me off," Ashley spat at me when I opened the door. "I just got a call from Alice something-or-other. Do you know where she was calling from? The Garda Station in Letterkenny. Do you know why she was calling from the Garda Station? Because Bernice something-or-other is behind bars. Do you know why she's behind bars? Because she tried to buy a silk scarf with nonnegotiable currency, and when the shopkeeper told her her money was no good in the republic but they'd accept plastic, she accused them of trying to steal her identity, slapped her money onto the counter, and walked out of the shop with the merchandise anyway. The police picked her up and hauled her off to jail! I hope you plan to head over there and bail her out, because, I mean to tell you, I'm in no condition to do it. So . . . what are you going to do? Why are you looking at me like that?" She narrowed her eyes at me. "What are those red welts all over your face and neck? They're really gross."

I couldn't think about Bernice right now, and I sure as heck couldn't deal with Ashley. I started to say as much, gave her an irritated look instead, then tore back across the room, leaving her standing in the doorway.

"I . . . I never! You Yankees are the rudest bunch. If the South had won the war, let me tell you, you would have learned some manners."

"I have an emergency here!" I shouted back at her as I applied pressure to Etienne's head wound.

"What kind of emergency?" She thumped into the room on her crutches and crossed to the sitting area, sucking in her breath when she saw Etienne's nearly naked body. "Holy shit! Is that real?"

"Do you know anything about head wounds?"

"Only that they bleed a lot." She hobbled closer. "What happened?"

"He must have been trying to straighten the picture when it fell on top of him."

"That's not surprising. I've conducted a few tours in

Switzerland. Those people are such neatnicks. I guess this kind of interrupted y'all's evening. That's too bad, sugar. Looks like you were in for a hot ride." She paused. "Are you sure that's real? Have you looked?"

"No, I haven't looked!"

"All right, all right. Is there anything I can do for y'all?"

"I've called the ambulance. I guess all we can do now is wait." I heard an annoying noise in my ears and suddenly realized it was more than just adrenaline roaring through my veins. "Actually, you could turn off the water in the tub. Doesn't look as though we'll get to use it tonight. And would you see if there's a blanket in the closet?"

As Ashley disappeared into the bathroom, I checked Etienne's pulse. Strong and steady. I checked my own. Rapid and thready. And my wrists and forearms were peppered with welts that looked like thousands of interconnecting mosquito bites. *Scratch scratch scratch scratch. Scratch scratch scratch scratch.* I pinched my eyes shut and tried to think about something other than scratching.

Scratch scratch scratch. Damn. I opened my eyes, my gaze falling squarely upon the portrait I'd hauled against the fireplace. What had Etienne said? That the children in the painting reminded him of someone? I studied the three barefoot children, my eyes roving their cherubic faces, their blue eyes, their fair complexions, their pale blond hair. They were absolutely beautiful children. If they'd lived to adulthood, they probably would have fallen into that elite category of people who could be called drop-dead gorgeous.

I heard the glide of the closet door behind me. "Don't see any blankets in here, Emily. Sorry. There's a pillow. You want that?"

Drop-dead gorgeous? Oh, my God! I'd been so blind. Why hadn't I seen it before? "Sure," I called out. I craned my head around, watching her as she made her way back across the floor.

"Here you go. Are y'all going to put it under his feet or his head? Sometimes it's good to keep the feet elevated above the heart in these situations." She had to maneuver so close to hand me the pillow that her cast bumped against my leg and allowed me a clear view of the toes that were deeply bundled within their little plaster casing—toes that were perfectly formed except for one detail.

There were no spaces between any of the toes. They were all stuck together.

"It's you!" I screamed at her.

Looking puzzled, she hobbled a step backward. "What's me?"

I pointed to her cast. "You're the one who's trying to give the castle a bad name."

"Whatever are y'all talking about?"

I pointed at the portrait. "You're the one who's related to the Ticklepennys!"

She regarded the portrait with blatant indifference, then laughed. "Their name's Ticklepenny? Let me tell ya, sugar, if my name was Ticklepenny, I'd do something about getting it changed."

My mind was racing at the same speed as my heart. "You have that innocent routine down so well. The *sugars* and *y'alls*. You're convinced no one would think there's another side to all that sweetness and light. And your job! You can breeze in and out of a place without stirring up any suspicion that . . . that you're a killer!"

"Ex*cuuu*se me?" Her chest puffed up like a prize pigeon's at the county fair. "Did you just accuse me of being a killer?"

"It's not an accusation," I fired back. "It's the truth!"

She lowered her voice and pinched her eyes into evil little slits. "You don't like me much, do you, sugar? You haven't liked me since you first set eyes on me. I'm used to jealous women spreading vicious gossip about me, but you've pushed the envelope too far this time. I'm gonna write you up, Emily. I'm gonna give the president of that little bank you work for such an earful about your maliciousness and misconduct that I'll be surprised if you *ever* work again! You got that, sugar? *Ever* again. I'm gonna ruin you!" She angled her way around to leave.

"It was easy for you to double-talk your way around the hauntings" I dogged her, "but how are you going to double-talk your way around webbed toes? You have the same defect as the family in the portrait! Look at all their little piggies. They're all fused together! Just like yours! Isn't it just a *little* obvious?"

She stood statue still, then turned back to face me. "Having webbed toes is as common as having blue eyes."

"Good luck finding a jury who'll believe that. Did you think no one would notice that your feet are an exact replica of the ghost's?"

"You do go on," she said flippantly.

"You really had me fooled, Ashley. I bet it took an incredible amount of expertise and planning to pull this scheme of yours off. But even if your toes are a dead giveaway, I never would have guessed you were the ringleader because of one . . . *tiny* . . . fact."

I noticed a tiny crack in her facade of invulnerability. A tenseness around her mouth. A hesitancy in her eyes. And I knew the exact comment that would infuriate her into singing like a canary.

She lifted her chin stubbornly and gave me a questioning look, unable to resist the bait. "What one tiny fact?"

"Who would have thought you had the brains? I mean, you're blonde!"

Her eyes spat fire. Her body stiffened. She drilled me

with a long, savage look, then curled her lips into a barracuda smile. Uh-oh. I didn't like the smile.

"My, my, my, aren't you the clever one. Morons! I told them the footprints should look like they belong to a small woman. *They* decided they should be historically accurate, so they made the toes webbed, ignoring the possibility that the trait might be traced back to the family. I'm related to morons!"

"You mean a real person didn't leave the prints?"

"Plastics, Emily. You can create anything out of plastic these days."

"And the wailing?"

"Major sound system. It cost a fortune. We operate it out of the dungeon."

"And the cold spots?"

"All part of the ventilation system."

I stared at her, disbelieving that she could be so cold-blooded. "You're responsible for the deaths of forty-eight people! How can you stand there and be so cavalier about the methods you used to kill them?"

"They were old, Emily. They had their best years behind them. I simply saved the health care system the added cost of hospitalization and long-term care."

"That's so sick! You frightened people to death just so you could buy back a stupid castle?"

"Hey! Ballybantry Castle belongs to me! Not to the McCrilly family. Not to a board of investors. To me! It's my birthright!"

"Someone should have told you—YOU LOSE YOUR BIRTHRIGHT WHEN YOU COMMIT MURDER!"

"This castle was stolen from my family four centuries ago, and no one is going to steal it away again. My ancestors would be proud of what I'm doing."

"Your ancestors would be appalled! Ticklepenny is

probably rolling over in his grave that he ever knocked up a serving girl whose descendants resulted in you!"

She jabbed her finger in the air at me, then paused. "Serving girl? What serving girl?"

"The one Ticklepenny got pregnant."

"He got a serving girl pregnant?"

"Umm, that's my theory. Someone had to have passed on the foot defect, and my money's on Ticklepenny. If his children died before they reached adulthood, the only way the defect could have been passed on is if he fathered a child outside of marriage."

"Excuse me? You think I'm the product of an illegitimate bloodline?"

"I was thinking more 'bastard' bloodline. That seems to suit you better."

Her voice grew razor sharp. "I will have y'all know that my bloodline's as pristine as they come. It's pure. Untainted. You see that girl in the portrait there?" She lifted her crutch to indicate the older female child in the corner of the painting. "Her name was Cecily. She fell in love with an Irish laborer and *legally* married him. *They're* the ones who passed on the defect."

Oh, sure. "He drowned in the moat and she died in childbirth. Didn't give them too much time to pass anything on."

"Time enough. Cecily died in childbirth . . . but the baby didn't."

Her words jolted me like a zap of lightning. "The baby? Oh, my God. I forgot all about the baby."

"Everyone always forgets about the baby."

"The baby lived?"

Ashley struck a pose on her crutches. "If the baby hadn't lived, I wouldn't be here."

Of course. The baby surviving explained so much.

Relationships. Motive. Podiatrist bills. Why hadn't I bothered to ask about the baby before? *Unh!* "The baby didn't die when the fever that killed the rest of the family swept through the castle?"

"Ticklepenny washed his hands of the baby right after Cecily died. The lout gave him back to his Irish relatives to raise. But no one ever forgot who the baby was, or what his origins were. The O'Conors have long memories."

"O'Conor? As in Nessa O'Conor, front desk clerk?"

"We're cousins."

"And let me guess, the rest of your cousins run a construction business in the village. Right?"

"How astute of y'all, Emily. It was the very construction company the board of investors hired to renovate the castle. Amazing what can happen when you lowball all the competition. Isn't that a coincidence? Of course, there were cost overruns, but the board was American. Americans expect cost overruns, so they don't blink an eye when you go over budget."

Had I called that, or what? And I bet I knew who her company foreman had been. "Some coincidence. O'Conor, you say?" I heaved myself to my feet and strode across the floor toward the bed. "Is that with one *n* or two?"

"One. Why?"

"I want to make sure of the spelling for when I report you to the police." I picked up the telephone.

"I wouldn't do that if I were y'all, sugar. Put the phone down."

I punched 999 and pressed the receiver to my ear. I glanced sidelong at Ashley to discover she was aiming the barrel of her cigarette lighter at my head.

"I won't warn you again, sugar. Put the phone down, or I'll shoot."

"Nice try," I said, dismissing her with a look. "I'm really afraid. You should consider chain-smoking. It kills people, you know." The operator answered. "This is Em—"

CHOOOOUNG!

I dropped the phone and hit the floor as a bullet zinged past my head and thunked into the wall. Okay. Now I was afraid.

"Do I have your attention, Emily? Be a good girl now. Hang up the phone and come on back over here."

I juggled the receiver onto its cradle and took hesitant steps back toward Ashley, my gaze riveted on the pistol in her hand.

"So what am I going to do with you, sugar? Too bad you know so much. That's gonna make it hard for me to let y'all live."

This might be a good time to reconsider my habit of screaming "It's you!" when I figure out the killer's identity. Something to think about. If I lived that long.

Knock knock knock.

I looked expectantly at Ashley. "It could be the ambulance."

"It's Ireland, sugar. Don't hold your breath. WHO IS IT?" she yelled at the door.

"It's Nana, dear."

She motioned me to a chair with her gun. "Sit down and don't move a muscle. If you try anything—anything at all—your granny's going to end up looking like a hunk of Swiss cheese. Understand?"

I nodded. "Did you know there's no such thing as Swiss cheese? It's called Emmen—"

"Shut up, Emily."

"Okay."

I sat worrying my lip and scratching my arms and neck

as Ashley opened the door. "Mrs. Sippel. Ms. Hovick. Why, come right on in. Emily's a little tied up at the moment, but I know she'll welcome y'all's company."

"We're here about Bernice," I heard Nana say as she crossed the threshold. She looked like a Concord grape in her Minnesota Vikings warm-up suit. Tilly followed close behind, dressed in her standard pleated skirt and leaning heavily on her walking stick. Nana waved across the room when she saw me. "Hello, dear. I just wanted to let you know that Tilly and me are takin' a taxi to Letterkenny to bail Bernice outta jail. Don't know why they decided to go to Letterkenny instead of Derry, but she got picked up for passin' bad money. Alice just called from the police station. She wanted to talk to you, but your line was busy, so she talked to us instead."

"Okay. That's great. You better wait out in the lobby for the taxi," I said, hoping to rush them out the door. "Be careful. Bye."

"She talked to Ashley earlier," Nana went on, giving Ashley a stern look, "but Ashley's only advice to her was to bugger off."

"You told Alice to bugger off?" I gasped at Ashley. "But she needed your help!"

"Hel-looo? Golden Irish Vacations guests aren't asked to fill out evaluation forms for the tour leader, so I can say anything I want."

"You're a poor ambassador of Southern hospitality," Tilly scolded.

Ashley shrugged. "I'll fill you in on a little secret. Southern hospitality? It's all smoke and mirrors. Pure hogwash. All right, ladies, I'm getting real tired of the small talk, so why don't we save some time here and cut to the chase." She played a little peekaboo with her gun, waving it at them with a theatrical flourish. Nana reacted by nearly choking on her breath. Tilly remained calm. Tilly had probably fended off hordes of flesh-eating cannibals in New Guinea, so this was no big deal.

"I'm not sure I understand what this is all about," Nana complained as Ashley herded them in my direction.

"Meet the Ballybantry ghost," I informed them.

"You're the ghost?" Nana exclaimed.

"Ta-da!" chimed Ashley.

"Is that gun loaded?" Tilly asked.

"It's loaded," I warned. "So, please, do what she says."

"You're the ghost," Nana repeated. "Oh, my word. OH, MY WORD," she cried when she saw Etienne. "What happened? He's not dead, is he?"

"The portrait fell on him. He's not dead, but he's bleeding badly."

"Did you call an ambulance?" she asked.

I nodded.

"What's that thing between his legs?"

"It's a cross between a G-string and a thong," I explained.

"It's his penis," said Tilly. "Although it's more typical in our culture to refer to it by its various euphemisms. Dick. Prick. Peter. Pecker. Mickey. Roger."

"I didn't know they could grow to that size," Nana said in awe. "You suppose it's real?"

"Of course it's real! Why does everyone think it's not real?"

"Have you looked?"

"I don't need to look!"

Nana gave a little suck on her teeth. "I'd look."

Tap tap tap.

"Kee-REIST!" screamed Ashley, glaring at the door. "What are we having in here? A freaking convention?"

"That'll be George," said Nana. "He'll be wantin' to let

us know when to expect the cab. He made the phone call for us. He's such a gentleman."

Ashley jabbed her gun at the two empty chairs near me. "Sit," she instructed Nana and Tilly. "And no funny stuff. Or else what happens, Emily?"

"Swiss cheese," I droned.

Nana furrowed her brow at me. "I thought there was no such thing as Swiss cheese."

Ashley thumped to the door. Nana angled her head to observe Etienne from another perspective. "I don't recollect your grampa's bein' that big. You s'pose your young man takes vitamins? Do you have any idea what kind?"

"Well, if it isn't George," Ashley enthused. "Come on in. Join the crowd."

"I just wanted to give Marion a message," he said as he crossed into the room. "The taxi will be here in— Is that a gun?"

"Bingo." She poked it in his face and motioned him toward us.

He raised his hands in the air like a nabbed TV bad guy and marched in our direction. "Does this mean we won't be needing the cab? I should probably call them back to cancel. I mean, that would be the polite thing to do. Holy cow!" he blurted when he saw Etienne. "What happened to him?"

"Picture fell on his head," said Nana.

"No. I mean about his roger."

"IT'S REAL ALREADY!" I shrieked.

George nodded matter-of-factly. "Looks like the trend to downsize is affecting more than just the Hershey bar these days."

We all stared at George with eyes as round as teacups. Nana's mouth contorted into an O of surprise before sliding into a euphoric smile. She caught my eye. "You can forget about those vitamins, dear."

Ashley stood to the side of George, panning her gun from left to right at all of us. "Well, are we all here? Or are we expecting more guests?"

"It would be nice if Jackie and Tom stopped by," Nana suggested. "They're a real interestin' couple."

"The ambulance should be arriving shortly," I reminded Ashley. "Are you planning to hold the paramedics at gunpoint too?"

"That pistol of hers only holds six bullets," George observed.

"And she's spent one already," I said. "So that leaves five. If you're hoping to kill all of us, you better hope there's only one paramedic, else you're going to be a few bullets short."

From a great distance, we heard a faint whir of a far-off siren. I cocked my head, straining to hear, then smiled. "I'd guess that's the ambulance now. Luck of the Irish. They're early."

She did a shifty thing with her eyes, looking a bit indecisive, before bolstering herself up on her crutches. "All right, y'all. Everybody up." She urged us to our feet with her gun. "Form a line now. Short people in front. And no arguing! It's not an exact science."

Nana took her place at the front of the line, followed by George, me, then Tilly. "I'd like to be at the back a the line once," said Nana, "just to get a different perspective."

"Very good," Ashley complimented us. "Now, very slowly, walk toward the closet."

"What are we gonna do once we're there?" asked Nana.

"You're going inside," said Ashley.

I saw Nana shake her head. "Tilly just come out of the closet. I'm not sure she's keen on headin' back in again."

Ashley shadowed along beside us as we marched to the deep-set mirrored closet that flanked the bathroom door.

"Stop right there," she directed when we were about five feet away. "Don't anyone move." She hobbled around us, slid open the closet door, backed inside, switched her gun to her left hand, then with her right, pressed something near the hanging rod that caused the wall behind her to glide open, revealing a hidden passageway of dark, unlit stone and a smell of dankness that hit us full in the face.

"Well, would you lookit that," Nana marveled.

"Secret passages," I muttered. That's how they'd been able to leave their bloody footprints, and rearrange furniture, and steal personal items, and scare people to death. They could come in through the closet and leave again without ever being seen. I wondered if the passages had shown up on the detailed map I'd seen in Ashley's tour bag. Duh! Why hadn't I been more curious?

"The whole castle is a maze of hidden passageways," Ashley explained as she hobbled back into the room. "Of course, no one knew that until we did the renovations. They're great to creep around in, but I think their real beauty is you can hide lots of bodies in there without anyone ever finding them." She brandished her pistol at us. "Poof! All gone." She motioned Nana into the closet. "Go ahead, sugar. Time's a wastin'."

This gave a whole new meaning to the term "walk-in closet." Nana poked her head inside the enclosure, gave it the once-over, and popped inside. George followed close on her heels. I knew if I stepped inside that closet, it would be all over, and I wasn't ready for it to be over. I didn't want to die! I needed a plan!

Scratch scratch scratch scratch scratch.

Ashley focused her pistol on me. "Stop that scratching."

"But I itch!" I felt a slight movement behind me. From the corner of my eye I saw Tilly's walking stick swing suddenly upward and drive hard into Ashley's wrist. *Wump!*

The pistol flew out of Ashley's hand and dive-bombed onto the floor. "Get her gun!" I screamed, lunging onto the floor to grab it.

Ashley knocked it away with her crutch. It skidded across the carpet. I scrambled to my feet. Ashley thump-hopped across the room after it, then whipped around, standing guard over it. Letting one crutch fall to the floor, she balanced herself on her good foot and cast and seized her remaining crutch as if it were a Medieval battering ram. "Stay where you are," she threatened, swinging the crutch by its footpiece in a broad arc. *Whoosh* to the right. *Whoosh* to the left. "I can decapitate someone with this thing!"

Standing a safe distance away from her crutch, I took my shoe off and gunned it at her. She whacked it with the crutch and sent it high-flying into the window. "Give it up," I warned, chucking my other shoe at her. She caught it on the fly and whacked it into foul territory in the other direction. She might be a miserable failure as a person, but she was an excellent hitter. "Did you play a lot of softball in Georgia?"

"Debutante's League. I had a four-oh-six lifetime batting average."

"Somebody throw me a weapon!" I cried.

I heard a flurry of activity behind me. A rush of footsteps. Tilly shoved a clothes hanger into my hand. I gauged the size of the hanger. I gauged the size of the crutch. I tossed the hanger aside. "I need something heavier!"

I glared at Ashley, trying to psyche her out. When she inched to her right, I inched to my left. When she inched to her left, I inched to my right. "Go for the gun and I'll be on you like green on a leprechaun," I taunted.

"Here you go, dear," said Nana, handing me the crystal paperweight with the colorful kites.

"Eh! I can't use that," I gasped, handing it back to her. "Etienne gave that to me. I think it's Waterford."

Nana checked the bottom. "Waterford. You're right. I wouldn't mind buyin' some Waterford while we're here."

More footsteps. The echo of sirens was getting louder, and closer. Ashley slanted a look at the window, then with an air of defiance, took aim at her gun with her crutch and batted it under the bed. "You want it?" she said, grinning at me. "Go get it." She cleared a path for herself with vicious swings of her crutch and limped toward the one escape route that was still open to her—the closet.

"Emily!" I turned toward the sound of George's voice and yelped as his artificial leg came rainbowing through the air at me. "Try that!"

Eh! I caught it against my chest with an *"Oof,"* then hefted it slightly to test its weight. Alone, it might have been too light, but with the steel-toed boot, it was perfect. I chased after Ashley, swinging the leg like a club. "Stop where you are!" I yelled at her.

She stopped and planted her feet. *Whoosh!* She swung the crutch at me, just missing my head. BOOM! I slugged the crutch pad and arm piece with George's leg, sending shock waves up her arms.

"Ow!" she whined. She jabbed the crutch at me again. I backhanded another powerful blow to the arm piece. CLONK! *Crrrrack.*

"Hit her again," George yelled, balancing one-legged behind me.

"Bitch!" she shrieked at me, staring at the splintered wood. "OooohhhHHHH!" She launched herself at me, swinging the crutch berserkly. I ducked. George didn't. The crutch caught him with an uppercut to his jaw. THUNK! He looked dazed for a millisecond, crossed his eyes, then

collapsed to the floor like a ton of bricks. Well, maybe half a ton, what with his leg detached and all.

"George!" screamed Nana. "You killed him! You killed George."

Ashley regarded him without remorse. "I hope he is dead. I'm so sick of all you helpless old people."

An odd look crossed Nana's face. She narrowed her eyes at Ashley, made a wavy gesture with her hands, then crying, "EEEEEYAAAA!" she executed four quick skips across the floor and—BAM!—snapped her leg out and kicked the crutch out of Ashley's hands.

Ashley's mouth fell open. My mouth fell open. "EEEEEYAAAA!" Nana raised her knee and with a rapidfire thrust—WOOF!—drove the ball of her foot into Ashley's gut. Ashley doubled over, gasping for air, clutching her stomach. "EEEEEYAAAA!" Nana jumped straight up in the air, spun around like a top, then with her knee up and leg straight—WHAM!—smacked the top of her foot into Ashley's cheek.

BOOM! Ashley slumped to the floor in a lifeless heap.

I stared at Nana, agog. "What was *that?*"

"A spinning roundhouse kick."

"You . . . How . . . *Where* did you learn to do that?"

"The senior center."

My voice was at a pitch that could shatter glass. "That's what they're teaching in senior aerobics these days?"

"I told you, dear. The step aerobics class filled up, so I had to settle for my second choice. Tae Kwon Do."

KABOOM!

I screamed as the door to the hall flew back on its hinges and Michael Malooley stormed into the room wielding a really big gun. "Don't anyone move!" he hollered, crouching into a defensive stance and two-handing his gun.

Shit. I forgot about him. "Behind you!" I yelled, pointing toward the hall.

He spun out of his crouch and leveled his gun at the door. I charged at him from behind, clutching George's leg like a caveman's club, and took aim at the back of his head. CLUNK! He wavered stupidly for a moment before he fell forward, crashing facedown on the carpet with a resounding THUMP!

Groans from Ashley. Writhing. Whining. Pathetic mewling sounds as she regained consciousness. Tilly stood over her with her walking stick poised to thwack her if she made a wrong move.

"I knew the two of you were in this together!" I called across the room at Ashley. "So who exactly is Michael Malooley? One of your relatives?"

Ashley rolled painfully onto her side to face me. "He's a bus driver."

"Sure he is."

I heard the ambulance squeal into the parking lot, engine roaring, siren screeching. I hunkered down beside Michael, removed his wallet from his back pocket, and flipped it open.

"Who does his driver's license say he is, dear?" Nana asked as she hovered anxiously over George.

"His driver's license identifies him as Michael Malooley. But he has another ID here that says—" I paused. "It says he's Detective Michael Malooley. Pearse Street Garda Station. Dublin. And it gives his badge number. Oh, look! Here's the badge. It was hiding."

I looked at the badge. I looked at Michael. I felt a familiar sinking feeling in my stomach. "Oops."

CHAPTER 15

"Dr. Mortimer, please dial four-one-six. Dr. Mortimer, four-one-six."

It was after midnight, and I sat with my legs dangling over the side of a gurney in the emergency room of the local hospital. Michael Malooley occupied a chair in the cubicle with me, pressing an ice pack to the back of his skull.

"I'm really sorry about your head," I apologized for the tenth time.

He shrugged. "A minor concussion. If it wasn't for the throbbing and the lump, I'd hardly be knowing anything was wrong." He gave me a wink. "I got off luckier than yer Swiss friend."

They'd whisked Etienne off to another part of the emergency room when we'd arrived, and despite my inquiries in the intervening two hours, I'd received no updates on his condition. It was driving me crazy. I rocked forward on the gurney, angling a look through the slit in the curtain that surrounded the cubicle. "They'll let me know how he is soon, won't they? I asked them to let me know."

"They'll be letting you know. I'll see to it."

Ashley had complained of head and stomach pains back at the castle, so the paramedics had called a second ambulance to Ballybantry to transport her to another hospital. George had regained consciousness and decided he was okay, so he stayed behind with Nana and Tilly, but the crew decided I needed to be transported with Etienne because I had the worst case of hives they'd ever seen and needed immediate medical attention.

So here I sat, dressed in a hospital gown that fit like a tent, looking like a tribal chief who was plastered from head to toe with ceremonial war paint—known to the rest of the world as calamine lotion. I was an utter mess, but thanks to a dose of antihistamines, at least the itching had stopped. "What's going to happen to Ashley?" I asked Michael.

"She'll be arrested, along with the people who helped run the operation. The desk clerk. The relatives in the construction company. Her cousin in the village police force who kept covering up for them. It was a clever plan they had. I'm suspecting they all expected to get rich when Ashley's family bought the castle back. These days, you can be renting a castle out for parties and catered affairs and asking fifty thousand dollars for a weekend. And there's those who can afford it, most particularly yer pop stars and Hollywood elite. That's a lot of money to come into a wee village in Ireland. It wouldn't take many of those weekends to turn ordinary laborers into the monied class. I fancy they were looking at it as their due for the wrong that was dealt them four hundred years ago."

"How did you get involved?"

"Too many deaths in a single place over a period of two years. A flag went up in Dublin. They decided to send me in undercover because the local authorities were being uncooperative. I'll be glad to be getting back to my day job, though, and leaving the damn bus behind. If the department wanted someone who could handle a bus, they should have been hiring an Italian."

"We're traveling to Italy next month," I said half-heartedly.

"You'll enjoy it. Italy is beautiful."

"Have you been there?"

"I've not visited it myself, but that's what people tell me."

I nodded. That was about right. I narrowed an eye at Michael as pieces of the puzzle kept sliding into place. "Did you find any evidence in the dungeon last night?"

"Jars of blood. Prosthetic feet attached to broom handles. A chart listing what family member was scheduled to work what night. Men's trousers. A ladies' bathrobe. A pair of really big fuzzy pink slippers. Video screens for the surveillance cameras. An incredible sound system. CDs labeled 'Ghost Howls' and 'Crying.' Microphones. Speakers."

"Surveillance cameras?"

"We haven't started looking yet, but we suspect they were hidden in every room."

"They were spying on the guests?"

"Best to know what's happening in a bedroom before you barge in through the closet to steal someone's possessions or rearrange the furniture." He furrowed his brow at me. "And how would you be knowing I was in the dungeon last night? I made sure no one saw me. I had a peek at the map Ashley left on the bus in her tour bag yesterday, so I entered through a concealed door."

"I saw the footprints you left outside the chamber door."

He slapped his knee. "No escaping that. The floor was about flooded because of the moat. The water from the outside keeps seeping into the dungeon. I'm surprised no one's been electrocuted yet." He gave me a curious look.

"But how would you be knowing the footprints were mine?"

"I don't mean to be rude, but I could tell by the smell."

He laughed aloud. "French cologne. A birthday gift to me from my mother-in-law. The worst-smelling concoction in creation, but it kept people at bay so I could be doing my work. Well, it kept most people at bay. You were something of a problem."

I forced a smile. "Do you think you'll be able to prove murder?"

"I'm thinking we'll be able to prove intent. When you target old people who are suffering from hypertension and heart disease and try to scare them to death, that's the same as pointing a gun in their face and pulling the trigger."

"Do you think the maid and custodian were frightened to death?"

"I do. I believe the maid suffered a fatal heart attack when she saw the bloody footprints, and I believe the custodian heard the false wall in the closet sliding open, went to investigate, and died right there as a result of whatever he saw. Whoever opened the secret panel left him where he fell and waited for some unfortunate guest to find him. Namely, yer grandmother."

"So there's no web-footed ghost of Ballybantry Castle? No wandering spirits? No blond-haired apparition roaming the halls and testing the door of every bedroom in search of her dead lover? The legend is just that? A legend?"

"There's no ghost, Miss Andrew. There never was. This is Ireland. Irishmen have fertile imaginations and they love spinning a good ghost story, whether it be true or not. It seems to help the tourism industry. That, along with the sale of Belleek, Waterford, Aran sweaters, linen, tweed scarves, Jameson whisk—"

"Oh, my God! Scarves! Bernice is in jail in Letterkenny

because she paid for a scarf with the wrong kind of money. I'm supposed to bail her out. Oh, my God. This could get me fired." I hopped off the gurney and gave the cubicle a frantic visual search. "Do you see my clothes?"

The outside curtain parted. A short-haired, middle-aged woman dressed in white pants and a matching lab coat poked her head inside. "Miss Andrew? Dr. Clery has received permission from Inspector Miceli to speak to you, so he'll stop by in a few minutes to brief you about the Inspector's condition."

"Is he going to be all right?" I asked breathlessly.

The nurse smiled with indulgence. "The doctor will give you all the details. Mr. Miceli's room is around the corner and down the hall to the left. You'll be able to see him after you talk to the doctor." And then she left, leaving me frozen on the spot, unsure how I could bail out Bernice and see Etienne at the same time.

"I think I'm feeling well enough to ring up the authorities in Letterkenny and convince them to let yer friend out of jail," Michael said. "You run along and check on yer boyfriend."

"But I'm supposed to wait for the doctor first."

"I don't recall hearing anyone say to wait for the doctor. Did you?"

I flashed him a grateful smile and squeezed his hand. "Thank you." I braced a hand behind my back to hold my gown together, looked both ways outside the cubicle, then turned back to Michael, remembering something. "What did Ira Kuppelman hand you this morning before we left for the Giant's Causeway?"

He crooked his mouth to the side and fished a folded sheet of white paper out of his breast pocket. Snapping it open, he held it up for my perusal. "Propaganda. What I have to do to adopt a macrobiotic lifestyle and why it's the right lifestyle for me. I suspect he gets kickbacks for any new members he signs up to join the Institute. Do you know they eat seaweed? Bugger me."

I scurried around the corner and dashed down the hall, peeking in all the rooms on the left until I found Etienne. *Eh!* He was lying in a bed, hooked up to a bunch of high-tech machines with mysterious readouts. An IV drip was plugged into his hand, an oxygen tube was attached to his nose, and a really substantial bandage was wrapped around his head. He looked so helpless that I felt my eyes well with tears at the sight of him.

"Hi," I whispered, entwining my fingers with his.

His eyelids fluttered open. He peered up at me, let out a startled gasp when he focused on my face, then blinked rapidly as if trying to clear his vision.

Oh, my God. What was wrong with him? I touched my hand to my face and suddenly realized what was wrong. "It's Emily," I soothed. "You can't tell it's me because of all the calamine lotion. I probably look like a ghost. They rubbed it all over me."

That calmed him down. He stopped blinking. "Emily?" he rasped.

"I'm here, sweetheart, and you're going to be fine."

He moistened his lips with his tongue. "I don't . . . feel so fine. What happened?"

"A painting fell on your head."

He paused thoughtfully, then tried to smile. "That's right. I remember. It was . . . crooked."

"You're too fastidious."

"Can't help it. I'm Swiss."

"Maybe you can lighten up a little after we're—" I bit off the end of my sentence. Etienne searched my face with his beautiful blue eyes.

"After we're what?"

I didn't want to come right out and say it. I mean, *he* was the one who said he had the all-important question to ask. But nearly losing him had crystallized my thoughts and firmed my resolve. I was through dithering. I wanted to be here for him while he recovered. I wanted to nurture him, and love him, and grow old with him. I didn't care where we ended up living or if I ever ate another Blimpie's grilled chicken sandwich. Those things were unimportant. I loved Etienne Miceli and I wanted to spend the rest of my life with him. I wanted our engagement to be official.

I smoothed my fingers over his hand. "This might not be the most romantic setting in the world, but . . . is there something you wanted to ask me?"

"About what?"

A prickle of alarm shot through me. "Earlier this evening, before the picture fell on your head, you said there was something you wanted to ask me."

He stared at me blankly for a time before I saw awareness creep slowly into his eyes. "You're right. I was going to ask you—" He broke into a sudden smile. "It was something about—" The smile wavered, dimmed, then faded. "Funny. I can't seem to recall what it was about."

"Miss Andrew?" a man called from the doorway. He was dressed in blue surgeon's scrubs and looked fairly official. "I'm Dr. Clery. May I speak to you in private, please?"

I joined him in the hall, casting a look back at Etienne. "He's going to be all right, isn't he?"

"We'll be keeping him for a day or two for observation, but I expect he'll recover fully. Any signs of memory loss should be only temporary."

"Oh, thank God." Relief flooded through me. I waited a beat. "Memory loss?"

"The kind of head trauma that the inspector suffered can sometimes produce lapses in short-term memory. A patient can often remember his mother's maiden name, but he can't recall more recent details, like what he ate for lunch, or what he was planning to do tomorrow. Of course, we've no reason to believe this will be the case with Inspector Miceli. We've grilled him on his day's activities, and he seems to be remembering everything quite brilliantly, so it seems you have nothing to worry about."

I took a taxi back to the castle in the wee hours of the morning, all the while trying to convince myself that things weren't as black as they seemed. So what if Etienne couldn't remember he'd been about to ask for my hand in marriage? He was alive, with excellent prospects of recovery, and if the memory loss was supposed to be only temporary, he'd remember to pop the question eventually.

Eventually. I supposed that could be anywhere from a week to a year. I could give him a month, but anything longer than that and I'd have to forget about the K of C Hall for the reception. Next on the list would be the banquet room at Perkins. *Unh.*

We pulled into the parking lot, I paid the cabbie, and then I walked through the front door of the castle with the weight of the world on my shoulders. Unwilling to give in to a full-blown depression, however, which would be very bad for my waistline, I told myself that things would look better after I got a few hours' sleep. And I did have a few things to be happy about. The hospital had given me a free sample bottle of calamine lotion, so I didn't have to go out looking for one. My itching had stopped completely. Michael had sprung Bernice out of jail. And I had several more days to enjoy the sights of Ireland. Blarney Castle. The Ring of Kerry. The Cliffs of Moher. The rocky Burren in County Clare. I'd heard that the Burren, with its vast limestone plateaus, was even more spectacular than the more touristy spots of Ireland. Etienne would probably be able to rejoin us by then. He'd need lots of attention, and I was anxious to give it to him. The Burren could prove to be a very romantic spot in which to pop the question. Okay. This was better. Things were definitely looking up.

As I approached my room, I noticed a woman at the far end of the corridor with her hand on the doorknob of Etienne's room. She was a small woman, with blond hair that draped over her shoulders and fell to the small of her back. She was dressed in a flowing white gown that looked almost effervescent, and if she was part of the tour, I didn't recall having seen her before. Had some new guests checked in to the hotel?

"Can I help you?" I called down the corridor. "If you're looking for the man who's staying in that room, he's not there."

The woman angled around toward me, her face sad, her eyes huge and soulful. She regarded me for a heartbeat, then turned her back on me and fluttered away as if on winged feet—to the end of the corridor and straight through the wall, disappearing before my eyes.

Uff da. I was stressed. I was tired. I didn't see that.

Did I?

POCKET BOOKS
PROUDLY PRESENTS

PASTA IMPERFECT

Maddy Hunter

Coming Summer 2004
from Pocket Books

Turn the page for a preview of
Pasta Imperfect. . . .

The main altar of St. Peter's Basilica in Rome is an oblong of white marble that sits beneath a soaring bronze canopy. Four black-and-gold corkscrew pillars the size of giant sequoias support the structure. I snapped several pictures of the sculptures atop the canopy, then, as I framed my next shot, heard a *click, click, click, click* of stiletto heels on marble. "Hold up, Emily," a voice echoed out in a throaty whisper.

I glanced over my shoulder to find a tall, glossy-haired brunette hustling toward me. She had the face of a madonna, the body of a supermodel, and a sassy style that turned the heads of most men. Her legs were long and tan, and she wore a sexy white mini-dress that fit like a coat of spray paint. She was all sleek angles, graceful curves, and exact proportions, except for her feet, which were big as snowshoes. Her name was Jackie Thum. Before she'd had sex reassignment surgery to become a woman, she'd been a guy named Jack Potter, and I'd been married to him.

"I'm so glad you told us about the dress code here," she

said, straightening the flutter sleeves that fell from her shoulders. "If you hadn't, I actually might have worn something totally inappropriate today."

I wondered what she'd consider more inappropriate than white spray paint. I regarded her arms. Oh, right. Spray paint without sleeves.

She removed what looked like a writing pen from her knit shoulder bag, held it to her mouth, and began speaking into it. "If you're visiting religious sites in Italy, check to see if there's a dress code. Bare arms and hairy legs aren't permitted in the church proper of St. Peter's, however, the clothes police might let it pass if you're planning to play bingo in the basement." She snapped the tape recorder off. "They play bingo here, don't they? It's a Catholic church. What Catholic church doesn't play bingo? Can you imagine the haul? I mean, this place can accommodate sixty thousand!"

She held her mini-recorder up for my perusal. "Doesn't this rock? It's the perfect thing to help me chronicle your every move. I'll be James Boswell to your Samuel Johnson."

Ever since Jack had become Jackie, she'd been searching for her new niche in life. After ending up on the same tour in Ireland with me last month, she'd decided she might like a job like mine, so she signed up for this tour of Italy in the hopes of recording the dos and don'ts of the successful tour escort. I tried not to let it go to my head, but it was kind of flattering.

I looked from the deep copper of her arm to the pale ivory of my own and felt a pang of envy resurface. Sunbathing with Jack had always been depressing. He'd turn warm and golden; I'd turn red and crispy. It didn't seem fair. "Where'd you get the great tan? I thought Binghamton was cloudy all the time."

She struck a glamour pose, pointing her high-heeled foot like a ballerina in toe shoes. "Flash Bronzer Magic Mousse."

"It's a fake bake?"

"Come on, Emily. Nobody tans for real anymore. Why do it naturally when you can achieve the same effect by doing it chemically? And the best part is, the chemicals they use in sunless tanning products haven't even killed anyone yet." She flashed me a smile that suddenly turned to horror. "Oh, my God! Where's your shoulder bag?"

"Mom has it. She wanted to free up my hands to take pictures. And bless myself."

"You gave it to your mother? Jeez, that was brave of you. I wouldn't dare let my bag out of my sight." She cast a furtive look around her. "Especially in this place."

I followed her gaze and swallowed slowly. "You wouldn't?"

"No way. I've read about what can happen here."

I forced myself to remain calm. "But this is the safest place in Italy. Nana said so."

"Where'd she hear that?"

"She read it. In a travel guide." I tried to swallow again but there seemed to be a hairball in my throat that I couldn't get around. "From the library."

"Jeez, I haven't checked anything out of the library for years. You know how current the stuff they let you take home is. The 1952 Mobile Travel Guide. The 1964 edition of *Frommers*. You're gonna find a lot of useful information in those babies."

A sudden disturbing thought struck me. What if the information Nana read was out-of-date? What if St. Peter's wasn't the safest place in Italy anymore? Oh, my God! What if someone snatched my shoulder bag? My phone. My sunblock. MY AIRPORT CONTACT NUMBERS FOR

MY MISSING LUGGAGE! I knew something bad was going to happen with my luggage. I knew it!

I broke out in a cold sweat as I searched out mom's face in the crowd. "You have to help me find my mother. I need to get my shoulder bag back."

"How come?"

I stared at her, wide-eyed. "Because of the *thieves,* Jack! Someone might steal my bag!"

"I thought Mrs. S. told you this was the safest place in Italy."

"She did! But you said—" I hesitated, my mouth hanging open and my mind a sudden blank. I cleared my throat self-consciously. "What did you read could happen here?"

"That you can get picked up by some really hot Italians."

I waited a beat before thwacking her on the arm with the back of my hand. "Jack!"

"What? I read it in *Europe's Sexiest Men and Where to Find Them.*"

"You're *married!* What are you doing looking for men?" She'd eloped a month ago with a hair designer named Tom whose specialty was corrective color and infliction of the choppy cut on unsuspecting heads.

"I'm married, Emily. I'm not dead." She hugged her shoulder bag close to her body. "So you can bet I'm not letting my bag out of my sight. With all these hunky guys wandering around, a girl never knows when she might need to touch up her mascara."

I rolled my eyes, thinking if I came down with another case of hives anytime soon, I was going to kill her.

"Okay, I made a list, and the next 'must see' in the basilica is"—she consulted a paper in the side pocket of her bag—"this way." She banded her hand around my arm and dragged me down the center nave. We stopped before a mammoth five-sided pillar to regard a bronze statue of a fuzzy-haired man with a beard. "St. Peter," said Jackie. He was seated in a marble chair beneath an ornate canopy, one hand raised solemnly like Al Gore in a vice-presidential debate, the other clutching a set of keys. I'd read someplace that the body of the statue might originally have been that of a Roman senator, with the haloed head and hands soldered on later. I had to compliment the Italians. St. Peter looked pretty darned good considering he might have been pieced together like Robocop.

"We need to get in line so we can kiss his toe," Jackie instructed.

I remembered back to my grammar school catechism and wondered what kind of spiritual reward we might receive for paying obeisance to this great saint. Partial indulgence? Plenary indulgence? In the days of the old church, the faithful accumulated indulgences like frequent flyer miles and could use them to get out of hell free. You didn't hear much about indulgences anymore. Wasn't that always the way? You just get locked into a great reward system and *boom,* all the perks expire.

"What significance does kissing his toe have?" I asked.

Jackie shrugged. "I thought it was the Italian version of kissing the Blarney Stone. Hey, look. There's some of the people on our tour up near the front of the line. You see the tall guy in the rose-colored polo shirt? Silver hair. George Hamilton tan. Looks like an aristocrat? That's Philip Blackmore, executive vice-president of Hightower Books. They tell me he's a legendary marketing genius. He's supposedly the one behind Hightower's switch from literary to more commercial fiction."

It was Hightower Books who was sponsoring this ten-day holiday to promote its unprecedented venture into the historical and contemporary romance market. The theme of the tour was *Passion and Pasta* and it provided an opportunity for romance fans and unpublished writers to rub shoulders with established writers, editors, agents, and other publishing luminaries. Guests were promised exciting excursions to historic venues, as well as daily lectures from the experts on how to write a best selling romance. My group of Iowans weren't particularly interested in the romance market, but when a slew of cancellations in the main tour occurred a couple of months ago, Landmark Destinations needed to fill up the empty seats, so they offered me some great discount prices and I'd scooped them up.

"And you see the woman standing to the right of Blackmore?" Jackie continued. "The one in the floral moo-moo with the horn-rimmed glasses and Cleopatra hair? That is none other than Marla Michaels. *The* Marla Michaels. I'm dying. *Dying!*"

I gave the woman a quick look-see. "Who's Marla Michaels?"

Jackie stared at me in disbelief. "Emily! Do you live under a rock? Marla Michaels. *The Barbarian's Bride? The Viking's Vixen?*"

"Oh. *The* Marla Michaels. The world renowned"—Barbarian? Viking? Of course!—"opera singer."

Jackie threw up her hands. "Marla Michaels is *only* the most famous historical romance diva in the world! Hightower lured her away from her old publisher by offering her a very lucrative contract that includes theme park rights and extended author tours to exotic places."

"She's a romance writer? How was I supposed to know that? I don't read romances." I cocked my head and smiled coyly. "But it seems one of us does. How do *you* know about her?"

"The seminar last night? She gave a talk? She autographed books? If you'd been less interested in complaining about your missing luggage and more interested in the theme of the tour, you'd know about her, too. So there." She nodded her head once, like a punctuation mark at the end of a sentence.

"Right. You read romances, don't you, Jack?"

She ignored me.

"Oh, my God. I bet you were reading them when we were married! That's why you were sneaking into the bathroom so much in the middle of the night. You weren't treating your athlete's foot. You were reading bodice-rippers!" Wow. He'd kept a lot of things hidden in the closet back then.

Jackie narrowed her eyes at me. "This is the thanks I get for cleaning scum from the toilet and scrubbing mold off the tile? We had the tidiest bathroom in the apartment building, Emily. How do you think it got that way? I'll give you a clue. Unlike an oven, it wasn't self-cleaning!"

"Hey, you didn't have to be so fastidious!"

"Yes, I did! You know how obsessive-compulsive I am!"

"Are you guys in line?" I heard a chirpy voice inquire behind me.

She was one of ours—a flaming redhead in her twenties who was snapping gum like a kid snaps rubber bands. The wording on her pink Landmark Destinations name tag read, *Hi! My name is Keely.*

"You're on the tour!" she said, aiming a finger at Jackie. "I recognize you from the seminar. I would kill for that leather bustier you were wearing last night. Can you believe this? Marla Michaels and Gillian Jones in the same room together? Did we luck out or what?"

"Gillian Jones?" I asked tentatively. "Another romance writer?"

"I'll say." Keely popped a bubble then sucked it back

into her mouth. "Sixty-four weeks on the *New York Times* bestseller list for *A Cowboy in Paris*. Eighty-six weeks for *A Cowboy in Sydney*. The reviewers said books about cowboys wouldn't have global appeal. Boy, were they wrong. She's the most successful writer of contemporary romance, ever."

"She's standing behind Marla in line." Jackie pointed her out.

Gillian Jones was waifishly petite with platinum hair cut close to her head and huge cactuses hanging from her ears. I suspected the over-sized earrings might be her trademark. Zorro's was a mask. Gillian's was desert vegetation.

"Marla and Gillian supposedly hated each other for a lot of years," Keely explained, "but now that they've signed on with the same publisher, I've heard they've become the best of friends. I want to learn so much from them. I don't mean to brag, but I've won every regional First Chapter contest ever offered."

"That's great," I enthused. I had a hard time writing postcards, so I admired anyone who could actually win a contest for putting words on paper. "But you're unpublished at the moment?"

"Pre-published," she corrected. "Unpublished gives the wrong impression."

Right. I guess it would give the impression that . . . you're not published.

"But I'm this close"—she flashed a quarter-inch space between her thumb and forefinger—"to getting published."

"Have you had any nibbles?" Jackie asked with girlish excitement.

"Not exactly." Keely blew a bubble the size of her head, then had to use her fingers to shove it all back into her mouth. "I need to complete the manuscript first, but finishing up should be a piece of cake."

"Are you close to the end?" Jackie wanted to know .

"Real close. Only thirteen chapters to go."

Thirteen *to go?* I couldn't imagine the fortitude it took to sit down every day and grind out page after page of fiction. I regarded her with even greater respect than before. "How many chapters have you written so far?"

"One. But like I told you, it's award-winning." She blew another bubble. I gritted my teeth. If she did that one more time, I'd be forced to make a finger puppet of her gum and stick it in her ear. "What I really need is an agent," Keely confessed. "That's part of the reason I'm on this trip. Gillian Jones's agent is here, so I signed up for an appointment with her. I'm hoping if she reads my stuff, she'll like it well enough to represent me. Her name's Sylvia Root. Ever heard of her? They call her 'the barracuda.' High-powered. Ruthless. She's every author's dream. The funny thing is, she looks nothing like you'd expect. I thought I saw her in line earlier."

She ranged her eyes over the people at the front of the line. "I don't see her now, but she's easy to miss. Medium height. Average weight. Hair the color of dishwater. Baggy clothes. No makeup. She kinda blends into her surroundings. You'd never guess she had *cajones* the size of Jupiter. Whoops, there's my roommate. Gotta run. She's supposed to take a picture of me in front of some famous pope's tomb."

The queue to reach St. Peter moved quickly. I kissed his little bare toe first, then pondered what other part of the statue I'd be kissing if the early Romans had worn wingtips instead of sandals. "If kissing the Blarney Stone imparts the gift of gab," I commented when Jackie and I were through the line, "what gift do you suppose kissing St. Peter's toe imparts?"

"I don't know, but if you start speaking in tongues, I'm

outta here." She wiggled her finger at my lips. "You left all your lipstick on Peter's foot."

I scrutinized her own glossy lips. "How'd you manage not to rub any of yours off?"

"You don't think I'd actually put my mouth where everyone else has put theirs, do you?"

I narrowed my gaze at her. "Correct me if I'm wrong, but I thought that was the *point!*"

"Hey, I got the job done! I kissed my forefinger and rubbed *that* over his toe. Which reminds me." She dug into her shoulder bag and yanked out a small plastic bottle. "You want some hand sanitizer?"

After oohing and ahhing over the magnificence of the dome and snapping some photos of the gilded candle sconces surrounding St. Peter's tomb, we headed back toward the entrance. "Hi, Jackie," gushed two blonde women wearing blue Landmark Destinations name tags.

"Hi there!" Jackie replied, waving her fingers enthusiastically. "See you on the bus."

A minute later a pony-tailed man with a trim beard and green name tag nodded at Jackie. "Ms. Thum."

"Mr. Fox." She nodded back.

I slanted a curious look at Jackie. "How do all these people know you?"

"It's called networking, Emily. Isn't that what a good travel club escort is supposed to do? Smile a lot. Be friendly. I attended the seminar last night, introduced myself to all the guests, and the dividend is"—she shot me a toothy smile—"they remember me."

"Of *course* they remember you! You were wearing a leather bustier!"

"If you lower your voice, I'll let you borrow it sometime." She sidled closer to me and spoke in a whisper. "That man who just acknowledged me? He's apparently a *real* biggie in the industry. Gabriel Fox. He's the senior editor at Hightower and is supposed to be editing both Marla and Gillian. Boy, I wouldn't want that job. Can you imagine the egos? Anyway, they call him the 'book doctor.' Isn't that cute? If there's anything wrong with a book, he's the guy who's supposed to be able to fix it. But you know what I don't get?"

I could see the red and green umbrella of our tour leader bobbing conspicuously in the air near the front entrance. "What don't you get?"

"All these wannabe writers are all in competition with each other, right? So how come they want to help each other so much? I mean, you should have been there last night. It was a lovefest! When a guy's in competition with you, he stabs you in the back and steamrolls you into the pavement. When a woman's in competition with you, she becomes your best friend! It makes no sense to me."

"Maybe you need to boost your estrogen level." I spied everyone in my group huddled around Duncan Lazarus and his umbrella. Even the newcomers were all in attendance. The Severid twins, Britha and Barbro, who were absolutely identical except for one characteristic, which they stubbornly refused to reveal. Holver Johnson, my high school English teacher. Anfin and Inger Amenson, owners of Windsor City's only independent bookstore. Mom, tilted at an odd angle with my bag slung over her shoulder. OH, THANK GOD! I breathed a grateful sigh of relief. When I got close enough, I was going to grab that bag off her shoulder and not let it out of my sight for the rest of the trip, no matter *how* much she insisted on helping me.

"Estrogen, smestrogen," Jackie sniped as she tried to keep up with me. "Women act really weird sometimes. And to think of all the money I spent to become one of you. I should demand a rebate."

I suspected Duncan must be from the Midwest because at precisely three o'clock he stabbed his umbrella in the direction of St. Peter's Square and led the charge out of the basilica. A wave of humanity followed him out the door, but I worried about the head count. Not everyone on the tour was from Iowa. What if someone was late getting back? *Uff da.* Was that the disaster I'd been sensing all day? Not that my luggage was going to stay missing, but that someone was going to get left behind?

Why is he walking so fast?" Jackie fretted as we emerged into blinding sunshine. "Jeez, he has old people on this tour. And young people wearing extremely sexy but *very* impractical stiletto slides."

"Why don't you lose the shoes? Barefoot might be easier on your feet."

"Oh, sure. With all the pigeon poop around here? I don't think so." She clattered down the ramp that funneled tourists into the square and stopped short when she noticed something in the service road that flanked the ramp. She motioned to me furiously. "Emily, you've gotta see this."

I scurried over. "Swiss guardsman," I said, cringing at the idea of having to wear blue-and-gold striped balloon pants with matching doublet and spats to work every day. I knew the guard formed a small army that protected the pope, but I figured if they expected to be taken seriously by an invading force, they might need to rethink their uniforms. I mean, that's why GI Barbie wore fatigues instead of spandex, right?

Jackie snapped a picture of the pike-holding sentry standing before his little guard house. "Emily, would you take a picture of me standing beside him? Maybe Tom can hang it up in the salon to show his clients what I'm up to these days."

I glanced back toward the entrance of the basilica. I didn't see any *Passion and Pasta* people lagging behind, but waiting a few minutes for stragglers probably wasn't a bad idea. I didn't remember seeing Keely leave with the crowd. Her red hair wasn't exactly hard to miss. Could she still be snapping gum in front of some tomb? I could be a big help to Duncan here. In fact, if I could prevent some tour guest the agony of getting left behind, I'd be a real hero, which would kind of make up for my not attending the seminar last night and introducing myself to the immediate world.

"Okay," I said to Jackie. "Hand over your camera."

I kept one eye on the front of the basilica and one eye on Duncan's umbrella as Jackie scooted down the ramp and up the service road toward the guard house. She said something to the sentry, who ignored her completely, then posed close beside him and smiled up at me. "Pizza!" she yelled.

CLICK. I listened to her camera rewind itself. "You're out of film!" I yelled.

"You gotta take one more for insurance!" She fished inside her shoulder bag and brandished another cartridge in the air at me. "You want me to throw it to you?"

I gauged the distance between the guard house and me. Unh-oh. Not a good idea. Given her recent sex change, she probably threw like a girl. "I'll come down and get it!"

Casting a final look behind me at the basilica, I hurried down the ramp. The rest of the group was filing helter-skelter through the nearest columns and emerging onto what looked like a street beyond, where the bus would no doubt pick us up. I jogged toward the guard house, reloaded Jackie's camera, and snapped a shot of her standing on the other side of the guardsman.

"Thanks, Emily." She took her camera back. "You want me to get a shot of you with Mr. Personality here?"

I waved her off. There was only one man I wanted to have my picture taken with, and he was in Switzerland.

As we hotfooted it back down the road, Jackie threw on her sunglasses and looked perplexed as she glanced around her. "Where'd everybody go?"

"Through those columns." I pointed to our right. Jackie stopped short.

"Hold up, Emily. I wanna get one last picture of the square. Have you noticed that the square really isn't square? Why do they call it a square if it's an oval?"

"Jack! Come *on!* Everyone's gone. They're probably on the bus already!"

"Just one more shot."

I hurried toward the shadow of Bernini's columns and passed through the relative coolness of the roofed colonnade, ending up on what looked like a residential street. But as I paused on the sidewalk, I noticed a minor problem.

Fifty-three people had come this way, right?

I looked left at the deserted street and sidewalk. I looked right at the deserted street and sidewalk.

So if fifty-three people had come this way, WHERE WERE THEY NOW?

Visit the
Simon & Schuster Web site:
www.SimonSays.com

and sign up for our
mystery e-mail updates!

Keep up on the latest
new releases, author appearances,
news, chats, special offers, and more!
We'll deliver the information
right to your inbox — if it's new,
you'll know about it.

SIMON & SCHUSTER
A VIACOM COMPANY
www.SimonSays.com

POCKET BOOKS   POCKET STAR BOOKS

2350-01

Visit
❖ Pocket Books ❖
online at

....

www.SimonSays.com

....

Keep up on the latest new
releases from your favorite
authors, as well as author
appearances, news, chats,
special offers and more.

SIMON & SCHUSTER
A VIACOM COMPANY
www.SimonSays.com

Pocket
Books

2381-01